LEFT
FOR
DEAD

ALSO BY CAROLINE MITCHELL

The DI Amy Winter Series

Truth and Lies
The Secret Child

Individual Works

Paranormal Intruder
Witness
Silent Victim
The Perfect Mother

The DC Jennifer Knight Series

Don't Turn Around
Time to Die
The Silent Twin

The Ruby Preston Series

Death Note
Sleep Tight
Murder Game

LEFT
FOR
DEAD

CAROLINE MITCHELL

Text copyright © 2020 by Caroline Mitchell
All rights reserved.

Published by Thomas & Mercer, Seattle

www.apub.com

Amazon, the Amazon logo, and Thomas & Mercer are trademarks of Amazon.com, Inc., or its affiliates.

ISBN-13: 9781542021791
ISBN-10: 1542021790

Cover design by Tom Sanderson

Printed in the United States of America

To Ben & Valerie, the best in-laws a girl could wish for.

PROLOGUE

Samuel relaxed into his leather chair. Elegant yet modern, his corner office gleamed with polished chrome and artful design. Like many contemporary spaces in central London, his windows were floor-length and wall-to-wall. None of his colleagues questioned the telescope fixed on the streets below. His unconventional approach to advertising had earned him his reputation as a people-watcher, and many tried to emulate him. If only they knew just how much he enjoyed getting under people's skin.

The vibration of his mobile phone diverted his attention, the image of his family flashing up on the screen. He answered without hesitation.

'Guess what, Daddy, guess what!' Megan's excited tones filtered down the line. People said she was the image of him, with her brooding brown eyes and mahogany hair. She was advanced, too. At the age of six, she was more than capable of dialling his number. However, such phone calls were strictly limited to special occasions. Megan had been fussing over her wobbly tooth for weeks now. The lisp in her voice warmed Samuel's heart. 'Oh, what could it be?' he teased. 'Has the cat had kittens?'

'No!' Megan giggled. 'Harvey's a boy.'

'So he is. Let me see . . . Has Mummy grown a beard?'

Another giggle. 'Don't be silly, Daddy.'

'You'd better tell me what it is, then.' Samuel's smile carried in his voice. Like his wife, he still retained his Essex accent and remained true to his roots.

'My toof came out!' Megan squeaked, barely able to contain her excitement.

'Nice one! You know what that means, don't you? The tooth fairy will be visiting you tonight.'

Unlike her older sister, Megan had been planned. Things were so much nicer this time around, now they weren't stressing over money. Megan wanted for nothing, which was exactly how Samuel liked it. As his daughter chatted, his eyes roved around the room. He called it 'splitting', his ability to interact in a perfectly normal way while at the same time giving the darker side of his nature free rein. He could easily conduct a presentation on digital trends while contemplating how much force was needed to keep a victim compliant but unbruised.

His eyes fell on the advertising masterpieces lining his walls. These were the campaigns that had earned him his large family home in Notting Hill. To his right, a framed photo of his wife and two children stood on his desk. To his left was an industry award. The necklace he had bought as an anniversary present for his wife was stored in the top drawer of his desk. The second drawer was locked, his own personal treasure trove. Samuel's thoughts returned to home as Marianne took over the phone.

'Put Laura on, I want a quick word.' Their older daughter had taken part in a school project – a mock *Dragons' Den* of sorts.

'She's out with her friends.'

'Again?' Samuel groaned. 'Why didn't you tell her to come straight home?'

'Like you did when you were sixteen?' Marianne replied. 'She's just gone for pizza. You can't control her every minute of the day.'

'What's that supposed to mean?'

'Nothing,' Marianne replied hastily. 'You're not working over the weekend, are you? Don't forget we've got the award ceremony Monday night. It would be nice to have some quality time before then.'

'This weekend I'm all yours.' Samuel tempered his troubled thoughts. 'I'd come home now, but I've some important clients over from Japan. I promised to show them the sights.'

When he said 'clients', there was just one. Mr Hamasaki was his alibi for the night. A few drinks, then on to a gentleman's club. Thanks to a sedative-laced chaser, Hamasaki would spend the rest of the night asleep, with little recollection of events the next day.

The voice deep inside him, smug and admiring, filtered through as he ended his call. *You lie so well.* His breath quickened, his heart beating a little harder in the confines of his chest. He could hardly believe he was going through with his plan. Would it live up to the fantasy? He leaned forward and buzzed his intercom. Naomi, his secretary, answered promptly. 'Yes?'

'Put everything on hold for ten minutes, will you, babe? I've got an important call to make.'

'Sure thing, boss.'

He smiled to himself. He could get away with the term of endearment when it came to Naomi. She wasn't the most qualified secretary, but she was warm, bubbly and down to earth. Most importantly, she was grateful for her job. His previous secretaries had acted like they were doing him a favour just by turning up for work. People used to look down their noses at him because he lacked their eloquence, and his Open University degree was initially frowned upon. But over the years, he'd earned his clients' trust.

Nowadays, his rags-to-riches story was compared to that of Lord Sugar, and Samuel was determined to emulate his success.

Plucking a key from his breast pocket, he unlocked the second drawer of his desk. Gently, it rolled on its runners, revealing its treasure within. Samuel's wealth gave him the ability to buy anything his heart desired, and holiday anywhere in the world. But the thrill of building his empire had faded after making his first five million last year, at the age of thirty-five. These days, everything came too easy, forcing him to look elsewhere for kicks. He picked up his black leather notebook, which contained thoughts too dark to voice. Each page was stained with the ink of his fountain pen, listing details and routines of the women who had caught his interest. It was more than a little black book; it was a murder list.

After thumbing through the pages, he reached for his most priceless possession. The carefully folded scrap of material represented an invitation into a euphoric world known to very few. He lifted up the handkerchief, his gaze falling on his other trinkets: a faded train ticket, a lock of hair. Each one signified a moment etched on the fabric of his being. They'd made him the man he was today.

Closing his eyes, he brushed the handkerchief against his face, evoking a scent that remained in his memory. It had come from a pack of seven, each one embroidered with the day of the week. It was threadbare now, but he did not see the frays or the material yellowed with time. All he saw was her face. The image burned into his psyche in his youth had followed him into adulthood. Now, more than ever, he found himself returning to a world he thought he had left behind. His arousal grew as he allowed himself to delve deeper into her memory. But this was not the place. Reluctantly, he opened his eyes, carefully folding the handkerchief and placing it back into the drawer.

He checked his watch. A few more minutes to think about what was to come. Focusing his telescope on the streets below, he watched pedestrians milling about, just as he did on his daily commute to and from work. The February sunshine was not strong enough to offer protection from the chilly breeze, and most people were wrapped in coats and woolly scarves. He trained his gaze on a thirty-something man in a business suit, waiting to cross the road. Did he have hidden desires too? Needs to be fulfilled? It gave Samuel a kick to think he was part of a secret society. How many people like him walked the streets of London? How many brushed against him as he boarded the Tube? He could blend into any situation. He was a father, a husband, a respected work colleague. Just an ordinary man you could pass on the street without a second glance. But his hobby took him out of his mundane life, releasing a tsunami of emotion buried since his teens. In his left breast pocket nestled a powdered white substance that would ensure his victim's compliance. Nothing had been left to chance. His thoughts were beautifully horrific, far removed from his phone call with his daughter minutes before.

CHAPTER ONE

Amy stared at her email, mumbling under her breath, 'What level of fresh hell is this?' Recently, she had coped with everything that was thrown at her. Losing her father had been devastating enough and discovering her true parentage would have knocked anyone for six. But this . . . Just when she thought things were getting back on an even keel, now the conductor of her misery was on his way over, acting as if he had done her a favour of some kind. 'Play nicely,' DCI Pike had insisted when she called to break the news of Donovan's visit. Play nicely, indeed. Her brow knitted in a frown as she read the rest of the message, informing her of future plans.

There was a soft knock on her open door. She fixed her expression to an impassive one as she raised her gaze. 'You're early.'

Donovan was not due to start until Monday, although he had been liaising with DCI Pike for the last couple of weeks. Having transferred from Essex Police to the Met, he had been chosen to take over DCI Pike's role. There was no love lost between Amy and Pike, but the suggestion in Donovan's email to involve a camera crew did not get him off to a good start.

'Nice to see you too,' he replied, not in the least bit fazed by her response. 'I wanted to let you know, there's an email winging its way to you.' His sleeves were rolled up to his elbows, the top button on his shirt undone. If it were anyone else it would have irked Amy that he wasn't wearing a tie, but the truth was, she was having a hard time tearing her eyes away from him. His body was toned and muscular. Somebody had been hitting the gym.

'I'm reading it.' She gave him a polite smile. 'Now, if that's all—'

'If that's all?' Donovan leaned against her office chair, his blue eyes unflinching in their gaze. 'We've got a lot of ground to cover, wouldn't you say?'

'And your official start date is Monday.' Amy pointed to her desk planner. 'I've got you pencilled in for a meeting at two.'

Taking a seat, Donovan chuckled, his smile fading as Amy arched an eyebrow in response.

'You're serious?' he said.

Amy nodded. 'Pike's farewell presentation is due in a minute. I'm sure our meeting can wait.' DCI Hazel Pike's retirement party had taken place a week ago, but Molly had organised flowers and wine from the team. Amy had prepared her speech, being as nice as she could be under the circumstances. There was no point in holding a grudge. Pike was leaving, and it was best for everyone.

'She's gone. Couldn't face saying goodbye. She asked me to pass on her thanks, but she preferred to slip away.'

'Oh.' Picking up her pen, Amy crossed a line through the event on her planner. She rose from her seat. 'I'd better tell the others then.'

'Already done. Looks like we have time for our meeting after all.'

'If you insist.' Amy's swivel chair creaked as she sat back down.

'Ah, here she is.' Donovan smiled as Molly walked in, balancing a tray in her hands. It held two mugs of coffee and a plate of jam tarts, all courtesy of the tea club funds.

'Any time,' Molly said before leaving. She had immediately warmed to Donovan. Out of everyone in the team, Molly would miss DCI Pike the least.

'She's not here just to make coffee, you know.' Amy lifted her mug from the tray. 'Why not ask Paddy or Gary? Just because she's a woman, you think—'

'Steady on,' Donovan replied. 'I didn't ask her, she offered.' He allowed the words to settle before continuing. 'Now, why don't you tell me what's really bothering you?'

'You need to ask?' Amy blew the steam from the top of her mug before taking a sip.

'Is it the TV crew? Trust me. We've worked with them in Essex, and it raised our profile no end. It's going to work wonders for the team. You might even enjoy it.'

'Easy for you to say,' Amy grumbled. 'You won't be the one with a camera shoved in your face.' She pushed a coaster towards him as he rested his mug on her desk.

Placing the mug on the coaster, Donovan smiled. 'You're going to have a hard time escaping publicity, so you may as well get on board. Everything happens for a reason.'

'If you say so . . .' Amy stared into the murky brown liquid that passed for coffee.

Donovan was well respected by his ex-colleagues in Essex Police, and her team was lucky to have him. But in all honesty, Amy was lashing out because she was hurt. She would never have forged a friendship last year had she known he would become her DCI. She had confided in him, opened up about her personal life. It was bad enough he was joining the team, but as a DCI? She had been told the rank was being made obsolete, but it seemed there was room for one more. Why wasn't it offered to her? It was easier to blame the impending camera crew than to open up any more.

Donovan downed a mouthful of coffee, his eyes never leaving Amy's face. 'The public loves you.' He rested his mug back on the coaster. 'You're the Met's secret weapon. We need to strike now, capitalise on it.'

But Amy was lost in thought. The newspaper coverage had gone well. The two-page spread in a leading paper had reported on her connection with Lillian Grimes in a favourable light. Much was made of Amy's ability to get inside the minds of serial killers. The article had described her as a 'psychopath-whisperer, the British equivalent to *Mindhunter*'s John Douglas', and gone on to say: 'leading an elite team, she hunts down Britain's most brutal killers by understanding what makes them tick'. Why they referred to her looks and five-foot-two-inch height, she did not know. Despite her serious expression, her photo had been mildly flattering, and she'd received a ridiculous amount of fan mail as a result. The only benefit for Amy was that she knew it would irk her biological mother in prison.

'Amy? Did you hear me? The documentary—'

'The documentary, yes, I heard you. It's the best thing since sliced bread!' Amy's grey eyes blazed as she returned her attention to Donovan. 'And call me Winter, like everyone else.'

Donovan shook his head. 'Oh, for God's sake, unclench, will you?'

'Unclench?' Amy gave a humourless laugh. 'You knew how much I hated publicity, yet you used the initiative to land the job. We were friends. You sold me out.'

'Friends? The second we got close you ran for the hills. Funny way to treat your friends.'

'Keep your voice down,' Amy whispered sharply, peeping out to ensure they were not overheard. 'I've already told the command team I'll cooperate with your little initiative. I don't have to like it.' She almost said she didn't have to like him either, but that wasn't strictly true. She liked him more than she cared to admit, which was why her responses were sharp.

'OK. Well, if you're not willing to discuss it, then I've got things to do.'

'Where do you think you're going?' Amy said as Donovan made his way to the door.

'I'm sorry?'

'We have a lot to get through, isn't that what you said?'

Bemused, Donovan returned to his seat. 'You're one in a million, you know that?'

Amy smiled. 'It's been said. Look. Believe it or not, I am glad you're here. It's the documentary I'm pissed off about. I'll get over it in time.'

'If you hate the idea that much, we can talk to the command team, see if we can come up with an alternative.'

Amy shook her head. 'I brought all this publicity upon us. I'm going to have to suck it up. The papers got one thing right. We *are* an elite team. And if the public backs us, then we might just get enough of a budget to do our jobs.'

'And you're OK reporting to me?'

'Me, report to you? Behave.' Amy snorted. This was her team, and she called the shots. 'Don't let my height fool you. *I'm* the one in control.'

Donovan shook his head. 'This is going to be interesting.'

CHAPTER TWO

'Check you out, slowing down outside the wedding dress display.'
As she walked down London's Oxford Street, Amy couldn't pass up
the opportunity to tease her older sister. 'Is Paddy going to pop the
question then?' It was a rare Saturday afternoon off, and there was
nobody Amy would rather spend it with than Sally-Ann.

'His divorce hasn't been finalised yet, but a girl can look.' Sally-
Ann delivered a sly grin. 'Besides, what about you and that hunky
DCI Donovan? I saw him in that police documentary last year.
Phwoar, I wouldn't kick him out of bed for eating crisps.'

'Paddy.' Amy rolled her eyes as she guessed the informant. 'He's
been telling tales again, hasn't he.' Paddy was Sally-Ann's partner,
and a sergeant on Amy's team. Amy knew that they sometimes
chatted about her personal affairs.

Sally-Ann could barely contain her smile. 'Apparently you and
Donovan have chemistry.'

'Well, you can tell Paddy he's way off the mark.'

'It's so easy to reel you in!' Sally-Ann chuckled, taking Amy's
arm. 'Come on, let's see what all the fuss is about.'

There *was* a fuss. Given it was February, the Valentine's Day theme had taken over the department store's window display. Half a dozen people had gathered, phones aloft and fixed on bridal gowns designed by Vera Wang and Vivienne Westwood. Standing outside the window, Amy caught sight of her reflection and withered at her passing resemblance to Lillian Grimes. Her biological mother's court appeal was well underway, and everywhere she looked, she saw the woman's face.

'Wow,' Sally-Ann gasped in unison with the crowd, her eyes alight as she took stock of the window display. 'Will you look at that?'

It certainly had the wow factor, with a realistic pale-skinned mannequin sitting on a luxurious red padded throne laced with gold. Luxury fit for a queen. In the midst of the busy London streets, a sense of quiet awe descended as shoppers took in the display. A pearl-encrusted tiara sat neatly on the mannequin's blonde hair. The diamanté and pearl droplets stitched into the fabric of the bridal gown made for a dazzling effect. It was as if she had been dipped in ice. Amy peered at her frozen face and scrutinised the bouquet of red roses, stark in the mannequin's ivory hands. Slowly, her smile evaporated.

'Blimey,' Sally-Ann chuckled. 'Have you got bride fever too?'

But it was not the gown Amy was interested in. Craning her neck, she moved forward for a better look. Pressing her hand against the window, she examined every inch of the display. The flowers were fresh, the mannequin's fingers laced around their stems. But Amy had never seen a dummy with a blue tinge beneath its nails before. And her mouth . . . Beneath the vibrant red lipstick and the blusher colouring her cheekbones, her skin had a purple-grey hue. *Please tell me I'm wrong*, she thought, her breath steaming the glass. But the dummy had a deathly pallor she had known from an early age. Amy's heart faltered as she caught the deadened gaze, along with the sliver of double-sided tape forcing open eyelids that were all-too-lifelike. 'That's no mannequin.' She turned to her sister as she slipped her phone from her pocket and dialled 999. 'She's real.'

A droplet of deep red blood leaked from the corner of the figure's mouth and dribbled down her chin. Coos of admiration turned to horror as a scream rose from the crowd. As the operator answered, Amy reeled off her shoulder number and their location, requesting the emergency services. Despite the bizarre circumstances, the call-taker took it in her stride.

'Can you take these?' As she pushed her way through the crowd, Amy thrust her shopping bags upon her sister, leaving her with little choice.

'Go, do what you have to do.' Sally-Ann waved her off, no stranger to the inner workings of the police. 'I'll give Paddy a ring, give him the heads-up.'

'You're a star,' Amy said, before making her way into the store. For now, her aim was divided into three tasks: close the store, check the victim and keep the public safe. As her police training kicked in, her focus became laser sharp. She knew in her heart that the bride was dead, but she had to try just the same.

'Your window display,' Amy said, grabbing a startled blonde girl with the name tag 'Brianna'. 'Is your mannequin meant to be bleeding? It's not part of some bizarre stunt?' The question seemed crazy, but bigger stores often employed artistic types to give their display the biggest impact.

'Bleeding?' Brianna looked at Amy as if she were insane. 'No, of course not!'

'Then get me into the window display – NOW!' Slipping her warrant card from her pocket, Amy flashed it in Brianna's face. To think she had almost left it behind when she ventured out for some shopping today. In the police, your warrant card was a vital accessory. You were *always* on duty and expected to carry it at all times. Failure to get involved would not only be alien to Amy, but a dereliction of duty too. CCTV was everywhere; she had known officers to receive severe warnings for not playing their role in circumstances that warranted a police response.

Warrant card or not, nothing was going to stop her getting into the window display today.

'You can't go in there!' the girl screeched as Amy searched for a way in.

'Listen to me,' Amy replied, in a tone that asserted her authority. 'Call your manager, tell them there's been an incident in the store window, and police and paramedics are on their way. Block off all access and shut down the store. Nobody goes in or out apart from the emergency services. Do you have shutters?'

The girl nodded dumbly, her mouth half open as the colour drained from her face.

'Then unless you want to be trending on Twitter for all the wrong reasons, get them down now.'

Tugging at the display door, Amy entered from the back, almost tripping over the raised platform in her haste. It was much to the interest of the growing crowd, who were filming her every move. 'So much for anonymity,' she muttered under her breath as she approached the silent bride. She hoped she was wrong, that her instincts had let her down. She could cope with looking an utter fool if it meant it was a dummy after all. But the scent of death reached her nostrils as she inhaled, and her heart plummeted in her chest. Not yet rigid, the body in the window was ice-cold, the blood dripping from her mouth too dark and sticky to belong to a living soul. After checking for a pulse that had long since died, Amy stepped back to allow the paramedics through. She shook her head to impart they were too late. At last, the *chukka-chukka* of metal rollers lowered the shutters down. Amy's stomach churned with disgust as members of the public crouched beneath them for a better look. What was it about murder that fascinated people so much? And why had the victim been put on public display?

CHAPTER THREE

'Why didn't you call me?' Donovan's words were spiked with irritation as he followed Amy down the hall. She had just returned from the crime scene and investigations were well underway.

'Monday's your official start date. Everything's under control. I'm going to briefing now.' Amy knew she was being petty, but she was not yet ready to relinquish her status as head of the team.

'I'm covering for Pike today, as well you know.' Donovan's voice echoed in the corridor as he strode beside her. 'You would have updated her, wouldn't you?'

'Yes, regular phone updates while she stayed at home.' It was true. Pike didn't like working extra hours and had been happy to let Amy shoulder the work. It was most likely one of the factors contributing to her forced early retirement.

Amy gave him a sideways glance, noting his sweatshirt and jeans. He must have rushed out of the door at breakneck speed if he hadn't given himself time to change.

A thunderous expression crossed his face. 'Imagine how I felt, at home with my feet up. Then I turn on the television to see you jumping into a store window display that's been confirmed as a murder scene. You should have at least given me the heads-up.'

Amy's clipped tones relayed that she did not appreciate being spoken to in such a fashion by someone who had yet to prove their worth. 'Like you gave me the heads-up about the camera crew joining us on Monday? Do you know how hard it's going to be with that lot breathing down our necks? But no – nobody asked the people who actually run the investigations.' She paused, closed her eyes and took a deep breath. Now was not the time.

Amy reached for her tag, ready to press it against the security panel outside the entrance to the high-profile crime unit. 'Look. I was going to call you as soon as I got back. So how about we both act like adults and get on with our jobs? I've got some paperwork you can sign off, and then there's the budget to sort as well as a meeting with the command team—'

'And you expect me to do all that?'

Amy frowned in response. 'You said yourself, you're taking over Pike's role.'

'And you said you don't answer to me. Which means I'll be rolling up my sleeves and mucking in with the investigation while you sort out the paperwork. You can't have it both ways.'

'We can't both be the SIO. I oversee the investigation, and you take care of the administrative side. That's the way it's always been.'

'It was until you kicked up a fuss.'

'Fine.' Amy's jaw set tight. 'I'll answer to you.' But her words were delivered in a mumble. She strode into her office with Donovan closely behind. She could feel her temper rising, along with the frustration of sharing ownership of the case. She used to hate that Pike wasn't more hands-on, but now she wondered if it had been such a bad thing.

'Sorry, what was that?' Donovan said, closing her office door behind them.

Amy turned to face him. 'I said, I'll answer to you. At least until we draw up some ground rules. Now, can you please sign off the paperwork? I'll have it sent to your office.'

'You mean Pike's office?' Donovan raised an eyebrow. 'I turned it down. Said I'll be sharing with you.'

This was met with a look of horror. 'Where are you going to sit – on my lap?'

'Tempting, but no. We have a new office now – the conference room.'

'How did you swing that?' Amy pulled out her swivel chair and sat down. She had been fighting for the conference room since she moved in. It was perfect for her needs, with a proper view of the street as well as her team.

'The power of television.' Donovan grinned. 'I told you, it worked wonders for us.'

'Hmm.' Amy was loath to agree. A bigger office *would* be better, but at what cost?

Donovan sat on the edge of Amy's desk and picked up a file. Sighing, he shook his head as the printed images of the victim's corpse came into view. She had not yet been identified but appeared to be in her early twenties. A young life tragically cut short. It was a sobering reminder of their priorities now.

As if reading her mind, Donovan met Amy's gaze. 'Look, I'm not sure what just happened, but can't we draw a line under it all and start again?' He glanced down at the pictures. 'She deserves the best from us, wouldn't you say?'

Amy cleared her throat, feeling thoroughly ashamed of herself. 'You're right. The body – it was elaborately staged, with attention to detail. It oozes arrogance. But worse than that . . .' The thought of their victim's final moments made Amy pause. 'There were scratch marks on the armrests. I think she was still alive when she was placed on that throne. The killer – they just left her for dead.'

CHAPTER FOUR

Amy opened the windows in the briefing room, in order to chase away the fresh paint smell. Outside, the sky was hazy, and the high-pitched beep of the nearby traffic lights signalled it was safe for pedestrians to cross. 'That's going to grate,' Amy said, wondering how many times a day the sound was activated. She watched her DS, Paddy Byrne, press a button on the wall.

'Air con,' he said. 'So you can shut the window. They installed it yesterday.'

Their spacious new location was an improvement on the old room, which would now be her shared office with DCI Donovan. She glanced across the rows of neatly laid-out chairs as officers filed in. Malcolm, their head crime scene investigator, gave her a respectful nod, while uniformed officers delivered furtive glances in her direction. Amy didn't need to eavesdrop on their whispered conversation to know what it was about. Lillian's appeal was gaining momentum, and public opinion was mixed. While Amy's own team had got used to the idea of her parentage, outside officers still regarded her as something of a curiosity. It was usual for her team to borrow officers from various departments to help with the groundwork, and Amy had kissed goodbye to the days when she could blend in like everyone else. She opened the button on her tailored suit jacket and glanced at Malcolm as he stood next to her.

'An update's just come in,' he said, his voice low. 'I tried to catch you before briefing but you'd already left.' Amy didn't like surprises, and the printout was Malcolm's way of ensuring she was equipped. She scanned the pages, which were titled 'Operation Glitterball' and marked 'sensitive'. The name had been chosen from a list of random titles, but given the amount of diamanté and glitter used on their victim, it seemed oddly apt. Amy's spirits plummeted as she absorbed the news. This was the last thing they needed right now.

'Thanks to those of you who have come in after booking the weekend off.' Amy raised her voice over the chatter in the room. 'We've got an update.' She turned to Malcolm. 'The floor is yours.'

'Thank you, darling.' Malcolm's plummy accent filled the room. If it were anyone else, it may have raised a snigger, but Malcolm was widely respected throughout the force. An ex-magistrate judge, he was known for his fairness and commitment, and they were fortunate to have him on the case. He stood confidently before them, trim and well dressed in his Savile Row suit. It made a change from the forensics onesies that Amy usually saw him in.

As officers quietened, Malcolm gazed solemnly around the room. 'Well now, it's come to light that a small heart-shaped wound had been cut into the victim's chest, about the size of a peach. It wasn't terribly deep, just enough to scratch the skin.' He paused for effect as his words sank in. If anyone enjoyed an audience, it was Malcolm. 'I've done some research and, twenty years ago today, a young Essex woman was found dead with a similar marking on her chest.'

'I thought it rang a bell,' a burly-looking officer in the corner piped up. 'What did the papers call it again?' He rubbed his beard as he tried to recall the details.

'The Love Heart Killer,' Malcolm replied. 'It was unusual, given there was only one victim, but a local rag nicknamed the murderer due to the circumstances surrounding the case.'

This was news to Amy, but if the murder had occurred twenty years ago, then she would only have been in her teens. Given the time frame, did it have any bearing on this case? She stood in silence as Malcolm continued to explain. 'Claire Lacey was a twenty-six-year-old schoolteacher, popular with her students. She was from a nice family, engaged to be married and had lots of friends. It came as a shock to the community when she was found dead on her bed with a heart carved into her chest. She'd had a very public domestic incident with her fiancé, who was arrested the next morning for her murder. At the time, it was believed to be a crime of passion.'

Amy observed her fellow officers. The tension in the room had heightened, and despite most of them staying late last night to conquer their workload, they appeared sharp and alert. Molly was sitting at the front, taking copious notes with a pink glitter pen. A blob of ink stained the sleeve of what looked to be the same blouse she'd been wearing last night. Paddy sat beside her, his long legs crossed at the ankles as he took everything in. He gave Amy a look as if to say, *Here we go again*. She acknowledged him with a slight nod of the head before returning her attention to the case. 'Her fiancé was sent down for murdering her,' she said, reading off Malcolm's notes in an effort to move his narrative on.

'Yes, indeed,' he replied, nodding vigorously. 'But the evidence against him was circumstantial, hinging on an argument he and Claire had that night. His family hired a top-notch solicitor and he was later freed on appeal.' Malcolm glanced around the room. 'I remember when it happened, a couple of weeks before Valentine's Day. It was bitterly cold that year.' He rubbed his hands together, as if feeling the chill. 'There was also speculation that Claire's murder was tied into a local occult group, but nothing was proved. The case has remained unsolved since.'

'And cause of death was blunt force trauma?' Amy said. The radiator behind her made a trickling noise. Spring may have been due to arrive soon, but there was still a nip in the air. She folded her arms across her chest, grateful the heating had kicked in.

'Yes,' Malcolm replied. 'Although reports state that the heart shape could have been scratched on to her chest while she was still alive. She was posed too, although not as elaborately as our current victim, to whom she has a striking resemblance.'

'We'll speak to Essex Police and request details of the case.' She gave Malcolm a grateful smile as he took a seat at the front of the room.

DC Molly Baxter raised her index finger. 'Ma'am, does this mean that we're dealing with a serial killer? Will the murders be linked?'

'It's too early to say,' Amy replied. 'Right now, I want to concentrate on the present day.' The murders could not be linked on a whim. Strategy meetings would have to be held, with an in-depth look at the similarities and a serious discussion of the implications of merging past and present investigations. They didn't even know the identity of their current victim yet. 'While we're in the storm of the golden hour, our focus is on our current case and chasing up leads.' Amy was talking about the crucial post-crime time period that could make or break a case. Every urgency was placed on taking early action. Time corroded evidence: witnesses forgot details, CCTV was taped over and forensics could be carried away by the wind.

Amy activated the electronic whiteboard, and an image of their store-window victim flooded the screen. It had been taken while the victim was still in her regalia, not long after life was declared extinct by the paramedics in attendance. She lay flat on her back in the window display, defibrillator tabs still attached to her chest where her gown had been cut open and CPR performed.

The temperature in the room seemed to drop as everyone took the image in. 'Someone must be missing her.' Amy's words cut through the silence. Officers had been tasked with checking recent reports of missing people. She pointed towards the elaborate head-dress as she brought the next image to screen. 'These props are key. Someone has supplied them to our killer. From the diamanté-encrusted shoes to the jewellery around her neck. They've all come from somewhere, and certainly not the high street – not from what I've seen.' She watched as officers nodded in agreement. 'Molly, pass around the list of taskings, will you?' She handed her a wad of freshly printed papers. Their priority was to identify the victim and understand the killer's motives.

Amy sipped her coffee, pulling a face as she realised someone had forgotten to put the sugar in. Regardless, she gulped another mouthful. She would need plenty of caffeine to get through today. Resting her mug on her palm, she turned back to her audience. 'The killer is proud of their work.' She closed her eyes and took a breath, the victim's image imprinted in the back of her mind. Her screams echoed in Amy's imagination as she sensed her killer looming large. 'They're taunting us. This is just the beginning. I can feel it in my bones.'

CHAPTER FIVE

Feeding coins into the machine in the corridor, Amy pressed the buttons to buy two bags of Minstrels. One for her, and one for Donovan: a sugar boost to welcome him on his official start day. Monday was like any other day to Amy, and despite officers racing through her list of tasks yesterday, they still had a lot to get through. But right now, she needed some peace. Personal matters were best left at home, but she had something urgent to contend with. Flora had come down with a debilitating cold. Pocketing the chocolate, she dialled her mother's number. Flora answered after the second ring. 'It's me.' Amy's voice echoed in the dim corridor. 'How are you?'

'I've had better days,' Flora croaked. 'Winifred's on her way over to force-feed me leek and potato soup.'

Amy imagined Flora pulling a face. Winifred's leek and potato soup was known by all. The vegetables came from a local allotment, courtesy of a Mr Charmer, an elderly widower who seemed to live up to his name. Amy wondered if her mother wasn't just a tiny bit jealous of Winifred's new-found friend. 'Well, make sure you eat it, you need to keep up your strength.' Amy raised a hand to massage her forehead. Flora had recently given evidence in Lillian's trial. The stress involved was bound to have had a knock-on effect. 'Keep me updated, will you?' Amy continued. 'Call me if you feel any worse.' Since her father's sudden death, Amy had been keeping a close eye on her mother's health.

'I will . . .' Flora's voice faded as she turned away from the phone. 'There's the doorbell. I've got to go.'

Amy drew breath to speak, but the line had gone dead. She walked towards her team's office, feeling as if she were heading into battle. Her mood darkened as she observed two men and a woman talking to Donovan in the centre of the room.

'No. Not now,' she moaned, as her eyes fell on their camera equipment. There was no chance of her slipping away to check on Flora. She watched as they dissolved into laughter, the woman tittering at something Donovan had said. Gritting her teeth, Amy forced herself into the office to meet the crew.

'Ah, here she is, the star of the show!' Donovan's smile wavered as Amy responded with a scowl. 'Erm,' he continued, less sure of himself this time. 'Amy, meet Ginny Wolfe.'

'Really?' Amy said, recalling the Virginia Woolf book her mother had left on her bedside table for her to read last week. Ginny appeared to be in her early twenties, with a nose stud and short, choppy black hair.

'Yeah, I know.' She grinned. 'Mum had a sense of humour.' Turning, she introduced Amy to her cameraman, Bob. A stout middle-aged man, he was sweating and red-faced after no doubt carrying in the bulk of the equipment. Dom, their assistant, hovered around them, his blue eyes alight as he took everything in. 'I've always wanted to be a police officer.' He rubbed the back of his gelled brown hair. 'I mean, I like filming . . .' He threw Ginny an apologetic glance. 'But the police . . . that's wicked.'

'Don't worry, mate.' Ginny patted him enthusiastically on the back. 'I'm sure they'll take you one day.'

'Is that all of you?' Amy said, hoping it was the case. In the background, Molly was chattering loudly on the phone about seized property from their last big case.

Ginny glanced around the room before returning her attention to Amy. 'Yes, it's just us three. It's not a big production, but that's what our followers like. We use two cameras. I usually give direction but there's times that I'll film too, to get that extra perspective. Our viewers like to feel as if they're part of the investigation, following you step by step.'

'It's pre-recorded though, isn't it?' Amy asked, checking her information was correct.

'Oh yeah, for sure.' Ginny shoved both hands into the back pockets of her faded jeans. 'We'll try not to get in the way.'

Amy smiled appreciatively. She wasn't an ogre, after all. If it helped raise their team's profile and put her in a better light, then perhaps it would be worthwhile. She observed as Donovan addressed their team, introducing everyone in turn. Her eyes rested on Molly, who was staring at Ginny with a burning curiosity in her eyes. After ending her phone call, she joined them, and heartily shook Ginny's hand. 'I'm a fan of your work,' she said by means of explanation, two pink spots lighting up her cheeks. Ginny smiled warmly, and as they gazed at each other, Amy cleared her throat. 'Right everyone, back to work. Ginny will let us know what she needs from us. In the meantime, we've got lots to do.'

Amy gratefully left Donovan to give Ginny the guided tour. She slid her mobile from her trouser pocket and reluctantly put it on silent mode. Winifred would call if her mum took a turn for the worse. She felt a pang of guilt as her focus wavered. This was her workspace. She should be concentrating on their victim instead of thinking about her mum. But her dad had died so suddenly, Amy couldn't help but be on tenterhooks. Returning to her office, she glared in disapproval at Donovan's desk. His workspace was the total opposite to hers, with papers and files in disarray. She could only imagine what it would have been like before the bulk of their work was migrated to computer programs. She snooped around his desk, looking for clues to his personality. There were no framed family photographs, but that wasn't unusual, given they had just moved in. Her mouth jerked upwards in a smile as she read the words on the mug on his desk: *I survived another meeting that should have been an email.* Amy could sympathise with that.

She stiffened at the sound of approaching footsteps and left the bag of slightly melted Minstrels on his desk. The little bit of appetite she had was evaporating. Just as well, given she was due to attend the autopsy in an hour. But the soft knock on the door did not come from Donovan, and she looked up to see Malcolm standing there. 'Twice in one day, people will talk,' she said, trying to inject some normality into her morning.

'Sorry, sweetie. I was wondering if you're going to the autopsy? Would you mind terribly filling me in when you get back?'

'Sure,' Amy replied. 'Have you turned up anything new . . . ? Because fresh leads are thin on the ground.'

'Nothing yet, I'm afraid. But whoever did this was calm and controlled, with a real eye for detail. We're talking about painstaking efforts to get everything just right.'

'I gathered that from the window display,' Amy said tersely. She delivered an apologetic smile, opening up her bag of chocolates as a peace offering. 'Sorry,' she said, as Malcolm took a few. 'I was the first on the scene. I can still see her face every time I close my eyes. She looked like a mannequin, her eyes forced open, staring into the crowd.'

'Fascinating,' Malcolm said, rolling the Minstrel around on his tongue. 'The diamanté, the glitter. If our suspect is a man, he knew how to apply make-up. And as for her hair . . .'

Amy sighed as Malcolm gushed. It was as if he were talking about a theatrical production instead of a real-life victim. But he had always been passionate about his work, and people dealt with things in different ways. Amy's irritation was all her own. Flora was at the back of her mind. Flora, and Lillian's awful trial.

'It was very ceremonial,' Malcolm continued, oblivious to her torment. 'Darling, this was planned.' He nodded, as if in agreement with himself. 'But I can't believe she was alive the whole time.'

'How did you get on at the department store?' Amy said. Door-to-door enquiries had not delivered anything new.

Malcolm stole two more chocolates from Amy's packet. 'With that much glitter and diamanté, we'd expect to find something. I don't think our victim was given her makeover there.'

'I don't think so either,' Amy agreed. She beckoned to Paddy to come in as she caught him hovering at her door. *One out, one in*, Amy thought, as Malcolm left her to it. It was always like this. It was a miracle she managed to get any work done at all.

Walking to her desk, she wrote a Post-it note reminder to update Malcolm on her return. She stuck it to the side of her computer monitor to join several others she had written that day.

Paddy cleared his throat.

Amy pushed back her sleeve to consult her watch. 'I've got the autopsy in an hour. Is it urgent?'

'A witness has come forward. They're in reception.' Paddy stretched his neck as he tugged his tie loose. 'She says she knows our victim from Facebook. Should I send Molly to speak to her?' Several videos had been posted to social media before being reported and taken down. Sliding a pen into her suit pocket, Amy grabbed her leather-bound police notebook from her desk drawer. There was no way she was letting an opportunity like this pass her by. 'Let me sound her out first,' she said, knowing she should delegate. But if someone had stepped out of the shadows with information on their victim, she wanted to hear it first.

CHAPTER SIX

Donovan didn't know Superintendent Jones all that well, but over forty years of police experience was evidenced in the lines in his forehead and his thinning hair. The pungent tang of cigarettes hung in the air. They weren't allowed to smoke in the building, but it clung to the superintendent's clothes. Donovan wouldn't be surprised if he had a bottle of Scotch in his drawer too: a throwback to days long gone.

Jones gestured at him to sit down, his phone handset pressed against his ear as he discussed authorisations for an ongoing case. Donovan hadn't had the best start with his new team. Amy cast a long shadow and Donovan was still getting to grips with being her boss. He crossed his legs, brushing a white thread from his black trousers. From the first moment he'd met Amy, he had been completely drawn in. Behind her sharp edges and frosty attitude was a vulnerability shown to very few.

After ending his phone call, Jones turned his attention to Donovan. 'Sorry about that,' he said, folding his arms across a shirt that was straining at the seams. 'How are you settling in?'

'Good, thank you, sir. Everything's going to plan.'

'I hardly call Winter jumping into a window display as "going to plan", do you? This is getting national attention.'

Donovan cleared his throat. 'To be fair, sir, I probably would have done the same thing.'

'Indeed.' Jones raised a finger. 'But you know why this would never happen to you? Instinct. You're a damn fine detective, don't get me wrong. But it was raw instinct that drew Winter to that window display – the same way it led her to the killer in her last case. Shame we can't bottle it.'

Donovan nodded, unsure of how to take his superintendent. The newspapers had relished Amy's handling of the child experimentation investigation. She had blown it wide open, but the risks she had taken to secure a conviction made him ill at ease. It was hardly any surprise that her last DCI had been forced to retire early. His senior officers had been clear about his role. He was to head up the team with Amy working under close supervision. Give her enough free rein to follow her instincts, but under his guardianship. She could never know. Their relationship was complicated enough as it was.

'There's a lot of eyes on our team. I hope we don't come to regret bringing a camera crew in.' Jones's voice cut into Donovan's thoughts.

'Winter's on board. We'll make it work, I give you my word.'

Jones nodded towards a black-and-white picture hanging on his wall. Rows of youthful officers in uniform sat with their hands on their laps. 'Robert and I joined the Met at the same time. He was a fine officer, and the legacy of his work lives on. But I'm retiring soon, and my successor won't be quite so accommodating when it comes to his daughter's behaviour. Don't get me wrong, she's a stellar detective inspector . . .' He gesticulated with both hands. 'But since her connection with the Grimes family hit the news, she's been sailing close to the wind.'

'Guv, what exactly is it that you want?' Donovan checked his watch; time was ticking on and he had so much work to do.

'Balance Winter's findings with some old-fashioned policing. Do the groundwork to support her theories, however wild they may seem. Any closer to finding out the identity of our real-life mannequin?'

'We've had a witness come forward. She's speaking to Winter now.'

'Good,' Jones replied, frowning as his phone rang. 'I'll let you get on with it. Keep me updated on any developments and keep a close eye on Winter. We can't afford any negative publicity.'

'Of course.' Donovan was about to offer further reassurance, but Jones had picked up the phone. In this world, there was little time for niceties. It seemed the superintendent would be keeping a close eye on them both. But Donovan was more than a glorified babysitter. The super's sentiment about his instinct had stung. Donovan had proved himself countless times while working for Essex Police, but now it felt like he was starting over again.

It was all the more reason to make the documentary a success. He trusted Ginny to get it right; he knew she would listen to him. Winter didn't know about their relationship, and he planned to keep it that way. At the moment, it felt like he was juggling lots of balls in the air. He only hoped that none of them would come crashing down.

CHAPTER SEVEN

Police reception was a depressing place, with painted brick walls and hard plastic seating screwed into the floor. A thick panel of safety glass separated police staff from members of the public, and although the tiled floor was regularly mopped, it still carried a putrid tang that was impossible to eliminate. There were nicer places to spend your day. Amy smoothed down her hair and tugged the hem of her jacket to straighten it out.

The witness, who gave her name as Rose, had been ushered into a side room reserved for initial contact. Molly would bring her through the building later if a statement or video interview was required.

Amy introduced herself as she entered. 'You're Rose, I take it?'

The young woman appeared to be in her mid to late twenties, with big brown Bambi eyes. Her fair hair was slicked back into a ponytail, and her suit appeared more expensive than anything Amy had ever owned. Amy gave her the once-over. Her designer bag, perfectly manicured nails and recently plumped lips: it all told a story.

'Yes, you can call me Rose,' she said, in a tone that suggested it was otherwise.

'What can I do for you?' Amy gestured at her to take a seat. The room was cramped but adequate, furnished with a basic table and chairs. It was unfortunate that it lacked windows, as it would have benefitted from a blast of fresh air.

Rose's eyes flicked towards the door, as if contemplating escape. Amy had seen that look before. Rose held a secret. One that could blow the lid off things. Her fingers tightened over the top of her handbag as an internal struggle seemed to take place.

'You've said you can identify the victim,' Amy prompted.

'Her name is . . . was Stacey. I've known her for years.'

'She was your friend?'

Rose shook her head, an expression of mild annoyance on her face. 'She was stupid, that's what she was.' She dragged out the plastic chair with a sigh of resignation and took a seat.

'Why don't you start from the beginning?' Amy mirrored her movements. 'We've got photographs we can show you, if it helps with the identity. We'll need a statement, of course—'

'I don't need to see any photos. It's her,' Rose interrupted, toying with the long silver chain around her neck. 'I won't be giving any statement. Her family will properly identify her. I can't have it coming back to me.'

'Why don't you tell me what *it* is? We can talk about statements later.' Amy was itching to get to the bottom of things. She had a lot to do and she couldn't spend all day cajoling her.

'It should have been me,' Rose blurted, her fingers winding around her chain. 'Stacey took my place.'

Amy straightened in her seat, her interest aroused. 'Took your place how?'

Rose's eyes dipped, her face conveying an inner struggle.

34

'If you're scared, we can protect you,' Amy replied, meeting her gaze. It was something she had said to countless victims in the past, but the words never lost their sincerity.

'I'm not scared.' Rose's eyes blazed. 'I just don't want this getting out.'

'Then let me put things in perspective.' Her patience exhausted, Amy folded her arms. 'Stacey was strapped to a chair with her eyes taped open in full public view. She experienced a slow, torturous death before her heart finally stopped beating. All the while, passers-by stared at her like she was part of a freak show. Now you're telling me that should have been you? Good enough reason to help us find the killer, don't you think?'

'All right . . .' Rose's hands fell away from her chain as she cleared her throat. 'I knew Stacey from uni. We shared a room before I packed it all in. After that, our lives took different paths. She got a job in a supermarket and I . . . well, I moved on. A couple of weeks before she was murdered, she came to see me. She was having money problems and wanted some advice.'

Money problems did not seem to concern Rose. But what line of work had she entered, after giving up on her university degree?

'I know what you're thinking,' Rose continued. 'Because Stacey thought it too. She saw my new car, my flat in Earl's Court. She wanted a bite of the cherry.'

'And what cherry would that be?' Amy said, presuming an element of criminality was involved.

'The girlfriend experience,' Rose replied, her chin tilted up defiantly, as if waiting for Amy's judgement. But it did not come. Amy was in no position to judge anyone, particularly given her parentage.

'At first, I got into escorting to help towards my student loan. Then I realised I could make far more money from the site than anything an arts degree could produce.'

'And what site would that be?'

'Sugar Babes.'

Amy delivered a slow nod. She had heard of high-class escort sites that students used to fund their studies. 'And Stacey became a member of this site?'

'It's very exclusive. You have to be nominated by another member to get in. She came around to mine, asking if I could help.' Rose pursed her lips as she recalled that night. 'She was struggling with money and saw it as an easy way out. Stacey was pretty, but she wasn't elegant. The girl had no class.'

'And you told her this?'

Rose gave a one-shouldered shrug. 'In so many words. If the site got complaints then it would affect my membership too. I'd set myself up with a nice little earner. I wasn't about to blow it over her.'

You're all heart, Amy thought. She watched as Rose checked the time on her Cartier watch, obviously impatient to leave. 'You said she took your place?'

'She must have hacked into my account after she went home. It was my own fault. She knew I used my date of birth as my password for everything. I should have changed it, but I didn't think she'd be so devious.' Rose opened her bag and took out a packet of cigarettes. 'Can I smoke in here?'

Amy pointed to the sprinkler overhead. 'Not unless you want a shower.'

Sighing, Rose pushed the cigarettes back into her leather bag. 'Stacey must have logged in under my username. But I don't see anyone without clearance from my handler. She vets all my new clients and monitors me when I meet them for the first time. Stacey must have bypassed all of this and agreed to a date.'

'And you've got a record of this date on your account?' Amy asked. 'When was it?'

'It was the day after she came to mine. She could have met the guy privately after that. Sometimes girls go off the radar to stop the handler taking a percentage of their earnings. It's not recommended practice.'

Amy could imagine Stacey, her eyes alight as she saw how much money she could make in one night. 'But wouldn't the client have taken one look at her and known it wasn't you?'

Rose shook her head. 'There were no shots of my face. Just tasteful black-and-white pictures of me in lingerie. Stacey and I are a similar size, similar hair colour. Physically, she could have passed for me. But she would have been way out of her depth. I bet she didn't tell anyone where she was.'

She hadn't been reported missing, as far as Amy knew. 'Do you think she arranged to meet him for sex?'

'The first encounter doesn't always lead to sex,' Rose replied. 'Sometimes they want to take you on a date, pretend you're in a relationship and show you off to their friends. Other times they just want you to listen. That's why it's called the girlfriend experience. We're not prostitutes. It runs much deeper than that. We kiss, offer intimacy, they buy the fantasy without any strings. But yes, Stacey arranged to meet him. It's listed as an agreed date on my profile.'

Amy leaned across the table, feeling a small flutter of hope for what could be their first productive lead. 'Can I have a look at his profile?'

Rose dipped her fingers into her bag. 'I closed my account. It's not active anymore.'

'You're not serious.' Amy's expression hardened at the thought of the missed opportunity. 'That could have been our last hope of getting in touch with him.'

'I printed everything out,' Rose replied, 'along with Stacey's details and home address. I wasn't being obstructive, I was scared.'

'I thought you said it was lucrative,' Amy replied, taking the paperwork from her hands.

'It is, but I've got a full-time sponsor now. I told him what happened, and he doesn't want me using the site anymore. Besides . . .' She hesitated, as if letting Amy in on a secret. 'There are lots more sites out there.'

Amy delivered a slow nod. This had all worked out quite well for Rose, considering. 'I'm going to need that statement.'

'Not happening,' Rose replied. 'You've everything you need in those printouts. Keep me out of it.'

Amy fingered through the paperwork. It seemed that Rose *had* printed copies of everything on her profile. But the date was arranged a couple of weeks before Stacey was found. Had the killer arranged to meet her again? 'Wait,' Amy said, as the young woman rose to leave. 'I need more. We can do a video interview if you prefer.'

But Rose was already pushing open the door. 'I'll come back this time tomorrow. You can have your statement then.'

'Then give me your details,' Amy said, reluctant to let her go.

Rose paused. 'I didn't *have* to come here. But I couldn't forgive myself if I didn't at least let you know. That could have been me . . .' She paled at the statement. 'But I've done all I can. I can't risk my livelihood.'

'And you're sure nobody has threatened you? You're not covering up for anyone?' It was unlikely, but Amy had to ask.

'As far as my date was concerned, he was meeting Rose. Maybe he got angry when Stacey arrived and had it in for her. It would have been obvious that she didn't have a clue. But he's got no reason to come after me because he doesn't know I exist. I like my job. I'm not being pressured into doing anything I don't want to do.'

Amy had a thousand questions, but she preferred to wait until her witness returned voluntarily rather than force the issue and have her clam up. At least they had a possible identification, and Stacey's family could be informed. Amy followed Rose out to reception, watching as she got into a cab.

Having delegated the task of identification to her officers, Amy poured over the printouts that Rose had provided, spreading them across her desk. The site was tastefully designed, with shots of Rose looking away from the camera, her hair shadowing her face. But it wasn't the images Amy was interested in, it was the correspondence between her and the man who had requested a date. His name was listed as Jonathon, and she was betting that the clean-cut image he provided was not his own. His contact with Rose was brief as he asked to hook up and it seemed that she had agreed. But an arrow was scribbled next to it, with the words *Not me. I didn't reply. My account was hacked.* Amy's pulse quickened as she read through their designated meeting place. It was a bar she recognised. 'Silly girl,' Amy tutted under her breath. But hope flared. She knew that street, and it was covered by CCTV.

CHAPTER EIGHT

'Have you had a lunch break today?' Samuel smiled at his secretary. Naomi's desk was situated outside his office. She was the gatekeeper for those who came through reception. Hers was an envied role.

'Yes, thanks,' she said, leaning over to pick up a pen that had rolled from her desk to the carpeted floor. Her blouse gaped open, revealing a glimpse of modest cleavage, and Samuel averted his gaze to a picture on the wall. 'What do you think of this?' he said, genuinely interested in her opinion. The framed poster displayed a British Bulldog racing a car with a chihuahua. It was part of a gif that had set social media on fire when it first launched. 'It's right in your eyeline,' Samuel continued. 'If you prefer something else, you only have to ask.'

'I like it.' Naomi smiled. 'It's clever marketing. The Bulldog oozes patriotism, a brand you can trust . . . but what do I know.' She laughed awkwardly.

'Every opinion counts, including yours.' Samuel glanced at the tiny plants on the side of her desk, which were resting on a miniature shelf.

Naomi followed his gaze. 'Do you want me to move them?'

'No, they're cute. But so small.' Chuckling, Samuel leaned in for a better look. 'Is that a miniature watering can too?' He picked up the tiny implement between finger and thumb. 'Does it work?'

'Yeah,' Naomi said proudly. 'I use an eye dropper to fill it. Microcrafting is my hobby. I made it myself.'

'And the cat?' Samuel poked at a miniature white feline.

'Made from real hairs.' Naomi grinned. 'I stole them from my sister's cat.'

'Well, I think it's adorable.' Samuel straightened. 'You'll have to tell me more about it sometime.'

Clearing her throat, Naomi turned her attention back to her iMac. 'Do you want me to hold your calls?'

Samuel checked his watch. Family time was important and always scheduled in. His kids were growing up so fast, with Laura looking more like her mum every day. It reminded him of when Marianne was a teenager, which stirred up so many memories of the past. 'Yes thanks,' he said, leaving Naomi to get on with her job.

Samuel had a workforce of fifty people, all highly talented and motivated. There wasn't an employee that he didn't know personally, and it was not unusual for him to take on his old work colleagues or friends. Everyone wanted a piece of him, now the company had been floated on the stock market and was making a mint. Such thoughts were enough to keep his mind racing. But not today. Today he had other things on his mind.

His smile dissolved as his office doors clicked shut. Like the flick of a switch, his mood changed. The phone call to Marianne could wait. The other side of him had come to the surface and taken a deep breath of air. If he suppressed his alter ego too long, it felt as if he were suffocating, pulled deep into the depths of his own hellish thoughts. Both sides of him needed time to breathe. Taking the weight off his feet, he stretched out on his chesterfield, leaning his head against the stiff armrest. There were times when he was tempted to give his darker side a name, but the thought of it having a separate identity utterly terrified him. He did not regret turning his fantasy into reality, but what if it consumed him whole? Crossing his feet, he told himself not to be so melodramatic. He was no serial killer. Those people took pleasure from death. Stacey was a challenging project, similar to the advertising campaigns to which he had given his all. Killing her was a necessity. He didn't need to watch the light leave her eyes. To witness the last breath escape her lips. Which was why he'd walked away at the end. But it didn't stop him wanting to do it again.

Raising his shirtsleeve, he checked his watch. He had ten minutes of alone time before he was due to call Marianne. Not enough, but it would suffice. Taking a soothing breath, his eyes fluttered shut as he allowed the memory to break free. A satisfied smile settled on his face as he relived the project he had planned so carefully. He had come out of it unscathed apart from two small scratches behind his ear, which he had managed to explain away. Touching them, he recalled the feel of the young woman's nails grating against his skin. His ability to overpower had been coupled with his need to possess. Her eyes were wild as she fought him, specks of her saliva hitting his face. She had screamed that her real name was Stacey, and she wasn't that kind of girl. It took her some time to realise that he didn't give a fuck either way. He remembered afterwards, when she was soft and compliant, the delicious *chink-chink* sound as he disposed of her tacky jewellery in the porcelain bowl. The palms of his hands tingled. He could almost feel the weight of the scissors as he trimmed her hair into a more fitting cut. Stripping Stacey of her personal possessions was one of his favourite parts of the ritual, and it gave him a hard-on every time it crossed his mind. Out went her loyalty card for Nando's and the unspent Tesco vouchers in her purse. Out went the dreadful stench of the cheap perfume she had sprayed behind her ear. If he *had* paid the requested five hundred pounds for her company, he would have asked for a refund. But luckily for him, all it cost was his time.

Basking in the memory of the cleansing, he recalled the moment when she was nameless, a living template of something once loved. For that night, she was all his. A groan of pleasure escaped Samuel's lips as he recalled what he did after that. Afterwards, placing her in a store window brought his artistic flair to light. True, it was daring, but therein lay the thrill. He didn't need to take pictures when she was immortalised on social media. Digital toxicity in all of its glory. His art would live forever, his title as the Love Heart Killer invoking fear and fascination whenever it was discussed.

His wandering thoughts were brought to heel as his mobile phone rang. It was Marianne, impatient to hear from him. Closing the door on his memory, he took the call.

CHAPTER NINE

As she lay naked on the stainless-steel table, the dead woman seemed to gaze at the ceiling in quiet reverence. Her blonde hair scraped back from her face, she was free of the make-up so cruelly applied. At least now she had a name and her family had been informed. Twenty-six-year-old Stacey Piper had made a meagre living working in a supermarket, despite having graduated from university with an arts degree. But now all of that was behind her. Today she had been weighed and photographed, her body combed for physical exhibits and scanned with UV light for bodily fluids.

Autopsies did not bother Amy. She had grown up with far worse sights, smells and sounds in her life. When she was young, the sour smell of decaying bodies had lingered in the background, although she did not fully understand back then. Besides, spending time in their forensic examiner's company was something she appreciated very much. Ray Goodman had worked on high-profile cases for over twenty years. What he didn't know about such examinations could probably fit on a postage stamp. Like Amy, Ray cared about the victims. They were more than cadavers to him. Ray respected both the living and the dead.

With his assistant following behind him, Ray entered the room with a slight waddle, which was either a limp or a side effect of his considerable weight. A kindly man, he had salt-and-pepper hair and permanent dark shadows beneath his eyes. Like Amy, he was gowned up and ready to deal with the young woman before them. 'Good to see you, Winter. How are things at home?' Ray's voice echoed in the open space. He had worked with her father in the past, and they had developed a mutual respect over the years.

'Good, thanks,' Amy replied. 'Mum still has her down days, but overall she's doing really well.'

'Lovely woman, your mother. A true lady. They don't make them like that anymore.' He flashed her a smile. 'Present company excepted.'

'Of course.' Amy returned his smile. 'How're the grandkids? You have five now, don't you?'

'Seven. Vicky had twins.' Ray came from a large family and Amy knew he would be in his element with the new additions.

'Wow. Twins. Congratulations! I bet they're keeping you busy.'

'I wouldn't have it any other way.' He turned his attention to the autopsy table. 'Which is why it breaks my heart to deal with a young woman of this age. Someone with their whole life ahead of them, reduced to a window display.'

Amy sighed. It was a tragic waste of life.

'Poor lass,' Ray said solemnly. 'No trace of the killer, I take it?'

'I'm afraid not,' Amy replied. 'We've had a fresh lead come in, but for now, the only person who can tell us what we need to know is Stacey.'

Ray tilted his head as he gazed at Stacey's face. 'Then I will speak to her, interpret her last moments, before her killer hurts anyone else.'

When it came to crime scenes of this nature, Ray worked on the basis that evidence of some type was always exchanged. Skin, blood, semen, saliva, hairs and fibres, the list went on. It was up to

Ray to capture the victim's last moments and it was a job he took seriously.

Stacey's skin was a pallid grey. Each piece of diamanté had been carefully peeled off, her nail varnish wiped away. She looked so different to the woman in the window. A tattoo of the tree of life embellished her shoulder, and on her inner wrist was a small butterfly. But they were overshadowed by the heart cut into her chest. It reminded Amy of the crude carvings often seen in the bark of trees. Why? What did it mean? She tore her eyes away as Ray switched on his Dictaphone.

'The measurements aren't exactly the same as before,' Ray said, referring to the love-heart shape. Amy already knew he had cross-referenced them with the previous victim's wounds. It was too early to assume anything, but they could not discount a link.

'You were alive when he cut you, weren't you?' Ray continued, his words directed at the corpse. 'But these bruises . . . not much in the way of defence wounds. Perhaps you were too numb to feel the pain.' His bushy eyebrows knitted together as he checked the body for unnatural markings. Amy noted each one with interest, hanging on his every word. 'Let's hope the toxicology reports will shine some light on things.'

A hush fell as he picked up his scalpel and made the initial Y-shaped incision. For this part, Ray exercised silence. Small talk was not appreciated as he made the first cut. All Amy could hear was the buzz of fluorescent lights overhead and the sound of her own heart as it drummed in her chest. She resisted bringing her hand up to her nose to block out the smell of decay. She had seen worse – far worse – and she told herself to get a grip. But Stacey's death had hit a nerve. She wasn't much older than the women her own biological parents had killed. The sour stench of death invoked memories she preferred to keep locked in the past.

Ray's assistant stepped in as Ray removed the internal organs and examined each one in turn. 'A meagre last meal.' Ray was still talking to the corpse as he examined the contents of the stomach. 'Looks like beans on toast, bless you.'

Amy watched as Ray held each organ with the same care you would offer a newborn child. It both touched and saddened her. What must it be like, performing procedures such as these, day after day? Did the dead return in his nightmares, or was it only Amy who experienced such nightly visitations? These thoughts floated in her consciousness as she continued to observe Ray at work. Taking great care with Stacey's heart, he described it in detail, noting the size and shape, along with any irregularities. After the body cavity was sewn up, Ray finally turned to Amy. 'There's no sign of strangulation. No physical injury apart from the restraint marks on her wrists. I'm confident the lab reports will reveal more.'

Amy nodded gravely as Ray's words echoed those of Malcolm's that she had heard earlier in the day.

'Now, we must wait,' he said, referring to the test results. 'But from what I've seen, cause of death is likely to be heart failure brought on by poisoning.'

After uttering his final observations and giving the current time, he gave his assistant the nod to switch off the Dictaphone. Then, softly and with reverence, he murmured a valediction to Stacey. They were the same words he said to every person Amy witnessed him perform a procedure on. 'Sleep well, my dear. Thank you.'

Amy fought to contain the question burning on her lips. As Ray peeled off his gloves, he turned to her. 'What is it, Winter? Spit it out.'

'I was wondering.' She stepped aside to allow the assistant to clean up. 'Why do you talk to them?'

'Respect.' The word came instantly, as if he had been waiting for her question all along. 'Most poor unfortunates I deal with experienced a trauma of some kind. Many were violated. Murdered. Held against their will. I know it's unusual, but . . .' He heaved a tired sigh. 'I don't want to be yet another person to handle their body without consent. I talk to them out of respect. I treat them with care. Just as I would want a member of my family treated if they had been through something as brutal as that.'

'I get that,' Amy said. 'And we'll work around the clock to get justice for Stacey.'

'I'd expect nothing less of a Winter.'

As she de-gowned and washed her hands, Amy spared a thought for her team. Had they uncovered any leads in her absence? DCI Donovan was on hand, if so. She felt a strange sense of disappointment. What had she expected to come from the autopsy? As Ray said, these things took time, and it could be weeks before they received any results.

'Thanks,' Amy said, turning to leave. 'Nothing personal, but I don't want to see you again for a very long time.'

As she reached the gloom of the corridor, Amy dialled her mum's number on her phone. But it wasn't her mum who answered, it was Winifred.

'She's still poorly, I'm afraid,' Winifred said, immediately recognising Amy's voice. 'I've sent her to bed with a Lemsip and turned her electric blanket on.'

'Do you need me to come home?' Amy's voice was brittle with worry.

'No dear, not at all. I'll stay with her until you finish your shift. I'm watching the reruns of *Agatha Raisin*. I'm going nowhere.'

Amy's heart warmed to know that Flora would not be alone. 'Thanks,' she replied, and urged Winifred to call should Flora take a turn for the worse. She knew that if it were the other way around, Flora would be there for her friend.

Taking a deep breath, Amy drew her car keys from her pocket and strode out of the door.

CHAPTER TEN

'Muuum . . . I told you already, I don't need a babysitter!' Laura groaned at her mother as she opened the front door. Standing in her unicorn onesie, she voiced her disgust. Icy cool air wafted through the front door as her aunt walked in.

'Is that any way to talk to your favourite auntie?' Karen closed the door behind her before rifling in a Tesco bag and plucking out a Toblerone. 'I brought chocolate.'

'Thanks, love you!' Laura snapped the bar from her grip before bounding upstairs.

'Sorry, she's in a funny mood today.' Marianne approached her sister, kissing her on the cheek.

'We were no different at that age,' Karen laughed. 'Where's the other munchkin?'

'Upstairs, writing a negotiation letter to the tooth fairy.' Marianne rolled her eyes. 'Takes after her father, that one.'

'Ooh, looks like her mummy's had a visit from the diamond fairy.' Karen peered at her sister's necklace. 'New bling?' She followed her into the living room, swinging her Tesco bag.

Marianne's fingers traced the necklace where it rested on her collarbone. It looked beautiful against her olive skin, the emerald-cut diamond complementing her wavy hair. 'It's lovely, isn't it?' she said.

'Stunning.' Karen's brown eyes roamed over the diamond centrepiece. But there wasn't a hint of envy in her voice. A security officer, Karen was four years younger and the more sensible of the two. Marianne couldn't believe it when she'd had all her brunette locks chopped off. The short style seemed harsh and regimented in contrast to Marianne's soft waves.

As she slipped the necklace off, Marianne placed it back in its black velvet box. It *was* lovely, but it made her into someone she could not reconcile herself with. Sliding across a picture on the wall, she accessed the hidden safe and placed the jewellery inside. It lay there along with the other pieces Samuel had bought her since the advent of his success. After clicking the combination number, she concealed their hidden treasures from the world. But even then it would taunt her. Stoke the embers of her guilt. She didn't deserve this. Everything she owned was paid for with Samuel's money. She hadn't held a job in years.

'Are you OK?' Karen muted the television, which had been on in the background. It was her favourite programme, a fly-on-the-wall production of life in the force, headed by a woman named Ginny Wolfe.

'I miss the old days,' Marianne said. 'Life was simpler when Samuel and I shared our little flat in Southend.' She remembered how hard they had scrimped and saved for the deposit, how happy they had been when they picked up the keys. It was the first time either of them had left home, and they were barely capable of boiling an egg. How Samuel's eyes used to twinkle when he spoke about the future, his face shining with hope as he promised to take her to far-flung places across the globe. 'Things were different back then. It was me and Samuel against the world.'

'Hmm.' Karen looked sceptical. 'You're glamorising it because you're viewing it from a comfortable place. You don't want to go back there.'

'I don't know,' Marianne said, feeling suddenly lost. 'I barely recognise myself anymore.' She began to wring her hands. Her conservative designer clothes, her dinner parties for the influential. She was stifled. In the old days, Samuel had carried an edge of darkness and it excited her. He had taught her how to shoplift, and how to smoke a joint without having a coughing fit. Back then, his world had revolved around her. Now they were just going through the motions and she didn't like it one bit.

'What about the bedroom department – everything OK there?' Karen said, her eyes flicking from the muted TV to her sister.

Marianne shrugged. 'Our sex life might be all right if I could physically get him into bed. When he's not working late, he's out with clients. This is the first weeknight we've spent together in ages. Sometimes he doesn't come home until three or four o'clock.'

'Really?' Karen's voice was tinged with suspicion. 'That doesn't sound right. Here, he's not carrying on behind your back, is he? Because if he is . . .'

Marianne shook her head as her sister voiced her worst fears. 'No. He wouldn't do that. And when we do get together, it's good.' A flush coloured her face. The truth was, she could barely remember the last time she and Samuel had made love.

'Why don't you turn that up?' Marianne pointed at the television. 'I wouldn't want you missing your favourite show.'

'They're filming from Notting Hill station next week.' Karen brightened as she turned her attention to the screen. 'It's just around the corner from here.'

Marianne tried to look interested, but her mind was racing ahead. Tonight, they were attending an award ceremony and she already knew how the night would go. He would come home and get ready, they would travel to the event in silence, and when he got there, he would tell everyone how in love he was with his wife. Their audience would fawn, and her society friends would press their hands against her arm and tell her how lucky she was. But there was something, or some*one*, stealing his thoughts. Samuel guarded his privacy, particularly his mobile phone. He was even more protective of his home office and kept the door firmly locked when he was out. 'I'm going to get ready,' she said to her sister. 'Make yourself a cuppa. There's chocolate digestives in the cupboard.'

Talking to her sister had focused her thoughts. She climbed the stairs to her bedroom, becoming more determined with each step. She wouldn't let things lie any longer. She would uncover his secrets, perhaps hire a private investigator. If her husband was having an affair, she would face it head on.

CHAPTER ELEVEN

With soft, swift strokes, Amy applied the cleanser to her face. Removing her make-up was a nightly ritual that helped her clear her thoughts. She sat at her mirrored dressing table, mulling over the catalogue of the day's events. Her main concern was the murder investigation, which was making slow progress. After consultation with the command team, they had released details of the murder to the press. But press exposure was also focused on Lillian's trial. Amy swept the cotton wool over her eyebrows and gently cleansed the mascara from her lashes. By the time she opened her eyes, she had refocused her thoughts. She crossed her bare feet beneath her seat. Dotty, her pug, was at her feet, having been Flora's bed companion for most of the day. As Amy threw the soiled cotton wool into the bin, a sense of gloom descended. Right now, all she wanted to do was curl up in bed with her laptop and watch something mindless on Netflix until she fell asleep. But the ring of her mobile phone put a halt to her plans.

It was her sister, Sally-Ann. 'Sorry, did I wake you?' she said, as Amy answered the phone. 'Paddy's just got in, so I thought I'd catch you before you fell asleep.'

'Sleep is a long way off,' Amy said. She sensed her sister's hesitation at the other end of the line. 'Everything all right?'

'Yeah . . .' Sally-Ann replied. 'I mean . . . are you worried about giving evidence? The thought of it is keeping me awake at night. I don't like to worry Paddy, he's got enough going on with the investigation and everything.'

Amy rolled her eyes. Her sister seemed to forget that not only did Amy oversee Paddy and the team, but she was first in line for the chop when things went wrong. Was it because she was a woman? Did Sally-Ann think that Paddy did more than her? Amy didn't always see eye-to-eye with her sister's old-fashioned views. 'We're not meant to talk about the court case,' Amy said, her words on a long exhale. Pulling back her duvet, she slid into bed. The crisp white cotton felt cool and comforting against her skin.

'But have you seen the momentum it's gaining in the press?' Sally-Ann said. 'I can't believe the amount of people supporting her now. I'm all for helping victims of domestic abuse but our mother hardly qualifies. I wish I could contact them and tell them the truth.'

'You'll get your chance in court.' Amy hoped she could change the subject. Lillian Grimes was the last person she wanted in her thoughts before she slept.

'It's not just domestic abuse groups,' Sally-Ann continued. 'She's getting tons of fan mail too. Mandy said she's had proposals of marriage, as well as letters from men wanting to date her, and some women too. They've even offered to put her up.' She snorted with disbelief. 'You'd think she was some kind of sex symbol or something. She's like a celebrity who can do no wrong.' Mandy was their biological sister, and she had always taken Lillian's side.

'It's called hybristophilia,' Amy said dully. Sally-Ann was obviously desperate to talk about it, and she wouldn't get any peace until her sister got things off her chest.

'His-what?'

'Hybristophilia. Also known as Bonnie and Clyde syndrome.' Amy leaned against her headboard, a pillow propped up behind her back. The psychology behind such fan mail had fascinated her long before Lillian's appeal. 'It's a sexual attraction for people who commit really dark crimes. Look it up. It's a thing. Some women have married serial killers who were on death row.'

'Why?' Sally-Ann said. 'It's not as if there aren't plenty of other fish in the sea – the non-murdering kind, that is.'

'But that's the very thing some women find attractive. Not the murders in particular, but the thought of being with someone who stands out from the pack. Some people like the attention; some get off on the shock value. It makes them feel special, like they're different to everyone else.'

'Jeez. It's sick, that's what it is.'

Amy was not going to disagree. 'There are lots of different reasons for this type of behaviour. Some women are in complete denial about the offences, and just enjoy being with someone who is strong in their masculinity or femininity. Others don't want the complications of real-life relationships.'

'I suppose you get women who want to fix them, too,' Sally-Ann said.

'Exactly that,' Amy agreed. 'They see the child behind the mask. They want to nurture them.' Amy opened her laptop and clicked on to Netflix. She would need some heavy-duty comfort viewing after a conversation like this. She settled on *RuPaul's Drag Race* and chose an episode to watch.

'Crazy,' Sally-Ann said mid-yawn. 'I can't imagine anyone wanting to date Lillian, much less live with her.'

'Hopefully it won't come to that.' Amy could not face the prospect of her biological mother being free in the world. But still there was a lingering niggle of worry that Lillian could soon be released.

'Paddy hasn't said much.' Sally-Ann's voice became low. 'He wants to support us both, but you know what he's like when it comes to feelings. He doesn't know what to say.'

'Just being there is enough,' Amy said, well aware of how Paddy struggled with expressing his emotions.

'That's what I told him,' Sally-Ann replied.

Amy could hear the smile in her sister's voice at their mutual understanding of Paddy's little ways. 'We don't talk about it at work.'

'I don't blame you,' Sally-Ann said. 'It's not healthy to dwell on such things.'

This amused Amy, as it was Sally-Ann who had brought Lillian up in the first place.

'What will be will be, as the song goes,' Sally-Ann continued. 'As for giving evidence . . . we have to do what's right. Even if Lillian does get out, I don't think she's a threat anymore. She's lost her wingman. She's powerless without Jack. She's a one-man band and she doesn't work that way.'

The words were said with such authority that Amy wanted to ask more. She opened her mouth to speak, but then changed her mind. She'd had enough of Lillian Grimes for one day. 'OK, sis. Well, I'm in bed now, so . . .'

'I'm heading off to bed myself,' Sally-Ann replied. 'Paddy's beat. I hope you solve this case soon. He's good for nothing when he's working twelve-hour shifts.'

A soft chuckle left Amy's lips. 'You'll get him back when we solve this case.'

'The sooner the better,' Sally-Ann said. 'I've got a ton of DIY waiting to be done.'

After ending the call, Amy stretched her arms, keen to shake off the stresses of the day. Snuggling beneath the covers, she found the warmth of Dotty's body near her feet. She switched off the light before returning her attention to her laptop, her sister's words resounding in her mind. But she couldn't dwell on them, not with a killer roaming the streets of London. Who knew what tomorrow would bring?

CHAPTER TWELVE

Marianne looked stunning in her backless black Givenchy dress. To Samuel, his wife was the most beautiful woman in the room. But award ceremonies had lost their shine and the buzz of winning just wasn't there anymore.

On the podium, the Mayor of London spoke in strident tones, preparing to deliver the accolade of UK Employer of the Year. Making the shortlist was a feat in itself, and Samuel had already been tipped the nod that he had won.

'The results are calculated from across twenty-five industry sectors,' the mayor said, envelope in his hand. 'Companies who champion their employees, who embrace diversity and equal opportunity, and create a strong and happy workforce. They are a shining example to others and it is something all employers should strive for.' As he opened the envelope, a smile crept to his face. 'I'm very happy to announce that the winner of the UK's best employer 2020 is . . . Black Media. Can we have a huge round of applause for Samuel Black, who was named Man of the Year just two weeks ago.'

The applause was thunderous as Samuel took to the stage. He could almost hear his stocks increasing in value. He likened it to the sound the old amusement arcades in Southend made when the machines paid out. *Ching-ching, you've won!* In his youth, Samuel Black had been a world away from the fat cats clapping in recognition of his award. But now it was *ching-ching-ching* all the way. He could make money in his sleep. Offering a dazzling smile, he shook the mayor by the hand and accepted the weighty engraved glass trophy.

'I don't deserve this award . . .' he said, pausing as his words were met with dismay. He smiled, with genuine sincerity. 'I don't deserve this award because my employees do. They have made my company what it is today. It is a privilege to be part of the most ambitious, passionate and ingenious workforce. Because at Black Media we are family. Sure, we may have our differences every now and again. But as the saying goes, if you get a job at Black Media, you're stepping into a dead man's shoes because nobody ever leaves . . .' He continued the speech he had memorised by heart, each word delivered with warmth and appreciation for his workforce. Rounding it off, he thanked the backbone of it all – his wife.

As he stood behind the heat of the spotlight, he recalled a time when he'd told himself that this would be enough. That when he'd made it, the urge to dominate women would dissipate. But now, at the height of his career, the truth dawned like a new morning. His secret and his success went hand in hand. Each side balanced out the other. Step by step he justified his desires as acceptable. People disappeared all the time. Planning his murderous project had given him a new lease of life. What's more, he had escaped capture. There was no reason he couldn't do it again. But why put himself in the spotlight by posing his victim in such an elaborate display? As he returned to his table, he mused on it. Perhaps his darker side wanted some recognition too. He laid his trophy on the table. Who didn't like being recognised for a job well done?

'That was amazing,' Marianne said, her eyes shining with pride. 'We've come a long way.'

And they had, from their humble beginnings in Southend-on-Sea. Everything was perfect. Which was why he couldn't stop now.

◆ ◆ ◆

You deserve a treat for this. The voice came as they were being driven home. Marianne was half asleep, resting on his shoulder, anesthetised by too many glasses of champagne. *It's too soon*, Samuel replied, his response spoken in his thoughts.

You've made all those plans. C'mon. All work and no play . . .

Samuel sighed. Now he'd had a taste, his urges were growing. His victim hadn't even been buried, yet he was itching to kill again. But winning the award was worthy of proper celebration. *I suppose it wouldn't do any harm to look in my little black book.*

He knew he was talking to himself, an internal conversation as he allowed his alter ego to take the reins. *Let's make this one even bigger and better than before.*

His wife shifted beside him and he paused to kiss the top of her head. *I'll think about it,* he thought. But deep down, he knew the decision had already been made.

CHAPTER THIRTEEN

Standing with her arms folded, Amy observed her team. No two mornings in her office were the same. The sounds of traffic filtered through the open windows, the hustle and bustle of London life. Amy knew it was never going to be easy, managing high-profile crime in the city she loved. If only she could strike a better balance between her private life and work. She had seen the headlines in yesterday's papers with regard to Lillian's court appeal. It was no coincidence that the camera crew were taking so much interest in her team.

'Try not to look at the camera.' Ginny dictated DC Steve Moss's movements as she set up the equipment in the corner of the office.

'But what are we allowed to share?' Steve took a swig of his protein drink. His biceps were straining in his shirt, which had become strangely tighter since the camera crew appeared. Unless Amy was mistaken, he'd also had a new haircut.

In fact . . . She cast her eyes over the rest of her officers. Molly was wearing make-up, something she rarely bothered with, and . . . were those high heels beneath her trouser suit? The last thing Amy needed was her team getting distracted when they had such a high-profile case on the go. 'The brief is to talk normally,' Amy said. 'It's not live. Anything confidential can be edited out later.' She looked pointedly at Steve and Molly. 'And for God's sake, relax. This isn't a Hollywood movie.'

'You mean Liam Neeson won't be playing my part?' Paddy piped up from behind Amy. 'Well, that's a kick in the teeth, for sure.' Paddy had come back from a recent trip to Ireland and his accent had grown stronger as a result.

'Yeah,' Amy replied. 'Liam really missed out there. Now, if we can focus on the case, I'd like to see where we're at.'

'Could you walk back into the room and speak to the team?' Ginny directed Bob, the cameraman, towards Amy.

'Is this really necessary?' Amy bristled. She was fine with five minutes of banter, as her team had worked non-stop all weekend, but she was damned if she was going to waste time replaying every movement.

'It won't take a second.' Ginny smiled as she approached. 'We need you to walk from there to here . . .' She pointed to the floor in the centre of the room. 'Now, if Dom can fit you up with a mike, that would be perfect. We don't want the sound boom getting in the way.' Amy cast Donovan a withering gaze as he entered the room. 'Perfect, you're all here,' Ginny smiled, oblivious to Amy's discontent.

'I can do it myself, thank you!' Amy said, threading the microphone up through her shirt. She hooked the small black box on the other end to the back of her belt. With the microphone fitted, Amy strode to the centre of the room. She could feel the film crew focusing on her every move as she spoke to her team.

'Thank you all for your professionalism and dedication to the case. I know that some of you have cancelled rest days to be here and it hasn't gone unnoticed. There's plenty of overtime available and we're drafting some more officers in to help.' Amy glanced around the room, ignoring the wide lens of the camera as it crept closer to her face. 'I urge you all to read the report from our criminal profiler.' She drew attention to the sheet in her hand. 'She believes our murderer is an attention-seeker. She compares the window display to a controlled explosion, planned for maximum impact. They may kill again.' The room fell silent as she relayed the report. The only sounds were the printer duplicating a batch of papers and the constant stream of traffic outside. 'Their risk-taking adds to the element of excitement and their actions display a hint of arrogance.'

'But if our suspect craves excitement, then why was the previous murder so many years ago?' The question came from DC Steve Moss.

'We still don't know that they're linked,' Amy said. 'But our profiler believes they are. It's possible they've been in prison, or out of the country.' She looked at Molly, who was studiously taking notes. 'Perhaps they were settled with a family, and now their life circumstances have changed,' Amy continued. 'But why the love heart? What does that signify? Was his victim random, was it a perceived act of love? Or is there a connection with Valentine's Day? These are the questions I want you to think about as you're going through this case. No theory is a stupid one. If you have a gut feeling then don't be afraid to explore it. Where are we with the CCTV?' Amy had the task flagged as a matter of urgency.

'It's been viewed,' Molly said. 'We can see Stacey waiting to meet her date. I was just going to let you know.'

'Good,' Amy said, as Molly drew it up on the computer. 'Have we a clear view of the suspect?'

'I'm afraid not,' Molly replied. 'She waited for half an hour, but he was a no-show.'

This was not the news Amy wanted to hear. If Stacey's one and only date was not their suspect then that would bring them back to square one. Were they wrong in thinking that their victim had met the killer online? Another thought occurred to her. 'Perhaps he stood her up so he could follow her home. Cross-reference the CCTV to see if anyone followed her.'

'But there's no sign of forced entry into her address on the night she died,' Molly replied.

Amy turned to Steve, who had been overseeing door-to-door enquiries. 'Her flatmates were out that night, weren't they?'

'Yes, ma'am.' Steve nodded. 'At a concert.'

Amy paused. It was rare for Steve to call her anything other than 'Winter', and it reminded her of the camera crew in the room. 'And nobody has seen anything? No mention of anyone noticing Stacey in the block of flats that night?'

'It's a busy street, people keep to themselves.' Steve tore his gaze from the camera as Ginny signalled for him to look away.

Amy folded her arms. Why couldn't the gods of chance give her a break, just this once? 'Officers on the ground can follow up on house-to-house enquiries, knock on the doors they got no response from first time around.' She turned to the rest of the team. 'Any joy sourcing the materials from the window display?'

'We have,' Paddy replied, holding a sheet of freshly printed paper. 'The display was put together by an outside company. Black Media. They're based nearby and source all the products themselves. Billy Picton, their employee, came in for a voluntary interview this morning. He's the chap who oversaw the design. He was also the only person with access to the building, apart from store staff.'

'And where are we on timings? Was he there the night Stacey was put on the throne?'

'He was, but two members of store staff were helping him with the display. We have them on CCTV coming in and out of the building.'

'Then why don't we have our killer?' Amy asked.

'Because the CCTV was disabled. Whoever did this knew where the cameras were located.' Paddy handed Amy the sheet he had just printed off, which contained a copy of Billy's voluntary interview.

'Couldn't Billy have come back?'

'He has an alibi,' Paddy said. 'He went straight from arranging the window display to a fundraiser in a pub. We've cross-referenced it with CCTV and it checks out.' Amy nodded as Paddy brought her up to speed with events. She felt a tug in her gut, an ingrained intuition that was not to be ignored. They may have been satisfied enough to cross this potential suspect off the list, but she wasn't. It was time to pay a visit to Black Media.

CHAPTER FOURTEEN

When investigating serious crime, it was preferable to speak to staff at home rather than notifying their workplace. But as Black Media had been commissioned to create the window display, it involved the company too. The receptionist at the building where they were based sat behind a wide chrome desk. She seemed unimpressed with Amy's credentials as she raised her warrant card in the air.

'All requests to speak to Black Media staff must go through Ms Naomi Blunt, Mr Black's PA. I can give you her number,' she said, clicking her ballpoint pen.

'Why don't you tell me where their office is? I'll take it from there.' Amy was in no mood to sugar-coat her words.

'They're on the tenth floor,' the woman replied. 'I'll let them know you're on your way.'

Amy stepped inside the lift, pressing the digital display panel for the correct floor. She avoided her reflection in the surrounding glass mirrors, staring at her shoes instead. Lately, she could barely stand to look at herself, because all she could see was Lillian Grimes's face. She wondered if there would be a time when she was not haunted by her biological mother's past deeds. She had heard whispers in the corridors where she worked: hushed debates as to whether Lillian would be freed. It was a very real possibility Amy had yet to come to terms with.

As the elevator doors parted, she was met with clean, crisp filtered air. It was the antithesis of her own office, which carried the tang of takeaway food intermingled with diesel fumes from outside. Every surface in this building shone, from ceiling to floor, and every window was sealed. There was no doubt she was in the right place, judging by the advertising artwork gracing the tiled walls. Black Media had won awards for its happy workforce, and Naomi Blunt's attitude was a testament to that. 'Welcome to Black Media,' she said, imparting a warm smile. 'Isn't it a lovely day?'

Amy paused, taken aback by her cheerful demeanour. 'Er . . . I guess so. I hadn't noticed.'

'What can I do for you? Can I get you a drink? Tea, coffee? Juice? We've got this delish flavoured water that we're promoting this week, almost calorie-free. Not that you need it or anything—'

'I'd like to speak to your boss, please,' Amy interrupted, wondering how anyone this chatty got any work done.

'Have you an appointment?' Naomi tapped her keyboard. But Amy was staring with unadulterated envy. It wasn't the top-of-the-range desk itself or her Mac computer Amy was mentally coveting, it was the colourful planners, notebooks and pens.

'I don't need one.' She flashed her warrant card for the second time that morning as she introduced herself. 'It's police business.'

Naomi regarded her in awe. 'Wow. That's so cool, a female DI. We don't get many of them in here.' She cleared her throat as Amy failed to respond, and tucked a wisp of fair hair behind her ear. 'Hi. I've got a Detective Inspector Winter here to see you,' she said, pressing a button on her phone. She returned her glance to Amy. 'You can go right in.'

Amy swallowed back the argument on the tip of her tongue. She had not expected such easy access to the elusive Mr Black. She absorbed further colourful posters lining the walls as she approached the double doors of his office. She recognised the campaigns from social media – she hadn't realised they all originated from the same company. It was hardly surprising he had grown so successful if this was the quality of his work. Taking a strengthening breath, she turned the chrome door handle and walked inside. Her face was a mask of impassivity as she greeted the man before her. Samuel Black was standing by the window, his hands deep in his pockets as he watched her approach.

'Mr Black, I'm DI Amy Winter. My officers have been trying to reach you for some time.' *It's all right for some*, Amy thought, surveying his office. It was big enough to house a chesterfield suite as well as a huge desk and several chairs. Full-length windows flooded the room with light, and Amy's attention was briefly drawn to the telescope fixed on the streets below. *So he's a people-watcher*, she thought, assimilating each clue. Many articles had been written of his 'rags to riches' success, but who was the real Samuel Black?

'I was about to call.' Samuel gestured towards the leather chair in front of his mahogany desk. 'Why don't you take a seat? And please, call me Samuel like everyone else.'

Amy glanced at the nearby chesterfield sofa and at the glass cabinet, which housed many awards. Like the corridor, the walls of his office were lined with advertising slogans and campaigns. Some were amusing, while others carried a more serious edge. Amy returned her glance to Samuel as he slid into his leather chair. He was a reasonably good-looking man with a firm jaw, short dark hair, and a slim but toned build.

'What can I do for you?' Samuel surveyed her with interest as she took a seat. There was something about the way he was looking at her, not in a leery or predatory way . . . It was as if his eyes were boring into her. His gaze was icy cold. Amy told herself she was being paranoid. She had a lot on her mind.

'I'm here about the Stacey Piper case. You're aware of it, aren't you? My officers have already made enquiries with your firm.' Amy wasn't sure why he was acting so innocent, but it wouldn't wash with her.

'Oh right, I see.' Samuel steepled his fingers, resting them beneath his chin. 'But you've already interviewed my staff. I presumed that was the end of it.'

Amy crossed her legs. 'There is no end to a murder investigation while the suspect is at large. Not only was your company hired to create the Valentine's Day display, Black Media sourced the products found on the victim's body.' She glared at Samuel as she drove her point home. 'We've got documented invoices signed by a member of your staff. The killer also had access to the building. No forced entry had been made.' Amy did not always share information so freely, but it was already public knowledge thanks to the press.

'But the body wasn't spotted until the next day. In fact . . .' Samuel's eyes narrowed as he stared at Amy. 'Hang on . . .' He pointed a finger in her direction. 'Wasn't it you who found her? I thought I recognised your face.'

'Yes, it was,' Amy replied. 'But we believe the victim was displayed the night before.'

'Hmm,' Samuel pondered, as precious seconds passed. 'How much trouble is Billy in?' He briefly broke his gaze to look out of the window. 'It's OK, he's told me everything. He said he's been interviewed at length.'

'He's helping us with our enquiries on a voluntary basis,' Amy replied stiffly. 'No arrests have been made. Why?'

'We look after our employees here at Black Media. I should know if Billy needs adequate legal representation.'

A smile hung on his lips a little too long. There was something about this man that made Amy ill at ease. 'I thought this was an advertising company?' she said. 'What has Black Media got to do with legal advice?'

'We offer all our employees full insurance, including legal representation. We're a family and we value every member of our team.'

The words sounded as if they had come from the back of a pamphlet. 'That's very commendable, Mr Black. But what I'd like to know is how the killer used props and products sourced from your company and accessed the store window without being seen.'

'Surely that's up to the police to investigate.' Samuel folded his arms. 'My job is to ensure that Black Media is not implicated in this . . . tragedy. After all, this doesn't just affect my employee, this reflects on my company as a whole. Our shareholders need to be kept in the loop.'

Amy scrutinised the man before her. He was purported to be a loving family man, but there was a deadness behind his eyes, a look known only to those trained to recognise it. This was the first time he had referred to Stacey's murder as a tragedy and the word seemed forced. Amy clasped her hands together as she tried to decipher his behaviour.

'What can you tell me about Billy?' she said, in an effort to move on.

'He's an old mate of mine. When he asked me for a job, I couldn't say no.'

Amy raised an eyebrow. Billy's statement mentioned nothing about being friends with Samuel Black. Samuel's company had funded his training and development. Perhaps that was why.

'When you say you go a long way back . . .' Amy said. 'How long?'

'We went to school together. Didn't he tell you?' Samuel frowned. 'That's funny. I thought he would have mentioned it . . .'

'I expect he thought it wasn't relevant.'

'Really? Seems pretty damned relevant to me, given what happened to our old schoolteacher.'

'I'm not with you,' Amy replied, pausing as his words clicked into place. 'Unless . . . Was your schoolteacher . . .' Her forehead creased as she made the link. Checks on the old case had begun in earnest, but the connection had not yet emerged.

'Claire Lacey.' Samuel finished her sentence for her. 'Maybe Billy presumed you knew. Besides, her boyfriend was in the frame for her murder.'

'It was her fiancé, and he was released on appeal.' Amy made a mental note to follow this up with her team. Just how watertight was Billy's alibi? In the meantime, Samuel was furiously backtracking on his earlier comments.

'But then, Claire dying had nothing to do with Billy. I mean, he was nuts about her. He wouldn't have harmed a hair on her head.'

'Billy had a thing for his teacher?' Amy's mind raced with possibilities. If Billy knew Claire, then so did Samuel – was he throwing his old friend under the bus?

'It was years ago.' Samuel paused for thought. 'He's a family man now. Well . . .' He smiled awkwardly. 'When I say "family" . . . he's just got divorced. Hit him hard . . . poor bloke. But we'll support him in any way we can.'

'Can I have a copy of his personnel files?' Amy said, expecting a firm 'no'. A court order would ensure they were turned over, but it was much quicker to ask.

Samuel shrugged. 'Sure. I'm always happy to help the Old Bill. If there's anything else you need, then you only have to ask.'

'Tell me about your relationship with Claire Lacey.' Amy watched as Samuel's face clouded over. 'Yours and Billy's, I mean. Did you see her outside of school?'

'Not me.' Samuel's smile faded as he checked his watch. 'But Billy had a real thing for her. He was a bit of a loner back then, and when she was nice to him, well, he got a bit obsessed. He used to bring her presents in class, and accidently-on-purpose bump into her after school. Everyone took the piss out of him. I think she secretly liked it, though.'

'What makes you say that?' Amy said.

'Because she didn't seem to mind. She had a lot of time for Billy. In *and* out of school.'

'Out of school?' Amy repeated.

'She used to give him extra tuition. Encouraged him to better himself.'

'And you? What about you?' Amy watched Samuel intently, but his body language gave nothing away.

'Me? God no, my wife and I were sweethearts, even then. I only had eyes for her.' He delivered a winning smile, but Amy was not so easily won over.

'I saw you on the box,' Samuel said. 'It wasn't just that footage of you in the store window . . . I remember now. Aren't the Beasts of Brentwood your parents?'

Amy frowned. This was not territory she wanted to cover. Certainly not with the likes of Samuel Black.

'It must have been hard, being a copper with your parents banged up for murder,' he continued.

Before Amy could respond, Samuel rose from his chair, his gaze on the streets below. 'I caught some of her court case on telly. They said you helped bring her appeal to light when you dobbed your old police colleagues in.' Samuel stood at the window, his hands back in his pockets. 'A new Banksy has popped up in Shoreditch this morning. Have you seen it?'

'No,' Amy replied. She monitored Samuel's intonation and movements as he kept his gaze on the streets below.

'I heard he paints for the love of it. He probably couldn't stop if he tried,' Samuel said sombrely. 'I bet he's always thinking ahead, working out what he's painting next.' The room darkened around them as the sun dipped behind a cloud. Instinctively, Amy knew they weren't talking about the painting anymore.

'Amazing, ain't it? How he displays his art so publicly, yet remains anonymous?'

'Somebody will find out who he is soon enough.'

'Not if he's clever.' Samuel delivered a devious smile. 'He must get a kick out of that.'

Amy's lips thinned. 'Nothing lasts forever. It's impossible to stay anonymous in this world.'

Finally, Samuel turned to face her. The expression on his face was frightening, and reminded Amy of one she had seen many times in her youth. It was the face of someone who was remorseless. Someone who would let nothing stand in their way. 'Then we'll agree to disagree.'

'Is there something you'd like to tell me?' Pressing her hands against the armrests, Amy rose from her chair. Within a split second, Samuel's expression reverted to normal, and already Amy was doubting what she had seen.

'Only that I'm a Banksy fan.' Samuel chuckled as he approached his desk. The dark cloud had passed, and his smile was warm again. But something had occurred between them and it was enough to turn Amy's blood cold. She knew exactly what he was getting at.

'Where were you the night of the murder?'

'Entertaining a client,' Samuel replied instantly. 'Japanese businessmen love being shown the sights. We were in a gentleman's club, then on to a few bars. I never left his side all night.'

'And you'll be happy to give a statement to that effect?'

'Of course. As long as you're discreet.' Samuel paused to check his watch. 'I'm afraid we've overrun. I had a meeting scheduled for ten minutes ago.'

Given he had a personal assistant, Amy doubted that very much. 'My officers will be in touch,' she said, wishing they had enough evidence to bring him in.

Samuel plucked a business card from his pocket. 'Here's my mobile number. Have them give me a call.'

'Here's mine,' Amy replied, ready with a card of her own. 'If you'd like to continue our conversation, you can get me here.'

Amy could feel Samuel's eyes upon her as he followed her to the door of his office. It wasn't until she was in the lift that she was able to take a deep breath and relax. What had just happened back there? Had Samuel alluded to being the killer? Amy tensed as she recalled their conversation. Every gesture, every inflection, told a story. One that only she could hear.

CHAPTER FIFTEEN

In the early days, Marianne used to visit Samuel at work unannounced all the time. Sometimes she would bring a picnic. Other times she would enter his office wearing a long coat and heels and little underneath. It had been a thrill: the wife of a respected businessman walking through the streets of London in her basque and suspenders. It didn't matter how busy Samuel was, he always made time to see her, and sex in his office had been so satisfying back then. Perhaps that was what their marriage needed: a good old-fashioned romp from time to time. Today she had been less daring with her clothing. The basque and suspenders were still there, but a knee-length black skirt and cream silk blouse protected her modesty. She smiled to herself as she imagined letting her skirt fall to the floor of his office. It would be just like old times. Back then, his office was tiny, the rent a fraction of what he paid now. She was in a lot better shape then, too. Marianne took a breath. Caught her thoughts. It didn't matter that she had put on weight. Not when her husband called her the most beautiful woman in the room.

But as the lift brought her to his floor, her grip on her handbag tightened and her confidence deserted her. What was she thinking? She was a mother now, and Samuel was a busy man. He obviously didn't look at her in the same way. If he didn't want to sleep with her at home, how was this any different? Her stomach churned as the elevator doors parted with a ping. On shaky legs she stepped forward, just in time to see a woman stride out of Samuel's office. Camouflaged by a pot plant, Marianne watched her husband at the door, and saw the admiration in his eyes as he observed the woman's every move. Marianne chewed her bottom lip as Samuel closed his office doors with a click. The woman was walking towards her now, to where she was standing near the lifts. She looked confident, bold and, disappointingly, attractive. She was short but athletic, with high cheekbones and long hair. Marianne touched her own dark tresses, which had lost their shine. Her hands fell to her skirt as she tugged it up over her stomach. She could feel the bump of the suspender belt, and heat rose to her face.

Naomi was behind her desk, staring at her computer screen. Marianne had warmed to her immediately. She was the girl-next-door type, all bubbly and chatty, not full of herself like some women her age. The two years Naomi had been in Samuel's employment, Marianne had never felt there was anything going on. She would have known by the way he spoke about her. If he was seeing someone, it wasn't Naomi. Taking a deep breath, she stepped forward, glaring at Samuel's visitor as she passed. Her eyes were grey, steely and unsettling. There was an air about her that made Marianne unsure of herself. Her confidence had all but dissolved as she approached Samuel's office. As Naomi hung up the phone, Marianne ducked into the toilets before she could see her. She would not go through the humiliation of speaking to Samuel's secretary. She would ring him herself.

'Hi,' she said, breathless with panic as he answered her call. 'What are you up to?' In a minute she would surprise him, tell him to meet her in the hall. Perhaps she could salvage today after all.

'Just had the meeting from hell.' Samuel sounded his usual cheery self.

A hesitant smile touched Marianne's lips. Perhaps the woman leaving his office wasn't as attractive to him as she thought. It wouldn't be the first time she had allowed her emotions to carry her away.

'Yeah, old Bernard Dunhill. I swear, that guy is ninety if he's a day. Came here laying down the law about their new campaign. It's hardly my fault if their product is crap. Self-adhesive dentures are a hard sell.'

Marianne paled as her breath locked in her throat.

'Babe, are you there?' Samuel added. 'I can't stay long, I've got to rally the troops, see if we can salvage things.'

'Sorry, bad line . . .' Tears brimmed in Marianne's eyes. 'I was just wondering what time you'd be home.' Pressing her hand over the phone, she muffled a sniffle. Her husband was lying through his teeth.

As usual, Samuel could not commit to a time, but told her he loved her before ending the call. Grabbing a tissue from the stall, Marianne wiped away the red lipstick staining her lips, rubbing until her mouth was sore. *You stupid, stupid woman*, she chanted under her breath as she stared at her reflection in disgust. She blew her nose before fixing her make-up, recalling the look on Samuel's face. Slowly, her upset turned to anger. *He may say all the right things*, Marianne thought, *but it's been a long time since he looked at me like that.* Her hands curled into fists. When she thought of all she had done for him. How she had supported him over the years, sacrificing any chance of a career as she helped him make it to the top. *If that bitch thinks she can walk in here and take it all away . . .* Marianne ground her teeth as she imagined them together. What had they been up to in his office? She was not putting up with this. But first she needed to know what she was dealing with. She inhaled a long deep breath as she grounded herself. Samuel wasn't the only one who could keep secrets. She would speak to a private detective, consider her options. Then she would put together a plan.

CHAPTER SIXTEEN

'Here, you look like you could do with it.' Amy handed Donovan a coffee as she entered their shared office. It was a bright and airy space, chilled from Donovan leaving the windows open all day. Amy scanned the corners of the ceiling for cobwebs, shuddering to think of the spiders that could make their way in. And she'd have to use a paperweight to stop any sudden gusts of wind sweeping her paperwork to the floor.

'Ta.' Donovan took the beverage from her grip. Despite the breeze filtering in, he looked flushed, no doubt from having to juggle several things at once.

'I've just been baited.' Amy placed her coffee on her desk before shrugging off her jacket and resting it on the back of her old swivel chair. It had been good to escape the office, if only for a little while.

'Eh?' Donovan replied.

Amy opened her planner before crossing a line through her list of tasks. 'I had the oddest meeting with the CEO of Black Media,' she said, eyes downward. 'Samuel Black is the strangest man I've ever met.'

'Well, that's saying something,' Donovan replied from behind his computer monitor. 'What happened? Wouldn't he cooperate?'

'Oh, he cooperated all right. Said we could have whatever we wanted. He's also got an alibi for the night Stacey died.'

'Have you been sniffing your highlighters? Because you're not making any sense.'

Amy blinked. Donovan was right. Ever since she'd left Samuel's office, she had been playing their conversation on a loop. 'Funny. What do we know about him?'

'From Molly's research, he's married, supports numerous charities and runs one of the best companies to work for in the UK. All-round nice guy, according to the web.'

That was nothing new. Pulling her chair towards her, Amy sat down. 'Yet his old schoolteacher was Claire Lacey, the original victim of the Love Heart Killer. Coincidence? I don't think so.'

'I know.' Donovan held a sheet of paper in the air. 'I've got the intel report. Samuel went to school with Billy Picton. She was his teacher too.'

Amy rubbed the back of her neck, unable to shake off the bad vibes she had picked up from being in Samuel's company. 'Yeah, he was acting really weird.'

'You tend to have that effect on people,' Donovan chuckled. 'What did he say?'

Shaking her mouse, Amy woke her computer up. She needed to put a tasking on the system for a full intelligence check on Samuel Black. 'It was more than just words. It was the way he looked at me, as if he was trying to gauge whether I was some kind of kindred spirit.'

Donovan glanced at the planner on the wall and the numerous Post-it notes stuck at the side of it. 'Why, is he an obsessive list-maker too?'

Amy ignored the comment. 'He was talking about Lillian Grimes. He hinted that I've been instrumental in getting her off the hook.'

'Oh.' Donovan tore his eyes away from his computer screen. Amy had his full attention now.

'Oh indeed.' She paused to sip her coffee. 'I'm used to people having a morbid fascination with me, but there was more to it than that. He was talking between the lines, about how Banksy creates art anonymously but craves an audience to see it. I think he was talking about himself.'

'What are you going to do?'

'I'm going to play him at his own game.' Amy's heart beat a little faster as she considered her next move.

Donovan's face clouded over. 'Sounds dangerous.'

'Yep, and he knows it. In fact, I think he gets off on it.' Amy frowned as she recollected something her biological father, Jack Grimes, was reported to have once said. When asked about being one half of a husband-and-wife killing team, he had replied: 'Killing is like sex, it's not as much fun on your own.' Amy frowned as the quote replayed in her mind. Samuel's comments about Amy helping with her mother's appeal . . . Was Samuel trying to confide in her because he thought she'd understand? The thought evaporated as Donovan spoke.

'I'm not being funny, but are you sure? Samuel Black is Mr Perfect. He hardly fits the criteria. He's probably messing with your head.'

'Maybe,' Amy said. 'But there was something about him that was so at odds with his reputation. It was like he gave me a brief screening of another side . . .' Amy stopped as she observed the confusion on Donovan's face. He didn't understand. How could he? Her instinct to sniff out the darkness in others had been implanted in her from an early age. Donovan was hardly likely to know how that felt.

'Just be careful. Black's a powerful man. From what I've read, he has friends in high places. You don't want to get yourself into hot water with the command team.'

'Oh, hang on, what was that?' Amy looked around the room. 'Sorry, for a minute there I thought DCI Pike had walked in.'

But Donovan failed to find amusement in her joke. 'While I'm managing this investigation, I'm responsible for what goes on. I'm your boss, Amy, like it or not. Document all contact with him, including today.'

Amy sighed. He was right. If Samuel Black was a potential suspect then every bit of contact should be recorded until they had enough evidence to bring him in. But how could they gain more evidence unless she got him to open up? 'You're right.' Amy forced a smile. 'I'll run things by you first.' She watched Donovan visibly relax. She knew his concern stemmed from more than his role as a DCI, and she was taking advantage of their friendship by treating him as anything less. She would toe the line – for now.

CHAPTER SEVENTEEN

Amy rested the phone on its cradle. The sound of Nasreen's voice had warmed her, as did speaking to any of her father's old acquaintances. But Nasreen was more than a friend; he was a useful contact too. Which is why she had been so pleased to see the woman who identified their victim stepping into one of his taxi cabs. Amy did not trust Rose to return, which was why she'd watched her closely as she left. As the owner of the taxi firm, Nasreen was more than happy to provide Amy with Rose's home address. Amy smiled to herself. Nasreen was twice her age, but such an old flirt. She slipped the address in between the pages of her planner. If Rose didn't make an appearance by tomorrow, Amy would be paying her a visit.

She stood to close the window, her spirits plummeting at the sight of the rain-streaked glass. She usually cycled the short journey home, but as the evening darkened, so had the clouds that passed overhead. She slipped her arms into her jacket, all set to leave. Like an ageing fairy godmother, Malcolm popped his head in, ready to answer her prayers.

'Fancy a lift?' Despite the late hour, he still looked perfectly groomed, and the faint smell of Old Spice wafted in through the door.

'I don't know if I deserve it.' Amy picked her leather handbag off the floor. 'I've been going non-stop all day, but I don't feel like I'm any further on.'

'I see Michael Richards has been spoken to.' Michael was the fiancé of Claire Lacey, the schoolteacher murdered twenty years previously. Amy had tasked local officers to obtain a first account interview so they could establish his recent whereabouts. His alibi was airtight. He was out of the country when Stacey was murdered. Staring but not seeing, Amy ticked off her mental checklist of the investigation to date.

'Earth to Winter, are you there, Winter?' Malcolm waved a hand in front of her face.

'Sorry.' She blinked. 'I was thinking about the autopsy. Ray told Stacey that we wouldn't give up on her, but I've no sense of who she was.'

'Then why don't we swing by her flat before I drop you home? Her flatmates have moved back in. I'm sure they'd be happy to show you around.'

It was unusual, to say the least – the head of crime scene investigation visiting with a DI – but Amy couldn't resist.

◆ ◆ ◆

Malcolm's 2009 Porsche Carrera virtually purred as he negotiated the traffic, which had eased now the evening rush hour had abated. It would have been easier to take the Tube to Whitechapel, but he rarely used public transport; driving was much more his style.

Malcolm tapped the steering wheel to the beat of a piece of music on Classic FM. Amy barely heard it. She was thinking about

Stacey in her Whitechapel flat. She had shared with two others who, according to Malcolm, were very amenable. Amy had read their statements, but nothing could compare to seeing them face-to-face. After making a quick phone call, the visit had been cleared.

As they approached the address, Malcolm slowed the car, turning off the windscreen wipers. 'At least the rain has cleared. Do you mind awfully if we park up outside the supermarket and walk down? There's CCTV covering the street. I don't want to come out of Grove Heights and find my car on bricks.'

'Sure, the walk will do us good.' Amy unbuckled her seat belt. She cast her gaze over the red-and-white building, recognising the location as the address where Stacey had worked.

They reached Grove Heights in just over ten minutes. Amy remained quiet as she imagined walking in Stacey's footsteps to the supermarket and back to her flat each day. What must her life have been like for her to turn to escorting as a way out? Something told her that Stacey would not have found sex with strangers as easy as Rose did.

As they entered the bowels of the high-rise block of flats, Malcolm turned his eyes skywards. 'Please God, Buddha, Allah, let it be working,' he said, jabbing the lift button for the twentieth floor.

Amy shared a smile as his prayers were answered and the lift doors opened with a ding. She imagined Stacey returning home the night she visited Rose. Had she wrestled with her conscience? Wondered how she was going to get away with impersonating her friend?

Amy and Malcolm's footsteps echoed in the corridor as they approached the flat. Life went on all around them. Muffled conversations behind closed doors. Televisions blaring too loud. Dogs barking to be taken for walks. The building wasn't what you would call dirty, but it did have a dank, depressing feel. Amy rapped her knuckles against the door.

'Oh, hi, come in.' A fresh-faced young woman opened the door wide as Amy introduced herself. She was wearing a rainbow-coloured jumper that slid over her bare shoulder and a pair of skinny jeans. 'I'm Emma,' she said. 'Lewis is inside.' Her flatmate was draped across a lumpy maroon sofa as Amy and Malcolm entered the living room. He was mixed-race, his face covered in sandy freckles, an unusual but attractive mix. 'Can I get you a drink? We're out of milk, so I only have black coffee, I'm afraid.' Emma gave Amy an apologetic smile.

'We're fine.' Amy took a seat. 'Thanks for seeing us at short notice. I've read both your statements, but I wanted to get a feel for where Stacey lived.'

'That's OK. Hey . . . I recognise you.' Emma looked at Malcolm. 'You're the forensics guy.'

Malcolm grinned. 'I have one of those faces that's hard to forget.' Silence descended. A clock ticked ominously on the wall, a muted television screen revealing a PlayStation game on pause.

'How are you doing?' Amy said, glancing around the room.

'It's hard.' Emma sighed. 'I keep expecting Stacey to walk in through the door.' Her gaze fell to her hands, which were clasped on her lap. 'I wish I'd spent more time with her when she was alive.'

'To be fair, she was a bit of a loner,' Lewis said. 'We asked her out for drinks loads of times, but she always turned us down—'

'She said she had no money,' Emma interrupted. 'But when we offered to buy her a birthday drink, she still wouldn't come. We kind of gave up after that.' She began to pick at her nail varnish, remorse written all over her face.

'You weren't close friends then?' Amy's words were probing but gentle. Their relationship had been covered in the police statement, but Amy wanted to hear the sincerity in Emma's voice. She had no reason to doubt her account so far.

Emma shook her head. 'I'm a student nurse and Lewis has just qualified as a paramedic. I know it sounds silly but . . . I think she was jealous of us.'

Lewis leaned forward on the sofa. 'She was in a slump cos she couldn't get the job she wanted. But we worked our arses off to get here. Meanwhile, she was stuck working at the supermarket and watching Netflix at night in her room.' He exchanged a glance with Emma as she delivered a disapproving look. 'What?' he said. 'It's true.'

'Did she have any other friends or boyfriends?' Amy asked. If anything, she admired their honesty. It was all too easy to sugar-coat the truth when talking about the dead.

'Sometimes she'd mention a girl called Lisa, who she went to uni with,' Emma said. 'But I don't think Lisa had much time for her. I feel bad now, I wish I'd done more.'

'It's natural to feel guilty when someone close to you dies,' Amy replied. 'But the blame for Stacey's murder lies firmly at the killer's door. Did she ever mention going out to meet anyone? Give you an insight into her personal life?'

'She lived here for a year, but we never met her family,' Lewis said, looking dolefully at Amy. 'Sometimes our mums would come to visit but it was a touchy subject with her. I offered to get her a ticket to that concert we went to, but she wouldn't come.'

Emma shook her head. 'I wish she had now. Maybe she'd still be alive.'

Amy knew she was talking about the night Stacey disappeared. Despite her reassurances, it was obvious that Emma was plagued with guilt. *Survivor syndrome*, Amy thought. She recognised it immediately as she had once had it herself. 'What happened to her?' Emma's face was strained. 'I can't sleep at night. What if her killer comes back?' A door slammed in the flat above, making her jump.

'Try not to worry, darling.' Malcolm's soft words delivered reassurance. 'Lightning rarely strikes twice in the same place.'

But Amy wasn't so sure. 'Isn't there anyone you can stay with for a while? Any friends or family?'

Emma stood with her arms tightly folded. 'I might go to my mum's for a few days, if Lewis does the same.' She glanced around the living room, her face haunted with the memory of her flatmate. 'I thought I'd be OK but . . .' Her shoulders twitched as she shuddered. 'How does something like this happen? I mean, how did Stacey even come on to their radar?'

'Did she ever use any dating apps?' The memory of Rose's visit was still fresh in Amy's mind.

'She wasn't a Tinder kind of girl, if that's what you mean.' Emma looked from Amy to Malcolm. 'Do you want to see her room? I haven't had the heart to touch it, but we'll need to advertise for another flatmate soon.' She sighed, pushing her hands into the pockets of her jeans. 'It's a horrible business, this. I'll feel better when the killer's behind bars.'

'That's why I'm here.' Amy followed Emma into Stacey's room. She knew Emma and Lewis had been offered safeguarding, as well as an alarm. But fear was an insistent emotion, with claws that dug deep. She glanced around the room. Like in many high-rise flats in London, it was an economic box space and the air within smelled stale. Quickly striding inside, Emma shut the blinds before turning on the light. 'I know it's silly, but I feel like I'm being watched.' She pointed to the cabinet, which was still covered with fingerprint dust. 'I need to clean that stuff off.' It was a sober reminder of Malcolm's work. The bed was still unmade, the sheets seized by officers in case they revealed any clues. 'Stacey's family haven't been in touch?' Amy said.

'Not yet,' Emma replied, picking up Stacey's hairbrush and laying it down again. 'I thought I'd box everything up in case . . . you know, in case they wanted it.'

Amy felt a pang of disappointment as she conducted a quick room search. It was hard to pick anything new out of old ground.

The only thing she had got from her visit was that Stacey was a private person who kept to herself. Her glance fell on the door. 'Don't you have locks on your doors?'

Emma leaned against the doorway. 'Nope. Stacey wanted to put up one of her own but DeeDee – the landlady – said she didn't want any drilling in the flat. She's a bit eccentric, if I'm honest, but she leaves us alone most of the time.'

'I see.' Amy glanced at drawers, cupboards, beneath the bed, behind the books on the shelf – every inch of the room had already been searched. She stared up at a poster on the wall – one of those motivational ones about life not changing unless you do. It seemed at odds with a character who was coming across as pessimistic. 'Where did Stacey get that, do you know?'

'Oh, that?' Emma followed her gaze. 'It was mine. I was throwing it out a couple of weeks ago, when Stacey asked if she could have it. I didn't think it was her thing.'

Neither did Amy. She peered closer. It was curled at the bottom and frayed with wear. Touching the top of the poster, Amy smoothed it down, pausing as she came to a bump in the wall.

'You can take it if you want,' Emma said. 'It's all got to go.'

But Amy was in no hurry to disturb the scene. Slowly, she peeled up the bottom of the poster, which was hanging loosely from two blobs of Blu-Tack.

'What is it?' Malcolm watched with keen interest. 'Have you found a hiding place?'

Given the absence of locks on the doors, it was possible Stacey had hidden her most private possessions in plain sight. As she peeped behind the poster, Amy's heart skipped a beat. 'Yep. It's a phone . . . quite a slim one . . . and it's taped to the wall.' But officers had already seized Stacey's phone. Did this second one belong to her? If so, what secrets would it reveal?

CHAPTER EIGHTEEN

Samuel stared at his bedroom ceiling, releasing his thoughts to a darkness far blacker than the night. *The police think killers hate their victims*, he thought, recalling recent newspaper headlines. *But I covet every breath they exhale.* He mulled it over. Refined his ideology. In his fantasies, he had overpowered and killed a hundred times. Pages of his notebooks were stuffed with daring scenarios and, thanks to social media, the beauty of his act was now immortalised forever.

To think he had risked everything by letting down his guard. He knew who DI Winter was and had tried but failed to play it cool. To use one of Laura's phrases, he had been 'a total fangirl'. But then, who hadn't heard of Jack and Lillian Grimes? Since the launch of Lillian's appeal, her relationship with her detective inspector daughter had been splashed all over the news. When Winter walked into his office, it was as if she had opened a door to his soul. Her resemblance to her mother excited him, and soon he was saying things he would not dare utter to another living creature. But it wasn't so much a sexual attraction as a meeting of minds.

Marianne turned to face him, sliding an arm over his waist. 'Can't sleep?' she said, jolting him from his thoughts.

Taking a deep breath, Samuel came back to himself. 'I was thinking about the necklace I bought you,' he said, coming up with an instant excuse. Such thoughts did not spring from the voice of a killer. This was Samuel the husband and father, the man who cared. 'Why don't you take it back and choose something you like?'

'I do like it,' Marianne whispered. 'It's just . . . it's more than I would have spent.'

'You deserve it,' he murmured into her hair, detecting the faint scent of coconut shampoo.

'Thanks,' she said, tilting her head to kiss him goodnight.

Regardless of his new-found hobby, Samuel had never been unfaithful to his wife. Sex was part of his compulsion, but the reward came in pleasuring himself. Marianne had been so full of life when they first met. What he would give to recapture her spark. The old Marianne was still there, buried deep inside. But for now he would take his pleasure where he could. It had taken him years to build up the courage to allow his fantasies to come to fruition, and now his cravings were a monster who was hungry for more. *They'll never catch you*, the voice inside him said. *It all comes down to evidence.* It was true. Every effort had been made, from washing Stacey in the bath to clipping her fingernails. He had read countless textbooks on forensic science and the disposal of evidence. His way of doing things had worked well.

He recalled Stacey's surprise after he slid out from under her bed days earlier, silencing her screams as he plunged the needle into her vein. Nobody had paid any attention to him as he transported the small wardrobe on a trolley to the unoccupied flat on the floor above. His victim was safely inside, silenced but still breathing. An old dear had even held the lift doors open as she greeted him in the corridor. His adrenaline had pulsed like never before.

Getting her to the department store had been easy. Another set of overalls, another anonymous man, this time pushing a trolley into the back of a loading bay. He had obtained a collection of uniforms, and each one enabled him to blend in. His imagination ran riot as he saw himself in varying roles: a waiter, a groundsman, a doctor in a white coat. Confidence was the secret, along with knowledge of the role he was about to play. It all tapped into his creative side, and learning was part of the fun. But the involvement of DI Winter brought things to a dangerous edge. He blinked in the darkness. He could stop now if he wanted to. Nobody would ever know.

But where's the fun in that? The voice came like rolling thunder, making him tense. Marianne was sleeping now, having turned her back on him. *One more time.* He licked the dryness from his lips. Why not? And he had just the person in mind. Creeping out of bed, he padded out of his room and down the corridor. Megan was fast asleep, her nightlight covering her ceiling in a plethora of stars. His heart warmed as he crept into her room and smoothed her hair away from her head. Satisfied she was comfortable, Samuel continued down the hall. He paused outside Laura's room, slowly turning the handle until the door opened with a click. He found her sitting up in bed, wearing a sheepish grin as she peeped from behind her iPad.

'Hand it over,' Samuel said, sidestepping her schoolbag as he approached her.

She did so without argument, snuggling beneath her covers as Samuel took it from her grip. 'Night,' she said with a yawn as he kissed the top of her head.

Feeling a pang, Samuel watched his teenage daughter settle down to sleep. Each time he looked at Laura, he saw Marianne.

He padded down the hall to his office, slipped the key from his dressing gown pocket and turned the key in the lock. Closing the door behind him, he locked it from the inside.

Within seconds he was sitting at his desk, bringing up the Sugar Babes app. Her profile came up instantly. Miss Kandi Kane. Her real name was Erin Johnson, which had been easy for him to find, once he had persuaded her to send him a picture of her face. A Google image search was all that was needed to link to her social media profile, which is where he learned even more. But it was her private Dropbox account that held the prize. Erin thought she was sharing a few provocative pictures, when in fact she was giving him her address. All he had to do was right-click the picture to bring up her GPS coordinates.

Erin was pretty, but natural with it. Samuel was not a fan of drawn-on eyebrows, fake tan or plumped lips. She was the perfect template for what he needed, just as Stacey had been. A green dot lit up beside her profile picture, which signified that she was online.

Hey you, are you up? he typed into his phone. William was his username. It had a nice, British feel.

Hi! Yup, long day at work. But now I can't sleep. How are you? her reply came.

William: *Looking forward to seeing you. Can't sleep either. I had to get up and sneak another look at your pics. Stunning, by the way. I can sleep happy now we've spoken.*

Kandi: *Charmer. Just wait until you sleep WITH me. *Cheeky wink* And urgh, the pictures aren't great. I need to get some proper photographs.*

William: *Well don't get them yet. Don't want you getting too many requests until you've met with me first. With any luck, you won't need to work for much longer. Not if I have anything to do with it.*

Kandi: *That's sweet of you to say. Can't wait to see you. When and where??*

William: *Soon, I promise. I just need to arrange a night that I can get away.* Samuel paused, watching the cursor blink in the dim light. *I've got to go, but listen, take care of yourself, will you? There's a lot of weirdos out there.*

Kandi: *Tell me about it, LOL. I've had some strange requests. I'm going to wait for you. As you said, if we hit it off, hopefully I won't need anyone else.*

William: *I'll message you soon. I'll move heaven and earth to be with you.*

Kandi: *OK sweetie, I'd best get to bed. Sleep well. I'll be thinking of you xxx*

After signing off with a suitable response, Samuel slipped his phone into the drawer. Only full sexual intercourse was classed as being 'unfaithful', wasn't it? He had better plans in store for Erin. He had told her what she wanted to hear, a list of stock responses that had worked well previously. Erin would make a beautiful canvas for his next work of art.

CHAPTER NINETEEN

Amy was known as being strait-laced when it came to police procedure, but since discovering her true heritage, she had found herself bending the rules. Was her inner Grimes pushing her boundaries from a dark place, deep inside? Amy had seen the autopsy pictures of the Grimes's murder victims, all young women in varying stages of decomposition. The sins of the father . . . Would she ever make up for what they had done? Guilt threatened to overwhelm her as Lillian's court case progressed. A court case that would never have got off the ground were it not for the evidence she had unearthed. She had acted by the book then, but was justice being served? Amy tried to ignore the niggling sense that she was drifting away from a core part of herself – but if she had to go against protocol to put Stacey's killer behind bars, she wouldn't hesitate.

Emma's eyes blazed with curiosity as Amy peeled the sticky tape off the phone attached to Stacey's bedroom wall. 'I've never seen Stacey with that. I didn't think she could afford an iPhone.'

Perhaps it was an investment, Amy thought, making a mental note to speak to the officers named on the police search record. It was an obvious hiding place which they should have found the first time around. By rights, Amy should return to the station and make a statement covering the seizure, then book the phone into the property system before requesting analysis. But they were still waiting for the analysis of Stacey's laptop and old mobile phone. It could take days, even weeks, depending on how busy they were.

'Here, use this.' Malcolm produced a clear exhibit bag from his jacket pocket. Any officer worth their salt carried them, along with a pair of PVC gloves. But Amy was in no hurry to seal it as she thanked Stacey's flatmates for their time.

'What's the betting she used this phone for the Sugar Babes site?' Amy rested the bag on her lap once they were back in Malcolm's car.

'Are you sure you want to switch it on?' Malcolm watched as she lifted the phone from the unsealed bag with a gloved hand. 'She might have installed a virus on it.'

Amy knew he was talking about the security measures some drug dealers took with their phones. If the wrong code was inserted, such a virus could delete everything. 'I doubt she's gone as far as installing a virus.' Amy tapped in Stacey's date of birth as she guessed her lock code. 'There, I'm in.' She smiled as the handset lit up inside the car.

With Malcolm paying close attention, Amy activated the Sugar Babes app. But it wasn't Stacey who was logged into the site, it was someone with the username of Alicia Cherry.

'Of course.' Amy bowed her head as she scrolled through the phone. 'Stacey didn't just want to steal Rose's dates. She must have known that she'd be found out. She used Rose's account to nominate herself as a new member with a different name.' Amy tutted as she reviewed the profile pictures. 'See that?' She pointed to the tree of life tattoo she had seen during the autopsy. 'Stacey had that tattoo. This is her page.' Amy pulled a face as she saw that all girls on the site were given starred reviews by their sugar daddies. Her disbelief grew as she read each one aloud.

'Beverly provided a great girlfriend experience, she was educated, beautiful, and knew how to have fun. I'll definitely use her again . . . Mimi was such a disappointment. It was obvious she was going through the motions during sex. She didn't look at me once.' Amy closed her eyes as she felt her anger rise. 'She probably didn't look at you because you're a disgusting pig,' she muttered under her breath, feeling nothing but sympathy for the girls who were reviewed. She checked over Stacey's profile. No reviews had been added yet. 'I bet she was more attractive to these pervs because she was new on the block,' she said, thinking aloud.

Malcolm remained silent as Amy scrolled through the messages. Stacey's inbox was bulging with propositions and, given her profile photographs, it was easy to see why. But these were not images that Stacey had taken. Like Rose's pictures, they appeared to be professionally done. In fact, she recognised the furniture in the shot. Amy's eyes narrowed. Somebody else had had a hand in this. She recalled what Rose had said about her handler taking care of things. Did Rose's handler approach newbies to the site and recruit them? It made sense for them to do so. It was easy pickings, finding them online, signing them up and taking a percentage of their earnings. In return they would organise a photo shoot, check prospective sugar daddies, ensure the girls' safety and show them the ropes.

'Where's the section with the confirmed dates?' Amy said to herself as the phone beeped a warning that it was running out of battery. But the messages in the Sent folder appeared to have been deleted.

As Malcolm pushed the car key into the ignition, he finally spoke. 'I'm kicking myself for not seeing that phone the first time around.'

'It wasn't your job to.' Such responsibility lay with the search team. But Amy knew her words would be of cold comfort. Malcolm prided himself on being thorough. She watched as he activated the windscreen wipers, frustration etched on his face. 'It was damned sloppy of me. I didn't think she'd have a second phone.'

'There's a psychology behind keeping the tools of your trade separate,' Amy replied. 'It goes a long way towards demonstrating how Stacey felt.' At least Amy now knew their victim a little better, which was the whole reason for visiting her flat. But the discovery of a second phone had thrown up a new set of questions.

How many dates had she been on? Had she been working in the supermarket those days? Such things were easily investigated, and Amy knew just the person who could help her out. For now, it was time to head home and catch up on some much-needed sleep.

CHAPTER TWENTY

It wasn't often that evidence dropped into Amy's lap, and the knowledge that they had found Stacey's mobile phone had made her awaken in an unusually good mood. Sweat trickled down her temple as she finished a set of squats with weights in her basement gym. Her punchbag session had been brief as she concentrated instead on toning her muscles and keeping her body lean. She was grateful for her strength when it came to situations that were impossible to talk herself out of. Picking up a towel, she pressed her face against the soft cotton, allowing it to absorb her sweat. She could almost hear her father's voice, instructing her on the importance of stretches and cool-downs. When she was young, he had taught her how to take her frustrations out on the punchbag rather than direct it inwards, like some of her friends did.

Half an hour later, and she was walking to work with a coffee in her hand. Malcolm had dropped her home last night and she was without her humble bicycle, which was safely locked in the station bike shed. A lorry rumbled past on the busy road, belching the bitter stench of exhaust fumes in its wake. Deep in thought, Amy sipped from her travel mug as she mulled over the last few days.

By 9 a.m., briefing was completed and Amy was standing on the doorstep of the woman who called herself Rose. But she wasn't Rose, she was Lisa, and Amy wondered what else she had to hide. Her flat in Earl's Court must have cost a pretty penny, and Amy wondered how many sugar daddies were funding her lifestyle. Keeping her finger pressed on the buzzer, Amy was met with an irate voice on the other side.

'Yes?'

'It's DI Winter, from the station,' Amy said. 'I need to talk to you.'

No answer came. Amy was about to press the buzzer for the second time when a middle-aged man in a well-tailored suit opened the door to leave. 'It's OK, I'm a police officer.' Amy lifted her warrant card as he gave her a sideways glance on her way in.

'You're not here for me, I hope.' He gave her a sheepish grin.

'Not this time,' Amy said with a wink, brushing past him. She followed the door numbers to Lisa's flat, pausing to press the bell. A delicate chime ensued, but no answer was forthcoming. 'Police. Open up, or I'll open it for you,' Amy shouted, loud enough for everyone to hear.

The sound of hasty footsteps beat a path to the other side of the door. Amy was met with a flustered-looking Lisa. 'What are you doing here?' she said, pulling her silk dressing gown tightly together.

Was she entertaining a client? The thought had not crossed Amy's mind until now. 'I need to speak to you,' she said, looking past her through the crack in the door. 'Are you alone?'

'Only just.' Lisa's lips thinned. 'You should have rung me first.'

'I would have, had you left your phone number. If you gave me a statement like I asked, I wouldn't be here at all.' The man leaving the building must have been Lisa's sponsor. *No wonder she's so jumpy*, Amy thought.

'Sorry.' Lisa began to close the door. 'But I can't help you any more.'

But the word 'no' rarely existed in Amy's vocabulary, and she wedged her boot against the door until it shuddered to a stop. 'We can have this conversation here, or you can let me in.' She began to raise her voice. 'Now, as I was saying . . . about this dating site—'

'Come in, come in!' Huffing, Lisa opened the door wide, then slammed it shut behind Amy as she made her way inside. Amy glanced around the room, which had a tasteful yet exotic feel. There were tropical plants in every corner. Pictures from far-flung lands graced the walls, and the scent of incense hung in the air. Amy peeped towards a bedroom door, which was ajar. On top of a tussled white satin duvet lay an array of sex toys.

Moving swiftly, Lisa blocked Amy's view as she shut the bedroom door. 'I've told you everything I know. Why are you here?'

'Stacey didn't hack into your site just to take your dates. She used your account to nominate a new one for herself.'

Lisa's beautifully arched eyebrows rose an inch. 'The sly cow. So that guy she agreed to meet in my name?'

'A stopover until she got her own account off the ground.' Amy watched as Lisa darted around, picking up discarded clothes and tidying up her flat. 'You mentioned having a handler. How did you meet them?'

'Can we do this some other time?' Lisa paused to check her watch. 'I've got someone coming in an hour and I need to shower and change.'

'I'll be out of your way soon. Your handler . . . did they approach you, or did you get in touch with them? How does it work?'

It was clear Amy wasn't leaving without answers. Lisa's features softened as she relented. 'We call her Mama Danielle. She found me on the site. She messages all the newbies to offer her services.' Lisa swept a hand over her hair. 'We're all busy little bees working on our backs for her.' Her arms dropped to her side as a thought occurred. 'You don't think she had anything to do with Stacey's death, do you? Cos I'm telling you now, it's not her style. There's no money to be made from a dead Sugar Babe.'

The truth was, Amy didn't know. She may have had her suspicions about Black Media, but she wasn't discounting anyone at this point. She avoided the question. 'She could be the last person who spoke to Stacey. It's important that I speak to her today.'

Lisa scratched the back of her head. 'I don't know . . . If she finds out I brought a cop to her door, she'll kill me.'

But Amy was ready with an answer, because she had already given it some thought. 'Tell her I'm an old friend, that I'm interested in becoming a Sugar Babe.'

Lisa sighed. 'I suppose it could work.' She extended her hand. 'Gimme your phone.'

Her pink-varnished nails tapped against the screen as she composed a text. 'Don't ring, she won't answer. This will do the trick.' She pressed the Send button and the phone signalled a text delivery. 'There. Done.'

Amy glanced at the screen as Lisa handed the phone back.

Hi, Rose recommended I get in touch. She said you might be able to help me earn some extra cash. Amelia x

'Sorry to be so heavy-handed.' Amy pocketed the phone. 'But Danielle might have the answers I need.'

'I doubt it,' Lisa snorted. 'She's very protective of us, she won't tell you much.' After checking her watch, she opened her front door in an effort to make Amy leave. 'Just keep me out of it. I don't need any grief.'

'I take good care of my informants.' Amy followed her to the door. 'If you think of anything else, you know where I am.'

'She'll arrange to meet you somewhere classy. Treat it like a job interview. She'll be testing your manner, your clothes, your confidence.'

'Thanks,' Amy said. Although she didn't need advice on how to handle Mama Danielle. She would figure her out soon enough.

CHAPTER
TWENTY-ONE

There were several different types of interviews, and Amy's team planned them with precision. A voluntary interview was offered to witnesses rather than suspects. These were more relaxed, and the interviewees were encouraged to speak naturally rather than being interrogated. The police's planned interview structure would not be obvious to the interviewee. Setting was important too. A comfortable seat and a cup of tea could go a long way towards putting people at ease. For now, the only proof of Billy's involvement in the case was that he had been assigned to create the window display. He was certainly a person of interest, and suspicion of his involvement was enough to arrest him, but sometimes it was better to build a strong case first, rather than bring them in and wind down the custody clock. The voluntary interview was strategic and could push things either way.

For suspects, the interview process and setting changed. Instead, open questions were asked, with verbal pressure put on them to confess. Each of Amy's officers had different approaches to interviewing. Steve was forthright and professional, while Molly had a more laid-back style. Her ability to engage with suspects often reaped its own rewards. It was why Amy had chosen her to speak to Billy. Interviewing was the job of a detective constable, but Amy could not resist monitoring from another room.

They had seated Billy in the vulnerable victim suite, a place usually reserved for victims of crime. His arms spread over the blue sofa cushions, he took up a lot of room. A camera was placed in each corner of the ceiling – a subtle way of capturing multiple angles of the interview. Soft carpet and pastel walls added to the ambience. Molly had been briefed to keep things low-key. A cup of freshly brewed tea was placed before him, and his red-socked ankle jigged where it was crossed over his knee. In his corduroy trousers and plaid shirt, he did not appear to be the artistic type, but Amy exercised caution when judging outward appearances in cases such as these.

'It was a straightforward job,' Billy said, in response to Molly's prompt. 'We hired an artist to dress the dummy while I organised the window display.'

'What about the materials? The diamanté, the costume?' Molly prompted.

'We sourced the costume and make-up. Then I forwarded what was needed to the artist.'

'So, to clarify' – Molly tilted her head to one side – 'who had access to the materials?'

'Anyone in Black Media,' Billy replied. 'They're kept in an office with all the other promo stuff. I had the larger items, like the throne and props, delivered directly to the store. A couple of assistants helped me put it all together. The artist prepped the mannequin the week before.'

Amy already knew that. Such information had been gained as part of their early enquiries and substantiated. The artist involved was a twenty-two-year-old graduate called Zoe, who was already in the clear.

'Talk me through it.' Molly was sitting in the seat across from him. Officers had already obtained a first account of Billy's version of events. Now Amy was watching to see if he tripped himself up. But Billy seemed too relaxed to be anything but an innocent bystander caught up in unfortunate circumstances.

'We were hired to create the display to showcase a new line of wedding gowns. I commissioned Zoe to dress the dummy and we met a couple of weeks before to talk things through.' Billy cast his eyes upwards as he explained. 'She was briefed to create a lifelike mannequin with a Valentine's Day theme. She got the dummy ready, and delivered it to the store after it closed, the evening before launch. I arrived with the props at just gone eight. Everything was pre-assembled so we were out of there by ten.' Billy talked about the lengths they had gone to, to ensure everything was just right.

But his account of events did not deliver anything new. As Molly asked him about access, Amy studied his behaviour for clues. If he was nervous he didn't show it, and he proceeded to tell Molly that he had attended a fundraiser for his daughter in his local pub. 'I was there until late,' Billy said when questioned about his alibi. 'Ask the landlord.'

Amy had already read the landlord's statement, which verified Billy's presence until well after closing time. But could he have been giving Billy a helping hand? She focused on Billy's narrative as he continued to explain.

'I couldn't believe it when I saw the video online. It turned my stomach to imagine that young girl being murdered in the very spot where we worked.' His brown eyes were turned downwards, his face ruddy from broken veins.

'She was still alive, drugged into submission,' Molly said, her gaze intense. 'She sat there, dying for hours. Her eyes were taped open, parts of her hair glued to the throne to keep her head in position. Can you imagine that?'

Billy's hand touched his mouth as it fell open. 'My God . . . Why? Why would anyone do that?'

'That's what we're trying to figure out,' Molly replied. 'So you need to give us every little detail of that night, no matter how insignificant.'

Amy shifted in her chair as she watched from the monitoring room next door. While the vulnerable victim suite was free, she would use it to her best advantage.

'I wish I could give you more,' Billy continued. 'To see my daughter grow up in a world where people are capable of such things . . . it's frightening.'

'What age is she?' Molly smiled. Talking about family often helped people relax. Amy had seen Molly chat to people about their cats, their hamsters or their favourite cars. Anything to help them open up.

'She's twelve. She lives in America with her mother.' Billy paused to check his watch. 'Will this take much longer? I've come straight from work and I'm looking after the neighbour's cat.'

Amy crossed her legs. Something had touched a nerve. She made a mental note to task the team with finding out more about Billy's relationship with his child.

'We've recovered the mannequin.' Molly cleared her throat, returning to the task at hand. 'It was dumped down an alleyway. It's with our forensics team. We'll need your fingerprints . . . for elimination purposes.'

'That's OK,' Billy said. 'Honestly, this has thrown me. I don't know how they got in. We locked everything up securely when we left.'

'And there was nobody else around? What about security? Any night workers? Any store staff?'

'Nobody. The place was deathly quiet.' Billy shook his head. 'Sorry – bad choice of words.'

'Black Media seems like a nice company to work for,' Molly said, changing tack. 'How long have you been there?' Amy was pleased with Molly's line of questioning. She was curious to find out more about Billy's relationship with Samuel Black.

'Four . . . nearly five years. It's brilliant. Everything they say about Mr Black is true.'

Mr Black? Amy thought. Samuel had said they were old friends. He'd even told Amy to refer to him by his first name. Why was Billy being formal? Molly would be thinking the same thing. Amy only hoped she would handle this with care. It was better to say nothing and allow him to lie.

'Sounds great,' Molly said. 'A friend of mine went there for an interview, but she was knocked back. You must have great credentials.'

Good work, Amy thought. They already knew his qualifications had been poor when he approached Samuel for a job. Billy could answer this question in one of two ways – tell the truth or lie.

Billy exhaled a long breath. 'I was lucky. When I joined, Black Media was in its infancy. It was easier to get in then.'

'Ah, friends in high places?' Molly winked.

'No . . . just good timing. Everyone gets treated the same there.' Smiling at Molly, he reached out for his mug to sip his tea. He continued to talk as Amy made notes, piecing together his version of events. Someone was lying about Billy's relationship with Samuel Black. The question was – who?

CHAPTER
TWENTY-TWO

Marianne told herself that today was a good day. She was taking back control. So why did she feel so nervous? Handing over some crumpled notes, she paid the taxi driver and stepped on to the streets of Shoreditch. She checked the address of the agency on her phone for the hundredth time. She had stopped taking her Valium. She needed a clear head.

The chipped grey-painted door was situated next to a bookies, and the presence of graffiti on the walls did little to reassure her. Shoreditch was meant to have been regenerated, but there was little evidence of it in this neighbourhood.

After pressing the buzzer as instructed, she was allowed into the building, and she manoeuvred the narrow space as she followed the sign up a winding flight of stairs. The area carried a sickly sweet smell, like one of those odd vape flavours – toffee apple or candy-floss. This was a female-only detective agency, one that specialised in dealing with cheating spouses, but the building she was entering showed little evidence of a feminine touch. Petra, the lady she had spoken to over the phone, had sounded nice enough. Marianne rested her hand on the doorknob, her stomach feeling like a host of butterflies were trapped inside. The building was old and tatty, with chewing gum stuck to the floor. Should she go in? An ugly vision floated in her mind. Samuel and that woman in his office together. The sudden flash of jealousy urged her on.

'Hi, you must be Marianne?' An over-tanned woman rose from behind an antiquated-looking desk and shook her hand. 'I'm Petra. We spoke on the phone.' She smiled enthusiastically, her blonde curls bouncing as she sat back down. Her top was low-cut, her teeth unnaturally white against her caramel skin. Marianne realised she was staring and plopped into the swivel chair in front of the desk. She was the same with every woman she met, making an instant assessment and then comparing herself in an unfavourable light. It was exhausting, and she'd had enough.

'Before we start . . . is this confidential? I don't want this getting out.' Her gaze swept over Petra's desk. She glanced at the vaporiser, a packet of Tic Tacs, a well-thumbed organiser and an array of pens. In the centre was a Mac desktop computer, which looked out of keeping with the rest of the room.

'We put the private into "private detective".' Petra delivered another dazzling smile. 'You've nothing to worry about.'

Petra had already explained on the phone about confidentiality, but Marianne could not relax. 'It's my husband . . . I think he's having an affair.' It was the first time she'd said the words aloud and she pressed a hand over her mouth as her last meal bubbled up from indigestion. 'Excuse me. This hasn't been easy.'

'I understand.' Petra leaned forward in her chair. 'I've been cheated on myself.'

'Really?' Marianne's eyes widened.

'It's how I got into this business.' She looked around the room. 'I know it's not much to start with, but this is a franchise. They've got branches of these agencies all over the UK.'

'And they all deal with cheating husbands?'

'Husbands, wives, child maintenance swervers, we deal with them all.'

'How does it work?' Marianne's breath had regulated now she was with someone who understood.

'It depends on what you want. A lot of it can be done online. Does your husband use social media?' She rested her hand on her mouse and clicked into a site. Her nails were long, red and pointed. Marianne wondered how she got any work done with them. But then again, with a job like this, it was in her interest to look like a Barbie doll. Marianne had read on the site that they specialised in honeytraps.

Petra turned the computer screen around, revealing a plethora of social media sites.

'He's on Facebook,' Marianne said, as Petra showed her various online profiles.

'We can do an online entrapment for as little as two hundred pounds. We've got several established profiles, so they don't look fake,' Petra said cheerily, as if talking about the most natural thing in the world. 'We start off by befriending their friends before sending them a request. Then we work with you to establish their interests – get an idea what to private-message them about.'

'But if he's already cheating with someone else, how does that help?'

Petra gazed at her with sympathy. 'I don't mean to be blunt, but people who cheat aren't always exclusive to their bit on the side. This method usually works well. We start by getting a conversation going, then steer it towards meeting up. At that point, we've a good idea of their intentions . . .' Another reassuring smile. 'The messages are usually pretty explicit by then.'

'And you reciprocate?'

Petra nodded. 'We always respond in kind. Sometimes they send us pictures of themselves. We keep you updated every step of the way.'

'I don't know . . .' Marianne wrung her hands, knowing how careful Samuel was online. 'He's in the public eye. I'm not sure that would work.'

'Then we can go for the surveillance method. It's a lot more costly, though. It can run into a few thousand, depending on what you want and how long it takes.'

'What's your success rate?'

'Overall, ninety-nine per cent. We usually find out either way. It's fifty pounds an hour minimum for basic surveillance, but we get the best results from using equipment. We've got trackers, audio bugs, spy software . . .' Petra stood to close the window behind her as an onslaught of traffic drowned out her words.

'I don't know,' Marianne said, doubt taking over. 'What if this gets out? I . . . I'm not sure if I'm ready for this yet.'

'I can't promise there won't be consequences, but we're mindful of damage control.'

'What's the divorce percentage?' Marianne felt queasy just saying the 'D' word. 'I mean, do many couples work it out?'

'I could lie, tell you they make up and their marriages are stronger than before.' Petra paused for introspection. 'But most of our evidence is used in divorce cases. The only relationships that improve are those whose partners haven't cheated. There aren't many of them about.'

Marianne nodded glumly. She wasn't sure she could place Samuel in that category. Equally, she didn't want a divorce. She just wanted things back to how they were.

'Why don't you think about it?' Petra tugged at her desk drawer then slid out a pamphlet. 'Here. Our price list is inside, along with some case examples.'

'I'd better not take it, in case he sees it.' Marianne waved it away. 'Money isn't an issue. But you're right, I need to think about it.' She pushed back her chair, feeling light-headed as she stood. It was always the same. She'd start out full of fighting spirit, but it didn't take long for her bravery to desert her. She had changed beyond recognition over the years. She gave Petra a regretful glance before walking to the door. 'Sorry for wasting your time.'

As she left the building, she tried to untangle her thoughts. She couldn't stand by and act like nothing was happening, but equally it was too big a risk to involve anyone else. What if Petra blew the whistle? Given the state of the detective's office, money wasn't rolling in. Marianne's imagination ran riot as she visualised Petra luring Samuel in. What if she fell for him? Or blackmailed him afterwards? Could she risk involving a third party when Samuel's career was going so well? How would he feel if he had done nothing wrong? She plucked her phone from her pocket, ready to call a taxi to take her home. If she was going to put her husband under surveillance, she would have to do it herself.

CHAPTER
TWENTY-THREE

'I can't believe we're doing this.' Sally-Ann tapped her foot as she waited outside the prison visitors' room. Apart from staff, they were the only two people in there. In the distance, the usual sounds echoed through the walls: heavy doors slamming, disgruntled shouting, shrill bells signalling a change in activity. This was not a place Amy liked to spend time in. The same could be said for Sally-Ann. She had lost weight in recent weeks and her light blonde hair was interspersed with fresh strands of grey. Thoughts of Lillian's ongoing trial had taken its toll on them. Soon they would be standing in the box, exposing their dirty past to strangers as they faced a barrage of questioning. It was why Amy had gone against protocol today. They shouldn't be here. Amy had called in favours for them both to visit Lillian prior to giving evidence. But Sally-Ann had seemed so troubled when they last spoke, Amy had felt that she had no choice.

'You don't have to go in.' Amy squeezed her sister's arm as she caught the worried look on her face. 'You owe her nothing.'

'I need to see her.' Sally-Ann's expression was almost childlike: lost and alone. 'I'll never survive the trial if I don't clear the air between us first.'

But Amy knew no good could come from their meeting. Their mother was a deadly spider who drew the most vulnerable into her web. She leaned towards her sister, uttering words that only she could hear. 'Don't underestimate her. She feeds on weakness.'

'You don't need to tell me what she's like,' Sally-Ann snapped. 'I grew up in that house. You only had it for a few years.'

Amy flushed, her gaze creeping to the prison staff, whose faces were impassive. She could have given Sally-Ann any number of sharp responses, but chose to let it go. She knew her sister had been through experiences she was not strong enough to share. Amy's own memory of past events was returning in fragments. She was grateful. It was more manageable that way. But Sally-Ann wore the scars of her traumatic past both physically and mentally. Amy told herself that Sally-Ann would confide in her when the time was right. That is, if the trial didn't reveal all first. The very thought of being plunged back into that world filled Amy with dread. She wanted to be there for her sister – but at what cost?

'Sorry.' Sally-Ann exhaled a low breath as she pulled her cardigan together. 'I'm nervous. I shouldn't take it out on you.'

'It's OK,' Amy said. 'But once we walk through those doors, there's no backing out.'

Finally, they were given clearance. With a nod of the head, Sally-Ann pushed through the double doors. Every time Amy visited her biological mother, she told herself it would be the last. News of Sally-Ann's survival had been broken to Lillian only recently. Up until then, the world had thought that she was dead. It was nothing short of a miracle that she had managed to survive her father's attempt to kill her. He had been drunk when he dumped her beneath a tarpaulin and left her for dead. Bruised and battered, she had escaped in the middle of the night, never once looking back.

The room was stuffy and warm, the familiar smell of Forest Fresh air freshener making Amy want to gag. The artificial stench triggered an association with her biological parents, who used to mask the smell of decaying corpses by hanging Magic Tree air fresheners around the house. After buying a job lot at the car boot sale, her father had put them to good use. Even now, the sight of one of those green cardboard trees hanging from a car mirror gave Amy the creeps. To think that she had once lived in a home populated by the dead. Did their ghosts linger in those spaces, waiting for justice? If such things existed, she hoped they were now at peace. Remains had been found in the garden, beneath the floorboards, behind the fireplace. And all the while the sickly stench of air fresheners had lingered as her father hung them throughout the house.

Today, Amy and Sally-Ann were far from the serenity of a forest woodland as they entered the visitors' room. Amy weaved through the blue foam-padded chairs towards the table where Lillian was sitting. The room had recently been painted a lighter shade, but it did nothing to elevate the atmosphere as she took a seat across from Lillian Grimes. Stiffly, Sally-Ann stood, before the strength seemed to leave her legs and she finally sat down with a plop.

If Lillian was surprised to hear about Sally-Ann, she was giving nothing away. 'I'm so happy to see you.' Lillian gazed at Sally-Ann as she cracked a smile. 'I knew you'd visit me eventually.'

'How could you have known that?' Amy piped up, unable to bite her tongue. 'Up until last week, you thought she was dead.'

'Did I?' Lillian's eyes flickered towards Amy. Two glittering black coals set deep in ivory skin. 'You say so much, yet you know so little.' Her words were glacial. She crossed her hands on her lap, her movements graceful, her demeanour calm. She returned her gaze to Sally-Ann. 'You deserved a fresh start. I wasn't going to deny you that.'

Amy was incredulous. Lillian was lying. Surely Sally-Ann didn't believe her? *Pfft.* Another soft burst of air freshener from the plug-in on the wall. Sitting here with the stench of the past brought Amy way out of her comfort zone, and she dug her nails into her palms as she fought to remain in control.

'You're happy to see me?' A smile wavered on Sally-Ann's lips.

'Of course I am,' Lillian chuckled. 'It's been hell on earth for me all these years being apart from you. The one thing that kept me going was the fact you escaped. You were strong enough to do what I couldn't.' Her gaze rested on Amy. 'You see, Poppy here, she blames everything on me. I've tried to explain that we're all in this together.'

'*In this together?*' Amy echoed her words. 'You murdered those women and children. We were innocents!'

Lillian fixed her tabard, seemingly unaffected by Amy's words. 'I was too scared to ask for help. Yet I'm the one in prison.'

'You should have reported it,' Amy spat, barely able to look her in the eye.

'Like you did?'

'Yes, like I did,' Amy replied, unaware that she was falling into a trap.

'Very well, then why aren't you blaming Sally-Ann?'

'What?'

'Why aren't you blaming Sally-Ann for not calling for help?' Lillian's words stung. She may as well have slapped Amy in the face. 'I . . . I . . .' Amy paused as she felt the beginnings of a stutter on her lips. The fact that Sally-Ann had escaped but not sought help was a truth Amy had not contemplated – until now.

'You see?' Lillian broke the silence. 'Life's not all black-and-white, is it?'

'I'm sorry.' Sally-Ann spoke at last. 'I was traumatised after I left. I could barely function. By the time I got it together, the police were already involved.'

'So Poppy beat you to it, the same as she did with me. I was sorting out a refuge because I wanted our family to stay together. I knew the social would rip us apart.'

'I've heard enough.' Amy lifted her hands to her head, as if swatting away an insect instead of Lillian's words. 'Sally-Ann. You only came here to say goodbye. Let's go.'

'But I'm not done yet,' Sally-Ann replied. 'I'd like some time alone with Mum.'

'You're not serious?' Amy said, catching the expression of smug satisfaction on Lillian's face. Another gullible person lured into her web of lies. Surely Sally-Ann could see what she was doing, turning them against each other?

'Perhaps it's best if you go.' Lillian grinned, pinning Amy with a gaze.

'I don't think it's a g . . . good idea . . .' The re-emergence of Amy's stutter exposed her inner turmoil. It had taken her years to shake off the side effect of her childhood trauma, and now it was threatening to return. Amy gave Sally-Ann a pleading look. But her sister set her jaw in determination. Amy had lost this argument before it had begun.

'Give me ten minutes.' Leaning forward, Sally-Ann squeezed her sister's hand.

'F . . . fine. I'm going to the toilet. Then I'll wait in the car.' Amy swallowed the lump in her throat, unable to utter another word. Waves of nausea threatened to overwhelm her. She could not stand another second in this place. She stood on shaky legs. As soon as her back was turned, she heard Lillian express her pleasure at seeing Sally-Ann again.

'You sound different,' Sally-Ann said to her mother. 'You've not sworn once . . .' She chuckled.

'I've changed . . .' Lillian's words faded as Amy left the room.

Amy barely made it to the visitor toilets in time. Clutching her mouth, she slammed the cubicle door behind her before falling to her knees. The stench of bleach rose up her nostrils as she heaved. Gripping the sides of the porcelain bowl, Amy gagged until there was nothing left. Still on the floor, she grabbed a handful of toilet paper and wiped her mouth before flushing it away. It was a small mercy the place wasn't busy. She scrubbed her hands in the sink, before waving them under the dryer. Her thoughts were on fast forward as she dragged herself out of the past. Taking a deep breath, she wiped her eyes before making her way out. *What am I doing here?* she thought. *I should be in the office, working on the case.* Seeing Lillian had been a mistake, but did Sally-Ann think the same?

As Amy sat in her car, a motorbike revved its engine, throwing her out of her thoughts. She checked her watch. Sally-Ann had been in there for twenty minutes. Alarm bells rose in her mind. She should never have left them alone. She knew things had happened to Sally-Ann that she was unable to share. Lillian could be turning the knife right now. She rested her hand on the car door handle, jumping when Sally-Ann bustled into the passenger seat.

'Sorry,' she said, her face flushed.

Amy turned to face her. 'Never mind that, are you OK?'

'I'm fine. Better than fine, in fact. It's all good.'

Tell that to your face, Amy thought, but kept the words to herself. She turned the key in the ignition. 'I was worried,' she said, driving out of the car park and activating the indicator. 'Lillian was getting under your skin.'

'She's sorry for everything.' Sally-Ann's voice sounded weirdly cheerful. 'She deserves a second chance.'

Amy tightened her grip on the steering wheel. The tick-tock of the indicator felt like a detonator counting down. 'You're kidding me, right?'

But Sally-Ann's face was deadpan. 'I wouldn't joke over something like that. I'm going to help clear Lillian's name.'

'Bullshit.' Amy spat the word as she merged with the traffic, trying to keep her eyes on the road. 'What has she got on you?'

'What do you mean?' Sally-Ann stared straight ahead. The wind was picking up, sending debris swirling on the streets and paths.

A storm had been predicted, and Amy turned on the wipers as an old newspaper page flapped on to her windscreen. 'I know what Lillian's like. It's not so long ago she had me jumping through hoops. I'll say it again. What does she have on you?' Sally-Ann did not respond. Minutes passed in silence, but Amy wasn't going to let this lie. She braked at a set of traffic lights, staring at her sister until she was forced to meet her gaze. 'Something's wrong. I've felt it for weeks. Tell me. What is it?'

'The light's green.' Sally-Ann pointed ahead.

'Sod the lights!' Amy's anger flared as the car behind her beeped in protest. Sighing, she drove on, forcing herself to calm down.

'Lillian's right, though, isn't she,' Sally-Ann said eventually. 'I'm no different to her. I should have got help, but I was too wrapped up in myself.'

'You're nothing like her.' All traces of anger had left Amy's voice. How could her sister think that about herself?

'But I am. Lillian and I are equally guilty. If I deserve a second chance, then she does too.'

As Amy negotiated the traffic, she didn't trust herself to say another word. Something had happened between Sally-Ann and Lillian. She would find out what soon enough.

CHAPTER TWENTY-FOUR

Sifting through his paperwork, Donovan made a separate pile for the shredder. A digital stamp was made online every time one of them printed off an incident report. It made a welcome change. In the old days, little thought was given to the environment, but now they were all held accountable for their carbon footprint. Last year, he'd even got a Valentine's Day e-card. His thoughts drifted to Amy. Should he buy her some flowers for Valentine's Day?

'Almost ready to go?' Ginny stepped into his office, clipboard in hand.

Donovan signalled at her to close the door.

'Nearly. How's things going?' He wiped down his desk and threw a handful of crumbs into the bin.

'We've butted heads a few times with your media department but we're happy enough overall.'

'I never said it would be easy.' Donovan glanced at her warily. 'Just be grateful you got the gig.'

Ginny smiled, taking a step towards him. 'I have you to thank for that.'

Donovan checked over her shoulder to ensure nobody else was about. 'Keep that to yourself. It's best if nobody knows.'

'But why?' Ginny's tone was playful as she tilted her head to one side. 'You're not ashamed of me, are you? Where's the harm?'

Donovan rested his hand on her arm and gave it a squeeze. 'We agreed. It's easier this way. I've just started here, and I don't want to rock the boat.' The scent of her body spray rose between them, a fruity citrus number that smelled like sunshine in a bottle.

'OK then, whatever you say . . . boss.' She winked. 'I can't get used to hearing people call you that.'

'It has a ring to it.' Donovan smiled. 'C'mon, we've got a briefing to go to. And remember. You can film now, but you'll be cutting most of it out later. There's no way you'll be allowed to mention Black Media – at least, not unless any of them are charged.'

'Believe me, I know,' Ginny replied, holding the door open. 'That's been made very clear . . .' She peered at Donovan as he walked towards her.

'What's wrong?' Donovan touched his stubbled cheek. 'Have I got something on my face?'

'Yes, you have . . .' She grinned. 'Wrinkles. Will we get the make-up lady in? Looks like you could do with a little help.'

'Get out of it!' Donovan exclaimed in mock annoyance.

The briefing was a quick, impromptu gathering, held in the main office area while Amy was away. He knew she would be back soon, rolling up her sleeves, but they didn't have a second to waste.

His colleagues joined him as they sat in a circle, some resting on desks, others having wheeled their chairs across. Donovan had declined tea. This was a quick and dirty round of updates before Amy returned. He knew she didn't appreciate his input, but he had a lot more to offer than damage control.

'What have we got so far?' He turned to DC Steve Moss, who seemed eager to jump in. Having been demoted from DI to DC last year, Steve was used to being at the helm. The cameras quietly recorded in the background and Ginny's presence was unobtrusive as Steve spoke. 'To recap, we've identified our victim as twenty-six-year-old Stacey Piper, who worked in a supermarket but is believed to have begun supplementing her income through the Sugar Babes app. Both her phones have been sent for analysis.'

Donovan listened as Steve brought them up to speed on Amy's visit to Stacey's flat the night before. She hadn't even run it by him. Another example of her intuition working in overdrive. This time her visit had been fruitful, but Amy's unpredictability drove him to despair. He was yet to come to terms with the fact that it attracted him to her too. He brought his attention back to Steve, who was waiting for his response. 'Chase them up daily until you get a result. Tell them the command team is all over this.' Donovan turned his attention to Molly. 'Get in touch with the company behind the Sugar Babes app. See what you can wheedle out of them . . .'

'I'm all over it, boss,' Molly replied, swinging her chair around. She had been updating the computer system while taking the briefing on board. Donovan knew she was absorbing every word. She was the best multitasker on the team. 'I've asked for profile details of the users who have browsed Stacey's online account, as well as any messages that may have been sent.'

Donovan nodded in approval. He liked that Molly worked under her own steam. He turned to DC Gary Wilkes, who was looking colourful in his pink shirt. 'Gary, dig a little deeper with Stacey's family, and friends from her home town. Any ex-boyfriends lurking in the background? Unsavoury people she could have been running away from? Ask her employer if there have been any unusual incidents in the time running up to her death. We need to look wider than Black Media and the Sugar Babes app.'

'Will do, boss,' Gary said, scribbling down notes with a chewed-up pen.

'No news on the toxicology report?' Donovan glanced around the room. With the blessing of bigger budgets, they were placed ahead of the queue, but these things still took time.

'Not yet,' Paddy said. 'It's been fast-tracked so we should hear back soon.'

'OK,' Donovan replied. 'And remember, folks, not a word to the press.' He gave a cautious eye to the camera he had forgotten was rolling. 'That includes you,' he said to Ginny. 'Remember what I said. You'll need to cut most of this briefing, I can't see much of it being approved.'

Ginny signalled at Bob to turn off his camera. She knew better than to argue with Donovan.

'Ask yourselves why . . .' he continued, scanning the room. 'Why would someone want to risk leaving Stacey in a public place? What connection, if any, does this have with Claire Lacey, our schoolteacher from twenty years ago? I want you to drill down into Billy Picton and Samuel Black's alibis, but be discreet.' He stood, stretching his limbs. 'If Billy Picton is responsible, then why would he implicate himself? Or has someone got a grudge against Black Media? The shares have been floated on the stock market. Is someone trying to bring them down?' He paused as the idea took hold. A rival company was something they had not considered before. 'Speak to as many members of his staff as you can.' This instruction was issued to Paddy. He could be trusted to delegate the task. 'Have one of the team go to their hang-outs. I want to know what Black Media is really like. But remember, discretion is key. We can't afford to raise Black's hackles. Not until we have something concrete to challenge him with.'

As Donovan ended the briefing, he felt pride in his team. Nobody could doubt their dedication, and they had welcomed him into the fold. But the unit was expensive to run, and their foundation was made of stilts. Samuel Black was a powerful man. A lawsuit from his company could bring the team crashing down. He had warned his DCs not to piss Samuel off, but Amy was the one who worried him the most. How did you control someone who was determined to go it alone?

CHAPTER
TWENTY-FIVE

'What's going on?' Amy swigged from her stainless-steel water bottle. Her throat still burned from throwing up, but she was back in the office where she belonged. Her requests for time off had only been granted because she had accumulated so much leave. But she bitterly regretted visiting Lillian in prison. She had hoped it would give Sally-Ann closure, but instead it had made things worse. It was a sleeping dog she should have left well alone.

The room was bustling with movement and an air of excitement lingered as the cameras panned around. Were they closing in on a suspect? Her first thoughts went to Samuel Black. That in itself surprised her when Billy Picton had been so involved.

'Good timing.' Paddy approached her, smiling like the Cheshire cat emblazoned on his novelty tie. 'We've tracked down Stacey's date.'

'How?' Amy's mood lifted. Being back at work made her feel in control.

Paddy turned away from the cameras, which were focusing on DC Steve Moss. 'Molly spoke to Sugar Babes' head office and they handed everything over without question. Credit card, address, the lot. They wanted to delete the guy's account, but Molly told them to wait. We don't want to spook him, not yet.'

'That's a stroke of luck.' Amy smiled. Usually sites like Sugar Babes were strict when it came to data protection. 'I suppose it doesn't pay to have a potential murderer on your books. Who is this guy? Any previous?' She was referring to police convictions or intelligence logged on their database. Officers in the public protection team were already working through lists of sex offenders, recent prison releases and sexual deviants in the area around the time of the murder.

'No,' Paddy said. 'But we've been cleared to call in on his home address. Get this – his account gives his name as Jonathon Stone, but his real name is . . . Norris Burke.'

'Norris?' Amy repeated. 'Hardly the name of a player. I take it that profile picture wasn't his own.'

'I doubt it,' Paddy said. 'He's in his early sixties and, according to the intelligence unit, married with three grown-up kids. Bradley Cooper he is not.'

In the corner, Molly blurted a laugh. 'You can say that again. Here, cast your eyes over this. The intel unit sent his picture through.' Amy walked around to Molly's side of the desk, feeling more in her element with each second that passed. On the left of the screen was a handsome Sean Connery lookalike, with broad shoulders and a chiselled jaw to match. 'He's not bad,' Amy said.

'That's his profile picture,' Molly chuckled. 'Expectation versus . . .' – she clicked her mouse and another picture flashed up – '. . . reality. Say hello to Norris.'

The image appeared to have been reaped from a company website that featured Norris as an employee. Amy tried but failed to contain her amusement. 'Oh dear.' The lilt of her laughter filled the air. 'He should be sued for false advertising.' Amy glanced at his address, a respectable terraced house in Hayes where he lived with his wife. 'Looks like Norris has been a naughty boy.'

'He must have overdone it,' Molly piped up. 'He's off sick from work with a bad back.' Amy watched as she scrolled through the intelligence gained to date. Today Molly was wearing a dress, her hair newly styled with highlights to lighten her brunette shade. The camera crew had been working in Amy's absence, interviewing members of the team. But who was this new look for, TV viewers or Ginny Wolfe? Amy had seen Molly's admiring glances when she thought nobody was paying attention. From her viewpoint in her office, Amy didn't miss a beat. Neither did she miss Ginny's camaraderie with Donovan. Despite the age gap, they were totally at ease in each other's company.

'You *have* been thorough,' Amy said, closing the door on her thoughts. 'How did you know Norris was off sick?'

'I looked him up on LinkedIn. He was the only Norris Burke listed there. Then I rang his accountancy firm to ask if he was in. I think the receptionist thought I was his daughter. I told her I was Molly – that's his daughter's name too.'

'And you didn't go out of your way to correct her. Well done, some first-class snooping there.' Molly's desk was awash with paperwork, some of it stained with coffee rings. A half-eaten chocolate muffin sat next to her keyboard, a sprinkle of crumbs on her desk. Nobody could question her dedication. Amy had high hopes for the youngest member of her team.

Molly's eyes twinkled. 'Thanks, boss. He's due back in at work next week. You should catch him at home.'

'He could have been the last person to speak to Stacey alive, so it's well worth bringing him in.' Paddy reiterated what everybody knew. 'I suppose you want to come along?' He dangled the car keys before Amy.

'You suppose right. No cameras though. This needs to be handled with care.'

◆ ◆ ◆

The house on Warwick Crescent did not appear to be the home of a playboy, much less a serial killer with an artistic flair. Amy glanced at the cheerful faces of the garden gnomes lining the path. Hanging baskets were stuffed full of colourful fake flowers, and a sign saying *Dun-Roamin'* hung above the front door. But villains did not always come with sharp teeth and bloodstained hands. The ordinary garden-variety folks were the most frightening of all.

Public opinion had swayed in Lillian's favour. She was a grandmother now, her most recent photo depicting her holding up a drawing from her grandson. Nobody wanted to comprehend a regular-looking woman being capable of such heinous crimes.

The doorbell was stiff as Amy pressed it, a soft chime announcing their presence. No matter how much she tried to focus, thoughts of Lillian still crept in.

'Yes?' A softly spoken woman answered the door. Her eyes were close together, her face ghostly pale. Amy glanced at her plaid skirt and woolly cardigan. She did not look at all like the wife of a sugar daddy.

'Is this the home of Norris Burke?' Paddy asked, after introducing himself and Amy.

The woman stepped back, one hand touching the string of pearls around her neck. 'Yes, that's my husband. What do you want him for?'

'I'm afraid we can't say,' Paddy replied. Amy would have added that it was nothing to worry about, but Mrs Burke had a right to be concerned about two police detectives rocking up at her door.

There was a shuffle of slippered feet as Mr Burke crept up behind his wife. 'I'm Norris.' He tugged at his tank top, his Adam's apple bobbing as he swallowed.

Amy narrowed her eyes. He was guilty of something – but what? She exchanged a glance with Paddy as Norris turned to face his wife.

'Emily, why don't you go inside? I'll deal with this.' He placed his hand on the small of her back and gently turned her around. The scent of flowery perfume left a trail as she began to walk away.

'But what's it all about?' she wittered, her voice high-pitched and bird-like as she stopped halfway down the hall.

Norris looked beyond Amy at an elderly man walking along the pavement. An overweight black Labrador trailed behind him on a lead, pausing to cock his leg against Norris's gate.

'Come in.' Norris guided Paddy and Amy inside, a hint of annoyance in his voice. He glared at his wife. 'We had a suspicious man hanging round the office last week, the police are here to talk about it – that's all.' Emily seemed to relax visibly before opening her mouth to speak. 'And before you ask, no, we don't want tea!' Norris snapped.

Emily retreated to the kitchen, giving the officers one last curious glance. Amy remained tight-lipped. It was not her place to get involved. She could not enlighten Emily until further information came to light. At the moment the only thing they had on Norris was the fact that he used the Sugar Babes site. It didn't make him a murderer – at least, not yet.

Amy glanced around the living room, which seemed stuck in a Seventies time warp. A pea-green sofa was pushed up against the wall, with ornaments of birds in flight overhead. Amy directed her attention to the paintings of butterflies and peered at the signature, 'NW Burke'. William was Norris's middle name, but the paintings appeared as if they had been created by a child.

Paddy informed Norris about the Sugar Babes site as he gently closed the door. He proceeded to caution him just in case any admissions were made. 'You're not under arrest,' Paddy added. 'But this *is* in connection with a murder case, so if you say anything we consider to be evidence then we can use it against you.' The initial police visit was often a time when suspects were at their most loose-lipped. Shock usually played a part, along with the desperate need to explain themselves, even if it would trip them up later on. A small part of Amy wanted the murderer to be Norris so that they could close the case, but despite her musings about ordinary people being killers, Norris lacked the strength needed to get a body from one location to another. Judging by the paintings on his walls, he lacked artistic flair too.

'This is highly embarrassing,' Norris said, finding his voice. 'Did you have to come to my house and do this in front of my wife?' As he glared from Amy to Paddy, it was as if the police were in the wrong, not him.

'We tried your place of work, but they said you were off sick with a bad back,' Paddy replied.

'You rang my workplace?' Norris squawked, taking a step towards him.

Paddy's expression turned taut as he fixed him with a glare. At over six feet tall, Paddy could be intimidating, and as a former firearms officer, he had faced far worse than the likes of Norris Burke. It had the desired effect, and Norris stepped back. 'We didn't mention we were the police.' Paddy folded his arms.

Norris's tongue clicked as he tutted, his hands clasped behind his back. 'Since when was going online against the law?'

'It's a little more than that.' Paddy's tone was serious. 'Stacey was murdered after she arranged to meet you.'

Norris's mouth fell open as he registered the news. 'But I didn't turn up,' he said miserably.

'It's a tactic some punters use,' Amy said. 'They arrange to meet someone for a date and then follow them home to get their address.' She was conscious not to turn their meeting into an interview, not here. Such things had to be planned. 'But this isn't the place to discuss it. We need you to come to the station.'

'And if I don't want to?' Norris peered through the living room's net curtains, most likely to check that the dog walker had moved on.

Paddy clamped a hand on his shoulder. 'Then I'll have no choice but to bring you in. But if your wife rings the custody suite, she'll be informed that you're there under arrest. I don't think you want that, now, do you?'

'All right, I'll come.' Norris frowned. 'But I'm telling you, I've done nothing wrong. I was just looking. Nothing else.'

Amy raised her eyebrows to suggest that she saw through his lies.

Pulling at his shirt collar, Norris squirmed beneath her gaze. He turned to Paddy, no doubt hoping to appeal to his masculinity. 'I was just window shopping . . .' He emitted an awkward laugh. 'I messaged a few girls, but that's as far as it went. When it came to meeting up, I couldn't go through with it.' He sighed. 'I thought about it plenty of times, but I've never been unfaithful to my wife.'

What do you want? An award? Amy thought, but kept her opinions to herself. How lucky Mrs Burke was to have such a wonderful man in her life.

'Membership to that site is very expensive,' Paddy said. 'I can't see why you'd pay the subscription and not go through with it.'

'Membership gives you access to their pictures, and you can talk directly to the girls.' Norris rubbed the back of his neck. 'It was nothing more than a fantasy. I didn't hurt anyone . . .' Amy watched Norris closely, his face growing darker as he spoke. 'Besides, if they're going to put themselves out like that then what do they expect?'

'Seriously?' Amy shook her head in disbelief. What a little weasel this man was.

They waited in the hall as he delivered a few more lies to his wife. Norris seemed no stranger to dishonesty, but he was no cold-hearted killer. She had someone else in mind for that role.

CHAPTER
TWENTY-SIX

Samuel did not need the finer details of his next project's life, only to know that she was accessible. It was why he had set up a dummy run. He leaned on his crutches as he stood on the concrete step outside the communal entrance door to her building. A beanie hat and a set of Beats headphones provided a light disguise. He resisted the urge to scratch his right foot, which itched from the fake cast attached from the ankle down. The cold night breeze offered a slight relief as it chilled the tips of his bare toes. Samuel craned his neck towards the murky sky. It was devoid of stars, a blanket of slate-grey clouds left in the wake of the storm. At the side of the building there was a rattle of dustbins as a fox foraged for food. Samuel smiled. He was not the only predator on the streets tonight. Stiffening, he caught an outline through the stained-glass front door as one of the tenants prepared to leave the building.

It's showtime. Every nerve ending tingled as he cradled his phone between shoulder and ear.

'Honestly, I'm fine.' He spoke loudly, with convincing cheeriness. 'Mum, I'm home now. It's a fracture, that's all.' He mouthed a grateful 'thank you' as a smiling Asian woman held the door open for him. As it clicked shut behind him, he pocketed his phone and stepped on to the cool tiled floor. He sniffed the air. Someone was cooking curry. As long as it wasn't his Sugar Babe – according to their flirty online messages, she was visiting a friend and wasn't due home until ten. He cast his eyes at each corner of the ceiling, grateful the block of flats had yet to invest in CCTV. It beggared belief, in this day and age.

After pulling on his leather gloves, he limped towards Erin's flat. It was down the corridor and around the corner, away from prying eyes. There were several ways to gain entrance through the old-fashioned wooden door. He leaned his crutches against the hallway radiator as he worked out his next move. He had perfected the use of the bump key, which worked on the majority of locks. Taking a quick look around, he slid the set of keys from his pocket and a screwdriver from his backpack. There were all sorts of useful things in there, but right now, all he needed was access to the flat. Pushing the key in the lock, he tapped it lightly with the head of the screwdriver, encouraging the pins inside the mechanism to jump. Turning the key at exactly the right moment cleared the shear line and allowed the plug to turn. *Bingo!* he thought, as the door opened with a slow creak. Erin was out, so there was no security chain on inside to contend with. If there had been, his telescopic rod could have sorted it.

A bead of sweat broke out on Samuel's forehead and he carefully dabbed it away. It was excitement, not heat, causing him to perspire. Slipping off his rucksack, he removed the fake ankle cast, pulled his right trainer from his bag and put it on. He was trembling now, the shot of adrenaline that flooded his system superior to any drug. His sense of empowerment grew with each breath he took. He stood before the hallway mirror, watching himself in delicious anticipation as he slipped his balaclava on. A wicked smile spread across his lips as he clenched and unclenched his fists. As he crept through the flat he remained on high alert, listening for every sound. The pipes knocked behind the walls, filling the radiators to chase the February chill away. In buildings as old as these, the boilers were often noisy, and Samuel did not flinch at the sounds. The place was reasonably clean and cosy, and reminded Samuel of the first flat he had shared with Marianne. He pushed the memory aside. There was no place for sentiment here. Happy he was alone, he made his way to Erin's bedroom, working out his escape route.

It was a lilac-themed room, with lilac-scented candles and pretty dried heathers tied and arranged in a vase. He glanced at the array of cushions in every shape and size that covered the bed. Dark thoughts circled the periphery of his mind as he imagined taking one of those cushions and pushing it down on Erin's face. How long would it take her to pass out? He could feel his excitement growing. His eyes flicked to the framed photos on her dresser. Erin, looking much younger, holding a baby in her arms. Then Erin with a little girl in a primary school uniform. But there was nothing. Not one iota of sympathy for the young woman that Samuel had set out to kill. Instead, a storm of emotions rose inside him: a heady mix of lust, excitement, power and control.

As he inspected her underwear drawer, he ached to remove his protective clothing and bring her garments to his face. Pushing his sleeve back an inch, he checked his watch. He closed the drawer. It was time to hide. She would be back soon. The plan was to case her place, take her front door key, then leave. The curtains were closed, the flat empty. He was alone – for now. He folded his crutches and fitted them inside his bag. It gave him a queer thrill to be here among Erin's things. He looked longingly at the bottle of water on her bedside table, which she would most likely finish off tonight. *You could pop a sleeping tablet in there right now . . .* He unscrewed the cap, before reaching into his pocket for the same bottle of crushed sedatives he sometimes used on his wife. He sprinkled some of the white powder into the water and gave the bottle a shake. He had a far stronger drug to administer later; this was simply a taste of what was to come.

Sliding under the bed, he took his backpack with him, grunting as he squeezed into the narrow space. Closing his eyes, he imagined her above him, his breathing slowing as he began to relax.

◆ ◆ ◆

The rattle of door keys snapped him from his slumber. *Shit!* he thought. *What time is it?* His heart began to pound in his chest. Erin's voice was high-pitched and chattering but as it echoed from one room to another, he realised that she was on her mobile phone.

'Can't I see her this weekend? Please, Mum. I miss her so much.' She uttered a sigh. 'But you promised . . . No, you never mentioned going on holidays . . . I could tag along . . .'

Samuel grimaced from beneath the bed. The conversation was boring, and he should have been home by now. From what he'd gathered previously, Erin had given birth to a little girl when she was sixteen years old. Her mother had reared the child and now Erin wanted her back. Which he guessed was where her escort work came in. She had been saving for a new life for them both. But judging from the phone calls, Erin's mother was shutting her out.

'I *am* saving,' Erin said, sounding despondent now. 'But it's not all about money. She needs to spend time with me too.'

Samuel rolled his eyes, wishing she'd get on with her evening. He didn't want to hear her boring life story. Erin was little more than a possession to him. He regarded her in the same way he would consider a luxurious piece of furniture, or a new car. At last, the phone call ended, and Erin plopped heavily on to the mattress. Soft sobs erupted from above as Samuel shuffled closer to the edge of the bed. Sniffling quietly, Erin kicked off her slip-ons, revealing her bare feet. Her toenails were painted pink, her ankles slender. Samuel stared with longing. They were so close, he could reach out and grab them both. He imagined her terror as she was brought to her knees, her screams as she came face to face with his eyes, steely and determined as he crawled out and on top of her. He reined in his impulses as she rose from the bed and left the room. But she had not gone far. He listened as the shower was activated, the sound of water spiking against glass bringing up another tempting scenario. In the shower, she was totally vulnerable, trapped within the confines of her tiny bathroom. She would have nowhere to go. Samuel's mind had a scenario for every occasion, each one ending with him in complete control.

His teenage daughter flashed into his mind without warning. Samuel jolted, as if he had been slapped in the face. It was an unwelcome thought and he tried to dismiss it, but lately it was happening more and more. What would Laura be like at that age? Would she be like him, caught in the grip of dark longings, or was she destined to become someone's prey? Closing his eyes, he tried to drive thoughts of her away. But as she grew, so did the voice of his conscience. *Forget about this. You don't need to kill again, just walk away.* But he couldn't. The urge was too strong. Billy had messed things up by not going straight home the night Stacey was so beautifully displayed. He'd never mentioned the blasted fund-raiser. Samuel stiffened. It was why he had to get it right this time. It all seemed so simple when it was laid out in black and white. Framing Billy for the murders would stop the police coming after him. His thoughts came to an abrupt halt as the shower stopped. He clenched and unclenched his fists, feeling the leather stretch across his knuckles. A puff of steam escaped the door of the en suite as he heard Erin step out.

All thoughts of his daughter evaporated as he became absorbed in his next victim's nightly ritual. She padded around the room, pausing to drink from her bottle before returning to the en suite to brush her teeth before settling into bed. He listened to the soft click of her Kindle, until the motion stopped and the device fell to the floor. Waiting for her breathing to deepen, he slid out from beneath the bed. He was hard now, blood pounding fast and hot through his veins. The room was dim, but bright enough for her to see him should she open her eyes. He willed her to, his breathing growing rapid as his eyes trailed over her form, settling on her blonde hair. She seemed peaceful, small smudges of mascara beneath her lids that the shower had not been powerful enough to remove. But he could. His hands twitched as he imagined washing her skin, her face, her nails. He checked his watch. He had been standing there for ten minutes, just watching her sleep. Slowly, he reached out, touching the tips of her hair. His breathing grew rapid as he leaned over her sleeping form. It was so tempting just to—

Later, his inner voice instructed. *You're too excited. Too greedy. You don't rush a fine wine, you savour it. Go home and sort out your wife.* Only when Marianne was sedated could he return. She would be his alibi if questions were asked later on.

Exercising his self-control, he backed out of the room, pocketing Erin's front door key on the way out. She wouldn't be needing it anymore. Minutes later, he was trotting down the front steps of the building. The next time they were together he would not be hampered by protective clothing or the constraints of time. He imagined the glint of the knife as he branded her with a love heart. Then his attention was drawn to a fox scuttling across the road with a slice of bread in its mouth. *See you soon, my friend*, he thought.

CHAPTER
TWENTY-SEVEN

Amy pinched the bridge of her nose as she tried to keep the dull throb of a headache at bay. It was the end of a long working day. Norris's account had been taken in interview and background checks revealed he was telling the truth. He may have flirted with Stacey online, but was nowhere near her the night she disappeared. Now all Amy wanted was to go home and curl up in bed with the book on her dressing table.

A phone call from Mama Danielle put an end to her plans. With so much going on, Amy had forgotten about Lisa's referral to her handler.

It was a challenge, finding a space in which Amy could talk privately. Discussing her enjoyment of no-strings sex was hardly appropriate in front of her team. And besides, nothing could be further from the truth. Her early years in such a promiscuous household had put Amy off casual sex for life. 'The girlfriend experience sounds perfect for me,' she lied, having found a space in the car park where she could not be overheard. 'I've been told that I have a nice body and I'm good in bed.' Heat rose to her cheeks as Paddy drove past. He seemed lost in thought, oblivious to her presence. Backing into the shadows, Amy concentrated on her call.

'It's not as simple as that,' Mama Danielle barked down the phone. 'Our clients can get sex anywhere. They're paying for the experience. They want elegance, class.' As she brushed her hair from her face, Amy strained to work out her accent. It was more US than UK. She wondered how Stacey had factored into Mama Danielle's list of demands as she reeled them off. 'I have a degree in philosophy and English lit,' Amy replied truthfully. 'I've been privately educated. I can hold my own.'

'Then we can meet. I'll be at The Ivy in Soho at 11.30. See you at the bar.'

As Amy returned to her office, she tried to work out the logistics. Requesting police clearance would mean rescheduling their meeting while Amy waded through the red tape involved. That would hardly go down well with Mama Danielle, particularly given her abrupt nature. Besides, Amy needed to test the waters before involving her team. The last thing she needed was the camera crew tagging along. Ginny had already voiced her disappointment that Amy had visited Norris without them. The crew were becoming as welcome as a fart in a space suit.

Amy checked her watch. It was time to make the most of her headache. 'Mind if I shoot off now?' she said, looking suitably pained. Their office was dim, with Donovan's table lamp casting his space in a soft orange glow.

'I ordered pizza.' Donovan paused as another thought emerged. 'You're not meeting Samuel Black, are you? Because if you are . . .'

'At this hour of the night? Of course not.' Amy rubbed her temples. 'Look, I can stay if you want, but it feels like someone's pushing a jackhammer into my brain.' She winced as she spoke, feeling guilty for Donovan's growing expression of concern.

'Are you sure you don't want to stay for pizza? I can give you a lift home afterwards. You don't want to be cycling at this late hour.'

Amy waved his concerns away. 'The fresh air will do me good, and there's a pasta bake in the fridge. I'll heat it up when I get home.' She picked up her bag from the floor, feeling him watch her every move. 'Honestly, I'm fine, just spending too long staring at my computer screen. Call me if any big developments come in.' Had he not been her boss, Amy could have told him about her meeting with Mama Danielle, but the dynamics between them had changed. She missed the camaraderie they used to have. The look on Donovan's face told her that he did too.

◆ ◆ ◆

It took Amy half an hour to get ready and a further twenty-minute ride to Oxford Circus on the Tube. She had chosen a slim-fitting black dress that gave a hint of cleavage while flattering her curves. But it could all be for nothing if Danielle recognised her from the off. Losing her anonymity was costing Amy dearly but there was little she could do about it now. Gripping her clutch bag, she crossed the cobbles on Broadwick Street and walked into The Ivy Soho Brasserie. It was a slightly cheaper alternative to the famous original, where celebrities were said to dine. Staff were younger, and it was as quiet as you'd expect for a Wednesday night. With a DJ at weekends, it gave off a trendy vibe. Amy admired the artwork on display. It only occurred to her when she reached the bar that she had forgotten to ask Danielle what she looked like.

'Amelia, I take it? Or should I say Amy?' The voice was distinct, and Amy recognised the accent as she swivelled around. It was not often that she was rendered speechless, but the last thing she had expected was to be rumbled this early on. 'Mama Danielle?' Amy glanced up at the tall athletic woman before her. She appeared to be in her mid-forties, her cropped blonde hair a striking contrast to her mocha skin. She oozed confidence, and as Amy discovered, was not so easily fooled. She fumbled with her purse as the barman asked what she would like to drink.

'I got this.' Mama Danielle winked at the barman, her bracelets jangling as she slid her purse from the pocket of her white designer trouser suit. 'Two pink G&Ts, honey, and one for your gorgeous self.' The young man smiled in appreciation before turning to mix their drinks.

'Thanks.' Amy straightened her stance, not one to allow her authority to ebb away. 'How did you know it was me?'

'Rose is a selfish brat, always has been. There's no way she'd share clients with a stranger she'd met in a bar.' Danielle snorted a laugh. 'I had that bitch sussed from the off.'

Amy accepted the drink as it was handed to her, smiling as Mama Danielle clinked her glass against hers.

'I was gonna play along and interview you, but I'm guessing your time is as precious as mine.' Danielle paused to sip her drink. 'You could have just asked, you know. I would have met ya anyway.'

In Amy's experience, people connected to the sex industry were less than keen to speak to the police. 'I appreciate that,' she said. 'This meeting is off the record, by the way. You can speak freely with me.' An understanding passed between them, and Mama Danielle nodded in response. 'Where are you from? I'm normally good with accents but I can't pinpoint yours. I'm guessing New York?'

'Philly,' Mama Danielle replied. 'But I've been living in London for a decade or so. I was cut up to hear about Stacey.' She glanced around the bar before continuing. 'Word's got out. Now my other girls are spooked too. Have you caught the bastard?'

'If I had, I wouldn't be here.' Amy rested her glass on the bar. 'Can I be frank with you?'

'Shoot.'

'Whoever killed Stacey . . . I think he found her through the Sugar Babes site. I need your help. I'm not interested in your operation. If anything, it's good that you're keeping the girls safe.' Amy's voice was low and even as she drove her message home. 'I want you to come on board. I need some inside information and you're best placed to help me.'

'Seriously?' Mama Danielle's eyebrows shot up. 'You want me to snitch on my clients?'

Amy leaned forward and looked her dead in the eyes. 'If it means catching the scumbag who killed Stacey, then yes, why not?'

Danielle grabbed her glass and for a moment Amy wondered if she was going to thrust the contents in her face. Instead, she knocked back the remainder of her gin. 'Are you recording this? You setting me up, is that what this is?'

Amy shook her head. 'I head a team who deals with high-profile cases, such as murders and kidnappings. It's not in the public interest to interrogate you and it's certainly not in mine.'

'All right,' Danielle said. 'That guy Stacey met through Rose's account, Jonathon Stone? He's a pest, trying to score freebies with the girls. None of them talk to him anymore. I guess he speaks to the newbies cos they don't know any better, but he's never threatened to hurt them.'

'I know about Jonathon. In fact, we've interviewed him. I don't think he's Stacey's killer.'

'Well then, I'm sorry to tell ya that I didn't get the chance to arrange any new dates. I wouldn't be surprised if she went off the books to keep the profits for herself.' She grimaced. 'They say to me, "Mama, you take too much, I'd be better off on my own." That's after I've helped them build a profile and helped with their portfolio . . . Ungrateful bitches.' Mama Danielle lowered her head as she mumbled under her breath. As she looked back up, Amy was surprised to see tears gathering in her eyes. 'I should quit this crap.

But those girls, they need me. Who's gonna take care of them if I don't?' She swiped away an errant tear. 'Stacey . . . she was naive, but she had things tough, ya know? She used to be in a street gang. Her mom threw her out of the house when she was sixteen years old. Caught her using. Couldn't deal with it. The girl got herself clean and started again.'

'I didn't know that,' Amy said. Stacey's mother had been a closed book when officers spoke to her.

'My girls, they're family to me.' Mama Danielle sighed. 'I make it my business to find out everything about them before I take them on.'

'Do you use the same photographer for all of the girls? The backgrounds . . . they look the same.'

'I take the photos, develop them in my apartment. The girls trust me.'

The atmosphere was charged with emotion. At least Danielle was onside. Slipping her hand into her clutch bag, Amy pulled out a business card. 'Call me the second you or your girls see anything suspicious. My mobile number is on the back.'

'It's been nice meeting ya, Miss Winter.' Danielle slid off her stool, her composure regained. 'You know, if you came to me as Amelia, I would have given you a job.'

'Get away with you,' Amy chuckled. She had warmed to Mama Danielle. Despite her profession, she liked the woman's no-non-sense attitude and the fact that she cared about her girls.

'You wouldn't be the first cop on my books.' But her smile dimmed as a thought seemed to cross her mind. 'You'll catch him . . . won't you?'

Amy didn't need to ask who she was referring to. 'I'll do everything humanly possible,' she replied, in her most reassuring tone. Samuel Black's face appeared in Amy's mind. Would she find answers once and for all?

CHAPTER
TWENTY-EIGHT

Standing at the bedroom door, Marianne gave her husband a weak smile. He returned it with a wink, making her heart melt, even after all these years. He continued telling Megan a story. Laura was fast asleep, but Megan had woken and tiptoed out of bed the second her father came in the door. The story was about a powerful princess who could do anything. Samuel didn't buy into the usual tales of helpless princesses who needed to be saved. In Samuel's stories, the princesses were the ones doing the saving. Which is why it felt so odd for Marianne to entertain her growing concerns. How could he be unfaithful, when he was such a wonderful role model to their children?

She walked away from the door, unable to watch anymore. These days, tears were never far away. He was late, which wasn't unusual, but there was something about his behaviour lately that felt off. It was like the flick of a switch. Most of the time, he was a normal loving husband. Stressed at work, yes, but always had time for his family. But sometimes, in the dead of night, she would awake to find him staring at her in the dim light. The expression on his face . . . it was as if he was a stranger.

It had been good, seeing her sister when she came to visit again yesterday, but there was something about Karen's presence that seemed to unnerve Samuel. He didn't say it in so many words, but he had become increasingly territorial and hated having Karen in their home. To be fair, he *had* caught her snooping inside his office as he popped out to use the loo. Marianne could count on one hand the number of times he had left the door unlocked. He didn't buy Karen's explanation that she was looking for his daughter's favourite toy. Megan wouldn't venture into the office any more than Marianne would. But why not? It was their home, after all. So why was his office out of bounds?

Perhaps it's where he keeps his second phone. The thought was like ink on white cotton, a stain on their relationship that would not go away. They had been coming more frequently these days – these suspicious whispers in the back of her mind. But surely he would be better off keeping a second phone in his office at work? What if she snuck in and had a peek when he was at one of his meetings? Marianne sighed. Naomi would never let her in, and even if she did, Samuel's desk drawers were probably locked.

'She's out like a light. Didn't make it to the end where the princess sets up in business for herself.'

The sound of Samuel's voice made Marianne jolt. 'Oh!' She clasped a hand to her chest. 'You made me jump. I was miles away.'

'Sorry, babe,' he chuckled, before following her downstairs.

'Hey, guess who came to see me at work?' Samuel poured them both a drink from a decanter on their new sideboard. 'I've been meaning to tell you, but I never got the chance.'

Your mistress? Marianne felt like saying. 'Dunno,' she said instead, curling her feet beneath her as she sank into their plush sofa. Megan's toys were still strewn on the floor, and there was a pile of dirty dishes to be loaded into the dishwasher. Since giving up her medication, her worries crowded her mind and she had little time or motivation to do the housework. Samuel refused to employ a cleaner as he didn't want a stranger in their home.

'Here,' he said, handing Marianne a small glass of whisky on the rocks. 'Looks like you could do with it.' Taking a seat beside her, he pulled out a teddy from where it was stuck in the cushions and laid it on the side. 'Amy Winter, aka Poppy Grimes.' He paused, reading her confusion. 'You know, the daughter of the Beasts of Brentwood. She came to see me at work. Don't tell me you haven't heard of her.'

Marianne sipped her whisky. She had heard of her all right. Karen's attempts at searching Samuel's home office had been frustrated by his locked drawers, but there was something of interest she had found spread across his desk. A collection of newspaper articles about Amy Winter. Some were old, but Marianne had recognised her as the woman she had seen at Samuel's work. She had made it her business to find out everything about her. Her adoptive father had died recently, and she was single as far as Marianne could tell. She worked in Notting Hill and was a well-respected officer, dedicated to her job. They could be neighbours for all Marianne knew. She glanced at her husband, realising he was waiting for a response. 'I remember. Her mother's trial has been splashed all over the news.' Marianne's jaw tightened. It was another thing Samuel had taken an exceptional interest in. He'd always had a morbid fascination for true crime and serial killers. It gave her the creeps.

'Amy's overseeing the murder investigation of that woman who was found in the store window display. She came to talk to me about Billy.'

'Billy? As in tweed-jacket-with-leather-patches Billy?' Billy had been dressing like a schoolteacher since he was a teen.

Samuel's face crinkled in a smile. 'The very one. He oversaw the display.'

'Hmm,' Marianne said, resting her glass on the coffee table. 'Nice to know you're on first-name terms with someone high up in the police. Maybe she'll let you off the next time you get a speeding ticket.' She knew she should be relieved that Samuel was telling her about Amy, but why had he lied about it when she was there?

Samuel's hand stretched across the sofa as he toyed with Marianne's hair. 'She's too busy catching murderers to worry about me.'

'Aren't you worried about the negative publicity?' Shielding her mouth, Marianne emitted a yawn. Tonight, she might avail herself of the sleeping tablets the doctor had prescribed. It was good that Samuel still worried about her. If it were not for him, she never would have asked for the prescription.

Samuel's voice broke into her thoughts. 'If anything, it's been a real shot in the arm. We've had more enquiries now than ever before.'

'But that poor girl. Could Billy have had something to do with her death?'

'They say it's the quiet ones you have to watch.' Samuel trailed his fingers down the back of Marianne's neck. 'What do you think it was like, growing up with Jack and Lillian Grimes?'

Marianne suppressed a shudder. 'Must be why she became a police officer – to atone for their deeds. Maybe she feels guilty about it all.'

'Maybe . . . Although reports say she's drawn to serial killer cases. You'd think she'd want to run a mile from them.'

'I don't get you.' Marianne wanted to go to bed, but she hadn't had Samuel's undivided attention in a very long time. Was he trying to tell her something? She stared at the blank television screen as she tried to decipher his words. He was a straight talker in business, but when it came to relationships he was impossible to work out.

Kicking off his shoes, Samuel stretched out his long legs. 'Did you know that when police used to tape-record interviews, the offenders could request a copy? They'd use them as currency in prison, swapping them with other inmates so they could get off on what they'd done. It was popular with sex offenders and murderers – until everything went digital.'

'You've lost me,' Marianne said. 'What's that got to do with Amy Winters?'

'It's Winter, not Winters,' Samuel corrected her, his face alight as he spoke. 'I have a theory. What if she's cleverer than her parents? Maybe she gets her kicks legally. She goes to crime scenes, talks to offenders, visits victims. Perhaps she interferes with evidence. You don't know, do you?'

'No way.' Marianne frowned. 'She'd be found out. She'd never get away with that.'

'You say that, but do you know why her mother's appeal has gone ahead?' He paused but no reply came. 'Because Amy blew the whistle on her colleagues to set her free. She found evidence that proved Lillian had been set up.'

Marianne's face soured. Amy this and Amy that. A pang of jealousy lit inside her as she watched her husband's animated expression.

'You should have seen her when she came to visit me,' he said. 'She gets off on it. I can tell.'

'And do you?' The words escaped Marianne's lips before she could contain them.

'Do I what?' Samuel dropped his hands to his lap, his expression unreadable.

'Do you get off on being with her? You know an awful lot about someone you've only just met.' The room seemed to dim as Marianne's anger grew.

'What?' A frown creased Samuel's face as his voice rose. 'Hang on, I know what this is about. It's Karen, isn't it? She's been stirring again.'

'This has nothing to do with Karen.'

'Yeah it has. I caught her nosing around my office yesterday evening. This is exactly why I don't want her in our home. She's poison, that one. Always was.'

Marianne could feel tears edging the borders of her eyelids, a lump growing in her throat. 'It's not that, it's just . . . I've been feeling neglected lately, that's all.' She looked around the room at the home they had built together: the handmade Italian furniture, the Louis De Poortere rug. But she would give it all up tomorrow to recapture their lost spark.

'You're feeling neglected?' Samuel blurted a laugh. 'I buy you jewellery, send you flowers, heap praise on you at social events. And now I'm not allowed to talk about other women? Do you know how ridiculous you sound?'

Marianne instantly regretted her outburst. The first piece of quality time she'd got with her husband was going to end in a blazing row. 'I'm sorry,' she said, knowing she had no choice but to back down. She moved to the edge of the sofa, wrapped her arms around herself.

'If I fancied Amy Winter, I'd hardly be talking about her to you, now would I? Honestly, Marianne, it's like this every time your sister is here. She's always pouring poison in your ear.'

'It wasn't Karen, honestly. I just . . .' She lowered her head, unable to meet his gaze. 'I miss you. I never get to see you anymore.'

'Here, finish your drink.' Samuel handed her the glass. His hand felt warm as he placed it on her back. He rubbed in circular movements and the anger left his voice. 'You're seeing me now, aren't you?' His expression softened. 'Look. This won't last forever. I'm working to build a secure future for us all. You've got to hang in there. I couldn't do any of this without you.'

'Really? Do you mean it?' Marianne knocked back the contents of the glass as Samuel placed his arm around her shoulders.

'Yes. I'd never leave you. Get that thought right out of your head. You're the only woman for me.' Marianne rested her head on his chest. If only she could believe he was telling the truth.

CHAPTER
TWENTY-NINE

It was a surprise to hear that Mandy was in reception, especially given Amy wasn't meant to be at work herself. She had only popped in this morning to check her emails before meeting with Donovan to spend the day with him.

Amy was the youngest of the four siblings brought up in the Grimes household. From what she could remember of Mandy, she came with hard edges and a strong sense of self-preservation. Amy steeled herself for their meeting before entering the room off reception where her sister had been told to wait.

Mandy was dressed in her usual outfit: a leopard-print jumper, and jeans too baggy for her skinny frame. It was rare to see her without a pushchair in tow. She fidgeted in her seat, toying with her bracelets as she watched Amy enter the room.

'What's wrong?' Amy asked, her chair scraping across the tiled floor as she dragged it out. 'Everything all right?'

'Nuffink, we're fine . . . apart from this sodding cold.' Mandy's voice was thick with congestion, the stench of cigarettes lingering on her breath. 'I want a quick word.'

'Is it about the trial? Because I watched you give evidence. You made Lillian sound like a saint.'

'I didn't see you in court.'

'I watched it on television.' Amy had promised herself she wouldn't go there, but she had to get it off her chest. 'The last time we spoke, you thanked me for calling the police when we were young. So how could you make out she was Mother of the Year?'

Mandy shrugged. 'I told you what you wanted to hear, hoping you'd throw us a few quid to help out.' She paused to examine her nails. It was an old trait that Amy recognised. Mandy avoided eye contact when she told lies. 'It wasn't Mum's fault. I've stuck by her all these years and now, thanks to my loyalty, she's sticking by me.' In the absence of a tissue, Mandy wiped her nose with the back of her sleeve.

'So it's money. That's what this is about.' Amy ignored the buzz of her mobile phone as it vibrated in her pocket. 'You may as well admit it. I know you, Mandy – more than you think.'

Finally, Mandy met Amy's gaze. 'She owes me. And don't look at me like that! I didn't have the advantages you did. Mum warned me what you were like, but I gave you the benefit of the . . . you know . . . wotsit.'

'Doubt.' Amy sighed. 'The benefit of the doubt.' Mandy had a right to be bitter. She had children. Responsibilities. 'Don't you remember what Lillian did? Putting the murders aside, she could have at least made sure we were clean and fed.' Amy rolled her tongue over her teeth. Her baby molars had been riddled with decay. A sporadic diet of sugary foods and fizzy pop had seen to that. The gaps in Mandy's teeth told Amy it had been no different for her. But unlike Mandy's, Amy's adult molars had grown through OK.

'I know only too well. So does Damien – he still has the scars.' Mandy pursed her lips, realising she had said too much. 'But she wants to make up for it. I mean, have you seen her? Her eyes are bad from being in the dark so long, and her joints are stiff and worn. She served her time. She deserves a bit of a life before she dies.'

'Before she dies?' Amy laughed incredulously. 'There's nothing wrong with her! She's putting it on. Can't you see? She's got you right where she wants you. But not me. I'm going to put them straight.'

'And who's gonna listen to you? You were four when the social took you in. You saw nuffink.' Mandy's voice broke into a sawing cough.

'I saw more than you think. I was there when she murdered Viv.' Amy's brow furrowed as the past clawed for her attention. Every second she spent talking about it dragged her back to those awful days.

'You wot?' Mandy shifted in her seat. 'You're making it up. You've got a grudge because your copper friends were caught stitching Mum up. You all stick together, you lot.'

Unable to stand it any longer, Amy brought her clenched fist down on the table with a bang. 'I was the one that brought the evidence to light!' Her inner Poppy Grimes had emerged, and just like before, she was fighting to be heard.

Flinching, Mandy recoiled, her eyes growing wide. But Amy was too lost in the moment to stop now. 'Can't you see?' She jabbed her finger in the air. 'I could have walked away. I could have burned that box of evidence and not said another word.' Spent, she sat back in her chair. 'I wish I had,' she said in a small voice. 'Because this is killing me.' In truth, it was. Since the discovery of her parenthood, she had lost a little piece of herself every day.

Mandy snuffled. 'It's easy to come across all moral when you live in a posh house in Notting Hill. I found a dead rat in my kitchen this morning. Some of us haven't had the luxury of being able to move on.'

Amy pulled a packet of tissues from her pocket and pushed them across the desk. 'I've got some contacts in housing. I'll speak to them. Ask to have you moved up the waiting list.' Amy hated asking for special treatment, but Mandy's was a desperate case.

'Nah . . .' Taking a tissue from the packet, Mandy paused to blow her nose. 'Mum's sorting it all out.'

'What's she offered you?'

Mandy replied with a shrug. 'All I want is a better life for my kids, and she owes me big time. Go ahead and give your evidence. See what difference it makes. Everyone's on her side now.'

Judging by the newspaper reports, they were. Support for Lillian was growing by the day. 'Here.' Amy pulled her wallet from her blazer and took out three twenty-pound notes. 'For the kids.'

'Ta.' Snatching the cash from her hand, Mandy shoved it down her top and into her bra. 'It's the only place where it's safe,' she said, in response to Amy's bemused expression.

Outside the door, she could hear someone arguing. People often wandered in from the street, fuelled by alcohol and up for a fight if a family member was being interviewed for an offence. Satisfied it was nothing to worry about, Amy tried one more time to get to the bottom of Mandy's visit. 'Why did you come here?' She hoped for the truth, now a truce had taken place.

'To tell you to go easy on Sally-Ann. You don't know what she's been through.'

'And you do?' Amy was half afraid of her reply. A decaying memory loomed on the periphery, of a time Amy had tried hard to forget. It involved Sally-Ann, sobbing downstairs. Lillian was there. Jack Grimes too . . . Amy blinked as the past closed in. She took a deep breath and pushed it away.

'She'll tell ya when she's good and ready.' Mandy seemed oblivious to Amy's torment as she stood to leave. 'Just . . . just don't go shoutin' the odds. We're all trying to pull together the best we can.' She tugged the strap of her handbag on to her shoulder. 'If you won't do it for Lillian, then think of Sally-Ann.' Her brows knitted together as another thought came. 'Anyway, this is family business. Best you keep your nose out of it.'

Those words . . . Amy drew a sudden breath. She had heard them once before. She stared after her sister as the door clicked shut behind her, a memory seeping through the cracks.

CHAPTER THIRTY
THEN

Poppy was used to hearing strange noises after dark, but tonight she recognised the voice howling in pain. Creeping out of her bed, she shuddered as ice-cool air brushed her skin. Winter had bitten hard, and the hot-water bottle that Mummy had filled had turned cold. Wrapping her cardigan around her shoulders, Poppy tiptoed from her bed, casting an eye on the vacant spot where her sister should have lain. But Sally-Ann wasn't there. She was downstairs, crying out in pain. The bathroom door creaked open, making Poppy jump. If it had been her father, he would have beaten her for sure. Tonight, she was lucky; it was Mandy before her, her face scrunched up in a scowl. 'What are you doing out of bed?' Her words were uttered in a harsh whisper, her stringy hair dangling around her face. Sally-Ann used to tell her off for not washing it, but Mandy was what her mother called 'a law unto herself'.

'I need to pee,' Poppy whispered, pleased she had managed to get the words out without stuttering. Another howl of pain from downstairs. Poppy's hands bunched up into her nightie, her eyes growing wide.

'Well, hurry up then!' Mandy spat, administering a firm fist between Poppy's shoulder blades as she pushed her into the bathroom. Poppy stood at the door, mouth open as she stared at her sister for help. 'But Sally-Ann?' She recognised the screams as those of her eldest sister. As terrified as she was of her parents, she could not leave her crying out in pain. But Mandy's lips narrowed into a cold thin line.

'That's family business. Best you keep your nose out of it. Now do your pee and get back to bed!' Mandy clicked the door shut, leaving Poppy alone in the bathroom. She counted to ten before opening the door to check that Mandy had gone.

Poppy tiptoed towards the banisters, her eyes wide as she took in the darkened scene. Clutching the wooden railings, she peered through the open living-room door. Mummy was hunched over Sally-Ann, who was lying on the sofa, her nightdress up around her waist. Poppy wanted to go to her, but Mandy was right, Mummy would be cross if she caught her out of bed. Poppy stiffened as her father strode from the kitchen with towels and a roll of bin liners in his arms. 'We should take her to the hospital,' he said. Despite the wintry night, his forehead was beaded with sweat. He was too caught up with Sally-Ann to notice Poppy sitting on the stairs.

Snatching the bin liners from his grasp, Lillian's words were harsh. 'She's barely thirteen. They'll lock you up for this.'

'What? It ain't my fault . . .' Jack's features hardened. A piercing scream broke their argument as Sally-Ann wailed in pain. Pulling out a strip of black plastic bags, Lillian placed them beneath her daughter before covering them with towels. 'Shhh,' she said to Sally-Ann, whose features were contorted with pain.

'I'm dying, Mum!' Sally-Ann cried. 'I'm dying.'

'You ain't dying, ya silly cow, you're 'aving a baby,' Jack said, leaning over to see the state of play.

Lillian's face was thunderous as she pushed her husband away with both hands. 'Yeah,' she shouted. 'And don't you know all about that. Now fuck off down the pub while I clean up your mess.'

'I told ya, it wasn't me!' Jack's fists were clenched as he turned on her. 'And if you say that one more time . . .'

Poppy's parents fell silent as they stared each other out. Nostrils flaring, Lillian looked fit to explode.

'What are ya going to do with it?' Jack pointed in Sally-Ann's direction.

'I'll sort it, like I sort everything. It'll be gone by the time you get back. Go on, sod off. You're not helping here.'

Teeth clicking, Poppy shivered as she tried to comprehend their words. She understood little of what was being said, apart from Sally-Ann having a baby. Where was it coming from? Why was she crying? None of this made any sense. A gust of icy wind shot up the stairs as her father slammed the door behind him. There was never any peace in this house. Damien and Mandy only slept through it because of the tissues they stuffed deep into their ears. Poppy leaned forwards, her lips parted as she gasped. She forgot the cold, her lingering fear, the hard step as she sat still for too long. All was forgotten as Sally-Ann made a harsh grunting sound and her mother shouted at her to push. *Push what?* Poppy thought, rising to the balls of her feet. Tiptoeing into the hall, Poppy peered from the doorway to see her mother holding a baby in her arms. Sally-Ann had stopped screaming. Her tears soft, she was mewing like the next-door neighbour's cat. Wrapping the baby in a thick brown towel, Mummy handed it over to Sally-Ann. A tuft of black hair spiked from a pink scalp, the bundle sucking furiously on its fist. Darting behind the coats in the hall, Poppy watched as Lillian tidied Sally-Ann up, then left the living room to put the kettle on to boil. Minutes later, Sally-Ann was made more comfortable and the baby was swapped for a cup of tea.

'Drink. It'll help you sleep.' Lillian took the baby from Sally-Ann's arms. With one hand, she pulled the throw from the sofa and covered up her daughter. 'You mustn't tell anyone about this, do you hear? Not a word.'

'But Mum . . . what are you going to do?' Sally-Ann cried.

'The less you know the better. You're far too young to be a mum and I've got enough on me plate.'

Fresh tears erupted as Sally-Ann pleaded. 'Please, Mum, don't hurt him. I'll do anything, please let him stay.'

'And what about your dad? You want the baby to be safe, don't you?'

Her words were met with silence.

'You don't need to worry. I'll find him a good home.' Within five minutes, the baby had been bundled into a cardboard box lined with blankets and a hot-water bottle to stave off the chill. As the door slammed behind her, Poppy took advantage of her mother's absence to creep into the living room. She did not possess the words to express how she felt. Poppy's emotions always seemed too big to vocalise, but she knew Sally-Ann understood. Her sister sobbed quietly, pausing only to raise the cup of tea to her lips. Her hair was hanging down her face, her eyes puffy and red.

'What's wrong?' Poppy tentatively crept towards her, listening for signs of her parents' return. Reaching out, she stroked Sally-Ann's hair as she took in the scene. A patch of blood stained a discarded blanket, making her heart pound. It was not the first time she had seen blood in this house, but she sensed this was different to before.

'It's OK, get back to bed.' Sally-Ann's words came slowly, as if the act of speaking was an effort in itself. The tea had smelled strange when Sally-Ann raised it to her lips. Sometimes Mummy drank stuff that made her act all funny. Once, when they had visitors round, Mummy danced on the table and took off all her clothes. Poppy pushed away the memory, one of a hundred she had rejected. 'The baby . . .' she said, breathing through her mouth. Her heart felt all funny again and she could not get enough air in through her nose.

'Promise me, Pops, don't talk about the baby again.'

Poppy offered up her little finger, hoping a 'pinkie promise' would soothe Sally-Ann. Locking fingers, their pact was sealed. Fresh tears fell from Sally-Ann's eyes, her face crumpling as she tried to speak. Poppy crept under the blanket beside her. She didn't care about the stains on the sofa or the fact that Mummy would be cross. Placing her empty mug on the table, Sally-Ann wrapped an arm around her, drawing her close as she kissed the top of her head. Poppy's heart ached to see the pain her sister was in. Why did grown-ups do such strange things? Where had Mummy taken the baby? And why must she never speak of it again? But answers would not come – at least, not now. She sighed, snuggling closer. Maybe when she was older she would understand.

CHAPTER
THIRTY-ONE

'*It's Weeeeekday Williams, and I'm dishing out some groovy Thursday tunes!*' Amy smiled to herself as Donovan tuned in to the cheesy Eighties station on his car stereo. They were driving to Southend, but this was no seaside jolly. This was work. Amy had barely slept last night, and this morning she had been tempted to stay in bed. The day off was long overdue, given they had both worked the weekend. When it came to rest days, most officers used their time wisely. Time with family and friends usually took priority, while others liked to play hard – going out on the lash in the evening and spending the next day recovering from the night before. Rarely did officers use their days off as an extension of their work. But Amy could not justify a trip to Southend during work hours, particularly given her rank. If there was legwork of such nature to be completed, then they usually asked a unit from Essex Police, or sent a detective constable to do the job.

It seemed that DCI Donovan shared Amy's thinking. Or was he using the trip to Southend as an excuse? She had a feeling he was keen for some alone time, away from the cameras and in the confines of his car. Before he'd joined the team, they had shared the briefest of intimacies. What may have been just a kiss to some was a huge deal to Amy. When it came to relationships, she either gave herself completely or not at all. Donovan had felt like a kindred spirit. Like her, he was battle-scarred from a previous relationship. He did not trust easily. But him joining the team had stalled their romance. Though it wasn't easy for Amy to hold back her feelings, especially when he looked as good as he did.

Her glance dwelled on his navy Hugo Boss sweater. Today she had worn her blazer, teaming it with black jeans, a white shirt and a pair of black Converse trainers. A mixture of casual yet smart wear for her day off. Her thoughts wandered to Sally-Ann. Amy had long battled the re-emergence of past traumas, but this time another piece of the puzzle had clicked into place. Sally-Ann was pandering to Lillian because she knew where her baby was. Why else would she lie in court?

'Welcome to my old stomping ground.' Donovan turned down the music as they passed the border into Essex. The last time they were in Essex was when Lillian Grimes showed them the graves of the three remaining murder victims, which she had hidden for decades. But Amy did not want to dwell on Lillian's misdeeds. She would speak to Sally-Ann when the time was right. For now, her focus was on finding Stacey's killer before he struck again. Today, they were visiting Michael Richards. His late fiancée, Claire, was the original victim of the Love Heart Killer. 'You started off here, didn't you?' Amy said, forcing another train of thought.

'Yeah, it was a baptism of fire. Weekends were my favourite. We used to drive around in the van and scoop up all the angry drunks as the nightclubs kicked them out at the same time. We'd dump them into custody then go straight back out again. By the end of the night, the cells were full.'

'And peace restored?'

'Yep.' He punctuated his sentence with a smile. 'Happy days.'

Amy had lived in Essex until she was taken into social care. There was nothing happy about her time in this county. She glanced at the seafront as Donovan pulled out of a junction. It was choppy today, the waves dark and brooding, much like her thoughts. It wasn't long before they were at Michael's seafront home.

Amy stood shoulder to shoulder with Donovan as Michael opened the door. His brown wavy hair touched his collar and his beard was neatly trimmed. From what Amy had read, he was still living in the family home he had inherited from his parents. He had a wife named Janet and two young children, a boy and a girl.

'Can I get you a drink?' Michael showed them into a spacious living room. Shafts of sunlight spilled through the windows, and the haunting cries of a flock of seagulls filtered through. Michael stretched as he closed the top windows, silencing the outside world.

For some reason, Amy had built up a picture of Michael as some lager-swilling hothead. This clean-cut man was not what she expected at all. 'No, thank you,' she replied. She had planned on buying Donovan some traditional fish and chips before heading back. She glanced around the room, taking in the family pictures and the toys littering the floor. Michael caught her gaze. 'Excuse the state of the place. Janet's taken the kids to the park. I've not had a chance to clean up yet.'

'Don't worry, it's spotless compared with most of the homes I visit.' Being stationed in Notting Hill, that wasn't strictly true. But Amy could imagine the work involved in the upkeep of such a busy home. 'You've got twins?' Her gaze rested on a canvas of Michael and his wife, each holding a baby in the crook of their arm. There was love there, it was clearly evident. This was a happy home.

'Double the fun,' Michael replied. But his grin slid from his face as he seemed to remember why the officers were there. 'Have you had news? About Claire?'

Amy shook her head. 'Not as such. There's been a recent murder that may or may not be tied to her case.'

Michael's eyebrows rose a notch. 'A murder?'

'In London,' Donovan added. 'The body of a young woman was staged in a store window. It may be just a coincidence, but the victim had a love heart carved in her chest.'

Running a hand through his hair, Michael looked at them, aghast. 'You don't think I've had anything to do with it?'

'You were away, weren't you?' Donovan asked. It had already been confirmed by his team.

'Yeah. In France, with Janet's parents. We just got back last night.' He frowned, exhaling a long breath. 'I don't know how to feel about this.'

'We'll be questioning lots of people. It's as much to eliminate them from our enquiries as anything else.'

'No, I mean I don't know how to feel about someone being murdered in the same way.'

Amy watched his movements closely. 'Apart from the love heart, the MO was different to before. It's unlikely to be a serial killer, given the time that's passed.'

But Michael was staring into the distance, sorrow etched on his face. 'I loved Claire. We were going to get married . . .' He sighed. 'I've never forgotten her.'

'Are you up to talking about what happened the night she died?' Amy interjected.

'I was interviewed for hours,' Michael groaned. 'You must have a record—'

'We do, and we're going to pick it up this afternoon,' Donovan interrupted. 'But we'd prefer to hear it straight from the horse's mouth.' Outside, the happy tinkle of an ice-cream van played.

Michael rolled his eyes. 'It's not even spring yet and he's on his rounds. Costs me a fortune, he does.'

'I used to tell my daughter that the tune meant he'd run out of ice cream,' Donovan chuckled. 'But she got wise to me soon enough. Kids, eh?' A knowing look passed between them, two dads trying to do the best for their kids.

'You'd better sit down.' Michael took a seat on an armchair. Seconds passed as he gathered his thoughts. 'We'd had a row – a very public one. I was young then. Jealous. Insecure. I regretted it the minute I got home.'

'But you didn't call her?' Amy asked.

'It's not like it is now, with technology at the flick of a switch. We didn't bother with mobiles back then. Besides, I was drunk. I went to bed, figured I'd make it up to her the next day.'

'What state was she in when you left?' Amy scribbled in the notebook resting on her lap.

'Drunk. Which is why I followed her to make sure she made it home OK. Then the neighbours said they'd seen me stalking her.' Michael raised his palms in the air. 'Me – stalking my own fiancée. I couldn't believe how they turned against me. People my family had known for years.'

'Can you talk me through it?' Amy tried to picture the scene, relieved Donovan had won him round.

'We went to our local pub, the Hare and Hounds. Claire used to complain that it was an "old fogey" pub, but it was close to home. I was grumpy because she was an hour late and we'd not seen each other all week.'

'And how was she?'

'Stressed. Soaked through. She'd got caught in a downpour. We were both in a bad mood.'

'Did you stay long in the pub?'

'Long enough to get drunk.' He regarded them gravely, with more than a hint of regret in his eyes. 'She'd stayed behind to help one of her students. Some scrawny teenager who had a crush on her. At first, I thought it was harmless. It's normal for students to fancy their teachers . . .' Michael's voice trailed off as he revisited the past. 'But then she told me he was showing up everywhere she went. But she wouldn't call the police. I began to wonder if there was more to it than that.'

'He was stalking her?' Amy said, turning a page.

Michael nodded. 'Claire said he'd had a rough upbringing. She felt sorry for him . . . until it all got too much.' He rubbed his chin as he cast his eyes upwards. 'The last time I saw her she told me he'd followed her home. But instead of having it out with him, she invited him inside. I couldn't believe it. I told her to report him to the police.'

'I take it she didn't agree.'

'That's when I accused her of encouraging him.' Michael sighed. 'It was stupid, I know. I was drunk, and pissed that she spent more time with her students than me.'

Amy could feel the depth of his sorrow as fresh as if it were yesterday. As she watched Michael's eyes moisten, Amy knew he was still in love with her ghost. 'What happened next?' Amy cleared her throat. She was a sucker for a tragic love story. If Michael was acting, then he was worthy of an Academy Award.

'She stormed off home. If only we hadn't rowed. I would have gone back to hers . . .'

'And the two of you could have been killed,' Amy replied. 'There's no point in beating yourself up. You weren't to know.'

'I swear . . . I would never have harmed her.' Michael looked away as he tried to compose himself. 'The next day, I woke up to the police at my door.'

'You must have been devastated.'

'It felt like my world had ended. Not only had I lost Claire, but people were pointing the finger at me. All because of that stupid row. It helped that her parents were on my side. The evidence against me was circumstantial. Her parents' support helped turn things around in the end.'

'And the student?' Donovan asked.

'Claire never said who he was, and the police said it was too brutal an attack for a teenager. During my appeal we brought up the theory that she'd disturbed a burglar, or someone saw her and broke in. Or it could have been part of some satanic attack . . .' Michael glanced from Amy to Donovan. 'But now there's another murder, and you're beating a path to my door. I just want to get on with my life. Is that too much to ask?'

'I understand.' Amy tried to offer reassurance. 'We won't take up much more of your time. But if the killer is linked to Claire then I'm sure you'd want us to find them.'

'I do. But equally, I want to move on. Sure, let me know if you catch the person responsible, but I don't want the cops coming to my house again—' He froze as a car door slammed on the front drive. It was followed by the chatter of young voices, and the jingle of keys.

'They're home. Can you go out the back? I don't want the kids asking questions.'

'Sure.' Amy rose from her chair. She had personal experience of keeping the past at bay. 'Here's my direct number.' She slipped him a business card. 'In case you need to call.'

By the way Michael shoved it in his pocket, Amy knew that the card would soon be in the bin.

'I'll see you out.' He ushered them into the kitchen. Amy exchanged a glance with Donovan. He had a right to privacy, and it wasn't up to Amy to make his wife aware of past events. Just the same, she hoped that she knew.

'What do you think?' Donovan said later, as they queued in a fish and chip shop – another one of his old haunts. 'Seems plausible enough, doesn't he?'

Despite Michael's earlier upset, Amy was no longer sure. 'Mmm. He was very keen to get us out the door.'

'Wouldn't you be, if you were accused of murder once before?'

'I find honesty is the best policy,' she said with authority. She was just about to order when 'You Sexy Thing' played out at full volume on her phone, and all eyes were suddenly on her. Red-faced, she rifled in her bag for her phone. 'Bloody Paddy. He keeps changing my ringtone for a joke.' She muttered a few choice words in response to Donovan's amused expression. But the smile dropped from his face as Amy's voice took on a serious tone. 'What? Again? Where? When?' she said in quick succession, barely giving her caller time to reply. 'We're on our way.' Ending the call, she glanced at Donovan, a fire of intensity behind her eyes. 'We've got to go. There's been another murder.'

CHAPTER
THIRTY-TWO

Donovan drove as Amy spoke to her brother on speakerphone. Craig Winter was a detective inspector in CID and currently working an opposite shift to her.

'We were going to take it for ourselves,' Craig said, 'until CSI saw the love heart carved on the victim's chest.' He was referring to ownership of the case, something Amy had argued with him about in the past. But today she was grateful for his team's early response. 'She's still in situ,' he continued. 'Malcolm's down there now with the on-duty DCI – everything is in hand.' Like before, the victim had been stripped of her identity, and now Craig's team were searching through missing persons reports to ascertain who she was. 'How the hell did they get into the Natural History Museum?' Amy voiced her thoughts. 'Surely the security would have been cast-iron?' The victim had been found in a display piece featuring the prehistoric age. Amy wondered if Black Media had been commissioned to create the piece. Surely not? But there was someone else who could help her with her enquiries.

'I'll call you back,' Amy said, after Craig finished updating her on the case. 'Keep me up to speed.' She turned to Donovan as she brought up a contact on her phone. 'I'm going to keep this on speakerphone so you can listen, but don't say a word.'

'Who is it?' Donovan replied, his gaze on the road ahead. They seemed to be exiting Southend at twice the speed they'd entered it, and Amy hoped none of the local units picked them up for speeding. Donovan was driving his own car, and they couldn't justify a blue-light run. 'Mama Danielle manages a group of high-class London escorts,' Amy explained. 'She's a valuable contact. I met with her last night and . . .' She stalled, remembering her lie.

'Ha!' Donovan barked. 'So that's where you went. Headache my backside.'

'You wouldn't have authorised it if I told you . . . boss.' Amy looked at him sheepishly.

'Huh, shame you don't understand the definition. This isn't good enough.' He caught Amy just as she rolled her eyes. 'You're putting the investigation in jeopardy by going off-grid. Not to mention yourself.' He flicked on the windscreen wipers as a sudden shower dimpled his view of the road.

'We can talk about it later.' Amy felt suitably chastised. 'Now, do I have to keep this call to myself or not?'

'Go ahead,' Donovan replied, negotiating his BMW around a bend. The car was only a couple of years old, and more than equipped to handle the speed.

Mama Danielle answered the call after just one ring. 'Ah, Inspector Winter. What's up?'

Amy was ready with a response. 'Look, this is strictly between us, but there's been a murder, similar MO to before. Any of your ladies missing?' A plethora of expletives left Mama Danielle's lips. 'I'll ring around. A couple of my girls haven't reported back yet. I've told them to check in with me night and day.'

'Don't tell them anything,' Amy warned. 'Not until we know more.'

'But—'

'Please. Keep it under your hat for now. We can't afford to have this leaked to the media.' Silence fell as Amy and Donovan exchanged a glance.

'All right.' Mama Danielle's long exhale relayed that she was smoking, her worries evident. 'I'll keep trying their phones. I'll ring you back if I hear anything.'

'There's no record of this Mama woman on our systems, is there?' Donovan said as soon as Amy's call ended. 'And you shouldn't be sharing confidential information without clearing it with me first.' He was out on the open road now, accelerating. The rain was coming down harder, the wipers swishing back and forth as they kept the windscreen clear.

'I trust her,' Amy replied. 'Not just for this case. She's a good contact to have.'

'Then register her as a CHIS and do it above board.'

'Are you saying I'm not above board?'

'You're not sticking to procedure.' Donovan's jaw was set firm.

Amy frowned. Why couldn't he trust her to do what was right? 'She agreed to meet me at short notice. It was off the record or nothing at all.' Amy didn't want to scare her off by making her an official covert human intelligence source. She was about to say more when her phone rang.

It was Mama Danielle, her words panicked as she spoke. 'Oh Lord . . . It's Erin. I can feel it in my bones. She's not at home and she didn't turn up at her day job.' Her voice broke. 'Please don't let it be her, please God, tell me I'm wrong.'

'Slow down, take a breath,' Amy said. 'Erin's one of your girls, I take it?'

'Yeah, a total newbie.' The flick of Mama Danielle's flint lighter rasped down the line as she lit another cigarette. 'I rang her mom, said I was a friend. She said she spoke to Erin yesterday but hasn't heard from her since. She's worried. Erin rings her daughter every morning before she goes to school.'

'She has a daughter?'

'Yeah. She lives with Erin's mom. She said it's totally out of character for her not to ring. Oh Lordy . . . not again.' The despair in Danielle's voice added to Amy's growing concern.

'OK. Can you text me a picture of her? I'll need her home address too. I'll send a unit around.'

'Sure. But show some tact, yeah?' Another exhalation of breath. 'Her mom doesn't know about the site.' Mama Danielle groaned. 'She's a sweet kid. I really don't want it to be her.'

Neither do I, Amy thought. As well as being a mother, Erin was someone's daughter. Someone's friend. 'I'll keep you in the loop. But not a word to anyone. Especially not the papers. Understand?'

'Totally,' Danielle said, before ending the call.

Both Donovan's hands were on the steering wheel, his knuckles white. He had a daughter living in London, around the same age as these victims. Amy knew the case would be getting to him too.

'It'll help with identification if this picture of Erin matches up.' Her phone beeped a notification and she stared at the image as it came through. Erin was blonde, pretty, and scarily similar to the previous victims. Amy's heart sank. It was the snippets of information on Erin's personal life that hit home. She had a little girl. She rang every morning before she went to school.

After saving Erin's photo to her phone, Amy forwarded it to Craig. *Does this look like the victim?* she texted, wondering what state the killer had left her in. *If so, I know who she is.* Amy knew Craig was on his way to the scene and it was killing her to be at least another hour away. Why hadn't she brought her police radio? Because it was meant to be her day off, and she wasn't expecting another murder victim on her patch. But as the thought entered her mind, Amy wondered if it was true. From the moment she met Samuel Black, that was exactly what she had expected. She stared at the phone as her brother's reply came through. *It's her*, the text read. *Call me*.

'Something's wrong,' Amy said, knowing her brother would be busy with the investigation.

'More wrong than a murder?' Donovan flicked his indicator to overtake an articulated lorry. 'He probably wants to give you an update.'

'Then you don't know Craig like I do. He's never been one to share. Not since we were kids. He only told me about the murder because he had to.' Gripping her phone, Amy made the call.

'What's up?' she said, as Craig came through on speaker.

'Where are you?' Craig's voice echoed around him, and Amy guessed he was at the museum.

'We're still in Essex. I'm with DCI Donovan. We're heading back now.'

'Then you'd better get yourself over here, because you're not going to believe this . . .'

CHAPTER
THIRTY-THREE

It had come as a shock to discover Erin was hanging on to life. Yet again, the killer had left his victim for dead, but could she be saved in time? As Donovan dropped her off at the crime scene, Amy was rigid with fury.

'Keep your cool . . .' Donovan leaned out of his car window as he made his demand. 'It doesn't reflect well on the team if you throttle whoever's responsible.'

'Whoever's responsible for this monumental cock-up, you mean!' Amy flared. 'How the hell did they not realise Erin was still alive? Basic policing. What's the first thing you do? You check for a bloody pulse!' She growled in exasperation, unable to believe the news.

'Do you want to swap? You go check on Erin, while I visit the scene?'

'No chance.' Amy tried to regain her composure. 'You go to the hospital. I'll be fine here. We'll meet for debriefing when we're done.' A detective from CID had been tasked with harvesting Erin's clothing and requesting a blood sample from doctors as a matter of urgency. Crime scene operatives were also in attendance, waiting to take swabs from Erin's skin and beneath her nails. But first, the medical team had the important task of saving her life.

Amy felt sick with annoyance as she pulled on her forensic suit and overshoes. How could Craig's team be so negligent? Erin could have identified the killer, and nobody had noticed she was still alive.

Amy watched her colleagues working, their voices echoing in the wide-open space. The museum was closed to the public. It was a huge undertaking for POLSA, and every inch of the building would be searched. She turned her attention to the exhibit as she took stock. *What's done is done*, she told herself. *Be grateful it's not your team who messed up.* Donovan was right. She needed to calm down. It wasn't just Erin causing her unusual outburst. Lillian's trial was looming over her and she needed to rein it in. Closing her eyes, she filled her lungs, breathing in through her nose and out through her mouth. The air smelled of leather, of recently applied glue, and something akin to mothballs. She stepped around the dummies, who were eerily lifelike. Posed on their knees, they worshipped the sun. At least, it was meant to be the sun. From what Craig had told her, Erin had been hung in its place, her arms and legs cuffed with leather bindings attached to a winch, which suspended her from the ceiling. Her clothing consisted of a loincloth and a leather top bound over her breasts. This time, there was no mistaking the love-heart shape carved into her chest. Her blood had dripped on to the floor below, splattering the head of a waxwork prehistoric man. Each stain was now marked by numbers, measured and photographed. Amy swallowed back the tightness in her throat. Another victim of the Love Heart Killer, another girl who had used the Sugar Babes app.

A trickle of sweat ran down the curve of Amy's back. The central heating was on full blast, enhancing the musty, leathery smell. She turned to Craig as he approached, her forensics face mask failing to disguise her disgust. 'How long was that poor girl hanging here?' She pushed her mask on to her forehead, narrowing her eyes as she glared at her brother. 'If the papers get hold of this, they'll have a field day.' She could have spoken about Erin, told him a little about her life. She could have made Craig imagine how Erin's daughter and mother would feel. But Amy knew her brother, and nothing would hurt him as much as the threat of bad publicity.

Craig stood with his hands on his hips, his suit rustling as he gestured. 'The alarms and the CCTV were hacked into and deactivated at around eleven o'clock last night.'

'And nobody noticed she was still alive?' The flash of a camera lit up the background as officers photographed the scene.

Craig's face was thunderous as he tugged on the neck of his forensic suit. 'Her eyes were half open, her lips blue. Staff presumed she was dead.' He folded his arms, staring up at the spot from where she had hung. 'She was so far under that the paramedics could barely find a pulse.'

Amy's forehead knotted in frustration. 'But you said she was in situ when I rang.'

'That's what I thought, but the second my officers got here, they took her down. I didn't hear the update straight away.' Craig heaved a sigh. 'I've been juggling a million things at once. If you want this case, you can have it. Seems it's better placed with your team. How did you know who she was?'

'Inside information.' With a gloved hand, Amy tapped the side of her nose. 'Speak of the devil.' Mama Danielle's number flashed up on her phone.

After leaving the crime scene, it was a relief to de-gown. 'Winter,' she said, answering her phone. She embraced the appearance of sunshine, welcoming the breeze that caressed her skin. Hopping on one foot, she stripped out of her forensic suit as Mama Danielle spoke, her voice imbued with concern.

'Is it her?'

'Looks that way, but I was given duff info – Erin's still alive.' There was an exhalation of relief on the other end of the line as Mama Danielle absorbed the news.

'You're kidding . . . Oh man, that's a relief. Does her mom know?'

Amy groaned at the sight of Ginny and the camera crew pulling up at the back of the building. A smartly dressed DC Steve Moss was with them, guiding them to the scene. *Shoot.* This was all she needed.

'Winter? Are ya there?'

'Sorry.' Amy ducked out of Ginny's view. 'Yeah, she's on her way to the hospital now, so best you stay where you are. Had Erin arranged to meet anyone last night?'

'Didn't you get my email?' Mama Danielle replied.

'I've been on the road. I'm heading back to the office now.'

'I haven't had a chance to schedule her any dates. Honestly, I tell them not to branch out on their own, but do they listen?'

But Amy didn't have time to listen to Mama Danielle complain. She kicked a stone as she prioritised her next move. 'Do you think our killer will go elsewhere if we have the site shut down?'

'Probably,' Danielle replied. 'There's plenty of sites to choose from, but they'll have to pay a hefty registration fee to access quality girls.'

Amy grimaced at the description. These were real people, not choice cuts of meat. 'Is there a pattern between the two victims? They're similar looks-wise, but you know them better than me.'

'I've worked out the similarities. It's all in my email. Get back to your office, toots. Call me from there.'

Amy was impressed. Mama Danielle may not be the most politically correct entrepreneur, but at least she had done her homework. She watched Steve trying to persuade the scene guard officer to allow the camera crew inside. Biting her bottom lip, Amy returned her attention to Mama Danielle. She could almost sense Donovan's disapproval, see his warning glare. 'Set up a dummy profile similar to the other girls. Make it irresistible to him.' She was breaking all the rules by going it alone, but strategy meetings would have to be held if she made it official. They would never agree to a decoy in time.

'And if he takes the bait?'

'Then name the time and place and I'll be there.' Amy's pulse pounded a little harder at the prospect of coming face-to-face with the man who had left Erin for dead.

'You? That's risky.' Mama Danielle paused to take what sounded like a drag on her cigarette. 'Shouldn't this be done with a team?'

'We don't have time for that.'

'But this guy likes blondes.'

'Take my word for it. He'll like me too.' Silence fell as Mama Danielle seemed to consider this. In the distance, Steve was still haggling with the officer on scene guard.

'Hey, I admire your guts,' Mama Danielle piped up. 'But this guy is a psycho. He doesn't mess around.'

'Then all the more reason for me to get involved. I'll have dinner with him in a public place and suss him out. If it comes to nothing, I'll make my excuses and leave.'

'I dunno . . .' Mama Danielle replied. 'Sounds dangerous.'

'I'll be prepared. Besides, I think I know who he is. I'm just flushing him out.'

'Oh jeez. That's not creepy at all.' Danielle's voice dripped with sarcasm. 'OK then, I'll do it . . . as long as you're sure?'

Amy imagined Erin hanging from the ceiling, staring helplessly at the floor. The image dissolved any lingering doubt. 'I've never been surer. Set it up, but the minute you get a nibble, let me know.' Pocketing her phone, Amy strode down the path. She was blind to the danger of her situation; in denial about the trouble she might be in. Her mind was focused on only one thing: apprehending the Love Heart Killer, before he struck again.

CHAPTER
THIRTY-FOUR

As he approached the hospital, Donovan ran a hand through his hair. The day was beginning to feel surreal since their trip to the seaside. Being in Amy's company was like taking a ride on one of those fairground waltzers he'd spent time on as a kid.

After pausing to ask at reception, he found the ward where the victim was being treated. The officer posted outside her door straightened as Donovan approached. 'Guv,' she said, quickly pocketing the mobile phone she'd been staring at just seconds before. Her cheeks were flushed, her blonde hair scraped into a ponytail, which rested high on her head.

He recognised her as DC Sophie Gooch, who was new to Craig Winter's team in CID. Donovan had already made the call to cancel his team's rest days. With another victim publicly displayed, the pressure was on. The fact Erin was clinging on to life offered them a crumb of hope.

'Any update?' Donovan asked, looking from the officer to the double doors. The corridors echoed with the sound of footsteps, as doctors and nurses scurried from one room to another. Like the police, they were under pressure, understaffed and overworked.

Sophie responded with a shake of the head. 'Not yet, boss. They've told me to wait here.'

'You rode with her in the ambulance – how's she looking?' Donovan said, not willing to leave it there.

Sophie drove her hands deep into her trouser pockets. 'Her pulse was faint. The injury to her chest looked superficial. I couldn't see any other wounds but she looked out of it.'

'Do you know if it was similar to before?' Donovan was talking about the previous victim of the Love Heart Killer. He needed to know if it was the same MO.

DC Gooch nodded. 'I'd bet my house on it being the same person. Whoever did this had gone to a lot of trouble to pose her . . .'

But Donovan was trying to catch the eye of the doctor exiting Erin's room. 'Excuse me!' he called, falling into step with the harassed-looking woman. 'DCI Donovan,' he said, fumbling for his warrant card. 'Can you tell me how she's doing? When can we see her?'

Briefly, the doctor met his gaze. 'She's comatose. We can't tell you anything until we know what drug we're dealing with.' Checking her watch, she picked up speed, and Donovan let her go. He returned to Sophie. There was no way of knowing how long such tests would take. 'Update Control the second you hear anything. Seize the harvested clothing and preserve as much evidence as you can.'

He checked his mobile phone as he returned to his car. Amy was yet to update him, and he hoped she had calmed down. His concerns rose as she failed to answer her phone. He turned over his car engine, carefully reversing out of the parking space. He should never have left her. Activating the speakerphone, he dialled Paddy's number. He answered on the second ring.

'Stacey's toxicology reports have come back,' Paddy said, after Donovan updated him on Erin. 'We're passing it to the hospital in case it's of any use to them. They found carfentanil-laced heroin in her system.'

'Carfentanil? What's that?' Donovan frowned, failing to recognise the name. He pressed down on the indicator, glancing left and right as he pulled out of the car park.

'It's used to tranquillise elephants in Africa, but now it's on the black market over here,' Paddy replied. 'A few grains can kill a man stone dead.'

As he joined the stream of traffic, Donovan shook his head. It was becoming increasingly difficult to keep up with the new drugs coming on to the scene. 'And the chances of someone pulling through after an overdose?'

'That's the problem,' Paddy sighed. 'It's hard to reverse once it's been taken. It's not always found in autopsies, either. We're dealing with lethal stuff.'

'That's not good,' Donovan replied. Any drug on the market with the power to kill was a huge cause for concern. He made a mental note to submit an intelligence report. They were battling a killer with access to drugs he hadn't even heard of. 'Get Molly to step up her enquiries with the Sugar Babes team. Have they *really* given us everything? Get the ball rolling with a court order. I'm pretty sure Erin was using their app. Is Winter there?'

'She was, but she took off again, said she wouldn't be long. Didn't say where she was going.'

Donovan inwardly groaned. Of course she didn't. 'What about Billy Picton, has he been brought in yet?' Uniformed officers had been issued with instructions for his arrest.

'Not yet. Attempts have been made.'

'Then the intel unit needs to carry out a deep search of his known acquaintances. Someone must know where he is.' The dashboard clock on his car told Donovan the day was running away from him. And as Amy's phone went to answer machine, it didn't improve his mood. 'Winter, where are you?' he said, as he left a message after the tone. 'Get yourself back to the office. I'll see you there.' His fingers tightened around the steering wheel. He could imagine the reaction from the press. If theirs was such a great team, why was the killer one step ahead?

CHAPTER
THIRTY-FIVE

Amy switched her phone to silent. She had just finished calling her mother, who was being taken out by Winifred tonight. It was a relief to see her back on her feet, now the worst of her illness had passed.

She put all thoughts of her home life behind her as she marched into the offices of Black Media. Today she was in no mood to play games.

Jumping up from her desk, Naomi pulled off her headset as Amy strode past. 'Excuse me, miss . . . I mean, Officer . . . Oh heck, hang on!' Tripping over herself, she wobbled in her kitten heels as she raced to Amy's side. 'Have you an appointment? If you haven't got an appointment you can't go in.'

Amy flashed her warrant card. 'This says I can.' She pushed her way through the door, not bothering to knock. Samuel was standing by the window, staring at the street below.

'I'm so sorry, Samuel,' Naomi chirped. Her face was flushed, wisps of hair escaping her ponytail. 'She barged straight past.'

'That's OK,' Samuel said, before facing Amy. 'Detective Inspector Winter. Why don't you take a seat?' He checked his watch before returning his attention to Naomi. 'You were in early, weren't you, Nomes? Why don't you take an extended lunch?'

Naomi looked at him as if he had given her the winning lottery numbers. 'Really? Gosh, thanks. I've just got some emails to reply to and then I'll shoot off.' Black Media's policies stated staff were entitled to at least an hour away from their desks. Amy had read up on their working practices. It was a far cry from the police force, where food was eaten on the go. At Black Media, all members of staff were provided with cover to ensure they got a lunch break each day.

Naomi closed the door behind her as she left. Amy knew this was more than just policy. This was Samuel gearing up for some alone time with her. Was he going to confess? Every muscle in her body tensed. Perhaps he realised the game was finally up. Or perhaps he had nothing to lose.

'What can I do for you, Officer?' Samuel gestured at the chair. 'Make yourself comfortable, take a seat.'

'I'm fine standing,' Amy said, keeping her exit in mind. First rule of policing: be aware of your exits and don't get complacent, no matter how engaging the suspect becomes. Watch their hands and be vigilant for a weapon. When the net is closing in, people could be unpredictable. In Amy's uniformed days, weapons were often hidden over door ledges or in umbrella stands beside the front door. Men like Samuel may be wealthier than most, but it didn't make them any less cunning. 'We're trying to reach Billy,' Amy said. 'He's not at home and I hear he hasn't come to work today.'

Samuel's fingers trailed his desk as he approached. He paused to straighten a framed photograph of his wife and children. His smile was cold and fixed to his face. 'He booked some time off. Something about an emergency dentist's appointment. Is this about the incident in the museum? Your officers have already been in touch.'

'I'm aware of that.' Amy monitored Samuel's every movement as he slid into his leather chair. 'Has Black Media ever been commissioned to work for the museum?'

'I've already told your officers, no. And we have no record of . . .' He paused, his eyes flicking to the ceiling.

'What is it?' Amy stepped forward, conscious of the time.

'You'll have to check with human resources, but Billy may have worked there in the past.' He returned his attention to Amy. 'But that doesn't mean anything . . . does it?'

Amy stared at Samuel, her gaze intensifying as she tried to work him out. Officers were already hunting Billy down and it was only a matter of time before they brought him in. Samuel Black was the real reason she was here. He folded his arms, his chair creaking as he leaned back. He was obviously comfortable with the silence, a half-smile resting on his face. It was as if he were daring Amy to cross the line.

'You know, our last conversation has been playing on my mind,' Amy said eventually. Her legs were getting tired, but standing over Samuel gave her a slight edge.

'I would have thought a woman in your position has lots of interesting conversations,' Samuel said. The shadows beneath his eyes suggested that sleep was a stranger. But what was it keeping him awake?

'I do, but your insights interest me. I presume you were using Banksy as an analogy.' She paused to check his face for the slightest reaction, but there was none. 'You suggested the killer enjoys the attention? That's why he leaves his victims in such a public place.' Amy folded her arms as she stood.

Samuel steepled his fingers together and pressed them against his lips. It was as if his body were telling him to keep quiet. Not to give too much away. 'Well, yes. But that's obvious, isn't it?' he said. 'You don't need me to tell you that.'

Amy smiled. But it was a dark smile. One reserved for very few. 'I grew up in a crime scene. You could say I have a nose for it.'

'I've been watching Lillian's trial,' Samuel said. 'The newspapers say you reported your own colleagues to help her appeal.'

Amy shot him a wry smile. 'Mr Black, you run a media company. You surely know you can't believe everything you read.'

Samuel stared up at Amy. 'Would you be insulted if I told you I see a bit of your mother in you? I don't mean her personality, just her eyes.'

Amy ignored his comment. 'Tell me, did Billy use the internet for personal use in work time?'

Samuel nodded. 'We scan all our employees' time online. After you left, we interrogated his browser history and found that he's been browsing hook-up sites.'

'Can we have a record of that?'

'It's already on its way.'

'Mr Black, is there anything you'd like to tell me?' Amy said. 'Because now is the time.'

'Like what?'

'Like your involvement in these murders?' How easily the words tripped off Amy's tongue. She leaned in, her palms flat on his desk.

'Is this an official line of questioning?' Samuel remained composed.

'Would you like it to be?'

'I'd prefer to keep things between us.'

'Very well. Is there anything you'd like to get off your chest? Just between us . . .' In the silence of the office, you could hear a pin drop. Amy knew she was playing with fire by not cautioning him first, but she needed to hear him say the words.

Samuel's smile was mischievous, his eyes dark. 'I've often wondered, how did your mother and father find each other? I mean, it's not as if you could put it on a dating site – "enjoys fishing, flower arranging and killing at the weekends".' Amy arched an eyebrow. 'Did they get off on being a serial-killing couple?' Samuel paused for thought. 'I suppose they did.'

'I don't know,' Amy said. 'We were talking about you.'

But Samuel carried on. 'It's not as if they could have come out with it. I mean, maybe the first murder was an accident, but there had to come a time when they agreed to cross that line.' He was perspiring slightly now, his gaze far away. As if he was reliving a special moment himself.

'Did you kill those women?' Amy couldn't contain the question any longer. Her breath was shallow as she awaited a response.

Samuel snapped his eyes shut before opening them again. In that split second, he had come back to his senses. 'Don't be ridiculous,' he replied, straightening in his seat. 'I'm a happily married man with two beautiful daughters. What on earth would make you think that?'

Damn, Amy thought. She'd had him. He was right there, but now the moment had passed.

If Samuel had a hand in things, he wasn't going to confess now. But she had one small ace up her sleeve. She watched his expression closely, taking in every movement. Every breath. 'Thank God we found the second victim in time.'

'Sorry, what?' Samuel's forehead creased. 'When the police said there was an incident . . . I presumed the young woman was found dead.'

'She's alive. Police are speaking to her now.' It wasn't entirely true, but the lie was worth the pay-off as she watched Samuel's eye twitch.

'Oh. I see. Is she all right?'

Amy smiled in satisfaction. 'We expect her to make a full recovery. I can't say much more than that. I'd appreciate it if you kept this to yourself.'

Samuel checked his watch. 'Right, well, if that's all, I've got a meeting . . .' He leaned forward, as if to rise from his chair. Amy watched as his knees weakened and he was forced to stay put. It was a tiny movement, one that would have gone unnoticed had she not been scrutinising him. The shadows under Samuel's eyes seemed to deepen as a look of dark knowing passed between them. Goosebumps rose on Amy's skin as the atmosphere chilled. She had all she needed. Samuel was rattled. More than that, he was scared. Outwardly, he was a dedicated husband and businessman, but Amy had glimpsed his inner demon. She knew exactly what he was.

CHAPTER
THIRTY-SIX

As the doors of his office clicked shut, Samuel exhaled a low breath. He picked up the remote and turned the air con up. It was a relief to feel cool air on his skin. His shirt was sticking to his back, a side effect of being in Amy's company. Every time he saw her, she raised his blood pressure a little more.

Erin was alive. The news had come like a sucker punch. He had struggled to keep his composure, with Amy standing over him like a panther ready to pounce. He still wasn't sure what side of the law she was on. He had been careful to disguise his steps, and paid a hacker to gain him access to the museum. On the dark web, nobody knew your identity, and his bitcoin payment had been untraceable. As for Erin . . . at least he had worn his balaclava when administering the drug. Instinct had told him to leave his disguise on. It was the way she looked at him from the depths of her confusion, as if she were trying to memorise his form. She had fought with every fibre of her being. Willed her body to carry on.

It would not happen again. He could not afford to have witnesses. Next time he would finish the job.

Speaking of next time . . . the urge was strong to kill again. He told himself to wait, tried to quieten the voice that persisted. But he was hooked, caught up in an addiction that was too powerful to fight. Lately, his memories were dragging him back to the past at breakneck speed. Groaning, he rolled his head on his shoulders until the bones in his neck clicked. He was spending too long in his office. His expertise in delegation had chained him to his desk. Arching his back, he thought about Marianne. He should book them both a surprise spa day. Have a couples massage, she'd like that. Walking to the window, he checked the weather outside.

His thoughts jumped from light to dark as they flitted between home and his plans to kill. His attention was drawn to the figure on the street below. A slow smile crept on to his face as he watched her leave his building, her mind no doubt racing after their contact. Was she thinking about him, or her dirty past? He knew all about her: where she lived, where she worked, who she hung out with. His hidden notebooks and maps featured every facet of her routine. Samuel's breath accelerated as he imagined bringing her to heel. He returned to his desk and pressed his finger on the intercom. 'Cancel my next meeting,' he said, his breath heavy. He would reschedule. Right now, he had plans to make.

CHAPTER
THIRTY-SEVEN

'That bitch, back for more.' Marianne's words were sharp with hatred as she watched Amy Winter leave. Their first meeting had caught her off guard, but since giving up her medication, Marianne was seeing things in a new light. Samuel didn't know she had gone cold turkey, stopping everything apart from the sleeping tablets. She'd never rest without them, not with the amount of thoughts now swirling around in her head.

Marianne's hands trembled as she snapped a picture on her phone. Murder investigation or not, Winter had no business visiting Samuel when his staff dealt with every enquiry. Amy Winter was a woman with an ugly past. She would soon lose favour with the public if they knew she was a homewrecker too. Marianne dropped her phone into her bag and pulled the zip across. It sat nestled at the bottom, next to the knife she had brought.

Taking quick strides, she followed the detective down the street and into the chill of the late-afternoon air. Traffic was heaving, and pedestrians were milling around, wrapped up in coats and scarves as they kept the cold at bay. Goosebumps rose on Marianne's flesh. She should have worn something warmer than her dress, but she was barely able to think straight. Her heart pounded as the woman before her gained speed, turning a corner as she took a left. Marianne's shoes were pinching now, her skin rubbing against the tight leather as she trotted down the road.

Her footsteps came to a sudden halt as she turned the corner, a strong arm dragging her to one side. It was Amy Winter, and she was mad as hell.

'Who are you and why are you following me?' she said, her eyes boring into Marianne's. Marianne squealed as she was slammed against a doorway, and stumbled to keep herself upright. She could feel Winter's breath on her cheek, smell the faint trace of her perfume. At this moment in time, Marianne hated her more than anyone in the world. Her handbag rested between them, and once again, her thoughts went to her knife. Not that she would have the courage to use it. The most she could do was warn her off.

'Hang on . . . I recognise you. Are you . . .' Amy peered closer. 'Are you Samuel Black's wife?'

'Yes,' Marianne blurted. 'And I know what you've been up to with my husband!'

Amy released her grip, confusion clouding her face. 'What *I've* been up to? What would that be, dare I ask?'

Marianne swallowed her disgust. 'You've been sleeping with him. Don't try to deny it. But he's mine, do you hear me? Back the hell off!' Spittle flew from Marianne's mouth. She was taller than Amy, but nowhere near as strong. She clutched the bag to her chest, as if it were a shield.

'Do you know who I am?' Amy asked. 'Because you've got your wires seriously crossed.'

'I know all about you, Miss Winter. You've been seeing Samuel for some time.' But her confidence evaporated as she took in Amy's confused expression.

'I'm a detective inspector. Didn't it ever occur to you that this might be police-related?'

'Constables do the groundwork,' Marianne said. 'Not inspectors. And why would you want to see my husband when he's done nothing wrong?' Her teeth began to chatter, a comedown from the adrenaline, which was wearing off.

'Where's your coat? You're freezing . . .' Amy's eyes trailed over Marianne as she looked her up and down. 'Why don't we get you inside to warm up? I'll call you a cab from the coffee shop.'

Marianne didn't know which was more disconcerting, the fact Winter was being kind to her, or that she was avoiding the question. Her head felt fuzzy as she was led inside a coffee shop, an old-fashioned building with a bell over the door.

'Two hot chocolates, please,' Amy said to the waitress who came to their table. She looked down at Marianne's feet. 'You're bleeding. Here . . .' She rifled in her handbag and pulled out two plasters. 'Put these on.'

'Thanks,' Marianne said, her words barely a whisper as she accepted the plasters with grace. She applied a plaster to each heel. Her shoes were white leather, which made the blood all the more obvious. What had she been thinking, wearing high heels and a dress on a freezing cold day?

She accepted the hot chocolate that was offered, inhaling the sweet smell of the mini marshmallows floating on top. 'I should pay . . .' She gazed down at her bag, which was resting on the floor. She didn't even remember putting it there.

'No need.' Amy waved her offer of money away. 'Call it an apology for rough-handling you. In my line of work, I can't be too careful. I hope you didn't get hurt.'

'Hurt? No. I'm fine.' She paused to sip her chocolate, embracing its warmth as it made its way down. 'Sorry.' She licked the cream from her lips. 'I was there the first time you saw my husband. He lied. He said he was with someone else.'

Marianne drew a sudden breath at the admission. There was something about this woman that made her open up. In her eyes she could see a deep understanding of what it felt like to get hurt. Given her history, it was hardly surprising. This must seem like small fry to her. Just the same, Amy arched an eyebrow as Marianne confided in her.

'Ah . . . Yes, I remember seeing you there. Look. I can't go into details about the visit, only that it was work-related.'

'You're investigating that case, the one where those two girls were found, aren't you?'

Amy nodded.

'I thought that was all dealt with. I couldn't see why he'd . . .' Marianne stopped herself for a second time. She was about to mention Samuel's newspaper clippings. If their relationship was all above board, then why was he so obsessed with her? But being in Winter's company, it was easy to see why. She was every bit as enigmatic as portrayed in the press.

'You were about to say something?' Amy questioned, before briefly checking her watch.

'Nothing . . . it's nothing.' Marianne dipped her head towards her mug.

'Then can I ask you something?' Amy rested her mug on the table. 'Has Samuel ever hurt you? Lost his temper? Scared you at any point?'

The tinkle of the shop doorway bell signalled new customers, and Marianne sat with her shoulders hunched. 'Why would you ask me that?' She looked at Amy dumbly as their conversation took a sudden turn.

'Because you don't seem well. Do you need help? Are you on medication? I can take you to a safe place if you need to talk.'

Marianne smoothed down her wild, unkempt hair. 'How do you know if I'm myself or not? You've only just met me.' She grabbed her bag from the floor. Felt the knife shift inside. Winter was talking to her with pity in her eyes. How dare she look at her like that? She couldn't believe she'd been reeled in by her fake sympathy.

Scrambling out of her chair, Amy followed her to the door. 'Wait, I'm trying to help. How about I call you a taxi? Get you safely home?'

'There's no need. I've got an app, I can do it myself.'

'At least take my card.' Marianne stiffened as Amy touched her arm.

'Leave me alone!' Marianne jerked away, her bag slipping from her grip. It landed with a clunk on the wooden floor. Silence fell between them as the knife skidded from the bag to Amy's feet.

In a split second, Amy had grabbed the knife and slipped it into her pocket.

Marianne froze, weak at the knees as Amy picked her bag up from the floor.

'Sit. Down.' The officer's words were firm. Yanking Marianne back to the table, she forced her on to the chair. 'What are you doing with a knife? Was that meant for me?' Amy began to root through Marianne's handbag.

Marianne swallowed as her world caved in. 'No,' she said, before coming up with an excuse that would get her off the hook. 'It's for Megan's pony . . . I mean, it's for cutting the baler twine on his hay. It's pony-share week at the riding school . . . I forgot to take the penknife out of my bag.' It was all a lie, of course, and Marianne hoped Amy would not check out her story. She remembered Samuel telling her once that you were allowed to carry a penknife if the blade was under five inches and it was being used for reasonable purpose. Although he never did explain why he had it in his pocket when she took his suit to the dry cleaners. Marianne had presumed it was for work.

Amy snorted, refusing to meet her eye. Frantically, she sorted through Marianne's bag, pulling out everything and laying it on the table. Make-up, chewing gum, hairbrush, tampons. It was embarrassing. People were starting to look. Her movements stilled as a zip was pulled across and Marianne felt her heart plummet in her chest once more. *Damn.* She had forgotten about the clippings she had put in her bag.

'What are these?' Amy said, throwing Marianne's belongings back into the bag but keeping the clippings to herself. 'Did you print these? Have you . . .' Her eyes narrowed. 'Have you been stalking me? Is that what this is about?'

'No!' Marianne's panic rose. 'They're not mine!'

'Where did you get them?'

Silence followed. Marianne's heartbeat thundered in her ears. She watched as the waitress approached them, received a warning look from Amy and walked away.

'My sister gave them to me. She found them hidden in a bunch of newspapers in Samuel's study. Then when he lied about being with you, and I saw you there again—'

'You added two and two together and came up with five.' Amy's words were stern. 'I could arrest you for possession of an offensive weapon. It's up to you to prove your innocence after that.'

Tears rose in Marianne's eyes as panic set in. 'Please don't. You were right. I'm not well. I haven't been taking my medication. I'm not thinking straight.'

'Has Samuel been violent? Is that why you're carrying a knife?'

'What? No! Of course not. I told you, it's for—'

'—the hay, yeah, sure.' Amy slid her business card from her pocket. 'This time take the damn card. If you've any concerns, then call.'

'What concerns? Is Samuel in trouble?' Marianne rested a hand on her chest. Her heart fluttered beneath her flesh, like a tiny trapped bird.

Amy pursed her lips, as if containing her words. 'Go home. Take your medication and look after yourself. If you have any concerns, call me. It's best we keep this to ourselves.'

Marianne was hardly going to disagree. Relief swept over her as she realised Amy was letting her go. She looked down at her bloodied shoes, swept a hand over her hair. Had she even showered today? No wonder Amy was looking at her that way. 'Thank you,' she whispered, slipping the card into her bag.

Amy shot her a warning glance. 'If I catch you with a knife in public again, you're under arrest. Understand?'

Marianne responded with a sharp nod of the head. Her energy had dissipated. She put up no argument as Amy took her phone to order her a cab.

As she stood outside and waited, Marianne watched the officer checking her phone before striding away. Why couldn't she be strong like her? There was no confusion in her eyes. There was a woman with focus, who knew her place in life. Marianne could not begin to decipher the conversation she'd just had. She needed her drugs. She needed sleep. Perhaps then it would all make sense. But behind the numbness in her brain, a muffled warning bell rang. There was something very off about the detective's connection with Samuel. Why had she asked if he was violent? And why was she so concerned for Marianne's safety?

CHAPTER
THIRTY-EIGHT

'Where have you been? And what's this I hear about you seizing a knife?' Donovan's questions came like bullets as Amy entered their shared office.

Amy's meeting with Marianne had taken on a surreal quality. She had been made to feel like the 'other woman' as Marianne regarded her with contempt. The presence of the folding knife was disconcerting, but it would have done no good to place her under arrest. Marianne's excuse may have been feeble, but she clearly knew the law.

Amy dumped her handbag on her desk. 'I take it you've been speaking to Malcolm.' She shrugged off her jacket, having come straight from a meeting with their CSI.

'He mentioned he'd spoken to you when I rang,' Donovan said curtly. He sat in his swivel chair, his computer dinging with notifications as numerous emails came through.

'Then he'll have told you that the knife was too small and blunt to have been used in the Love Heart Killer crimes.' Amy took up residence behind her desk, drilling down her list of things to do. 'I bumped into Marianne outside her husband's office. We went for a coffee and I saw the penknife in her bag. She handed it over without question. I figured it was worth getting it checked out.'

'You went for coffee in the middle of an investigation?' Donovan's face was stony, in complete contrast to hours before. 'Didn't you get my message? You should have been here. You missed briefing . . . *again.*'

'Sorry, boss,' Amy responded half-heartedly. 'Paddy had things under control.'

'A victim hanging in the Natural History Museum is hardly being "under control". The press has got their teeth into this. It's all over the news.' Donovan rose from his desk as a reminder beeped on his watch. 'We work as a team in this department. Go solo one more time and I'm taking you off this case.'

'You . . . you can't do that.' Amy felt suddenly breathless. 'This is my team. You've only just come on board!' She glanced out of the window of the office, hoping none of her team could hear. But their heads were bowed as they worked. There were phone calls to be made, CCTV to be viewed, enquiries to be chased up. The drone of printers and the clamouring ring of telephones had drowned out their words. She returned her attention to Donovan, surprised to see him staring her down.

'Why do you think we share an office?' he said. 'Do you really think this room became available, just like that?'

'You said it was because of the documentary,' Amy said, taken aback by Donovan's spiralling mood.

But Donovan shook his head. 'They put me here to keep an eye on you. You can't be trusted to work on your own.'

'I don't believe you.' But the sincerity in his voice hit Amy hard.

'Look.' Donovan pushed back his chair as he stood. 'This comes from them, not me. How many times have I told you? You need to toe the line.'

Amy sat with her fingers tightly interlinked. She could not find the voice to disagree. Donovan had warned her to rein it in, but she hadn't realised the instruction came from the top. She knew she had been acting recklessly since news of her relationship to Lillian broke, but nobody cared more about her team than she did.

'I've got a strategy meeting with the command team.' Donovan's eyes flicked to the clock on the wall. 'We'll talk about this later.'

Amy watched him leave. She had underestimated her new DCI.

The door had just clicked shut behind him when her phone rang. 'Hello?' she said sharply. 'I'm a bit busy, can it wait?'

'I'm fairly up against it myself.' Sally-Ann sounded equally harried. 'I'm just returning your many calls.'

'Sorry,' Amy replied, wondering why she was apologising. It was a struggle, grovelling to her sister when *she* was the one who had blanked her. But now she knew about the baby, Amy could put some perspective on things. She missed her sister. They needed to talk. In the background, Amy could hear distant buzzers and the jangle of cups and saucers as a tea trolley wheeled past. 'I remember . . .' she said, her voice low. 'About the baby. I want to help.' The words felt foul as they left her tongue. But the memory was too vivid, too ugly to be a product of her imagination.

'I don't want to talk about it.' Sally-Ann heaved a weary sigh. 'At least, not until after the trial.'

Because of Lillian and her precious appeal, Amy thought. But she didn't dare say the words aloud. Challenging Sally-Ann about Lillian would only increase the widening gap between them. She would have to trust her sister to do what was best. 'Does Paddy know?'

'Yeah, he knows. But I don't want him getting involved.' Sally-Ann's words came to an abrupt halt as her name was called. 'Listen, I've got to go. You don't need me there when you go to court, do you? The cameras, the press. Once I've given evidence, I won't want to go back.'

'No, no, of course.' Amy cast her eyes downwards, a pang of disappointment hitting home. 'Just keep in touch, yeah? I miss you.'

'I miss you too, and I promise . . . we'll talk soon.' Sally-Ann's voice was imbued with sincerity. 'And hey, watch out for the defence barrister, Prunella. She's like Batman's granny, that one. There's no stopping her.'

Amy chuckled as they said their goodbyes. But a vein of awkwardness had run through their conversation. Would things ever be the same between them again? She unpeeled a Post-it note from the side of her computer. Another box had been checked.

'Cheers, Paddy,' Amy said, as he entered her office with mugs of coffee in his hands. She steeled herself for their conversation as he gave her the rundown on the investigation to date. In the corridors of her mind, there had always been rooms she did not want to enter. But now the doors were flung open and she was powerless to stop the memories flooding in.

'I've been talking to Sally-Ann.' She sipped her coffee. 'She said you know about the baby.'

'Aye.' Paddy rested his mug on the edge of her desk. 'She was barely a teenager when she had him.' He ran a hand through his wavy hair. It held more than its fair share of grey, gifted from investigating cases such as these. Offences involving children were the most traumatic of all.

A myriad of ugly questions rose in Amy's mind. Had Jack been the father? Was this mystery baby a product of incest? And what had Lillian done with the baby that night?

'Has she said anything to you about it?' Amy hoped Paddy could give her the answers her sister was unwilling to provide.

Paddy blew out his cheeks. 'Far be it from me to upset her. She doesn't want to talk about it.'

Amy understood. This can of worms held implications for them all. 'I remember . . . Lillian wrapping the baby up with blankets and a hot-water bottle. It was winter . . .' Amy cast her grey eyes to the ceiling as she searched her mind for more. 'At least, it was cold outside. It's possible she left the baby somewhere to be taken in.'

'Or left it to die,' Paddy replied. 'Why would Lillian show a baby mercy after everything she did?'

It was a fair point, but not an outcome Amy wanted to contemplate. She swallowed a mouthful of coffee, drawing back from the memories that caused so much pain. She was parting the darkest of curtains, opening them a chink as she peeped at something too horrific to view in full light. She thought about Sally-Ann, sweating and shivering as she cuddled Poppy on the sofa that night. Then Lillian coming home, her strong arms pulling Poppy from the settee as she carried her back to bed. There had been a tiny sliver of compassion as she smoothed her hair. Sally-Ann had followed, too exhausted to cry any more.

Amy swallowed, realising that Paddy was staring at her. 'You all right?'

'Yeah. Fine.' She cleared her throat. 'Should we look for him? Put some feelers out?'

'Wait until after the trial. Then we'll figure out what to do.' They were wise words, but the prospect of waiting did not comfort Amy. What further surprises were in store?

CHAPTER
THIRTY-NINE

It gave Samuel a tingle of excitement to stalk his prey so close to home. Marianne's sleeping tablets were doing their job and she had not heard him creep out of the house. Tomorrow morning, she would awaken, and it would be as if he had never left. He knew she wasn't buying his suggestion that Billy was responsible. He had seen the way she looked at him, with a measure of suspicion in her eyes. With the police closing in, this had to be his last kill. *The last as the Love Heart Killer*, the voice deep inside him added. But today Samuel was not going to quieten it. He was in hunter mode. He was akin to a junkie prepping a needle to plunge into his vein. It was too late for recriminations or regret. The lust for power and control was all-consuming. It was all about the next hit.

It was fortunate the streets were quiet as he slipped inside the townhouse with minimum effort. Tiny alarm bells rang a warning in the back of his mind. What had happened to taking his time? But he had planned every movement. His conquest was known to him. He licked his lips in anticipation as he prepared to see her again. He thought about her job – the one she would never return to. Right now, the precious seconds of her life were ticking away. His leather gloves stretched over his knuckles as he clenched his fists. *Soon . . .* he thought, his breath heavy as he relished the moment. *Soon she'll be home.* Slowly, he crept up the stairs, instinct leading him to her bedroom.

He glanced at the framed photographs, picked up a discarded book next to the bed. He did not hear the door creak until it was too late. It couldn't be her. Not already. He darted behind the door, his pulse racing as a grey-haired woman in a white night-dress drifted in. *What is she doing here?* he thought, panicked. He knew his target lived with her mother, but she was meant to be out tonight.

'Hello?' she said, her voice feeble. 'Are you home, love? I thought I heard you come in . . .'

In she wandered, her slippers shuffling on the deep carpet.

Shit! What now? Samuel's thoughts darkened as he worked out his next move. With two sudden strides he was behind her, clamping his gloved hand over her mouth. Her skin felt loose and saggy, and she emitted a muffled moan as she collapsed beneath his grip. *What the hell?* Samuel's sense of control slipped away as she dropped to the floor. *Has she fainted? Had some sort of heart attack?* Her eyes were open and unmoving, her lips devoid of breath. Panting, Samuel stared at the body lying motionless at his feet.

There was no remorse as he closed over her mouth and pinched her nostrils shut. But she was already dead. Perspiration soaked Samuel's balaclava. He could not afford to get a droplet of his DNA on the body lying crumpled at his feet. Grunting, he scooped her up, his biceps straining to manage the dead weight. He caught the scent of perfumed talc wafting from the woman's skin. Lily of the Valley, his grandmother's favourite back when he was a child.

Down the hall he trudged, his breath laboured as he nudged open her bedroom door with his foot. He'd known it was her room, not just because the door had been left ajar, but because of the old-fashioned framed photos on display. With little grace, he tipped the woman back into her bed, and left her facing the wall. He fixed the duvet, pulling it over her shoulder. She looked as if she were sleeping, should anyone poke their head in.

Obscenities skimmed Samuel's lips. All the planning in the world could not allow for idiots breaking their routines. But he had a backup plan: soon, Billy would take the flack. He checked his sleeves. It only took one flake of skin to place him at the scene. Opening his pocket, he prised out a clear plastic bag, shaking out one of Billy's stray hairs. If they failed to discover that, they would get enough of the 'killer's' DNA from the tumbler inside Samuel's duffel bag. But the clock was ticking, and soon his conquest would be home. Returning to her bedroom, he gathered up his backpack and hastily shoved it under her bed. Panicked thoughts rose to greet him as a door slammed downstairs. What if she found the old woman dead before she came to bed? What if she called the police? *Calm down*, the voice inside him reasoned. *She's not going to start shaking her at this hour of the night.*

The heat was stifling as he settled himself beneath the bed. He imagined his sweat seeping into the carpet fibres, and he could feel his control slipping away. Then he heard it: the steady tap, tap of feet climbing the wooden stairs. The creak of a floorboard on the landing. He held his breath. Was she checking on her mother? He waited for a scream. A cry. A sob of grief. None came. Then the flush of a toilet. Taps gushing forth water. The gentle click of the bedroom door as she entered at last. A pause. Did she sense her mother's death? Samuel peered out from beneath her bed, just as he had done with the girls that came before. He was every woman's nightmare. He was the monster under the bed. He kept his breathing shallow and light, despite his heart clamouring for more. At last, she was here. A gentle peace swept over him as she began to undress. He heard clothes being folded, the jangle of hangers. Change emptied from pockets and left on the dresser. A mobile phone was plugged into a charger. Cleanser was applied. He smiled at the delightful ching of jewellery being dropped into something ceramic. A sigh of relief as a bra clasp was undone. He would never get tired of this ceremony. He watched her feet as she stood next to the bed and pulled back the duvet. As she climbed into bed, Samuel was grateful she did not have a divan. Nothing had the effect on his psyche of being able to lie beneath her, just like all those years ago. He touched the mattress, euphoria washing over him as he relaxed in the knowledge that it was just the two of them. Knowing her mother was dead in the next room added spice to the proceedings. Nobody would disturb them now. He listened as she slid the book off her bedside table and settled back to read. That was fine, he would give her a little longer. He waited for her soft snores. For when he could climb out from beneath her bed.

CHAPTER FORTY
FIFTEEN MINUTES EARLIER

Amy checked over her shoulder before pushing her key into her front door. This case was giving her the creeps. The killers she dealt with fell into different categories. Crimes of passion were easier to deal with, because once you isolated family members there was little likelihood of them harming anyone else. Then there were the random kills, where the victims were in the wrong place at the wrong time. But the planners and plotters worried Amy most of all. That's where the Love Heart Killer came in. There were so many unanswered questions. She hoped tomorrow would shed light on things. Erin was being brought out of her induced coma. She was lucky to be alive.

Amy's instincts told her that the Love Heart Killer had little emotional connection with his victims, but he knew their routines inside out. The killer was too clever to risk getting caught. She imagined him like the police in reverse, planning the murder, then working backwards to ensure his forensic footprints were absent from the scene. Relieved to be inside, Amy closed the door behind her and quickly turned the lock.

Sighing, she shrugged off her jacket and hung it on a hook in the hall. She needed a holiday. Lately, she was thinking like a killer, stepping into her biological mother's shoes. They were dirty, ugly shoes that she did not want to put her feet inside. *But they're so comfortable*, a voice spoke in her mind. It was Lillian. She recognised it instantly. Would she ever give her peace?

At least she had cleared the air with Donovan, after taking his earlier warning on board. It was a brief chat, but enough to plan a way forward for them both. They were both still finding their feet. Lillian's court case had played havoc with her emotions, while Donovan was coming into an established team whose first allegiance was to Amy. Padding towards the kitchen, she paused to glance upstairs. *Flora must be asleep*, she thought, placing one hand on the banister. She could not shake off the creeping feeling that something was wrong. As she climbed the stairs, Amy strained to hear every sound. *This is getting ridiculous*, she thought. *What are things coming to when I can't relax in my own home?* But thoughts of the case invaded every facet of her life. She paused outside Flora's room. The door was half open, her curtains billowing as the light of the moon peeped through. Amy waited to hear her usual snores, but there was no sound. 'Mum?' she whispered, stepping inside the room. She hovered over her mother's sleeping form, reaching out to touch her shoulder.

Her hand stalled in mid-air. Best to leave her be. Her outing with Winifred had probably exhausted her. A lump formed in Amy's throat. She looked so tiny, alone in the double bed. She vowed to take her out soon and spend some quality time with her.

Slowly, she backed away and tiptoed down the hall, pausing outside her own door. Her hand froze on the doorknob as she heard a shuffling noise. Surely not . . . She pressed her ear against the door just in time to hear a rasping breath. Someone was in her room. Her heart was thundering now, the swish of blood pounding in her ears. There was definitely someone inside. Goosebumps rose on her flesh. She should go downstairs and arm herself, or better still, dial 999. It could be a burglar. It could be . . . Taking a deep breath, she pushed open the door.

CHAPTER
FORTY-ONE

Amy liked arriving at work at the crack of dawn, before the rest of her team filtered in. For once, she'd had a good night's sleep. The presence of her pug, Dotty, in her bedroom had been a pleasant surprise when she returned home last night. She had been so preoccupied with the killer she had completely forgotten about her. She imagined her mum smiling as she deposited Dotty in the room. Today, the camera crew were almost finished filming, and she hoped things would return to normal soon. Even with her office window open, she could still smell last night's pizza in the air. At least some things never changed.

With his shirtsleeves rolled up and a dirty cereal bowl cluttering his desk, Donovan appeared to have been there for some time. Tiredness was etched on his face; his new role was clearly weighing heavy on his mind. Their team was under the spotlight and there was pressure on them to perform. But it was about more than budgets and the constraints of red tape – there were lives at stake.

'Have you been home?' Amy said, taking in the shadows beneath his eyes.

Donovan brightened as he saw her. 'Fell asleep at my desk. If you look really close, you can see the indent of the keyboard on my cheek.'

'Muppet.' The word slipped out of Amy's mouth before she could stop it, but it was accompanied by a smile. The boundaries between them had changed since Donovan had asserted himself. She was about to apologise when he spoke.

'May I refer you to my new office sign, DI Winter?' Donovan pointed to a printout he had sellotaped to the wall: *Everyone brings joy to this office. Some when they enter, and some when they leave.*

'In that case, I'll leave – to make you a coffee. You look like you need it.'

'No need.' Donovan raised his hand, his face growing serious. 'I'll do it in a minute.'

Amy looked at him in wonder. Donovan offering to make anything was not a good sign. She pulled out a flask from her bag, containing an unappealing green goo. 'I'm trying this detox juice thing.' She laid the bottle on her desk, dropped her bag next to her chair and analysed his expression. 'What's happened? Has something come in?'

'I'm afraid so. We don't know if it's connected to the Love Heart Killer yet, but it looks to be that way.'

'What?' Amy's voice rose an octave. She couldn't believe she was exchanging office banter when another murder had come in. 'Why didn't you call me? When did it happen?' But she had to rein in her anger, because these were the questions that Donovan had asked her when she'd failed to notify him about Stacey.

'It's under control.' Donovan looked at her sagely. 'I've been to the scene. CID are putting together a handover. It'll be with us soon.'

Another handover? Amy knew her brother would be unhappy about that. Each team was judged by their detections – each positive outcome when investigating a case. But the hours Craig's officers worked on this case would come to nothing if they handed it over to Amy's team. 'Give me the low-down,' she sighed, wishing she had made that coffee after all.

'A neighbour called it in after seeing a couple acting suspiciously as they left a townhouse not far from where you live. At first she thought they were drunk, as the woman was having trouble walking. But the man helping her out had a balaclava on his head. She said it was weird – he was acting normally, it was the headgear that spooked her. Get this – the woman's been identified as Naomi, Samuel Black's PA.'

'Ah, no . . .' Amy replied, remembering how warm and friendly she had been. 'Another link to Black Media. I can't believe he'd shit on his own doorstep like that.'

'There's more,' Donovan said. 'We've searched the townhouse. Not only is Naomi gone, her mum was found dead in her bed.'

Amy's hand rose to her mouth as she inhaled a sharp breath. 'Murdered?'

'It's too early to tell if it's a heart attack or if the killer finished her off. She was lying, both hands under her face in a sleeping position, her body facing away from the door.'

'Did she have any carvings on her chest?'

'Nope, nothing.'

'And no leads for Naomi?'

'CSI are turning her place over with a fine-tooth comb. She must have been well-off to live in a townhouse in Notting Hill.'

'Or it could have been inherited, like with my family,' Amy said. 'Some of the residents on my street have been there for generations.' A breeze rose outside, causing the blinds to rattle back and forth. 'It couldn't have been a domestic?'

Donovan leaned back on his swivel chair as he gave the question some thought. 'It's doubtful. According to Tara, her sister, Naomi was a popular girl, but she didn't have time for relationships. When she wasn't working, she was caring for her mum. Tara wanted to put her in a home, but Naomi wasn't having it. She worked around the clock to look after her.'

Amy nodded. She could identify with that. 'He's getting sloppy. Making mistakes . . . Unless he meant to kill her mum all along.'

'Doubtful,' Donovan replied. 'Tara was meant to take her overnight, but she cancelled at the last minute because she came down with a stomach bug.' He tutted. 'Ironic, really – she didn't want her mum falling ill. Now there's no sign of Naomi and her room has been freshly hoovered – just like before.' It had been noted in a recent forensic report that Erin's bedroom carpet had been recently vacuumed too.

'Under the bed?' Amy asked, remembering the wording on the report. 'And the hoover bag is missing too?'

'Yep, on both counts. Once could be put down to the victim being clean, but twice . . . that's more than a coincidence.'

'So that's where he's lying in wait . . . under the bed.' Amy fought an involuntary shudder. She was going online and shopping for a divan bed as soon as she got home.

'Creepy as hell, eh? Floyd the FLO is with her sister Tara now.' Floyd was the family liaison officer who was called in during cases such as these. He would monitor the family dynamics and ascertain Naomi's daily routine.

Amy couldn't begin to imagine the regret Tara must have felt for not having her mother as planned. 'I reckon he was lying in wait for Naomi when her mum disturbed him. There's no way he could have taken Naomi without waking her mother up.' A cold chill enveloped her as she recalled returning to her own house last night.

How she had peeped in on her mother in bed and decided to leave her be. It could have just as easily been her. 'Any signs of a struggle?'

'If there was, he's cleaned it up.' Donovan's bones cracked as he stretched in his chair. 'Although we did recover a glass in the kitchen that seems to have been used. No blood, which at least is hopeful. From what the neighbour said, it sounds like Naomi was drugged. Officers are checking museums, galleries, window displays and the like.' It was no mean feat.

Amy drew up the CAD report on her computer and began to read for herself.

'No sign of forced entry,' Donovan continued. 'He's like a ghost travelling through walls. Winter? Are you with me?'

'Sorry.' Amy stepped out of her thoughts. She had been think-ing about last night again, remembering the cold metal of the key in her hand as she shoved it in the lock of her door. The unsettling feeling of being watched.

'I'll put the kettle on.' She took an empty mug from her drawer. 'We'll need to chase up that handover package for an update on all arrest attempts. Serious consideration needs to be given to bringing Samuel Black in, too.' She glanced at the mugs on Donovan's desk, trying to pick out the cleanest one. Soon she would be rallying her team to action and the day would run away with her. They had to make a breakthrough. This was way too close to home.

'I don't think you should be alone at night.' Donovan's words made Amy pause. 'At home, I mean. Naomi's mother was in her early seventies. This job has echoes of you and your mum.'

He was right. Amy couldn't imagine Naomi using the Sugar Babes app. She was well paid for her time at Black Media and every hour in her day seemed to be accounted for. The killer was playing with fire, choosing one of their own. But then, criminals didn't always play by the book. Sometimes they did stupid things, pan-dering to their own ego instead of worrying about repercussions.

'You're too close to this case.' Donovan pushed his chair back as he stood. 'What if this was a message? It's more than a coincidence that Naomi lived with her mum, like you.'

'If I couldn't leave my home every time I felt threatened, I'd never get to work.' Forced laughter escaped Amy's lips. But this was about more than her; it involved her mother too. She couldn't bear for anything to happen to Flora. And Dotty wouldn't be able to defend either of them against the balaclava monster who hid under women's beds.

She was warmed by the concern in Donovan's eyes as he approached. She took in his tousled hair, his full lips, the way his eyes crinkled when he smiled. This was more than a workplace friendship. Much more.

'I think I should stay with you for a while.' He was standing before her now, tense with concern. 'I'd ask you both to come to me, but it's a tiny flat and it wouldn't be fair on your mum.'

'Don't you live with your daughter?' Amy said. 'She's almost Naomi's age, isn't she? You don't want to leave her alone.'

'She's off to Disneyland Paris soon with Daisy, and the dogs are booked into kennels. How about I stay for a couple of nights until this dies down?' Daisy was Donovan's granddaughter, the apple of his eye.

'I'm quite capable of looking after myself,' Amy grumbled, although she was tempted by his offer.

'But is Flora? Look, this isn't an excuse for a bunk-up. I'm happy to kip on the sofa.'

'As if Mum would let anyone sleep on her precious sofa.' Amy smiled.

Donovan ran his fingers through his hair. 'Sorry, I'm not doing a very good job of this, am I? One minute I'm telling you to be more professional, and the next I'm offering to stay over at yours. I'm just looking out for you, Amy.' He emitted a throaty chuckle.

'Forget I mentioned it.' He met her gaze as he tried to read her expression. 'I'll leave you to chase up the handover, while I nip home and grab a quick shower and change of clothes. I'll bring you back a Starbucks. Better than that tar that passes for coffee in the tea club.' But Amy was not done with their conversation just yet.

'You're welcome to stay in the spare room,' she blurted. 'God knows how I'm going to break the news about Naomi to Mum.' Flora would be beside herself when she learned that the murderer had struck nearby. Amy's emotions were getting the better of her. Recent events had taught her how fragile her world was. Flora wasn't getting any younger, and her sister had switched loyalties. She had never felt so alone. Regardless of his position, it was time to let Donovan in. Brick by brick, she could feel her defences crumbling away. 'I won't be waiting on you hand and foot, mind,' she added. 'You'll have to take care of yourself.'

'Believe it or not, I'm a good cook.' Donovan's voice was deep and reassuring as his hand brushed against hers.

Amy tensed as another spike of embarrassment flared. 'We'd better get moving on this caseload. The team will be in soon.' They weren't due in until eight, and it was ten to seven now, but Amy had exhausted her reserves when it came to her personal life. Right now, her priority was finding Naomi. She only hoped they weren't too late.

CHAPTER
FORTY-TWO

Samuel paced his office, struggling to tone down his exhilaration. He had barely slept last night. He imagined the police scouring Naomi's home, searching for clues. Had they found the glass with Billy's DNA on it yet? Discovered the hair he'd left in the old dear's bed? His smile spread as he recalled Naomi, restrained in his special place. She was like a fine wine he had taken from his cellar. He had employed her, put her right in his eyeline, knowing that someday he would possess her completely.

Billy was at work, despite the police's frantic search for him. Last night he had slept in his office, hiding from the world after they all went home. Samuel struggled to wipe the smirk from his face. It seemed he was too scared to go home.

'Billy, good to see you. Take a seat. How are you?' His words came in quick succession as Billy approached. He patted the man's back, trying to hide his disgust. Billy's clothes were crumpled and his breath reeked of stale beer. He was a sorry excuse for a human being, but now he would finally be of some use.

'I've been better,' Billy said glumly, as he shuffled in his seat. His curly hair was wild and untamed, his face pimpled from a shaving rash.

'Of course, stupid question.' Samuel sank into his chair on the other side of the desk. 'How's your daughter?' Samuel's heel tapped beneath the table and his right eye twitched. He was nervous and unfocused. He needed to calm down.

'So far so good, thanks for asking. It's hopeful, as long as the treatment continues, but it doesn't come cheap.'

'Of course.' Samuel was well aware of her treatment in the US. 'I wish there was more we could do, but we've clamped down on charity donations. The shareholders are disgruntled about the amount of money we're giving away.' It was a lie. Samuel had brought the charity donations to a sudden halt. He had reeled Billy in six months ago, drip-feeding payments until his family were dependent. He had kick-started their daughter's treatment. Now he was leaving them high and dry.

'Yes . . . yes, of course.' Billy's face fell as Samuel confirmed his worst fears. 'You've done enough.' His shoulders slouched; he heaved a weary sigh. 'You've been very generous, everyone has. But Hollie's illness has really taken it out of me . . . and now all this business with the police. I feel like I'm free-falling down a black hole. It was bad enough, that woman dying in the store window, but now they're trying to pin the girl in the museum on me too.'

Wait until you hear about Naomi, Samuel thought. 'Unfortunate business, that.'

'I swear, I didn't do anything.' Billy shook his head in disbelief as he rested his elbows on the armrests of the chair. 'It had nothing to do with me.' A low whirr sounded overhead as filtered air flowed into the room.

'Billy, mate, it goes without saying. God knows you've had enough to contend with this past couple of years.' Samuel delivered a sympathetic smile. 'You know . . .' – he lowered his voice in a conspiratorial tone – 'I have friends in high places. Apparently the police are under pressure to get a result for this one. Sorry . . .' Samuel warmed inside as he watched Billy's face fall. 'I'm not trying to make you feel worse. I just wanted you to know that your legal insurance is still valid.' He paused for effect as the next piece of his plan fell into place. 'As well as your other insurance policy, of course.' He waited for Billy to take the bait.

'What other insurance policy?'

'Oh . . . don't you know? If you're charged with an offence that results in a custodial sentence, your next of kin receives a payout in the event that you lose your job. We put it in place because of the background of some of our ex-offenders. I wanted their families to be covered in the event of something going wrong.' Samuel's chair creaked as he fed him the line. Beneath the desk, his hands were trembling. Everything hinged on Billy taking the bait.

'I've never heard of that.' A sense of wonderment crept into Billy's voice.

'We don't advertise it, as it's a substantial amount. It's amazing what you can get insured these days. I mean, for something like murder . . .' Samuel pursed his lips and whistled. 'We're talking two hundred and fifty thousand for life imprisonment.'

'Really?' Billy straightened in his chair. 'A quarter of a million pounds? And that would pay out if I got life imprisonment?'

'Well, yes . . .' Samuel gestured. 'But I'm sure it won't come to that – after all, you're innocent and—'

But Billy wasn't listening. Samuel could see him mentally doing the maths. That amount of money could save his daughter's life. It wasn't just a number Samuel had plucked from thin air. The updates were as regular as clockwork on her JustGiving page. Hollie had been diagnosed with acute lymphoblastic leukaemia – a cancer of cells in her immune system. Remission rates were 85 per cent, but unfortunately for Hollie, she fell into the 15 per cent for which chemotherapy did not work. After a gruelling year of treatments, her family had been told that Hollie's illness was terminal. She was twelve years old. But then her mother had discovered a clinic offering a revolutionary treatment named Kymriah, which had saved the lives of hundreds of children just like Hollie. Treatments did not come cheap. Her parents had already sold their London home to pay for the bespoke blood infusions costing $475,000. Fundraising had generated a quarter of a million pounds on their JustGiving page, but with the total cost of hospital charges, they were still $250,000 short. They had reached a critical stage of Hollie's treatment, and Samuel knew they could not stop now. It was a bargaining chip he held tightly in his fist.

'All I ask is that you keep it to yourself.' Samuel tapped the side of his nose. 'God forbid, but if you *did* get convicted it would reflect badly on the company if people knew you were receiving payment from us. People could campaign. Kick up a fuss. They might even have the payment stopped.'

'I won't say a word.' Billy breathed through his mouth as he assimilated the news. 'If the worst happened and I was charged . . . how quickly could the payment go through?'

Samuel gave himself a mental high five. 'I'd personally ensure it was processed as soon as you were found guilty in court. There would have to be a trial, but I'd imagine it would happen quickly, given the nature of the crimes.'

'And you're serious? There really is a policy?'

Opening his desk drawer, Samuel slid out a manila envelope and pushed the contents across his desk. Billy's eyes darted left and right as he read through each page of the policy in turn. It was there in black-and-white.

'I'd let you keep it, but I can't afford this getting out.' Samuel reclaimed the official-looking paperwork. 'At Black Media, we're like protective parents. Once we take you under our wing, we support you every step of the way.'

'And you have.' Billy's demeanour completely changed. There were tears in his eyes. A weight was lifted. There was hope. 'I can't tell you how grateful I am. You've dug me out so many times.'

'At least you know your family will be taken care of in the event of anything happening.'

Billy sniffed. 'I'd give up my life for my little girl.' The words were mumbled under his breath, but Samuel strained to hear each one.

He rose from his desk, a signal for Billy to go. He felt tall. In command. 'Let's forget this conversation ever happened – for the sake of the company.' Samuel extended his hand, taking Billy's in a firm grip. 'And Billy, you have my word. I'll personally oversee that your insurance is paid.' He delivered a dark chuckle. 'Just as well you've got me fighting your corner – the shareholders would never allow it.' An unsettling change had occurred. The conversation had veered from Billy not being guilty to Samuel ensuring the insurance paid out.

Billy blinked as Samuel squeezed his hand, driving his message home. He could not afford for him to mess this up. 'You should look on YouTube. There's footage of serial killers being interviewed – it's fascinating stuff. They talk about their motivations in real-life interviews. Of course, we never hear from the ones who get away. They could be right under your very nose.' Samuel's eyes narrowed a fraction. He saw a flicker of confusion in Billy's eyes. Finally, the penny dropped. Billy's arm grew limp, and he seemed to weaken at the knees. He knew who the real killer was. Samuel had told him without having to utter a damning word. 'Why don't you take the rest of the day off?' Samuel continued, in the same cold tone.

'Yes . . . I . . .' Billy paused for breath. A sweat broke out on his brow. Samuel could see the conflict in his eyes. If he accused his boss of murder, he could kiss goodbye to the insurance payout. Billy glanced down at the paperwork one more time. Perhaps now he could see that the papers were a little thin, the logo on the header not quite right.

'Yes?' Samuel spoke as their eyes met. 'You're looking a bit pale. Are you OK?'

'The money . . . it's guaranteed?'

'Billy boy, I'm a man of my word. I'll pay it out of my own pocket if I have to. Anything to help that little girl of yours.' He picked up the paperwork and held it in the air. It was a metaphorical gesture. Billy's daughter's life, hanging in the balance. 'Do we have a deal?'

'Yes . . . I know what I have to do . . .' Billy's voice trailed off. Samuel watched as he sloped out of his office without saying another word.

CHAPTER
FORTY-THREE

Her arms tightly folded, Amy sat watching the monitor in a side room as Billy's interview progressed. He had been placed under arrest at lunchtime, having strolled into the station in response to the messages on his answerphone from her team.

Billy was visibly shaking, which was hardly surprising given the severity of the crimes he was accused of. He had tripped over his feet on the way in and knocked over his tea before the interview got underway. Could such a clumsy man be the sleek, professional killer they were looking for? Today, they had new evidence to put to him, as Erin had come round. In a hoarse voice, she had described a strong man in a balaclava, who smelled of expensive aftershave. But the only smell emanating from Billy was musty clothes, cigarettes and stale alcohol. Amy watched his hands as Molly progressed. Was it nerves or an alcohol addiction making them tremble? Beside him sat the duty solicitor, a quiet, elderly man who rarely intervened. That suited Amy and her team just fine.

Amy had briefed Molly to take a first account from Billy, one offence at a time. Question him briefly about Stacey, then Erin, then move on to Naomi as quickly as she could. Their main priority was to ascertain her whereabouts, not that they expected Billy to comply.

Such questioning could go on for hours, even when the killer admitted to the crime, because there was nothing to stop the suspect changing their story later on. Officers would pick out every thread of Billy's account.

It was interesting to see how suspects reacted to female officers, particularly ones known to murder women of a certain type. Molly had light brunette hair but was around the age of those killed previously. If she ran into trouble, then DC Steve Moss was on hand. Their questioning would be conducted in a calm and clear manner, extracting information in the same way a dentist would extract a rotten tooth. Painlessly, swiftly, and without fanfare. Molly was equipped with an earpiece, so Amy could communicate if need be. It was something they rarely used in interview, but Amy's instincts had urged her to take advantage of the technology today.

She watched as Billy was asked about his part in Stacey's death.

'I killed her.' He stared unblinkingly at Molly and Steve. 'Charge me now. I did it all.'

Amy's heart skipped a beat as Billy confessed. She had not seen that coming. Not for a second.

Molly's expression did not change, but Amy knew she would be doing cartwheels inside. 'You're telling me that you murdered Stacey, attempted to murder Erin and kidnapped Naomi?'

Billy's eyes widened. 'Naomi?'

'Yes.' Molly's eyes narrowed as Billy expressed his surprise. 'Can you tell us her whereabouts?'

The question was warranted. Officers had stepped up the hunt for the young woman, but she was nowhere to be found. But judging by Billy's reaction, he was unaware.

'The first person I killed was Claire Lacey, my old teacher,' he said. 'I don't know anything about Naomi. I liked her . . .' His voice faded as he stared into the distance. 'I didn't mean to do her any harm.'

'Who? Naomi or Claire?' Molly said.

'I told you. Claire,' Billy snapped. 'She found me in her bedroom, we had an argument and she got hurt. It was me. I murdered her.' Staring at his hands, he began to pick at his nails. His fingertips were nicotine-stained, a world away from Samuel Black's manicured hands. 'I thought about Claire a lot over the years,' Billy continued. 'Wondered what it would be like to kill again. Then I found Stacey. I drugged her and brought her back to my place. When I was done with her, I made her into a display.'

'We're going to need more detail than that.' Molly folded her arms.

Amy watched, entranced. Normally she would be thrilled to get a confession, but Billy's explanation was stilted. Rehearsed. Nothing added up.

Pressing a button on her microphone, Amy spoke into the earpiece Molly was wearing. 'Ask him about his motivation. This doesn't ring true.'

Molly nodded, a barely noticeable movement of the head.

'You're a father, aren't you? Our victims were somebody's daughters . . .'

Silence descended as Billy closed his eyes.

Amy peered at the camera as she scrutinised Billy's face, waiting for a flicker of regret. Was he thinking of his little girl? She was well aware of their relationship, having insisted on a full background check. But the expression that emerged was one of steely determination. His jaw was set firm, his hands curled into fists on his lap.

'Why did you do it, Billy?' Molly spoke with purpose. 'What drove you?'

'It's a process,' Billy replied. 'It doesn't happen overnight. First I depersonalised them. Saw them as an object instead of a living, breathing human being.' He shrugged his shoulders. 'I enjoyed it. No other reason than that.'

He fell quiet, picking at his nails. Amy thought about Erin's description of her abductor. Strong, confident, and wearing expensive aftershave. Molly broke the silence with another question, moving from past to present. 'You said the first person you killed was Claire Lacey. Why the gap before you killed again? Can you explain that?'

'There wasn't the physical opportunity to do what I wanted to do.' Billy avoided all eye contact with his interviewers. 'I started off looking at soft porn, but soon I was craving more potent stuff. It became an addiction. The harder stuff gave a sense of excitement. It heightened the risk.' He risked a glance at Steve before returning his gaze to his hands. 'I wasn't a pervert. I led a normal life. But I had this destructive part of me that I hid from the rest of the world. But soon violent porn wasn't enough. I needed more.'

'Why the public displays?' Molly asked.

Billy shrugged once more. 'I wanted them to be found. Their families deserve peace. They were someone's daughter, after all.'

'But you could have left them anywhere,' Molly said. 'Why take that chance?'

Shifting in his seat, Billy's words were flat and devoid of emotion, as if he were reading a script. 'It was a shrine, the public display. I was paying homage to them. You need to lock me up and throw away the key.' He talked about Erin, and how he'd thought she was dead. But he continued to refuse to answer Molly and Steve's questions about Naomi.

Amy shook her head, her suspicion growing. There was something familiar about his words. Amy had researched the most famous serial killers. She now knew it was something deep in her genes that had drawn her to them. A passion quickly extinguished when she discovered the identity of her biological parents. But now those old interviews were proving valuable as she recognised the words used.

'It's odd,' Amy thought aloud. 'One minute he's depersonalising his victims, but the next he's describing them as someone's daughter. It goes against the grain.' She stared down at the notes she had made. His so-called addiction to porn smacked of a Ted Bundy interview she had heard. Regardless of Billy's sudden confession, Amy was not convinced.

Turning to her computer screen, she brought up YouTube and played back an interview with the serial killer Jeffrey Dahmer. At the same time, she brought up the transcripts of a Ted Bundy interview. Billy had basically repeated their accounts word for word. Amy felt a surge of disbelief. She had come across some strange behaviours in her time, but this took the biscuit. Didn't he realise that when the interview was played in court, people would realise his testimony was plagiarised?

Paddy had crept in beside her to monitor the interview, smelling of freshly smoked cigarettes. 'Great result, eh?'

But Amy failed to share his enthusiasm. 'I'm not convinced.'

'The forensic results say different,' Paddy said. 'We've got Billy's DNA on a glass found at Naomi's flat, and one of his hairs on a sheet in her mother's bed. There's that, and the links to his workplace. Sounds watertight to me.'

'Seriously?' Amy's face creased in a frown. 'Would anyone be that careless? He hoovered up after himself—'

'Not all our suspects are criminal masterminds,' Paddy interrupted. 'The CPS will run with this. Prima facie.'

Paddy was right. The CPS would view it as an open-and-shut case. An image of Samuel Black floated into Amy's mind as she imagined him in his office, a smug smile on his face. 'Brief Molly for the next interview,' Amy said. 'Drill down into his motivations, beginning from his childhood. We need a thorough psychological profile. Go into every aspect of his relationship with Samuel Black. He's had a hand in this, I can feel it.'

'Whatever you say, boss.'

'And chase up the Sugar Babes company. There's a definite link between the victims. We need their user data before Billy is charged.'

Amy stared out of the window long after Paddy had left. She would not rest until she uncovered the truth. As for Naomi . . . the clock was ticking down. Would they find her in time?

CHAPTER
FORTY-FOUR

Samuel stood at his office window, feeling on the edge of a precipice. Today, his thoughts were crowding in, making it hard to breathe. He tugged on his collar. His shirt was sticking to his skin, despite the air conditioning. On days like these, he fantasised about taking the lift to the top floor and free-falling off the roof. It was the heroic thing to do – sacrifice himself in order to save the lives of the young women he would invariably continue to kill. He imagined tearing through the air as gravity pulled him down. The sight of the ground rising up to greet him before he smacked on to the concrete kerb. Would the world mourn his passing? Pay tribute to him? Perhaps they would feature him on *Sky News*. He pressed his hands against the glass, his breath fogging the pane. But then people would ask why. A slur would be placed on his good name.

Not today, Sam. You've got work to do. He stepped away from the window, taking steady breaths to calm his accelerating heart. He had one more ace up his sleeve.

He had no qualms about pulling in a favour now things were getting tight. Infiltrating Notting Hill police station had not been difficult, not when he had connections with someone on the inside. He would leave Billy with the knowledge that Samuel could get to him wherever he was. He should have told Billy about Naomi, but doing so strongly implicated him evidentially. Samuel had managed to get the message across in just a firm handshake, a steely gaze and a few well-chosen words. But now panic gripped as his contact in the police force told him Billy had yet to be charged.

'Why haven't they charged you yet?' Samuel barked down the phone as Billy came on the line. He had been taken to the shower cubicle, the only place without CCTV glaring down on him.

'Samuel? Is . . . is that you?'

'Don't say my name aloud, you idiot!' Samuel grimaced. *What a cretin*, he thought. Billy sounded like a little boy who was about to cry. Not even a day in custody and already he was losing the plot. 'We had an agreement. Why haven't they charged you yet?' There was no time for niceties anymore.

'I . . . I don't know,' Billy whined. 'I was very convincing. I studied YouTube videos of Ted Bundy and Jeffrey Dahmer, I repeated what they said word for word.'

'Word for word?' Samuel rolled his eyes. 'Word for fucking word?' He growled under his breath – a low, rumbling sound. Billy was lucky he wasn't in the room right now or he wouldn't be making it out alive. 'Who do you think you're dealing with, the Keystone Cops? This is Winter's team. She's the daughter of serial killers, for Christ's sake. Why didn't you answer "no comment", you stupid twat!'

Billy's breath hitched. 'I needed to make it convincing and I figured . . .' He caught a sudden breath. 'I figured—'

'Shut up, I'm thinking.' The line fell silent as Samuel paced the room. 'Listen, we don't have much time. I need you to remember this. It's enough to get you incriminated. But if this comes back to me . . . if you point the finger at my fucking door . . . I'll get to you, just like I got to you today. And I'll make sure that daughter of yours doesn't get another penny. She'll die, and it'll be all your fault.'

'I won't, I promise. I just need some help.' Billy was crying now, snivelling into the phone.

Samuel massaged his forehead, his head bowed as he spoke. 'Tell them when Claire died it affected you. Turned you on . . . Are you listening?' The line had gone very quiet.

'Yes. Yes, I am.' Billy's voice was a whisper.

'Years passed. You tried to put it behind you. But you were stressed. Frustrated. Obsessed.' Samuel paused for breath. 'Then you stalked your victims, hiding under their beds. You always cleaned up after yourself, using their hoover and removing the dust bag. That's important. Make sure you mention that.'

'Yes, I will.'

Samuel's pulse was accelerating now; it felt so good to offload. Reliving the moments of power and control delivered a mini-surge of satisfaction as he said the words aloud. But if he was going to fully admit his culpability, it would not be to the likes of Billy bloody Picton. 'I've contacts on the inside. The police never make all the details of the crime public. That's why you need to give them this story. Don't embellish it. Anything you're not sure about, tell them you don't remember, or you're too upset to talk about it. They check everything. Give them the bare facts and leave it at that. Comprende?'

'Yeah, sure.' Awkward laughter jangled down the phone. 'And you don't need to worry, I've kept you out of everything. They don't even know we were friends.'

Friends? Samuel rolled his eyes. They were never friends, Billy was nothing but a hanger-on. It didn't matter that their stories conflicted, not if Billy did as instructed. Another sniffle crossed the line. He just needed to grow some balls first. 'Man up. You're a killer, Billy boy. Don't forget that. It's you. It's *always* been you.' But still . . . Samuel felt a pang of sadness in his chest. For a loser like Billy to take credit for his work. It was hard letting it go.

'And the money?'

Billy's voice brought Samuel back to reality. 'Paid in full upon conviction. I'll even arrange an advance as soon as you're charged. But keep it under your hat. If the cops hear about it, they'll see it as motive to confess to a crime you didn't commit.'

'What about Naomi? They keep asking what I've done with her.'

'Focus on the past murders and nothing else.'

Samuel got Billy to repeat everything back to him.

'Better,' he said, after Billy relayed his account. 'And none of this serial killer bullshit. Tell them you're a normal guy who got wrapped up in an addiction. Don't analyse it any more than that. Remember. They check everything. Don't fuck it up.'

'I won't. And Samuel?'

'What?'

'Thanks.'

A sly smile crossed Samuel's face as he ended the call. He had managed to pull things back from the brink just in time. He had gifted Billy to them, all wrapped up in a pretty bow. The CPS would run with it for sure. They would all pat themselves on the back. And Naomi? Her time was coming to an end.

CHAPTER FORTY-FIVE

As she nibbled on her tuna sandwich, Amy failed to share in the jubilance of her team. Billy's last interview had taken an about-turn as he'd filled in the gaps. As he discussed the scene, he'd revealed information only the police and the victims themselves were privy to. So why did Amy feel so flat? It was more than Naomi's disappearance, although that in itself was troubling enough. It was Billy. She simply didn't believe him. Perhaps she had too much faith in her own judgement, her ego inflated by the media coverage of her so-called special skills.

Was their killer really a clumsy, nervous man who couldn't wait to spill his guts? But if Billy wasn't the killer, then why confess? Amy turned the idea over as she automatically chewed and swallowed. Perhaps Samuel had set Billy up this whole time to take the fall. But Billy's account seemed to fit. A lusty teenager under the bed who got more than he bargained for. Billy was a misfit. She couldn't envisage the ambitious Samuel being friends with him in school. Billy had claimed that the stress of his daughter's illness made him desperate for a form of escape. His explanation may not have been perfect, but it was plausible. And now Erin's user data had finally been made available from the Sugar Babes app. Her conversations with a 'William Picton' were printed off and added to Billy's file, complete with his address. He must have been the only man using the app to give his real name.

It was all a little too convenient, and an involuntary shudder drove its way up her spine. The thought of someone lying under her bed as she slept . . . a man in a balaclava creeping around her room when she was at her most vulnerable. It was enough to keep anyone awake. She tried to imagine Billy behind the balaclava, his chubby form stealthily gaining access to each flat. Could he even fit under the bed? Amy tipped a bottle of water to her mouth. Why was Billy so tight-lipped about Naomi?

'Cheer up.' Donovan interrupted her thoughts. 'We got him!' He jabbed a thumb over his shoulder as Ginny followed him in. 'They want to do a quick piece with you on the result. What a great way to end the show.'

'A great way to end the show would be finding Naomi.' Amy's voice was flat. 'He's given us everything. Why withhold on her?'

'He's got her holed up somewhere, probably in revenge,' Donovan replied. 'She told her boss that he gave her the creeps.'

'Shame no one else was around to hear that conversation.' Amy ran her tongue over her teeth. It wouldn't do to be on-screen with the remnants of a tuna sandwich on show. It felt wrong, making entertainment while Naomi was still missing. The ripple effect of a job like this spread far and wide. 'All right then,' Amy relented. She owed Donovan some slack.

'Erm, if you could pop this up through your blouse.' Dom handed a small microphone to Amy. Donovan watched, amused, as she clipped it to her clothing. 'There you go,' he said as they readied the scene. 'All set.'

'It'll be the same as before,' Ginny explained. 'I'll prompt you with some questions. My voice won't be aired, it'll just be you answering . . . erm . . . Is that OK?'

'What she means is, can you stop scowling?' Donovan chuckled. 'We're trying to encourage people to join the police, not frighten them away.'

Sitting with her hands on her lap, Amy displayed her teeth in a forced smile.

'My God, that's frightening, can you turn the volume down a bit?'

Amy glared at Donovan. 'And why don't you fu—'

'We're all set here,' Bob interrupted, as he aimed the camera in Amy's direction.

Amy straightened in her chair as they began to record.

In a rare moment of downtime, Amy had the office to herself. She had vowed not to watch the televised report of Sally-Ann's testimony, yet found herself streaming it on her computer just the same. Due to recent changes in legislation, Lillian's appeal was being piloted for television. Amy couldn't tell if it was a blessing or a curse. She sighed as her phone call to her sister went straight to answerphone. Paddy had reassured her that Sally-Ann was fine, but Amy needed to see for herself.

Donovan was in the control room, monitoring the team set up to take calls with regard to the appeal for Naomi's whereabouts. Floyd the FLO had done a stellar job, guiding Naomi's next of kin through the TV appeal.

As Lillian's face came on to the screen, Amy felt herself transform from within. She was Poppy now, the little girl who grew up in the Grimes household. Every word Lillian uttered dragged her back to a past life, which was re-emerging at a frightening rate. Lillian maintained her story of having called a women's refuge three decades ago to plead for help. But the refuge had no record of her calls. During questioning, the manager admitted that on a busy night they may not have taken Lillian's details. That was before the advent of computer files. Paper records were sometimes lost. There was no way of knowing now. That, coupled with old hospital records of Lillian's injuries . . . piece by piece, the evidence against her began to fall away. She had been portrayed as a monster when the story of the Beasts of Brentwood first broke. But in court, she did not fit the profile. Behind the glass panels in the dock stood a diminutive, frail woman with her hair coiled loosely in a bun. She was a grandmother, just like many other women her age. Regular people did not commit such atrocities against women and children. Because if they did, it meant nobody was safe. But behind the gentle smile, Amy saw amusement. Lillian had them all fooled – except for her. She swallowed hard. This was not looking good. But surely Sally-Ann's testimony would count for something?

The defence barrister, Prunella Fisher, appeared competent. A pair of Harry Potter-style glasses were perched on her beak-like nose, her face set in stony concentration. Sally-Ann confirmed she was the eldest child of Jack and Lillian Grimes. Amy felt a bloom of sympathy for her sister, who was struggling to catch her breath as nerves took hold. Sally-Ann had a better memory of events than Amy, and she did not envy her sister that. But now the record would finally be set straight. Years of abuse, beatings, neglect. Lillian and Jack's vicious fights, in which both parties came away injured. How Lillian had encouraged Jack every step of the way. Evidence against Lillian may have been planted but she was every bit as culpable as Jack.

'What sort of a mother was Lillian Grimes?' Prunella continued.

Sally-Ann cleared her throat. Her face was chalk-white in contrast to her black shift dress – a far cry from her usual colourful clothes. 'A good one,' she replied, exhaling a sigh.

Amy jabbed at the volume button on her computer. She must have heard her wrong. But yet the barrister did not ask her to clarify.

'And how do you come to that conclusion, after everything that happened in your home?'

Sally-Ann leaned forward, her fingers gripping the lip of the bench as she stood in the box. 'Mum was a victim, the same as the rest of us. We were all terrified of Jack.'

Prunella nodded in response. The camera panned over the courtroom and back to her face. 'Yet you fled, believing one or both of your parents had set out to kill you.'

'That's not true,' Sally-Ann replied. 'Jack thought he'd killed me, but Mum hid me away to keep me safe.'

Prunella's eyebrows raised. 'That's not what you said in your original statement to the police.'

'I've had time to think about it. Things are a lot clearer now. Mum sent me to stay with relatives and told Dad she'd buried me. It was the only way to keep me safe.' Gravely, Sally-Ann locked eyes with Lillian Grimes. A current of whispers grew in the room as the onlookers digested the news.

'No!' Amy groaned, her voice rebounding into the corners of the empty office. She had suspected this might happen, but her sister's lies still cut her to the quick.

'Why didn't you call the police?' Prunella continued, her black gown billowing as she moved around the room. 'You must have known your siblings were in mortal danger.'

'Mum said she was going to a refuge as soon as the time was right and would call me when they were safe.'

'But that time did not come.'

'No,' Sally-Ann replied in a small voice. 'My youngest sister, Poppy, spoke to social services and they got involved.'

'Yet nobody listened to your mother's pleas of innocence!' Prunella exclaimed in the silence of the room. 'Why do you think that was?'

'Because of the evidence planted against her. After Jack died, the public were outraged. They wanted someone to pay for what he did.'

'You're saying your mother was a scapegoat?'

'Jack was devious. He had a way of making you do things whether you wanted to or not. We were all terrified of him. She should have got help sooner. But she's paid for her mistakes.'

'Indeed.' Prunella waved one hand theatrically in the air as she paced. 'Why didn't you come forward when your mother was arrested?'

Sally-Ann looked around the room. She appeared lost, in need of someone to latch on to. Yet she had flatly refused to allow Paddy to attend. Finally, her gaze rested on Prunella as she delivered lines that sounded rehearsed. 'I was severely traumatised. I couldn't bring myself to get involved. The police had all this evidence against her and I . . .' Tears filled her eyes and the camera zoomed in. 'I thought that perhaps she *had* been involved after all. If they had evidence against her, then it was game over. I'm not proud of myself. I walked away. But I'm here now and I want to put things right.'

'It must have been difficult for you, coming forward and revealing your identity.'

'It was.' Sally-Ann sniffed as she dabbed her eyes with a tissue she had plucked from the sleeve of her dress. 'People treat you differently when you're a Grimes. They distance themselves, as if you're carrying an infectious disease. I've had eggs thrown at my front door and my walls spray-painted. I don't feel safe in my own home anymore.'

Amy frowned. Was this true? Paddy had never mentioned any of it. How would people know where she lived, for a start? Was this an effort to tug on people's heartstrings? Sympathy for the daughter drew sympathy for the mother. Why else would Sally-Ann be lying through her teeth?

'I wish there was something I could have done to save those girls,' Sally-Ann said, in response to further questioning. 'But we weren't brought up in a normal, rational household. We were taught not to ask questions. Nobody knew the truth about Jack until it was too late.'

'Stop lying,' Amy whispered at the screen. Sally-Ann was painting Lillian as a victim, instead of the monstrous, vile creature she really was. Such testimony was bringing Lillian dangerously close to being freed.

'Have you ever seen Lillian assault or murder anyone?'

'No.' Sally-Ann shook her head vehemently, pushing back a strand of blonde hair as it came loose. 'There were sex parties, although I didn't understand them at the time. People came and went. Jack had a violent nature. It was my job to keep the kids quiet and out of his way.'

'Did your father beat anyone in particular?'

'Damien often got the brunt of it, but Mum did what she could to protect us. She rowed with Dad all the time, and sometimes their arguments came to blows.'

Amy gazed at the screen in disbelief. Sally-Ann was being truthful for once. She remembered the times Jack and Lillian had laid into each other. Sometimes, they would come away with bloodied faces or a broken tooth. Amy paused the recording as it panned across the courtroom once more, catching a warning glare from Lillian as she stared at Sally-Ann. Her nostrils were flared; it was clear she was unhappy about this nugget of truth being exposed. Amy recognised her disapproval. As a child, she had seen it many times.

'So, your mother beat your father?' Prunella continued. 'The violence went both ways?'

Her head hung low, Sally-Ann began to back-pedal. 'Only in self-defence.' She swallowed, the lie streaked across her face.

How could she lie like that? Amy shut down her computer. She couldn't bear to watch any more.

CHAPTER
FORTY-SIX

'You could have gone to the pub with the others. You didn't need to stop in with me.' Amy was curled up on the sofa next to Donovan, her belly full after a delicious home-cooked meal. A good-looking man who could cook – he was definitely a keeper. They would sort their differences out. But now that Billy had been charged with murder, she had no right to ask Donovan to stay. They both skirted around the fact that the reason for his presence had been negated. Flora already knew about the crime, thanks to the gossip network that was her friends. She had dealt with it far better than Amy had given her credit for. Even the profiler felt that they had got their man. A misfit all his life, he seemed resentful of others' success, connecting the murders to Black Media in the hopes of taking the company down. Stress was Billy's constant ally. His growing dependence on alcohol and cigarettes were testament to that. Black Media had stopped funding his daughter's care in the US, and it had all got too much. Perhaps the victims had laughed at him, and this was Billy's way of taking control. It was feasible.

He repeated the words of famous killers in the hopes of following in their footsteps. Respect had been in short supply. He wanted to be feared rather than mocked. Yet unease lingered in the back of Amy's mind. A nagging feeling of doubt that would not go away.

'I'd much rather be here with you.' Donovan curled an arm loosely around her shoulders. She could feel their shared weariness, having exhausted their enquiries in the hunt for Naomi. Flora had gone to bed, unable to hide her delight at seeing Donovan again. It was a while since Amy had had anyone around to visit, much less a man.

Amy stretched like a kitten next to him. It felt good to be held again. What's more, Donovan wasn't rushing her. Everything was at her pace. But she had already made up her mind. Despite her tiredness, she wasn't sleeping alone tonight. Her stomach flipped at the prospect of what the evening would bring. On the television, the credits of the movie they were watching came to an end. As the local news began, a segment on Lillian's case flashed up on the screen.

'You want me to turn it off?' Donovan reached for the remote control.

The old Amy would have shrugged with indifference and told him she didn't care. Then again, the old Amy had opened her heart to very few. But being with Donovan was different, and she found herself nodding in response. 'I'm dreading giving evidence.' She gazed at him, her grey eyes filled with pent-up frustration. 'They've got what they wanted from Sally-Ann and Mandy. I don't know why they need me too.' But Amy had been tied up in Lillian's case from the start. At the tender age of four she had confided in children's social care, and thirty years later she had uncovered a shoebox filled with evidence that suggested Lillian had been framed all along. The Grimes family tree felt like gnarled vines. Dark and twisting, each aspect of Lillian's life wrapped around Amy as tendrils of despair. But being in Donovan's arms made her feel whole again. He reassembled the parts of her present-day self that Lillian had worked so hard to chip away. She was falling for him, and they had exchanged nothing more than a kiss.

'It'll all be over soon.' Donovan squeezed her shoulder. 'The worst is over. She has no hold over you anymore.'

But Amy's fears for the future emerged as a tightness in her chest. She could only repress her concerns for so long. 'I work so hard to separate myself from the Grimeses, but I'm a part of them. That will never leave me. Sometimes, I can't bear who I am.'

'Then make it your strength. That's what attracted me to you in the first place. You're different. You have insights . . .' Donovan paused for thought. 'Go into that courtroom and show her she doesn't intimidate you anymore.'

Amy smiled. It was easier said than done. 'She said something once: that I'll always be drawn to her. That I couldn't walk away from her, even if I tried.'

'I'm drawn to people who murder,' Donovan replied. 'We deal with them in our job. Does that make me like them?'

'Of course not. But their blood doesn't run through your veins.'

But Donovan wasn't prepared to agree just yet. 'If a baby is born as a result of rape, what does that make them? What about Sarah Reynolds? You saw her last month, didn't you? Is that what you told her?'

Sarah's case was one of many Amy had shared with Donovan during one of their late-night phone calls. A victim of rape, Sarah had kept her baby, and Amy had dealt with her case until her attackers were jailed. It was a nasty incident, given the attack was a result of gang crime. Two years after the attack, Sarah had visited Amy at the station to show off her son, Jerome. The little boy was adorable, and despite everything Sarah had been through, there was no disguising her love for her child. Jerome was an innocent, regardless

243

of the circumstances of his conception. 'You're right.' She smiled at Donovan. 'Pay no heed to me.' Her fingers found Donovan's, and soon all thoughts of Lillian dissolved from her mind. 'I suppose I'd better go . . .' Donovan said, his hand brushing her cheek.

'You don't have to . . .' Amy tilted her chin to meet his. Tentatively, Donovan pressed his lips to hers, then pulled back to examine her face. 'Are you sure?'

Amy's heart was beating wildly. She could have said that the spare room was all made up, but they both knew that wasn't what she meant. Curling her hand around the back of his neck, she pulled him in for a kiss. This time there was no hesitation, and she enjoyed the feel of his mouth against hers. Their kisses were hungry now, after what felt like an eternity of longing had built up between them. Flora would be asleep, having taken Dotty into her room to give Amy and Donovan some peace. 'Come to bed.' Amy rested her hand on his chest as they parted for air. 'My room is on the top floor.'

CHAPTER
FORTY-SEVEN

Amy could hear Flora pottering about downstairs as she made breakfast for them both. Should she have woken Donovan up an hour earlier to give him a chance to leave? His jacket still hung on the hanger behind the front door, his shoes resting nearby. When it came to relationships, Amy was not one to skulk about. She was a grown woman and could see who she pleased. Besides, Flora would be nothing but happy for her.

Today Amy was due to give evidence in court. Normally, cases were not heard on Saturdays, but due to the publicity surrounding Lillian's trial, her hearing was an exception to the rule. Last night, Amy had clung to Donovan like he was a raft on a stormy night. Would she feel this way when it was all over and she could finally move on with her life? How would she cope if he let her down? Would she have enough strength in her reserves to start again?

Her concerns faded as Donovan's hand snaked around her waist. 'Morning.' He nuzzled the back of her hair. She leaned into him as he spooned her, their bodies a perfect fit. Amy's skin erupted in goose bumps as his warm breath skimmed her ear.

'No time for that now.' Regretfully, Amy extracted herself from his grip. 'You need to get to work.'

'Should I mess up the bed in the spare room?' Donovan grinned. 'I feel like I'm a teenager again.'

'Too late for that.' Amy pushed her hair back from her face. 'Thanks for last night.'

'Happy to be of service,' Donovan chuckled, in no hurry to let her go.

'No . . . seriously. Thanks for being there. I don't know what I would have done without you. Whatever happens between us in the future . . . I'm grateful for that.'

'I care about you, Amy. I think you've always known that. And I'll always be here for you.' Slowly, Donovan ran his fingers over her body, pausing to draw circles on her thigh.

Emitting a soft groan, Amy turned to face him. 'Ditto,' she said. It was as much as she could commit to, before dragging herself away. 'C'mon. We've both got a busy day ahead.' This was a day she had come to dread: facing her biological mother in court. She reached for her phone, checking for messages. Lillian wasn't the only person who had haunted Amy's thoughts last night; Naomi had too. CID were covering and had spent the night reviewing CCTV for sightings. In a busy city like London, it was an unenviable task. 'No news on Naomi,' she sighed, her frown deepening as she scrolled through her phone.

'Then there's still hope. We'll find her.' Donovan grabbed his T-shirt from the carpeted floor.

A sense of sadness overcame Amy as she watched him pick up his discarded clothes. They would never have a normal relationship as long as the status quo prevailed. She had come into this world with a debt on her shoulders. A debt to the victims who lived beneath the floorboards of the Grimes home. She could never rest, never fully toe the line, as much as Donovan asked it of her. Because she would do whatever it took to bring killers to justice, to save those ensnared by their charms. It was the only way she could live with herself.

CHAPTER FORTY-EIGHT

As predicted, Flora had prepared a full breakfast for them both. Amy loved how Donovan conversed so effortlessly with Flora, obviously enjoying her company. Most men would be put off by having to meet her mother so soon. She had sent Donovan off to work, on the end of a knowing smile from Flora, before setting off herself.

It was astounding how quickly Lillian's appeal had progressed. Her lawyer had set the wheels in motion last year, and public outcry demanded a swift conclusion after new evidence was revealed by the press. Now the wheels of justice were turning at a rapid rate. Lillian's case had been heard at the Court of Appeal, where barristers made submissions to bring the latest evidence to light. It was more than enough to cast doubt on the safety of the original conviction. Following that, the Crown Prosecution Service had applied to retry the case. Now Lillian's trial with a new jury was well underway.

The sense of desolation in the old court building was tangible as Amy prepared to recount her ordeal. The worst part about giving evidence was waiting to go in. Not everybody who entered through these doors received justice, and not all perpetrators of crime were punished sufficiently. Amy stood in the room devoted to witness care. Her suit felt itchy and tight; her new pointed leather shoes pinching her toes. She had come here countless times during her role as a police officer, willing her witnesses to turn up. Not all of them did. Now Amy could see why.

Every minute felt like an hour until she was called. By the time it was her turn, her armpits were moist with sweat. She was grateful for her black blazer, which hid the damp patches breaking through.

As she walked through the double doors, she delivered a respectful nod to the judge and inhaled a deep breath of stuffy courtroom air. The room was packed with bodies of every age, shape and size. Every seat was taken with journalists, support groups, Lillian's newfound groupies, and some of the victims' loved ones. They watched Amy intently as she took her place on the stand. From the corner of her eye she could see Lillian's form behind the glass panel on the other side of the room. The cameras panned towards Amy as they waited for her response. This was nothing short of a circus and it was Amy's turn to perform, but she would not give her biological mother the satisfaction of meeting her gaze.

Preliminaries over, the barrister for the defence launched into her spiel. *Batman's granny*, as Sally-Ann had called her the last time they spoke. She wore the same round glasses as yesterday, perched on the end of her nose. Today she looked tired, her skin as grey as the wig on her head. 'Ms Winter.' She spoke with a voice that defied her diminutive stature. 'What was life like in the Grimes household?'

Amy's stature was rigid, her hands clasped before her, as if she were part of a passing-out parade. But the question was too broad to return a satisfactory reply. 'I was four when I was adopted,' she said. 'But I remember the neglect and abuse.'

'Indeed.' Prunella glanced around the room. 'Your statement relays your account in explicit detail. Nobody can deny you and your siblings suffered considerable neglect. But the case of neglect has already been answered.'

No question had been asked of Amy, so she offered no response. She listened as Prunella read from the statement she had provided. Amy confirmed the accounts she had given were true. She knew what was coming: the part of her statement where she detailed Vivian Holden's murder. Just as expected, Prunella read extracts from her account. They detailed how Amy, then named Poppy, had crept down the stairs during a New Year's Eve party and hidden behind the curtains in the living room before falling asleep. How Lillian had come home and found Vivian half-naked on the sofa with Jack, and how Amy had witnessed the violent acts that Lillian had committed against Vivian after Jack went to bed. But Amy would not take herself back to that day. Instead, she sang a Simon and Garfunkel song in her head. It was something she had heard Donovan humming the other day. 'The Sound of Silence' soothed her mind as her alter ego, Poppy Grimes, lay dormant. Prunella turned from the jury to Amy, obviously enjoying her part in proceedings – which were making her a household name. It had all the theatrics of the O.J. Simpson trial, just on a smaller scale.

'In your statement, you have stated that Lillian Grimes is guilty of Vivian Holden's murder. I put it to you that you have, in fact, what is deemed a false memory. It was Jack Grimes, your father, who was responsible for her death.'

Amy's jaw tightened as Prunella referred to Jack as her father. She wanted to scream a retaliation, but forced herself to stay calm. Her hands were rigid as her fingers interlocked, and she knew viewers would be watching her body language for clues. 'My memory of events is crystal clear,' she replied, without inflection in her words. It had come as a blow when Amy's telephone recording with Lillian was ruled inadmissible evidence. The woman had practically admitted to strangling Vivian, but the evidence had been dismissed.

'Hmm.' Prunella tapped her chin. 'Are you sure about that?'

'One hundred per cent.' *Just get on with it*, Amy thought. *Why drag this out?*

'Am I correct in saying that you discovered evidence in your adoptive parents' loft?'

'Yes.'

'You found other things up there too, from your time in the Grimes family home. Is that correct?'

'Yes.' Amy cast her eyes over the gallery, seeking a friendly face. How could Sally-Ann, the sister she had loved so dearly as a child, let her down now? Amy had been adamant that Flora was not to attend. The same went for Donovan and Paddy. She did not want her present relationships to be infected by her past. But Sally-Ann was one of the few people who understood. Amy forced her attention back to Prunella, still keeping her emotions in check. She imagined herself as a statue. A cool slab of rock, unmoving and strong.

'Can you describe what you found?' Prunella continued, relishing the onslaught.

'Some drawings,' Amy replied. 'A dress belonging to Sally-Ann that I'd saved, and a doll.'

'The doll mentioned in your statement, is that correct?'

'I believe so.' Amy took a breath. All of a sudden she felt as if she were being pushed towards a cliff edge. Where was the barrister going with this?

'Either it was or it wasn't, Ms Winter. Was the doll you recovered from the loft the same one you kept from the Grimes family home?'

'As far as I'm aware.' A chill enveloped Amy as the sweat on her back cooled.

'But a few minutes ago, you said your memory was one hundred per cent.'

'It's the same doll,' Amy said firmly.

'What *type* of doll was it?'

Amy paled. She had forced the discrepancy with the doll to the back of her mind – until now. This made her look like a liar. Someone who could not be trusted. She looked Prunella in the eyes, feeling the heat of Lillian's glare. 'It's a Cabbage Patch Kid.'

'Indeed. I have the item here, exhibit AK13. Is this the doll you owned as a child?'

'If it's the same one seized from my adoptive parents' house, then yes, it is.'

'I'd like you to read the section in your statement in which you refer to your childhood doll.' Prunella's eyes were sparkling now, two dark jewels of intent. All traces of tiredness had evaporated from her face. She was going in for the kill.

The barrister for the prosecution jumped to her defence. Despite his youth, he carried an air of confidence. 'Your Honour, is this relevant?'

'I think you'll find it is relevant to Ms Winter's recollection of events,' Prunella replied.

'Continue,' the judge commanded, 'but don't labour it.'

'Very well.' Prunella approached Amy, handing her a copy of her statement. 'Can you read this paragraph of your statement? It pertains to the day Jack and Lillian Grimes were arrested for multiple murders.'

Amy did as instructed. 'DC Griffiths tried to reassure me when I lashed out,' she said. 'I remember holding my favourite Raggedy Ann doll. He said her head would come off if I wasn't careful. He was able to calm me down instantly as I stopped to check if it was OK. That doll had special importance to me, as Sally-Ann once showed me its button heart and told me the doll was alive.' A lump formed in Amy's throat and she struggled to swallow it back.

'Yet it wasn't a Raggedy Ann doll, was it?'

'It seems not,' Amy replied stiffly as a murmur of whispered voices travelled the length of the room.

'And there's little likelihood of there being another doll, is there? Can you tell the court what is drawn beneath the dress of your Cabbage Patch Kid?'

'A h . . . heart.' Amy faltered as the word tripped on her tongue. The re-emergence of her stutter brought a smile to Lillian's face. Amy cursed herself for catching her smug satisfaction. Even now, the woman held power over her. But her ordeal wasn't finished yet.

'What did you say to your adoptive mother, Flora Winter, when you found the doll?' A hint of triumph carried in the defence barrister's words.

Only now did Amy realise that Flora had told the police about that day when she became confused after finding the doll. Nobody else could have known. Amy had no choice but to reply. 'I told her I remembered it as something else.'

'Indeed. You were quite shocked that your memory had betrayed you. Is this correct?'

Dropping her gaze, Amy stared at her feet. 'Yes.' She was quiet now, for fear she might stutter. There was no turning back from this. She thought of all the people watching, doubting her account.

Prunella stabbed the air with her finger in Amy's direction. 'I put it to you, Amy Winter, that none of your memories can be relied upon. Indeed, we are about to hear expert testimony that states it is common for victims of trauma to have false memories as they come to terms with their experiences.'

Amy stared blankly at the woman before her. It did not matter what she said after this; the jury would never take her testimony seriously now. She wished she had never found the doll. Wished she had never gone snooping in her parents' loft. But there was no turning back the clock. With the limited evidence against her, Lillian Grimes may well be freed.

CHAPTER
FORTY-NINE

Bloody vegans, Samuel thought, as he faked interest in his department's presentation. Was it too much to ask for a Saturday off? All he wanted was to sit at home and watch highlights of Lillian Grimes's court case. It wasn't unusual for his team to work over the weekend, but these new clients had insisted on him overseeing this latest campaign. As one of them caught his eye, Samuel forced a smile. Such digital campaigns were Black Media's bread and butter, but as the clients went through their list of demands, he inwardly rolled his eyes. Their hotel chain catered only for vegans and, as they termed it, 'eco-friendly warriors'. *Pass the puke bucket*, Samuel thought, wriggling his toes inside his expensive leather shoes. His smile broadened. 'Our theme is ethical luxury – stay in comfort, without compromising your values,' he said, gesturing to a screen on the wall. 'And Todd here is going to show you a presentation that will blow your minds.'

Samuel sat, arms loosely folded, as the presentation played. They had managed to rope in some mid-list celebrities to give a one-liner about the benefits of veganism – for a price that would be added later to the hotel chain's bill. The celebs would also attend the hotel for a complimentary stay in return for a picture or two. Everyone would be happy, and the proposed campaign, #EthicalLuxury, would go down a storm on social media. At least Todd, with his ethically sourced notebooks and sustainable clothes, was doing a great job of impressing them. If he pulled it off, this would be worth a cool half a million to Black Media.

But Samuel was finding it increasingly difficult to focus on work. There had been a short period of shock when the news about Billy and Naomi broke. But the young go-getters who worked for his company did not dwell for very long. They were all out to make an impression, and several had asked about Naomi's job. They knew the way to the top was to get close to the boss. There had been a few bumps along the way for Samuel, but Billy was well and truly stitched up.

Samuel's mind began to wander as he idled through his memories, each one a precious gift. He thought about his youth. At just sixteen, his gangly body had surged with hormones that drove his moods to despair. Having grown up in a houseful of men, women had held an air of mystery from an early age. His fascination grew when puberty took hold, and his lust for his teacher had hit him with force. A soft sigh escaped his parted lips as he remembered her wispy blonde hair. Every day it had started off tied back in a bun, and by afternoon, half of it had fallen free. He recalled the lilt of her laughter. The smell of her Angel perfume. He had once shoplifted a bottle for himself, so he could spray it on his bedclothes before he went to sleep. Claire was a drug he could not get enough of. But he'd never imagined just how far he could push the boundaries until the night she died.

As the presentation came to an end, Samuel left Todd to seal the deal, returning to his office for a few minutes alone. Rain beaded the windowpanes, the sky so dark that the lights automatically switched on. On the street below, pedestrians ran with newspapers over their heads as they took shelter from the sudden downfall. It reminded him of another rainy night, when he was in his teens. Unlocking his drawer, he took the memento from the past, enjoying the texture of the handkerchief as he held it between finger and thumb. Sighing, he reclined on the sofa, giving the past free rein. The only way to clear his thoughts was to return to when it all began.

◆ ◆ ◆

A storm had taken the sky hostage, enveloping the usually starlit night with grey rolling clouds. In the distance he heard the rumble of thunder, but it could not match the steady beat of his heart pounding in his ears. It felt as if he was electrified. His obsession with Claire had grown to fever pitch. Which was why he had broken things off with Marianne. She was one of the few people who truly understood him, having also come from a one-parent family. But it was only a matter of time before she walked out on him, just as his mother had done. But not Claire. In his fantasy world, she was his, and his alone. Why else did she give him special treatment? She had more than a soft spot for him. Why else was she about to end things with her boyfriend? That day, he had all the proof he needed when he overheard Claire talking in the staffroom to Miss Hart. 'I don't know if we have a future anymore,' she'd said, a mug of tea in her hand. 'He's jealous of anyone and anything that takes me away from him.'

'You need to nip it in the bud,' Miss Hart replied. 'If he's like that now, what will it be like when you're married? Being a teacher is a labour of love. It's more than just a job.'

Which is why he had followed Claire home. The rain was hard and heavy, soaking him to the skin. Claire's dedication to her role was something Sam was willing to take advantage of as he knocked on her door. He had been watching her for weeks, building up the courage to follow through with things.

'Sam, what are you doing here?' Claire's face registered surprise as she wrapped her dressing gown tighter around her. She didn't need to. He had already seen her naked when he peeped through her bathroom window on the nights she forgot to shut it tight.

'Sorry . . . can I come in?' He hooked his thumbs into the corners of his jean pockets, his head hung low.

But Claire did not greet him with the enthusiasm he had hoped for. 'I'm getting ready to go out. Can we do this another time?'

He lifted his face to look at her, perfectly displaying the bruise on his cheek, which he had given himself earlier in the day. It was difficult, overriding his natural instincts as he punched himself.

'Your face . . . what happened to you?' As she opened the door wider, her big blue eyes flashed with concern.

Sam responded with a crooked smile, basking in her warmth. 'I got into a tussle. But it's not what you think. I did it for you.' Reaching into his back pocket, he pulled out the fine gold necklace he had found beneath her desk at school the week before. It had once belonged to her grandmother, but the clasp had become loose and it had slid from her neck. He could have given it to her that day. But he knew her gratitude would increase the longer he made her wait.

'My necklace!' she gasped, ushering him inside. 'Where did you find it?'

Absorbing the pleasure from the touch of her skin, Sam pressed the jewellery into her palm. 'I can't say, only that they put up a fight.' He chuckled good-naturedly. 'They were about to pawn it when I helped them see the error of their ways.' It was his father's terminology, used when he was punishing Sam if he crossed the line. But the look on Claire's face was worth the thumping his dad would give him when he got back. As if reading his mind, Claire's relieved expression turned to one of guilt. 'Let me ring your dad, explain what you've done.'

'Would you?' Sam rubbed his bruise, happy to buy himself some extra time. Anything to make her a little late for the date with her boyfriend tonight. 'Thanks.'

'Come into the kitchen, I'll get you a towel. You're soaked through.'

Sam's heart picked up speed, thudding a warm beat in his chest. Pulling off his sweatshirt, he stood topless in her kitchen, hoping she liked what she saw. She would be overcome with emotion, fall into his arms – because that was the way it happened in the movies, wasn't it? He didn't understand women, and he certainly didn't understand romance, but he had taken a punch for her. Surely her feelings were just as strong as his? Were they bubbling under the surface, harnessed by the constraints of her job? As she arrived back in the room, towel in hand, a crimson blush rose to her face.

'Sam . . . I'm grateful for my necklace.' She looked away, thrusting the towel towards him. 'But you're my student. This isn't appropriate . . .'

Sam opened his mouth to speak, but the words wouldn't come. This was his chance to impress her, to take her breath away. But all he could do was stand there, holding the towel up to his chest. 'Uh . . . sorry. I thought maybe you had a dryer?'

Sighing, Claire took his top. 'OK. It can dry while I ring your dad. Sit down, wait there. I need to get dressed.' She checked her watch, was about to say something but then seemed to think better of it. 'I'll be back in a minute. There's squash in the fridge.'

Squash? Sam frowned. He wasn't a kid. He drank beer with his dad at home, why not here? A little voice piped up inside him, one that told him Claire would never take him seriously. He was kidding himself if he thought any different. This was never going to work.

That night, Claire had thanked him before sending him home.

'You've not been following her, have you?' His dad had glared at him with laser-beam eyes when he walked in the door. Sam's habit of following women developed at an early age. 'I told you. I stopped someone pawning her necklace, then I went round there and gave it back to her.'

But Sam's reassurances failed to lift the frown from his father's face. 'Just you stay out of trouble. We can't afford to have the social services around here again.'

'I'm going to bed,' Sam grumbled. 'I don't feel so good.' But he didn't stay there very long. He waited for his dad's walrus-like snores before creeping out of his bed. Humiliation burned from within. She thought he was just a kid. He would show her how wrong she was.

CHAPTER FIFTY

Amy returned to work without fanfare. The atmosphere in the office carried a sense of urgency, and furtively, she watched Donovan cross the room. It had taken all of her self-control not to call out his name. She headed towards the kitchen, empty mug in hand. Theirs would not be the first clandestine relationship in the station, but Amy had provided enough gossip for now. The clock was ticking down, hope fading with each hour that passed. A hunt was under-way for Naomi, with droves of officers working overtime to search buildings, warehouses and offices. The cost of this investigation was spiralling upwards, and the pressure was on to bring Naomi home. They could not be lured into a false sense of security just because Billy was under lock and key. Specialist officers were inter-rogating his computer, and his flat had been thoroughly searched. Samuel's employees had all been spoken to, and while they had their reservations about Billy, nobody had a bad word to say about their boss. Yet it was at Naomi's flat where they gained the most evidence: a glass of water with Billy's fingerprints and DNA. His hair was found in the bedclothes, then there was the Sugar Babes account set up in his name. Unless . . . Echoes of Lillian's case rose in Amy's mind. Maybe Billy was being set up too. Was that why he had denied being friends with Samuel? Was he scared of him?

'How's it going?' Paddy said, lifting the kettle as it bubbled noisily on the counter. He plopped a teabag into a mug before filling it with boiling water.

'Don't ask,' Amy replied, spooning coffee into her mug. She paused to peek behind him. 'You know, I'm still half expecting the camera crew to come in through the door.' They had wrapped up their filming earlier today after saying goodbye to the team.

'I can't say I miss them,' Paddy sighed. 'At least now we know how Miss Wolfe and her team got the gig.'

'We do?' Amy replied. There wasn't much going on that Paddy didn't know about, and when it came to the camera crew, she was all ears.

Paddy gave her a knowing smile. He had a way of saying things without words. 'She's a bit young for him, mind. I can see why Donovan would want to keep it quiet . . .'

'Keep what quiet?' Amy's spirits plummeted.

'They were seen arriving at work together, looking very pally.' Paddy snorted a laugh. 'Like nobody would notice.'

'Maybe he was giving her a lift.' Amy's spoon clinked against her cup as she stirred.

Paddy gave the milk a quick sniff before pouring some into his mug. 'At that hour of the morning? Do me a favour. Have you seen them together?' He handed the milk to Amy. 'Good luck to him. It's not as if he's married.'

Amy stirred in the milk. 'Indeed. Who are we to judge?' Her comment put an end to the conversation. Paddy had held more than his fair share of secrets over the past year. He walked out of the kitchen, unaware of the bombshell he had left in his wake. Amy swallowed hard. She had been stupid to imagine what she had with Donovan was any more than a fling. But she was an expert at denying her emotions. And she had the case to concentrate on now. The burden of responsibility lay heavy on the shoulders of Amy's team. They desperately needed a win.

◆ ◆ ◆

'Before you ask, I don't want to talk about court.' Sitting in her office, Amy glared at Donovan. Her appearance had been dismal, her humiliation caught on camera for all to see. Then to return to the gossip about Donovan seeing a younger woman . . . She repressed the urge to ask him about it. This was not the time or place.

Donovan seemed weary as he spoke. 'Forget about court. Lillian's had enough of your energy for one day.'

Amy reined in her frustration as she turned her focus to her team. Public opinion may be currently in their favour, but things could change in an instant. She couldn't take her eye off the ball. 'I take it we've had no new leads on Naomi?'

Donovan turned down the police radio resting on his desk. He liked to keep his ear to the ground, and Amy had got used to the constant background chatter from officers as they went from job to job. 'The public appeal reaped a lot of calls,' he said. 'But no solid leads as of yet.'

'And Billy's family? They've been spoken to?' It was one of the many taskings Amy had set for the team.

'His wife's in shock.' Donovan stifled a yawn. 'She said Billy wouldn't hurt a fly. Naomi's sister wants to appeal to Billy directly. I think we'll have more luck with his wife.'

'Or we could put the squeeze on Samuel Black. He knows more than he's letting on.' Samuel had been thoroughly interviewed and there was no justification for his arrest.

'Be careful with him,' Donovan's brow creased in concern. 'As far as the command team are concerned, we've got our suspect.'

Amy picked up a pen and began clicking and unclicking the top. She liked bouncing her thoughts off Donovan. He was a huge improvement on his predecessor, DCI Pike. 'But what if we're wrong?' she replied. 'What if he and Billy are in it together? He could be holding Naomi captive for all we know.'

'Then work with me to make your case watertight.' Donovan's voice trailed behind him as he rose to close the window. 'Black is a member of the Masons, did you know that? And he's not the only one. He's pally with some high-ranking officers in the Met. You'll have to tread carefully if you're going after him.'

'Yeah, I get it. He's a nice guy. But so was Ted Bundy. He was an educated, intelligent family man, just like our Mr Black.' Samuel regularly donated money to charity and played golf with members of the command team.

'I hear you,' Donovan said. 'But be careful. Document everything and don't meet him alone.'

A knock on their office door brought their conversation to a standstill. It was Molly, and she carried an air of excitement as she allowed herself inside. Today she appeared more like her normal self, dressed down in a V-neck sweater and loose-fitting black trousers.

'Sorry, boss, have you got a sec? I did some digging on Samuel Black like you asked. Found out some interesting stuff about his mum.'

Amy had instructed the checks on the basis that Billy and Samuel could have been working together as a team. 'What have you got?' She indicated for Molly to continue.

'When Samuel was four years old, his mum brought him to the train station. They were due to visit her sister in Leicester.' Molly glanced from Donovan to Amy as she relayed the account. 'She bought a ticket, but then five minutes later she calmly dropped her suitcase and bent down and told Samuel to stay where he was . . .' Amy didn't like where this was going. She watched as Molly glanced at the printout in her hand. 'Then she left him on the platform and stepped in front of a freight train. She was gone in the blink of an eye. Samuel suffered from PTSD, although it wasn't diagnosed until years later.'

'Oh God . . . that's awful.' Amy could only imagine the trauma four-year-old Samuel must have endured. It would have taken some serious covering up to keep it out of the public eye.

'Get this . . .' Molly continued. 'His mum fits the description of our victims. Early twenties, blonde hair, blue eyes, average build.'

'Where did you get this info?' Donovan took the paperwork from Molly's outstretched hand.

'A relative spoke to me off the record. Our Mr Black was generous when it came to family donations, but the money was given on one condition – that they don't discuss his past. Same went for what happened at the station. The police have witness accounts, but they've all been buried deep.'

'Hush money,' Donovan said, sliding a scanned image of an old photograph from the paperwork Molly had accumulated. 'Will you look at that . . .' His words faded as he took in the striking similarities between Samuel's mother and the Love Heart Killer's victims to date.

'Apparently, he still keeps mementoes,' Molly continued. 'A lock of his mother's hair and the train ticket from that day.'

'This is good work,' Amy said, her suspicions validated at last.

Molly reciprocated with a smile. 'When he was young he used to follow women around, looking for his mother. Sometimes he'd go up to them and try to hold their hands. It's heartbreaking really. His dad fell apart after his mum died. Little Samuel was left to his own devices a lot of the time.'

'And when he got older? Any insights on his teenage years?' Amy had already guessed the answer. A child growing up with serious abandonment issues fitted the profile of many world-famous serial killers. Their chaotic teenage years were a reflection of their disturbed minds.

'He was a bit of a scallywag before he met his wife, Marianne. They said she gave him focus. He turned things around.'

Just a scallywag? Amy thought. She had expected worse than that. Her hand fell to the silver necklace that Donovan had fastened this morning. He had helped her through so much. Had Marianne been Samuel's life raft in the storm?

'Does this relative think he's involved in the murders?' Donovan asked, still scanning the page.

'They wouldn't say it outright . . .' Molly replied. 'But I could tell they had their suspicions. They said they knew Billy back then. They didn't think he had it in him.'

'But Samuel did?'

Molly shrugged. 'That's as much as I could get out of them. I mean, we've got Billy's confession and forensics are strong but . . . I've interviewed him for hours. I don't think he knows where Naomi is.'

'Samuel's the brains behind this operation. Billy was his accomplice,' Amy interjected. But still, it didn't sound right. Why didn't Billy dob him in?

'OK, thanks, Molly.' Donovan pressed the door handle as he showed the young detective out. 'Can you do me a favour? Keep this to yourself until I run it by the command team.'

'Am I hearing right?' Amy glared at him as Molly left. 'Why are you covering this up?'

'I'm not.' Donovan's face clouded over. 'But we can't go barrelling in. We need to build a case against this guy. I'll speak to the command team about organising surveillance.'

'They won't agree to that.' Amy's face creased in a frown. 'And if they do, the paperwork will take forever to clear. Naomi needs our help *now*. Samuel Black knows where she is.'

'You think I don't know that?' Donovan's voice rose a notch as he held the paperwork aloft. 'You don't think I'd like to bring that fucker in here and throttle the truth out of him?'

'Yes, but—' Amy drove her fingers through her hair.

'How many cases fail at court because of botched investigations?' Donovan interrupted. 'How many offenders walk away with a smile on their face? I'll get you your surveillance. It'll take twenty-four hours max. Promise me. You'll sit on this until then?'

Reluctantly, Amy nodded. But after what she had heard, she owed Donovan nothing, and her fingers were crossed behind her back. Her morning in court had taught her that justice didn't always prevail. She was doing this her way. She was bringing Naomi home alive – whatever the cost.

CHAPTER
FIFTY-ONE

The National Portrait Gallery could easily have become the setting for the Love Heart Killer's next victim, had security not been so tight. The building was steeped in history, much of its artwork echoes of the past. You would not find any of Black Media's advertising campaigns here. It seemed a fitting place for Amy to meet her next contact. As she saw it, Mama Danielle was the only person who understood the situation. Donovan was doing his best, but he wasn't prepared to break with protocol – no matter the consequences.

She smiled an acknowledgement as Mama Danielle fell into step next to her. Her hair was short and spiked, her red lipstick dramatic against her clothes. Dressed in white, she seemed like an earthly guardian angel, watching over her girls. It might seem fitting, were she not making so much money from their nocturnal activities.

'Thanks for calling me.' Amy was relieved to be in the company of someone who understood. 'I'd like us to work together. Not just on this case, but future cases too.'

'I never saw myself as a snitch,' Mama Danielle mused, as they stood before a portrait of King Henry VIII. 'But I like you. You've been around the block. And I mean life experience, before you get all offended.'

'Ah.' Amy gave her a furtive glance. 'You've done your homework.'

'I like to know who I'm dealing with. Especially when we can be of mutual benefit.'

'Agreed,' Amy said, kind of liking this new side of herself. Why not? With the camera crews bigging her up as some sort of psychopath-whisperer, and the publicity surrounding her relationship to Lillian, the pressure to solve cases was stronger than ever. She needed help wherever she could get it, and it felt good to meet people outside her usual circles. She knew Flora would frown upon such acquaintances. *There but for the grace of God go I*, Amy thought.

'Have you got something for me?' Amy felt a twinge of excitement as she caught the twinkle in Mama Danielle's eye.

Responding with a nod, Danielle guided Amy away from a group of children to a quieter part of the museum, featuring contemporary art. 'It's Naomi,' she whispered, as they stood in a corner of the room. 'She used to be a Sugar Babe.'

Amy's jaw became slack as she registered the news. She stared at Mama Danielle for confirmation. 'No. We carried out checks. She's clean-cut.' She rubbed the back of her neck, conscious of her audience. 'Not that the other girls weren't—'

'It's OK, I get your meaning. She has money, a good job and family commitments. She's not the type. But things were different a few years ago, when she was living on her own. She used the site to make ends meet.' Mama Danielle glanced from left to right before continuing. 'I barely recognised the girl. She's lost a hell of a lot of weight. I reckon she's had a nose job and a boob reduction too. She quit the site when she moved in with her mom two years ago.'

'The same time she got the job with Black Media.' Amy caught her breath as another piece of the investigation slid into place. Despite their police checks, there was no way to recover deleted Sugar Babes accounts. Apart from schoolteacher Claire, all three victims were linked to both the site and Black Media in some way. Samuel must have met Naomi through Sugar Babes. But why employ her? How many Sugar Babes were acquaintances of his? 'So, what next?' Amy watched Danielle slide her phone from her Prada bag.

'I've narrowed it down to one guy who used all three girls. I've read through all the messages and I reckon it's him.'

'I know.' Amy felt a pang of disappointment. 'William Picton. We've got him in custody.' She watched as tourists took selfies in front of famous portraits. People were happy and smiling, oblivious to their conversation, which had taken a dark turn.

'It can't be him,' Mama Danielle whispered as the tourists passed. 'Not unless he's got a phone on the inside.'

'You mean he's still online?' Amy's pulse beat a little quicker at the news. Danielle gave Amy a dry smile as she opened up her Sugar Babes account. 'Honey, not only is he online, he wants to meet you tonight. What do ya want me to do?'

CHAPTER
FIFTY-TWO

'Boss, hang on!' Donovan turned towards the voice calling his name. Grappling with his paperwork, he tried to open his car door. The station car park was full today, and he struggled to slide through the gap between his car and the next.

'Here, let me get that for you.' Trotting towards him, Amy grabbed a blue folder from under his elbow as it began to slide from his grip. 'Where are you off to?'

'HQ. I told you I'd get your surveillance, didn't I?' But the look on Amy's face relayed something was wrong. 'What is it?' He placed his paperwork on the back seat. She had been in a bad mood since her court appearance this morning and now her hesitancy was worrying him. 'Get in.' He gestured towards the car. 'I can spare you a few minutes before I go.'

The car felt like an ice box, chilled from the wintry weather that showed little sign of letting up. Donovan started the engine, activating the heater, which began clearing the condensation from the windows.

Today had been another busy day, and he'd had little time to think of his night with Amy as he was buried under paperwork. Last night had been mind-blowing, and it wasn't just the sex. He had a connection with Amy that could not be denied. His predecessor, DCI Pike, had spared Amy the duller side of the job, but Donovan had more to offer than administration and was feeling increasingly frustrated by it all. 'What's up?' He turned to face her.

Amy's face was animated, her cheeks flushed pink from running to catch him. 'I've been talking to Mama Danielle.' She paused for breath. 'She believes our sugar daddy is still using his account.'

Donovan stared at Amy as the implications of her words hit home. 'Have we proof? Is he online now?'

'He's deleting his sent messages. He thinks he's undetectable. But we have her word.'

'So she's spoken to him?' Donovan asked. This changed everything.

Amy nodded in response. She pulled the lapels of her jacket together. 'It's freezing in here.'

'Will Danielle give us a statement?' Donovan asked, activating the heated seats.

'Well, no, but . . .'

Donovan groaned. He knew it was too good to be true. 'So if she won't give us a statement, then all we have is an intelligence report.'

'We could have a date,' Amy blurted. 'Or rather, I could. She's ready to set it up.'

Donovan couldn't believe what he was hearing, after everything he had said. 'Let me get this straight. You want to set up a honeytrap with the same person who's been using the Sugar Babes account to meet our victims?'

Amy nodded, her face animated. 'It's Samuel Black. I know it.'

But Donovan didn't share her enthusiasm. She was raring to go, and sense was taking a back seat. 'Then all the more reason to tread carefully. You've not arranged to meet him, have you?'

'No.' Amy's gaze did not waver, but he had been taken in by her lies before. He could not risk any more reckless behaviour. Not when they were on the cusp of getting surveillance approved.

He pointed to the pile of paperwork on the back seat. 'Do you know how much work is involved in getting surveillance? Are you aware of the implications when things go wrong?'

Amy scowled. 'Of course I am. I wouldn't be a DI if I wasn't.'

'Then tell me,' Donovan said. 'I want to know.'

'Don't be silly.' Nervous laughter left Amy's lips. 'I'm not going through all that.'

Raindrops speckled Donovan's windscreen, casting the station car park in a blur of grey. 'So you know our request for covert surveillance has to be proportionate, lawful and ethical.'

'I know all about RIPA . . .' Amy was referring to the regulation of investigatory powers – the legal framework involved.

'That's comforting, because I thought you'd completely side-stepped it,' Donovan replied. 'So you understand collateral intrusion? The right to a private life? What about the investigatory powers tribunal? You know, the guys who chew your arse off if you get it wrong?'

'And what about Naomi?' Amy snapped. 'How are we meant to do our jobs if we're buried in paperwork?'

'How can we not be?' Donovan replied. 'Say you go galloping off without authorisation and it all goes wrong? That's the end of the team. For the sake of one person, you've cut the lifeline for all future victims. Is that what you want?'

'All right!' Amy blurted. 'You told me to be upfront. I came to you, just as you asked.'

Donovan looked into the same grey eyes that had captivated him the night before. Amy acted as if she were a cat with nine lives, and seemed oblivious to the danger she was putting herself and the team in. But he wasn't, and he couldn't allow it – even if it meant pissing her off. 'I'm grateful that you came to me. But now you can go home. You're off the case.'

'You what?' Amy shifted in her seat, rigid with annoyance.

'You what, *sir*,' Donovan corrected. 'I'm authorising three days' holiday. I'm saving you from yourself.'

'You're thinking of yourself, more like . . . *sir*,' Amy rebutted. 'And it wouldn't be the first time—'

'Maybe I am,' Donovan interrupted. 'Because I don't want to end up like Pike. Her forced early retirement was down to you. Either we work together or not at all.' It was easier for Donovan to blame the job than own up to how protective he felt over her and the team. A few days away from the case might make her see sense.

'The super's not going to like this.' Amy fidgeted in her seat. She was grasping at straws.

'Superintendent Jones has already approved it. Anything to keep you out of trouble until this case is wrapped up.' That was not strictly true, but Jones had given Donovan his blessing when it came to the well-being of their team.

'Do you know how disrespectful you're being, treating me like the little woman who has to be kept under control? Would you speak to Paddy like this, or Steve?'

'Damn right I would,' Donovan said, insulted by her remark. His views were far from sexist. They could make a powerful team if they could work the system to their mutual benefit.

'Fine.' Amy gritted her teeth as she pulled on the car door handle. 'But if Naomi turns up dead, that's down to you.'

'Amy, wait!' Donovan said, as a blast of cold air infiltrated the car. As she turned to face him, he was chilled by the anger burning in her eyes. He had made the right decision. He sighed. 'Give me your harness. I'll lock it away safely for you.' She handed over her harness, which held her CS gas, handcuffs and baton. The look on her face was thunderous. But he couldn't risk her going it alone, not like this.

CHAPTER
FIFTY-THREE

Amy fixed the clasp of her fitted navy dress before checking her reflection in the mirror. These days, she barely recognised herself anymore. Her physical features were tainted by her resemblance to Lillian, her actions so out of character from her old self. She had gone from being supremely in control to veering towards self-destruct. But there was a reason behind it. One that was difficult to face. Going it alone would make it easier for her team if things went wrong. They would carry on without her. Too much money had been invested for them to be shut down. The fact she had given this some thought told her all she needed to know. Deep down, she didn't feel worthy of her job. She was living a lie, masquerading as a police officer, with the blood of serial killers running through her veins. Her fledgling relationship with Donovan had shone a light on her failings. He was an exemplary officer, but she had made a mistake by letting him in. Now he couldn't get shot of her quickly enough. If she was going to be kicked off the team, then some good would come of it first.

Nervousness twisted her insides into knots, but at least her reflection gave nothing away. Regardless of her bloodlines, she appeared cool and serene, ready to take on the world. Her throat clicked as she swallowed. Her adrenaline was flowing, her body preparing for battle. But what lay ahead?

Her thoughts returned to Donovan as she made the taxi journey to the restaurant where she had agreed to meet her Sugar Babes date. Why had he slept with her if he was seeing Ginny as well? Was it morbid curiosity, or sympathy? Was that all she meant to him? She forced the thought away as her taxi came to a halt.

It was Saturday night, and the place was crammed with revellers enjoying the weekend. Street vendors weaved around the tables selling roses, even though Valentine's Day was still a week away. 'No thanks,' Amy said as one of them approached her.

After an hour of sitting alone, she decided to call it a night. As she exited the restaurant, she didn't see the car pulling up alongside her until the driver slid the window down.

'Ms Winter, can I offer you a lift?'

She recognised the voice the moment the man said her name. How clever of him. By bumping into her outside, he was not implicated in the date. 'Mr Black, we meet again.' Amy approached the open window. They were both playing games tonight and she had a feeling the fun didn't end here. But the safety of a public place would be very far behind her if she accepted his invitation and got in the car.

'I was supposed to meet a client for dinner, but he rang to say he couldn't make it. Looks like you've been stood up too.' He leaned his elbow on the open window. 'I like the hair, by the way, it suits you. Nice to see you looking more relaxed.'

Amy forced a smile as he remarked on her straightened hair. She was pretty sure her male colleagues didn't have to put up with comments on their hair or clothes. 'You know what they say, a change is as good as a rest.'

'Why don't you get in?' His words were firmer this time, insistent. 'We have unfinished business, wouldn't you say? I won't keep you long.'

Amy hesitated, her fingers gripping the lip of her handbag. She knew how expertly the Love Heart Killer overpowered his victims, using drugs to make them comply.

Samuel's smile was rigid as he awaited her response. 'I want to show you something. But it's a time-limited offer. I'm flying to the Far East tomorrow. You were lucky to catch me tonight.'

Amy leaned into the car window, catching the scent of his expensive cologne. 'You wouldn't be propositioning me, now would you, Mr Black? Because last time I checked, you were a married man.'

'A very happily married man,' Samuel added with a grin. 'It's work, not pleasure. But if you'd rather not . . .' He checked his rear-view mirror as a car flashed him from behind. Central London was not a place you could park in for very long.

The hairs prickled on the back of Amy's neck. She shouldn't get in the car. But he was going away tomorrow, God only knew for how long. This could be her last chance to find Naomi alive. She justified her actions as her mind played tug of war. She wasn't like the other victims. She was prepared. There was no way that Samuel would hurt her. She didn't fit the profile and it was too big a risk for him. She glanced around for CCTV, but Samuel was too clever for that. He had picked her up in a blind spot. He had been waiting outside all along.

Opening the door, she slid on to the leather seat, her instinct to help Naomi overriding her concerns.

'Where are we going?' Amy stiffened as he pulled away from the kerb.

'It's no fun if I tell you.' His fingers tightening around the steering wheel, Samuel stared straight ahead. 'Don't worry, I'm not going to hurt you – not in a million years.'

'Why on earth would I think you'd hurt me?' Amy replied, injecting as much confidence as she could into her voice.

'Oh come on, we both know our meeting was no coincidence. I want to run a project of mine past you. Something I think you'd like. But I can't do it under surveillance.'

'There's no surveillance,' Amy replied haughtily. 'Why, is there something you'd like to get off your chest?'

'You could say that.' Samuel's smile faded. 'But forgive me if I don't take you at your word.'

As the car pulled up at the traffic lights, Samuel turned to face her. 'The doors aren't locked. You can walk away any time you want.' But they both knew the temptation would be too much for her to resist. She watched as he negotiated traffic, driving deep into the night. It was just the two of them now, as he had obviously wanted. And nobody knew where she was.

CHAPTER
FIFTY-FOUR

Blinking away her tears, Marianne drove a safe distance behind her husband. He was too preoccupied with the woman in his company to notice her following behind. So much for his meeting with clients. Her fingers tightened over the steering wheel as she imagined what he and Amy Winter were about to do. But why had he waited outside the restaurant before picking her up on the street?

'Because she's a common whore . . .' The words were sharp with hatred as Marianne answered the question aloud. *But it doesn't make sense*, the rational part of her brain thought. *None of this does.* These days, very little made sense for Marianne. Samuel was too preoccupied with work to notice she was falling apart. She tried to quieten her thoughts and concentrate on the road. But it all came back to one thing. Was Amy Winter *really* investigating the Love Heart Killer, or was it all a front?

For too long, Marianne had told herself that there was no connection between Claire and the present-day victims. How could there be, when they were decades apart? Unless . . . Had something flicked a switch in the killer's mind? Sparked something that had lain dormant all these years? Her stomach clenched as she remembered that night. The memories were old now, stored away behind closed doors in the recesses of her mind.

As a teen, she'd had her suspicions about Claire for some time. It was obvious her boyfriend was infatuated. It was 'Claire this' and 'Claire that'. She was all he could talk about. That night when he ended their relationship, she'd known exactly why. 'It's so you can be with her,' she'd screamed. 'Isn't it? You want her more than me!'

Sam's face had flushed, as it always did when he lied. It was a trait he had rid himself of as he left his youth, but that night it told her all she needed to know.

'It's not working, babe,' he'd replied. 'That's all.' His eyes were dark and conflicted, the pain etched on his face showing he still cared.

Hot tears streaming down her cheeks, Marianne had galloped down his stairs, rattling the front door on its hinges as she slammed it shut behind her. A speckle of rain had hit her face as she watched Sam close his window blinds. That's when she decided to hang around. She knew he would go to her soon enough.

The old treehouse in the garden gave a perfect viewpoint of Sam's bedroom window. Marianne had wrinkled her nose as the stench of dry rot rose, flapping away the cobweb brushing against her cheek. She even ignored the stack of porn magazines in the corner next to a crumpled Coke can. Her face knotted in determination, she'd sat cross-legged on the floor, her fists buried in her denim jacket pockets as she kept watch. Just ten minutes after the lights went out in the Black household, Sam edged out of his bedroom, quietly shimmying down the metal drainpipe. The rain had picked up, sounding like hard nails hammering against the roof of the treehouse. Marianne's lips thinned into a white line. Even the rain could not stop Samuel as he proceeded to get soaked through.

Rooting in her rucksack, Marianne pulled out an umbrella, remembering how Sam used to tease her about the ladybird motifs. She followed him down the path, pouting as she observed his cocksure walk. *Nobody* dumped her, and certainly not for a schoolteacher with a boyfriend of her own. Following in his muddy footsteps, she took the path to Claire's house. Such was their tight-knit community that everyone knew where everyone else lived.

Her stomach churned with disgust with every step she took. Sam was her world, and now he was going to *her*. Saliva pooled in her mouth as a wave of nausea overcame her. Shaking, she edged closer to Claire's house, just in time to hear Claire ask Sam in. As she approached the cracked kitchen window, white-hot anger burned inside her. Sam was standing there, topless, wearing a lopsided grin. He didn't waste any time.

Standing in the shadows, she planned her confrontation. But yet her sensible side whispered in her thoughts. What if she was wrong? What if it was all one-sided? She watched Claire throw him a towel before looking away. But it was easier to believe Claire had lured him in, rather than face up to the fact that Sam didn't love her anymore. *It has to be her fault. She's his teacher*, Marianne seethed. *She encouraged him.* As she watched Claire leave, Marianne prepared to follow. It was time to have it out with her.

Yet silently, Marianne pursued her, saying nothing as she entered the pub. As Claire went to her boyfriend, Marianne bought herself a glass of juice, then parked herself in the next booth, so she and Claire were practically back to back. But Claire was too busy apologising to her boyfriend to notice her. 'Hey, Michael, sorry I'm late,' she gasped, flicking her wet hair as she pulled off her jacket. 'I was held up at Mum's.'

'Are you sure about that?' Michael's words were low thunder as Claire took a seat next to him. 'Because I rang your mum and she's not seen you all day.'

'What? You're checking up on me now, are you?'

'Sounds like I'm justified. Where were you, Claire?'

Marianne's fingers tensed around her glass. She both dreaded and needed the answer, and her breath locked in her throat as she awaited a response.

'I had a visitor,' Claire replied in a small voice. 'Just some kid from school. I couldn't turn him away.' Silence fell. The slam of an empty glass as it hit the table. 'I need another drink,' Michael eventually said.

'And me,' Claire replied. 'Make it a double.' The evening progressed into small talk, with Claire asking Michael about his work. But for every drink Michael downed, Claire matched him with a double, and they were soon both the worse for wear.

'It was that lad again, wasn't it?' The question came through Michael's gritted teeth as the conversation took a sudden turn. 'The one who's been bugging you? Who is he? I'll sort him out.'

A beat passed between them before Claire replied. 'He needs my help. He's got no one else. I can't turn him away.'

He has no one else? Marianne chewed on her thumbnail. *The cheek of it.*

'Are you fucking him?' Michael's words were loud and abrasive, bringing the pub to a standstill. Patrons at the bar fell silent. It felt like the world was listening in on the argument, which had been spoken in harsh whispers up until now.

'What . . . ?' Claire replied on the inhale. 'I can't believe you just said that!'

'What else am I supposed to think? You stand me up on our anniversary, then lie to me about where you've been.'

'Our anniversary . . .' Claire replied. 'Oh babe, I'm sorry. I forgot.'

'Only cos you had something more important on the go. Roll out from under him, did you, then come to me for seconds?'

'You're disgusting.' Claire's voice rose an octave as she sprang from her chair. 'Who do you think you are, speaking to me like that?' Heads turned in her direction as she grabbed her bag from the floor.

'Claire, wait . . .' Michael's words were tinged with a regret that came far too late.

'Go to hell!' she shouted, tugging on her coat and making for the door.

But Marianne didn't believe her outburst, because everything suddenly made sense. If Claire was sleeping with a pupil, she had a hell of a lot to lose. That's why she'd made such a big fuss of things. Michael was right. She had virtually rolled out from beneath Sam to go to him.

Marianne's thoughts had consumed her as she'd wandered the streets in the rain that night. It wasn't as if anyone would miss her. Both from one-parent families, she and Sam were kindred souls – at least, until Claire had turned his head.

Now, Marianne eased her foot from the accelerator as the past continued to rear its ugly head. Dark and foreboding, a sense of dread loomed. History was repeating itself as she followed her husband all over again. She thought of Claire, and of how things had ended between them. If only she had left things alone. She should never have followed her home.

CHAPTER
FIFTY-FIVE

Storm clouds loomed in the night sky, an ominous backdrop to the high-rise building ahead. Amy's mind raced as she hunched her shoulders against the rain. The block of flats was located in Whitechapel, not far from where she had once lived. Samuel had brought her here on the condition that she hand over her phone. Her only line of defence was her wits – and her fists. But she was accompanying him of her own free will – so far.

'It's not that I don't trust you,' Samuel chuckled. 'Aw, who am I kidding, of course I don't trust you! But that makes this exciting. I'm letting you in on a secret, and it will blow your mind.'

Amy trotted along beside him, taking two steps for each of his long strides. She was breaking all her own rules by going it alone. But Samuel would be out of the country by the time the surveillance came through. If she could pinpoint Naomi's location, then she could enlist help. But the tower block was huge. It would take them forever to search each flat. She needed more. 'Where are we going?' she said, as they stepped out of the lift on to the fifth floor. 'Is Naomi here?'

'Patience.' Samuel confidently moved to one side to allow a young mum with a buggy to go past. He was edgy but excited. Whatever was ahead of them, he was getting off on it. Shoving his hand in his trouser pocket, Samuel pulled out a set of keys. 'In here,' he said, glancing left and right before pushing the key into the lock. The corridor walls seemed to close in around them as Samuel's lips stretched into a creepy smile. A sense of trepidation made Amy turn cold. She knew she should run away and call for help, but her feet were rooted to the floor. 'Go,' Samuel whispered in her ear. 'If that's what you want. But I won't be here when you get back . . .' His eyes roamed her face. 'And neither will what's behind that door.'

Flashing him a look of defiance, Amy stepped inside. She had already planned her escape. A well-timed kick to the groin would disarm Samuel long enough to grab his keys and run. She could activate the fire alarm in the hall, flooding the corridors with people, before getting to a phone. She had crossed procedural lines, but surely it was worth it to find Naomi alive? She found herself in a small hallway, dotted with closed doors. A single light bulb flickered as she stood on the cracked linoleum floor. Inhaling deeply through her nostrils, Amy gauged her surroundings in the dim light. There was no dead body smell here, but there was something else on the periphery. Bleach, possibly. Or some kind of cleaning fluid. A flash of memory: Jack Grimes hanging air fresheners from the ceiling of her childhood home.

Samuel glanced at the door to the right before turning to Amy. 'I need to check you for a wire before I can let you in.'

'A wire?' Amy tried to laugh it off. 'You've been watching too many cop programmes.'

'Says the TV celebrity.' Samuel's dark eyes shone with admiration. 'Exceptional exposure, isn't it? It must be nice to be recognised for your work.' He raised his hand in the air, pointing at imaginary headlines. 'The psychopath-whisperer does it again.'

Monitoring his every movement, Amy tried to keep one step ahead. 'Is that why you brought me here? To talk about the case?'

'Enough with the questions.' Samuel's tone grew serious. 'Unzip your dress and turn around. Don't worry, I won't touch you. It's just so we can keep this conversation nice and private.'

'Damn right you won't touch me.' Reaching around, Amy did as instructed, her eyes firmly on Samuel. If it were anyone else she would have told them to go to hell, but the stakes were too high. Satisfied she wasn't wearing a recording device, he signalled for her to zip her dress back up. Goosebumps had risen on her flesh. Her muscles were tensed, ready to lash out at a second's notice. She did not trust him one iota.

'Good.' He clapped his hands together, making Amy jolt. 'Now we can get to the fun part.'

'And that would be?'

Samuel's keys jingled as he unlocked the door on the right. 'Your reward, of course.'

'Wait.' Amy raised a hand. 'If this is you making a pass, it's not happening. I have a boyfriend.'

'Your DCI. Yes, I know.' Samuel's fingers gripped the door handle. 'He's not good enough for you.'

Amy was stunned to know that Samuel had been stalking her too.

'He wouldn't do this for you, would he?' Samuel opened the door and waved her inside. Biting her lip, Amy followed him in. She stared at her surroundings, dread rising in her gut. Plastic sheeting lined every wall in the room. Behind it was a wad of padding – home-made soundproofing. Even the floor and the ceiling had a coating of thin blue plastic sheeting attached. A wire hung down, with what must have been a 100-watt light bulb. But Amy didn't focus on that for long. Her gaze was on the woman lying on a metal bed.

'Isn't she glorious? I brought her here for you.' Samuel's voice was animated now, his eyes wide as he took in Naomi's form. Amy had seen that look before. He was on a high.

Amy glared in horror as he sought her approval. It was as if he were a cat, bringing home a mouse. Billy had taken the credit for his actions and now Samuel wanted a slice of the glory. Her shoes rustling on the sheeting, Amy rushed to Naomi's side. The mattress was old, the stale smell of urine rising from the sheets. Naomi was propped up on an array of dirty pillows, her blonde hair splayed around her face. At least she was dressed, in a blouse and skirt. A small breath of relief escaped Amy's lips. She was alive. 'Naomi.' Amy shook her shoulder. Her flesh was cold, her eyes rolling to the back of her head.

Amy could feel Samuel's eyes burning into the back of her neck. She turned to face him. 'Samuel Black, you are under arrest on suspicion of the murder of Stacey Piper, the attempted murder of Erin Johnson and the kidnapping of Naomi Blunt.' She knew he may have murdered Naomi's mother, but she couldn't bear for Naomi to find out in such a way.

'Don't forget her mum . . .' Samuel's mouth curled into a smile. 'I presume that's who the old bag was. She did me a favour. Dropped dead all by herself.' Samuel's smile did not falter as he appeared to read Amy's mind. He gestured towards Naomi. 'She can't hear you, not properly. She's wayyy out of it. I didn't think you'd want to fight her, not for your first time.'

Amy frowned as she caught the manic glint in his eyes. 'First time for what?' Samuel had been fascinated by her background. Perhaps it was safer to play up to his perception of her right now.

'We both know who you are. You just need a little push in the right direction . . .' Samuel's breath was heavy as he slid his hand into the folds of the mattress. A thin sheen of sweat coated his brow as he pulled out a carving knife.

'I'm not my mother. I'm a police officer . . .' Amy's gaze locked on to the knife.

'Same dog, different fleas.' Samuel smiled. 'Come on . . . I've done all the groundwork by getting her here. Say you'll finish her . . . Say you want to.'

'Give it to me, then.' Amy's palm was open as she asked for the weapon. Her heart thrumming, she prepared to defend Naomi with her life.

But Samuel stood, unconvinced. Gritting her teeth, Amy lunged for the knife.

A sudden flare of pain exploded as Samuel drew back his fist and punched Amy in the gut. Wheezing, she gasped for breath, her knees weak from the impact. Before she could move another inch, Samuel's knuckles slammed against her face. Her eyes watered as he closed in. Samuel had taken her off guard by feigning admiration, and now she could barely draw breath. Holding her aching jaw, Amy tried to regain her balance, only to be met with a knee in the stomach. Groaning, she climbed to her feet, willing her breath to come. Tears streamed down her face.

'I saw a little bit of fight in your eyes,' Samuel said. 'You've been winded, no damage done.'

Dragging in thin breaths, Amy clawed at the bedclothes as she tried to stand.

As he grabbed her hair, Samuel forced Amy on to the bed, his breath warm on her face. 'Pick up that pillow and smother her. I'll kill you if you don't.'

Amy tried to focus as a wave of nausea overtook the pain. Samuel didn't want to kill Naomi, he wanted Amy to finish her off. She tuned back into his narrative as he whispered in her ear.

'You've nothing to feel guilty about. All those doubts and recriminations, I've taken them away.' Another sharp tug on her hair as he pushed her towards Naomi. 'Kill her, or I'll gut you both.'

Amy gritted her teeth as Samuel pressed the blade to her throat. She knew too much. There was no way he would let her go now – not unless she did as he said. Was this what her life was leading up to? Perhaps Lillian was right, she *was* destined to be a killer – just like her. A sting of pain sharpened Amy's senses as Samuel tightened the blade against her throat. A warm trickle of blood made a path down her neck, blooming red flowery patterns on the sheets. She was on all fours now, desperate to keep her balance as Samuel forced her on to Naomi. Lillian would have carried out his instructions. Had she hesitated with her first kill?

'Do it!' Samuel growled. Amy felt his growing excitement as he pressed himself against her. Her fingers gripped the pillow. She had no choice.

CHAPTER
FIFTY-SIX

As Samuel pushed the blade against Amy's throat, he knew there was no turning back. He groaned in satisfaction as he felt her relent, watched her fingers wrap around the pillow as she picked it up.

He remembered when he'd found Naomi on the Sugar Babes app. He had been weak back then, too scared to hurt her for fear of repercussions. But having her in his employment brought him that bit closer to making fantasy a reality. Naomi was special enough to share, and Amy would thank him in time. Then he could tell her how it all began. Memories of the past were never far away.

He used to love being in Claire's room. There were no phone selfies back then. Every moment of her life was reflected back in the photos pinned to her bedroom wall. He had broken in after she'd left for the pub that night. As the rain clouds parted, the light of the full moon flooded the room. He glanced at the clothes hanging on an exercise bike. Took in the beaded necklaces snaking across her crowded dressing table. Bottles of perfume sat with lost lids, the boxes discarded on the floor. He paused to spray a puff of scent, inhaling deeply as he drew it in. Delving his hands into her drawers, he ran his fingers through her underwear, bringing a pair of pink lacy knickers to his face. He stuffed them in his pocket as a key scratched in the front door. His heart stalled. She was back early. He could leave . . . or he could spend more time with her.

What would it be like, to hear her fall asleep? To spend the night with his love. His mind made up, he darted beneath her double bed, disturbing the dust bunnies beneath. Holding his sneeze, he listened as Claire stumbled into the room. She kicked off her shoes, swaying on her feet. She seemed drunk, but thankfully alone. He watched, entranced, as she stepped out of the puddle of clothes that fell on the floor. The bed bounced beneath her weight as she threw herself on to it, and within minutes her breathing became snores. Sam absorbed the moment, raising his hand to touch the mattress from beneath the bed. Closing his eyes, he matched his breathing with hers. But their moment of intimacy evaporated as the bedroom window opened with a creak.

A pair of black Dr. Martens touched the floor. Sam's heart stalled as an intruder entered the room. Shock pervaded his system. How could two people invade Claire's home in the same night? As the stranger approached the bed, fear coursed through Sam like iced water in his veins. Whatever happened now, he had to stay put. He could not risk getting caught. What if it was her boyfriend, playing some kind of kinky game? Sam's Adam's apple bobbed as he struggled to swallow. His heart felt like it had crawled up into his throat as the intruder's feet came to the side of the bed. But when the intruder spoke, everything changed.

'Hey, cradle-snatcher, wake up!' It was Marianne, sounding furious. Claire's scream was muffled in an instant. 'Shut it or I'll cut you,' Marianne growled.

Sam's world tilted as he felt the heat of Marianne's anger. He had no idea she cared that much for him. The bed rocked from the weight of them both as Marianne climbed on, and Sam's breath grew heavy as he imagined them both on top of him. He had never felt so turned on. 'Consider this a warning,' Marianne said. 'Stay away from Sam Black, or I'll tell everyone what you've been up to.'

Sam drove his hand inside his jeans. The heat of the moment made the room feel electrically charged. A groan escaped his lips, but the women above him did not hear over the sound of Claire's muffled whimpers. What was Marianne doing? The thought of her holding a knife to Claire brought him to the edge. Above him, the bed creaked as the two women fought. Ripples of ecstasy ran through his body as he shuddered to a climax beneath them. He had never felt anything like it in his life.

'Stop it! Stop it or I'll—' But Marianne's words were cut short as a knife skittered across the floor. A sudden struggle. A thump of flesh against metal headboard, then . . . eerie quiet. Two sets of heavy breaths were now only one. 'No.' The anger in Marianne's voice was replaced by undiluted fear. 'No, no, no.' A shake of the mattress. A slap of contact; a palm against flesh. 'Claire. Wake up, Claire. Wake up!' But there was no response.

Taking Claire's underwear from his pocket, Sam cleaned himself up. He shoved it back in his jacket, his breath shallow as all became still. The brief flash of headlights through the window made him freeze as a car drove past. What had just happened above him? With relief, he watched Marianne's Dr. Martens make contact with the floor. Her breath was trembling in short and staggered intakes. She stood, unmoving for seconds, and Sam could barely breathe either. What if she felt his presence? What if she looked under the bed?

Slowly, she crept around the room, before exiting the way she came. Sam waited a few minutes before rolling out, his heart hammering in his chest. Every nerve ending tingled as he stared at Claire, lying on bloodstained sheets. Had Marianne murdered her? For him? Claire's hair was matted, blood infiltrating her blonde strands. A small jagged slash was etched on her chest where Marianne had pressed the knife into her. Sam froze as a soft gurgle left the back of Claire's throat, and he pulled out the balled-up handkerchief that Marianne had shoved into her mouth. She was still alive. Sam's frown deepened. And therein lay the problem.

Marianne could go to prison. He should never have ended things with her. His legs trembled from the force of emotions welling up inside him. Nobody needed to know they were here. Taking a pillow from the floor, Sam approached Claire's body, excitement building once again. Fear and lust made for a heady cocktail as he exerted control over her. Marianne was the one woman in his life who would never desert him. He wouldn't allow his girlfriend to go down for this. He glared at Claire's bloodstained face before pressing down on the pillow with every ounce of his strength. He felt powerful. He felt like a god. He felt as if his heart was going to burst. He was invincible. Claire became limp.

His arms aching from holding the pillow, Sam scouted around the room, removing all evidence of their visit. He pocketed Marianne's handkerchief before rolling Claire over and ripping off her duvet cover. But what if there was more? His gaze fell on the small folding knife that had fallen to the floor. Unless . . . unless they wouldn't look for Marianne. Why would they, when Claire had told her friend that her relationship with Michael was on the rocks? But how could Sam make it look like *he* had been here? *True love will find a way*, he thought, palming the knife and turning back to Claire. *It's Valentine's Day soon*, Samuel thought, formulating a plan. *You hear about domestic murders reported on the news, of love affairs gone badly wrong.* A love heart would both implicate Michael and let Marianne know he cared. Perhaps, one day, he could tell her that he had been there all along.

CHAPTER
FIFTY-SEVEN

Marianne's breath trembled as it left her lips. What would Samuel think when he saw her, clutching his keys? It had not been difficult to get a copy made, not when he was so distracted with his illicit affair with Amy Winter. But why bring her here, to this dingy flat? She stared at the key in the palm of her hand. Did she *really* need to go in? Not a day passed that she did not regret what had happened with Claire. She wished she could go back in time and stop herself from murdering an innocent woman in cold blood.

As thoughts of Samuel whirled like a tornado, Marianne brought herself back to when she stood outside Claire's home. She was right in the eye of the storm, climbing through her bedroom window, her chest tight as anger burned from deep within. Stealthily, she planted her feet on the floor, a knife tightly held in her grip.

Twitchy and restless, she listened to Claire's drunken snores. Her face was pressed into her mascara-stained pillow, her room stinking of cheap perfume and booze. Marianne's eyes narrowed as she revisited every imagined encounter between Claire and Sam.

Their first kiss. The first time they had sex. Was it here, in her bed? It had to be. Michael was her fiancé. If he didn't know the truth, then who did? But if Claire thought she was keeping Sam for herself, then she could think again. Marianne's breath was fast now, adrenaline pumping through her veins. She imagined wrapping her hands around Claire's throat. Gaining satisfaction as she drew her last breath. But this was a warning, nothing more. She didn't have the guts to go that far.

Unable to contain her fury, she pushed Claire hard in the chest. 'Hey, cradle-snatcher, wake up!' Her knife felt heavy in her hand. She wanted to cut the bitch up.

'What the . . . ?' Claire cried, wild-eyed, as she was tugged from sleep. Blinking, she inhaled a lungful of air to scream. But it was muffled as Marianne shoved her handkerchief into her mouth. 'Shut it or I'll cut you,' she warned. Claire instantly complied, her nostrils flaring. She shrank back into her pillow as Marianne pressed the blade against her chest.

'Consider this a warning!' Marianne spat. 'Stay away from Sam Black, or I'll tell everyone what you've been up to.'

Dimples of blood prickled Claire's skin as Marianne scratched her with the knife. Wriggling beneath her, Claire began to buck like a bronco. This wasn't meant to happen. She was drunk. She wasn't supposed to fight back. 'Stop it! Stop it or I'll—' Marianne's words were cut short as Claire lashed out, sending the knife skittering across the floor.

But Marianne still had the winning hand. She was the one on top. Grabbing a handful of Claire's hair, she rebounded her head against the metal bedstead. The woman slumped like a puppet whose strings had just been cut.

Marianne's anger gave way to the sudden realisation that she had gone too far. She'd only meant to warn her off. But her possessiveness came with a temper that was like a snapping dog's.

Later, she had been stunned to hear of Claire's death, having fooled herself into thinking she was alive when she left. Her school friends mistook her guilt for grief. Everyone was talking about the love heart on Claire's chest, blaming Michael for her death. Had she scratched a love heart on to her body? If she did, it wasn't intentional. But it was too late to admit the truth. Nobody would believe a word she said. It was Sam she dreaded seeing, but he was nonchalant.

'Her boyfriend's been arrested,' he said. 'They had a row in the pub that night.'

'Oh?' Marianne was grateful the pub didn't have CCTV. 'What over?'

'Dunno.' Sam tugged his school bag over his shoulder.

'How was she when you saw her last?' Marianne tested the waters. She was surprised Sam wasn't more cut up. There was a twinkle in his eye, a glimmer of perverse interest, but nothing more.

Then he uttered the words she longed to hear. 'Babe . . . That night, I was all over the place. I just got scared you were gonna leave me one day and—'

'I'll never leave,' Marianne sniffled, fighting her tears. Samuel's hand was warm as it clasped hers.

'Then forget about Claire. It's you and me – always.'

As her anger evaporated, Marianne knew she'd got things wrong. Whatever crush he'd had on Claire was as fleeting as that night.

CHAPTER
FIFTY-EIGHT

As she crept down the corridor of Samuel's secret apartment, Marianne prepared for a showdown. Samuel would be forgiven. She would plaster over the cracks, just like before. But Amy Winter . . . she was a liar of the worst kind. First, she had tried to gaslight Marianne, who had almost fallen for it. Then she'd implied that Samuel was violent in an effort to drive a wedge between them.

Samuel wasn't the strong man he portrayed himself to be. He was weak. This woman had come into his life and completely turned his head. Marianne pressed her ear against the nearest door, bristling in disgust as she heard Amy groan.

Her stomach lurched. Was she ready for this? She pushed the key into the locked inner door. She had her family to think of now. As she opened the door, she blinked against the stark white light. It temporarily disarmed her – that and the plastic sheeting that coated the walls and floor. Just what kind of kinky stuff did they get up to in here? Every rustle of plastic seemed magnified as she crept in. Samuel did not hear her until it was too late.

Blinking, Marianne struggled to comprehend the scene. Yet there was her husband, pressing a knife against Amy's throat. Marianne peered at the form beneath them as she made out a pair of feet in tights. The blonde hair, the slight build. It was Naomi. 'What are you doing?' Marianne cried, her words a half-scream. Amy's eyes were wild, her face bruised. Marianne watched with horror as the blood trickled down her neck. This was no sex game.

'Marianne.' Samuel dropped Amy like a rag doll. Naomi appeared unconscious, oblivious to it all. A thin layer of blood dripped from Samuel's knife as he stepped off the bed. 'How did you get in?' His eyes were dark and monstrous, sweat patches blooming on the armpits of his shirt.

'I had a spare key made.' She answered automatically, but her words seemed far away. This was her husband, the man she trusted and loved. Yet she knew if she had come in seconds later, he would have cut Amy Winter's throat.

'I found them here,' he panted. 'I was just going to call the police.'

'No, you weren't.' Marianne shook her head. 'It's you . . . isn't it? *You're* the Love Heart Killer. You've been murdering these women all along.' As Samuel locked the door behind her, it told her all she needed to know.

Taking a tissue from his pocket, Samuel wiped the knife. 'Babe . . . I've been wanting to tell you for so long.'

Bile rose in Marianne's throat as she watched Amy Winter struggling to get off the bed. But her movements were slow and jerky. Samuel had beaten her up. 'What were you doing to her?' Marianne's eyes grew large as she flashed Samuel a look.

'Babe . . . it's not like that.' Samuel clasped a hand on Marianne's shoulder, his fingers pinching her skin. '*She* found *me*. Her involvement wasn't part of the plan.'

'Now what?' Marianne wailed. 'Are you going to kill me too?' Her world had imploded. It took all of her strength just to stay on her feet.

'Of course not.' Samuel looked at her with incredulity. 'Why would I hurt a hair on your head?' He brushed his bloodied knuckles across her cheek. 'Hey, you're shaking. Relax.'

'Relax? Are you mad?' Marianne felt as if she had wandered into an alternate universe. The situation was on a knife edge. The door was locked behind her. Amy was incapacitated and Samuel was holding a knife.

'Sweetheart, we're the same, you and me,' Samuel replied. 'I was there the night you attacked Claire. I was lying under her bed.'

Confusion crossed Marianne's face as she tried to take it in. 'What?'

'That night, it all became clear. You were the only person in the world who would kill for me.'

'No.' Marianne wrung her hands. 'I didn't mean to . . .'

'. . . to leave her alive?' Samuel finished her sentence. 'I know. I found your hanky stuffed in her mouth. I've kept it to this day. I finished what you started. I did it for you.'

A sob escaped Marianne's throat. 'All these years . . . I thought I killed her. Claire was alive when I left?'

'Yes. That's why I carved that heart in her chest. For you. And now you're here. We can relive old times.' He laughed, the whites of his eyes flashing as he clutched the knife in his hand.

'Yes.' The word was a whisper on Marianne's lips. Physically, Samuel was stronger than her. There was no way she could say no to him and escape this room alive.

CHAPTER FIFTY-NINE

Through the fog of her concussion, Amy strained to hear the conversation between Samuel and his wife. Just moments before, she had been hit by the sudden realisation that she was going to die. The second Amy grabbed the pillow, she knew she couldn't hurt Naomi. Her hesitation was rewarded with Samuel's rage as he delivered blow after blow. 'Do it!' he'd roared, before landing another punch. She had tried to fight back but Samuel quickly overpowered her, pressing the blade to her throat. She should never have gone there alone.

Slowly she blinked, hiding her strength as it returned; but she lacked the power to fight them both. Now Samuel was trying to win his wife around. She caught Marianne's eye, but the woman was impossible to read. A sharp stab of pain made her catch her breath. There was an injury, it was internal, and something was very wrong.

'I want her.' Marianne pointed at Amy. 'Because you like her a little too much.' A wicked smile lit up her face. 'Just like before.'

'We could do it at the same time.' Samuel's excitement was evident. 'We can burn your clothes, get rid of the evidence. I've got spares.'

'I want it like before,' Marianne whispered. She glanced over Samuel's shoulder as Amy tried to get to her feet, and gave her a tight shake of the head. Relief flooded Amy's psyche as she figured out what was going on. Marianne needed Amy to fight the monster she had married. But she had to get control of the knife.

At least, she hoped that was the case. If she had interpreted it wrong, she may not be getting out of there alive.

Wrapping her arms around her husband's neck, Marianne kissed him full on the mouth. He responded hungrily, his hands roaming her body until they pulled apart. 'My heart's beating so hard. Can you feel it?' Marianne placed his hand on her chest. 'I came here because I thought you were having an affair, just like before.'

'It's good to have you back,' Samuel said, kissing her once more.

Marianne's body language relayed that she was getting no joy from this. Samuel was delusional, seeing what he wanted to see, just as he had done with Amy.

Amy played weak as Samuel scooped his hands beneath her and laid her next to an unconscious Naomi. Even if she could get away, Naomi stood no chance without her help.

'Get under the bed.' Marianne gestured to Amy. 'I'll do her, then I'll watch you finish off the other one.'

Samuel looked as if he were going to explode with excitement, and his eyes filled with renewed admiration for his wife. He glanced at Amy as her eyelids fluttered shut. 'You're really gonna do it?' he said to Marianne.

She was breathing heavily now, her words filled with renewed confidence. 'Look.' She slid her phone from her pocket. 'See these pictures? They're her. I've been watching her for some time.' Her face hardened as Samuel scrolled through her phone. 'I was carrying a knife when I followed her. I wanted to cut her up.'

'Oh, babe,' Samuel said, almost crying with relief. 'It's so good to have you onside.'

'I love you,' Marianne replied. Amy's stomach clenched as the words were delivered with sincerity. Just who was playing who?

'Don't do it until I tell you.' Samuel handed Marianne the knife before sliding under the bed.

Amy heard his trouser zip come down, a soft grunt as he made himself comfortable. 'Take your time, enjoy it,' he said from beneath the bed. 'No one's coming. Give her hell.'

Amy's eyes snapped open as Marianne walked around the bed. Putting a finger to her lips, Marianne signalled at Amy to be quiet.

'You bitch,' she said. 'You're going to be sorry for coming between us.' Climbing on to the mattress, Marianne handed Amy the knife.

'Oh yeah, babe, do it now.' Samuel's voice was breathless as it came from beneath the bed. A soft groan told them that he was getting a kick out of this. Marianne delivered a few words of threat but there was undisguised fear in her eyes. Tears rose as she looked at Amy for instruction. Nodding, Amy climbed on to her knees and waited for Samuel to roll out.

CHAPTER SIXTY

For a while Samuel had thought Amy would share his fantasy, but she had glimpsed the darkness inside her and its power clearly terrified her. As soon as Marianne agreed, it felt as if he had come home. Marianne knew what he was, and she loved him for it. Like a bird in a cage, she had been waiting for him to set her free.

As silence descended above him, he hitched up his trousers and rolled out from under the bed. It was time for round two. Getting to his feet, he expected to see Amy Winter cut open, or with a pillow over her head. As the knife flashed in the air, he reacted too late. A sharp gash of pain sliced across his forehead and blood ran down his face. Taking two steps back, he convulsed in shock and horror as warm blood entered his eyes. Marianne had betrayed him. Some secrets were never meant to be shared. Grasping at the air, he searched for something to hold on to as the two women climbed off the bed. Winter's face was bloodied, her eyes fiery as she delivered a roundhouse kick. As his legs were swept from beneath him, she straddled his torso, pulling his belt from his trousers and wrapping it around his wrists. 'Sit on his legs!' she shouted at Marianne, as he kicked out in fury and howled for release. In the few seconds he had been disorientated, Amy Winter had immobilised him. It seemed her strength had returned. How could his wife have let this happen? Why wasn't she stopping her? 'Marianne, no!' Samuel shouted. 'Don't let her. You'll go to prison for this!'

'Give me your scarf!' Amy instructed as Marianne began to cry. Any moment now, Amy would call for the police on Marianne's phone. He had to stop her. There was still time. He had to try. 'Think of our girls.' Samuel struggled beneath their weight. 'They need you! You'll never see them again.'

Gathering up the scarf, Amy shoved a chunk of it in Samuel's mouth before reeling off the police caution for a second time. Gritting her teeth, she climbed off, one hand clutching her side.

But Amy could not be everywhere at once. Samuel's attention switched to his wife. Behind a veil of red, he watched her pick up his knife. Hope flared as she approached Amy, tears streaking down her face.

'Marianne.' Amy paled, wincing as she gripped her side. 'Put the knife down.'

Laughter gurgled up in Samuel's throat. He should have known Marianne wouldn't let him down. But his jubilance turned to horror as she knelt beside him and pressed the blade to his chest. 'All these years,' she hissed. 'All these years, I thought I killed her, and she was still alive.'

'Marianne.' Amy's voice was firm. 'Listen to me—'

'Back off or it goes in!' Marianne hissed, the tip of the knife firm against Samuel's chest. 'A part of me died the day you killed Claire,' she cried, tears streaming down her cheeks. 'Have you any idea of the guilt I felt? Of how it ate me up inside?' She wrapped both hands around the handle of the knife.

Samuel's eyes grew large as he froze beneath her, looking to Amy for help.

'You could have saved her,' Marianne continued. 'You could have let her live. And those women . . .' Her face crumpled as Naomi emitted a moan. 'What has this poor girl ever done to you? You're a monster.'

'Kill him and your daughters will lose you both.' Amy's movements were cautious as she approached.

'He deserves to die,' Marianne cried, flecks of spittle landing on Samuel's face.

He watched through blurred vision as Amy gently took the knife from her grip. 'And your phone,' she said, before using the mobile to call the police.

Within minutes, there was a crash at the front door. There were one, two, three heaving thumps of the police enforcer, and the weak door hinges broke away. This was followed by the call of officers as they shouted 'All clear'. Heavy footsteps echoed in the corridor as they approached the room. A demand followed for the door to be opened, but nobody was in any fit state to move. Samuel watched Amy rest the knife on the floor. Any one of them could be tasered or handcuffed if the officers misunderstood. 'Stay on your knees, put your hands on your head,' Amy shouted at Marianne, as she cowered in the corner. Then all hell broke loose.

CHAPTER
SIXTY-ONE

Amy could not wait to leave hospital, having spent the last few days undergoing tests. A bruised spleen had caused internal bleeding, but it was nothing she couldn't overcome. She packed the cosy socks her mum had brought in for her into her rucksack, along with the rest of her belongings. She could still hear the clamour of the police forcing their way into Samuel's flat. He had been immediately detained while Marianne was led away, crying and whimpering in shock. Amy hadn't realised just how intimidating it was to be on the other side of a police raid. It served to reaffirm her commitment to her team. Police surveillance had brought them to the area, as they'd tracked Marianne's car, but it was Amy's phone call that delivered the whereabouts of Samuel's lair. Donovan had rushed down the corridors, as her exact location was updated by police control. Concern furrowed his brow as he saw the gash on her neck, and he had escorted her to the waiting ambulance on the ground floor. Now he was back at her side as she prepared to leave. He could have made her life hell for going against him. He could have had her kicked off the team. But things had changed. Amy already knew where she had gone wrong. They had come to an agreement, one she would not break this time. Together, they would be a force to be reckoned with. She picked up the huge bouquet of roses, his Valentine's Day gift to her.

'Why don't you come back to mine?' Donovan watched her wince as she pulled her blazer on. 'I can look after you. I'll take a few days off work.'

'You have met my mother, haven't you?' Amy grinned. 'I'd never deny her the opportunity for some serious mollycoddling.' She pursed her lips as she remembered something that had left a bitter taste in her mouth. 'Besides, what would Ginny think?'

She tilted her head upwards, trying to appear nonchalant, but the truth was, Paddy mentioning Donovan and Ginny together had hurt.

'Ginny? What's it got to do with her?'

Amy shrugged, cursing the blush rising to her cheeks. 'Your personal life is your business. Even if she is young enough to be your—'

'Daughter?' Donovan ended her sentence. 'That's because she is.'

Amy stalled as everything clicked into place. No wonder they had been familiar with each other. 'So, *Ginny's* gone to Disneyland Paris with her little girl?'

Donovan nodded. 'I didn't want the team thinking she was getting special favours. You know what they're like.'

'But her surname is different to yours.' Amy's cheeks were burning now. How foolish she had been.

Donovan smiled ruefully. 'Takes after her mum, that one. A free spirit. That's why she has her surname.'

Amy relaxed her grip on her flowers. 'I've been so silly . . .'

'Forget about it,' Donovan smiled. 'She likes you, by the way, despite how prickly you've been.'

'Oh dear . . .' Amy cringed, linking his arm as they both left the room. 'And what about my job? Have I shot myself in the foot there too?'

'Not at all, you're in the clear.' Donovan seemed happy as he relayed the news. 'Marianne's account tallies with yours. You acted in self-defence.'

'Good to hear.' Amy recalled kneeling on the bed, her fingers tightening around the knife as Samuel rolled out. Slashing his forehead was less harmful than plunging the knife into his chest. As the blood had seeped into Samuel's eyes, it bought her enough time to restrain him. If Marianne *had* sided with Samuel, things would have been a whole lot worse. Even in hospital, Amy had taken to checking under the bed.

Marianne would face consequences for her actions, but given she had dependants and no previous convictions, she would likely avoid a prison sentence.

'You were right about Billy.' With Amy's rucksack on his arm, Donovan pushed each set of doors open for them both. 'Samuel offered him a pay-off to confess. He wrapped it up in the guise of an insurance policy, telling him his wife would get a quarter of a million if he was sent down for the crimes.'

Amy knew Billy's daughter was undergoing treatment in the US. 'Wow. He was willing to sacrifice himself to save his child. Imagine . . .' Her voice echoed down the corridor. 'Falling on your sword like that. Shame his daughter won't get the payout.'

'You don't know the half of it.' A gush of fresh air greeted them as the double doors parted to the outside. Donovan smiled as he spoke. 'Their story went viral and they've raised the money on their JustGiving page. There's even talk of a movie. Can you imagine it?'

But the glint in Donovan's eye made Amy suspicious. 'Hmm, and I don't suppose you'd know how the media got hold of that information?'

'Why, DI Winter, I'm mortally offended . . .' But Donovan's face said otherwise as he led her to his car. Amy would not mention it again. If some good could come of this then it would be the silver lining to a very dark cloud. Donovan paused to take Amy's roses, gently laying them on the back seat of his car.

After opening the passenger door, Donovan ensured Amy was comfortably settled before sliding into the driver's seat. 'Aren't you going to watch Lillian's verdict?' Drawing back his shirtsleeve, he checked his watch. 'It'll be coming in soon.'

'Nope,' Amy said. 'I don't want to know.' It was a lie. She *needed* to know, but she was too scared to look, at least on her own.

'We can watch it together, have a couple of drinks . . . soften the blow.'

'All right then,' Amy replied, 'but only if you've nothing better to do.' It would be nice to have someone in the house other than Flora. She loved her mum, but her nervousness was infectious, and Amy felt bad enough as it was.

'How are Erin and Naomi?' Amy groaned as she reached for her seat belt. Her bruised body was a reminder of her own limitations. She had not expected Samuel to turn on her like that.

'Here, let me do that.' Donovan clicked it into place. 'They're doing well. Naomi wants to thank you in person when you're up to it.'

Amy jerked her shoulders in a shrug. 'I was only doing my job.'

'But that's the thing, you weren't.' Donovan started the car before turning to face her. 'If you were doing your job, you would have waited for surveillance, and you certainly wouldn't have made a honeytrap.' Donovan shook his head in exasperation. 'Honestly, what were you thinking? You could have got yourself killed.'

In her official statement, Amy had said that Samuel had picked her up off the street. Samuel had not contradicted her account. Amy was painfully aware of how much trouble she could have been in. Donovan had done a stellar job of extricating her from the mess she had created, but it came with a warning that this would be the last time. His arm over the steering wheel, Donovan turned to face her. 'Amy, you've got to place more value on your life. You're not immortal. What would your mum do if something happened to you? What would I do?'

Amy stared into the distance, because she didn't know how to respond. She could try apologising, but such words did not come easily. The rumble of her stomach broke the silence. 'You should get me to a drive-through then, before I fade away.'

'No chance. Your mum's got enough home-made lasagne for us both.'

'Well, that's a bit presumptuous.' Amy pouted, relieved she was off the hook.

'You forget, Ms Winter, you're not the only one with special powers. I can make you *and* your mum putty in my hands.'

'Oh yeah?' Amy snorted. 'You've got no chance—' Her words were cut off as Donovan sealed her mouth with a kiss. The outside world melted away as she leaned into his embrace. His lips were warm and comforting, his arms strong. She was about to unlock her seat belt when he drew away, a bemused smile on his face. 'You were saying?'

Amy relaxed back into the passenger seat, feeling a warm glow of happiness inside. 'I've got a craving for lasagne. Best you get me home.'

◆ ◆ ◆

Amy's happiness was short-lived; that afternoon, they settled down to watch the verdict on television. She held her breath as the jury returned. It had taken them less than an hour to determine a unanimous result. 'Please say guilty, please say guilty,' Amy whispered, her fingers interlocking so tightly she could barely feel them anymore. Flora was to her left, Donovan was on her right. At least she wasn't alone.

'How do you, the jury, find the defendant?' the judge boomed. Amy's heart throbbed against her ribcage. It felt like all the air had been sucked out of the room. The camera panned the jury, each face sombre, giving nothing away.

'Not guilty,' the spokesperson said, her eyes flicking to Lillian's. A gasp rose from the crowd. Amy's breath stilled as the jury found her not guilty for each of her crimes. She had heard wrong, hadn't she? But the screams from the victims' families confirmed that she had not. 'Murderer!' cried a red-haired woman. 'Rot in hell!' roared the man next to her. But their words were soon drowned out by another section of the crowd, cheering and clapping hands. Lillian smiled at them appreciatively, tears shining in her eyes.

'It's wrong . . .' Amy gasped. 'It must be wrong.'

A strong arm slid around her shoulders and gave her a squeeze. 'I'm so sorry,' Donovan said, drawing her close.

'It's my fault.' Flora began to sob. 'I shouldn't have given evidence. I should never have told them about that doll.'

'I don't believe it,' Amy said, ill-equipped to reassure her. Blinded by shock, she kept repeating herself. 'I don't believe it. I won't.'

◆ ◆ ◆

That night, Amy had asked Donovan to stay over as he tidied up after their meal.

'As long as you promise to rest,' he'd said. 'You need a good night's sleep.' Gently, he touched the yellowing bruise on her cheek. 'I could have lost you, Amy. Don't put me through that again.'

He was right. She *had* behaved recklessly. But she had little hope of rest tonight. Would Lillian start again with a new name? Public opinion had changed. The world needed protection. What were her plans? Where would she live? Would she kill again? She would give a convincing performance as an innocent victim, and most likely become rich from it. It was why Mandy had sided with her. She saw her as a sure thing. And how *were* the others feeling? Mandy, Sally-Ann? She had yet to hear from her sisters and did not have the stomach to make the call. Tomorrow, Amy would feel stronger. For now, she'd take comfort in Donovan's arms. It was the only way she was getting any shut-eye tonight.

CHAPTER SIXTY-TWO

Tears threatened to rise as Amy sat alone in her car. She hadn't cried properly in years. Even her father's funeral had not invoked a tear. But since Lillian's acquittal, she had been put through the emotional wringer like never before.

She needed to speak to her sister, but Sally-Ann still wasn't answering her phone. She had received a text asking to meet at Mandy's – and now Amy could not drag herself out of the car. She imagined Mandy twisting the knife, gloating now Lillian had been freed.

Free. The thought of that monster roaming the streets was chilling. Amy sighed, bowing her head to the steering wheel. It was easy to become overwhelmed by it all. 'C'mon, Winter, pull yourself together,' she said, before opening the door of the car. Such moments of self-pity were short-lived.

When she stepped out of the graffiti-smeared lift on the tenth floor, Sally-Ann was waiting for her.

'Thanks for coming.' Sally-Ann paused for a hug, drawing away as Amy stiffened beneath her touch. Sally-Ann's linen dress hung loosely on her frame. She had lost even more weight since Lillian's trial. But their relationship had taken a battering and Amy still felt betrayed.

Sally-Ann sighed as she pulled her pink cardigan over her chest. 'Sorry I've not been around . . . It can't have been easy, standing up for what was right.'

'I can't believe she's out,' Amy said, the topic of Lillian's freedom an unwelcome one.

Her sister's response was instant. 'Sometimes we have to make ugly choices. Decisions that go against the grain.' The fluorescent light above them harshened every line on Sally-Ann's face. Every wrinkle, every hollow was carved from a life of pain.

'It's because of the baby, isn't it? That's why you testified in Lillian's favour in court.'

Sally-Ann's chin wobbled. 'I tried to tell you, but it's hard, you know. Reliving it all. We've been through so much.'

'And whose fault is that?' Amy sensed her sister wanted sympathy, but this needed to be said. 'Lillian put you through hell, yet you stood up in court and defended her.'

'I've got a son,' Sally-Ann blurted. 'And as soon as I've done what Mum asks, I'll find out where he is.' Tears glistened in her eyes. 'So please, Amy, don't kick off. Do this for me.'

Amy frowned. What had Sally-Ann planned for her? Her sense of dread grew as she followed her into Mandy's flat. It was every bit as awful as Mandy had described, but her sister had made little effort to improve things. The rooms were long and narrow, the stench of chip fat competing with the cigarette smoke yellowing the ceiling and walls. From behind a door to the right, a dog barked to be freed. A giggling child greeted them, his soggy nappy hanging heavily in his pants. His eyes were wide and blue, his expression one of happy innocence. Amy recognised him as the child who had been with Mandy when they first reunited. 'This way.' Sally-Ann's voice was grave as Amy took in the sounds and smells.

Another reunion with Mandy had been on the cards as Sally-Ann tried to patch things up. But as the living room door was opened, the blood drained from Amy's face.

'Hello, Poppy, nice of you to join us.' The voice was not Mandy's. It was that of Lillian Grimes.

CHAPTER
SIXTY-THREE

'I want to speak to my daughter alone.' As she sat with her grand-child on her lap, Lillian's eyes burned with intensity. She was sitting in front of the window, framed by sunlight dappling a set of orange curtains.

Amy felt Sally-Ann tense beside her as the atmosphere cooled in the room.

Resting her hands on her hips, Mandy spoke up. 'I don't fink that's a good idea, Mum.' Her child jumped off Lillian's lap, picking up on the uneasy vibe. He ran to Mandy's side, burying his head in her hip. Absent-mindedly, she rubbed his hair. Amy knew Mandy would keep a close eye on Lillian with her brood. She did not trust their mother any more than Amy did. But she seemed willing to compromise her morals to look after her loved ones financially.

'I'm unarmed!' Lillian chuckled in mock surrender as she raised her palms in the air. 'I'm not going to hurt her. I just want to talk.'

'It's fine,' Amy said. 'This has been a long time coming.' Before now, their conversations had been stilted by the presence of the guards watching over them both. Today, Amy shrugged off the constraints of being a detective inspector. She was Poppy Grimes. It was time she accepted the truth.

As her sisters closed the door behind them, Amy knew they were not far away. 'I thought you'd be in a hostel.' Amy sat on the armrest of the sofa, which was frayed and torn with wear.

Lillian smiled in a look of wonderment. 'Why? I've done nothing wrong. I'm an innocent woman . . .' She glanced at the plethora of newspapers on the coffee table before her, all featuring headlines about her case. 'And I'm certainly in demand.'

'Why here? And don't give me your bullshit about family. I bet you've already been online, learning the joys of internet chat rooms, mixing with people just like you.'

'There's a lot of fun to be had on the World Wide Web.' Lillian's smile was unwavering as she crossed her legs. It was odd to see her dressed in regular clothes. To see her out in the world. 'I've been gifted a laptop. Would you believe it? Someone tweeted my Amazon wish list and people haven't stopped sending me things. Some inmates told me about the dark web. I may even look some of them up online. It's amazing how these little cliques form.'

But Amy refused to be rattled. She knew Lillian was baiting her. 'Aren't we done yet? Hasn't our chapter come to an end?'

'It will *never* end. You're so tied to me, I may as well be holding the umbilical cord in my hand.' Lillian's foot bobbed as she spoke, the price sticker still on the sole of her leather boot.

Amy grimaced at the image. 'Perhaps you're right. There's no getting away from it, is there? I am what I am.'

'Yes.' Lillian smiled perversely. 'That's why I show myself to you and nobody else. Your sisters . . .' She kept her voice low, her eyes flicking to the door. 'They're not very bright. But you . . . A thin line separates us. It's why you gave up that evidence so I could be freed.' She licked her lips, taking obvious delight in her words. 'Your knowledge of forensics will benefit you. You certainly helped me. I wouldn't be sitting here today if it wasn't for you.'

But this time Lillian's verbal arrows failed to hit their mark. 'What do you want from me?' Amy replied. She had heard it all before.

'You know what I want.' Lillian uncrossed her legs, pausing as Mandy's children screamed in the hall. The *thump-thump* of footsteps signalled they were out of earshot as they both ran away. 'You said it yourself, there's a whole new world out there – a community of people doing things you wouldn't believe. I want to embrace that side of life, but I can't do it on my own . . .' Lillian paused as she examined Amy's features. 'Death has always fascinated you, hasn't it?'

'Do you honestly believe that?' Amy's face was impassive and she gave nothing away.

'Of course. And now it's time for you to embrace your true self. There's no shame in it. Society had you brainwashed. I can introduce you to people who will treat you like a queen.'

Amy arched an eyebrow. She had heard these words before. 'And here was me thinking you hated me. Remember my prison visits?'

Dust motes sparkled in the sunlight as Lillian shifted her weight. 'You're right. I wanted to destroy you. But then I saw that spark – Robert Winter's conditioning crumbling away.' She stopped to light a cigarette, with little thought for the children who might inhale her fumes.

'Then I found the evidence that set you free,' Amy replied, unable to resist poking the coals.

'Join me. The police will never suspect you.' Smoke curled from the corner of Lillian's mouth. 'Imagine, you could investigate your own murder case. Only we would know your secret side.'

'I've always been different,' Amy said truthfully. 'Growing up, I could never put my finger on it.'

'But you're not alone,' Lillian replied. 'Not anymore. These people you help, they don't deserve it. What have they ever done for you?'

Amy delivered a dry, slow clap. 'Bravo. How long have you been practising that speech?'

'Longer than you can imagine.' Lillian's mouth twisted in a smile before sucking on her cigarette once more. 'You might not be ready to accept it yet, but my words will play on your mind.' Children's laughter filtered from another room. A normal family with evil under its roof.

'You're wrong,' Amy said. But Lillian wasn't listening.

'You won't know till you try it. One day you'll find someone like Jack, someone you can shape and mould. You'll explore the darkness together, just as we did.' She exhaled a plume of smoke. 'It feels good to be able to talk freely.'

'I *have* been there.' Stretching her legs, Amy sat next to Lillian. She was forced to inhale her smoke, but she didn't want her to miss a word. 'There *was* a man. He was handsome, dark, living that black-and-white life: loved by the public and a devil in private. He wanted me to experience what it felt like to kill. He knew all about me . . . and you too.'

'Describe it. Give me detail.' Lillian stubbed her cigarette on a cracked saucer, her eyes alight. It was sickening, a mother asking such a thing of her daughter, but Amy conceded just the same. The sounds and smells of the outside world fell away as she described the scene. 'The room was soundproof, with plastic sheeting lining the walls and the floor. Things had happened there. Bad things.

You could feel the despair. All I could see was our old basement, and when he spoke, all I could hear was you. For the briefest of moments, I wondered if that's what my life had been leading up to and perhaps I *should* stop fighting it. Surrender myself to it all.' Amy kept her gaze on Lillian as she absorbed every word. 'He held me hostage, along with Naomi, another woman in the room. She was drugged, lying on a bed.'

Lillian's breathing had deepened as she relished every word. 'Did he hurt you?'

'He winded me with a punch then forced me on to the bed.'

'Did he undress you?'

'Oh no,' Amy replied. 'He wanted me as an ally, not a victim. He told me to smother Naomi, so I'd know how it felt . . .' She paused as she revisited the scene where she could have lost her life. 'He said he'd kill me if I didn't. It was my life or hers.' Amy glanced at her hands. 'I picked up the pillow. I brought myself there. Nobody knew where I was.'

'And?' Lillian moved to the edge of her seat, captivated.

'I looked at Naomi's face and felt such release. Because then and only then did I know who I was. It didn't matter what happened after that, because I was free.'

Reaching forward, Lillian gripped Amy's hands. Her face was waxy, her fingers icy cold. 'My Poppy. It's good to have you back.'

Amy jerked back her hands. 'I knew I wasn't a killer. I would rather have died than hurt her. I wasn't scared. I was free.'

'No.' Lillian's voice was small as she withdrew. 'Tell me you did it.'

But Amy shook her head. 'He beat me up for not going along with it. With each punch he screamed at me to change my mind. Then his wife found us and he was arrested.'

'No.' Lillian slumped back.

'I owe myself the biggest apology for thinking I could be like you.' As Amy stood, she felt stronger and more complete than before. 'But you're right, I *will* be watching you and I *won't* be able to stay away. I'll be monitoring every step you take. And when—' She raised a finger to silence Lillian as she opened her mouth to speak. 'And *when* you put a foot wrong, I'll send you down so fast and so hard your head will spin.' Amy's eyes blazed with conviction. 'Expect to see a lot of me in future. I think Mandy and I will be the best of friends. So enjoy your new laptop, and thanks for telling me your future plans. I'll be in touch real soon, *Mother dear.*'

Turning her back on Lillian, Amy opened the door and walked through. The touch of her hands, and even calling her 'Mother' no longer bothered her. She had not expected to confront her, but the words had flowed from a place deep in her heart. It was only now that she could see how powerful Lillian's hold over her had been. She looked at her sisters as they stood, speechless, by the open door. Glanced one last time at Lillian. She meant nothing to her anymore.

CHAPTER
SIXTY-FOUR

It was a novelty to have some time off to recuperate. Amy used it to go shopping, but this time without Sally-Ann by her side. She dearly loved her sister, but a sense of mistrust lingered. Sally-Ann had given her up to Lillian without warning. She didn't know her sister at all. At least now she knew herself. She wasn't a murderer, and nor did she have tainted blood. She was Amy Winter, and proud to bear the name. She would spend the rest of her life atoning for Lillian's misdeeds. That was the real reason she was drawn to her profession. It was also why Lillian had affected her so profoundly when she got back in touch. But the woman held no more power over her. Amy was finally free. She would see Lillian behind bars again. As for her, her conscience was clear.

Her arms ached from carrying shopping bags bulging with presents for her new nieces and nephews. Amy had not been able to forget their faces after visiting Mandy's home. It was never too late to make up for missing out on their lives. They were the vulnerable ones. She had already contacted children's social care about the state of play between them and Lillian Grimes. If Mandy was too blind to see the danger, Amy would not let them down. Squeezing past a group of tourists, she gravitated towards the store she had visited with Sally-Ann. Her life had changed monumentally since she had stared at the woman in the wedding dress. Now, it felt like she had climbed a mountain and planted her flag in the soil. This time, she did not recoil in horror as she gazed at the window before her. She saw her reflection in the glass and smiled.

AUTHOR'S NOTE

I'm very fortunate to bump into my ex-police colleagues from time to time, and pleased when they tell me they're reading my books. I usually ask them to forgive any creative licence I have used in order to keep the story fresh and interesting. They nod and agree, knowing only too well the realities of police procedure that would bring any fast-moving story to a trudging halt. However, I try to make up for condensing the boredom with injections of authenticity, such as the feeling of being part of something bigger, and the entertainment value when it comes to working with such strong personalities. This features with the complexities of juggling a personal and a working life in the police.

In this book, I ask you the reader to give me a little leeway when it comes to Lillian's case being televised for TV. I don't know about you, but when it comes to high-profile American court cases, I have always found myself gripped. I can think of nothing more interesting than having a case like Lillian's televised for UK audiences. It's not too big a stretch of the imagination, as at the time of writing this it has been reported that recent UK legislation may soon allow cameras into the courtroom to film high-profile cases such as these.

Whether they'll go as far as filming juries and witnesses is another matter, but for the sake of this story I ask my readers to make an exception, just this once. Of course, I could have easily got around this point by having Amy attend all of her mother's hearing, but there is something very enticing about watching Lillian play up to the cameras, as Amy fights to keep up her guard. I do hope you enjoy this latest instalment in the series – there is more to come.

All the best,
Caroline

ACKNOWLEDGMENTS

It warms my heart to be releasing the third book in my Amy Winter series, and to be currently writing the fourth. You never know how readers are going to react when a new detective arrives on the scene in the world of fictional crime. There are so many fantastic thrillers out there – is there room for one more? Thankfully for Amy Winter, it seems there is. I would firstly like to thank my valued readers for championing Amy's story and helping to spread the word. Thanks also to the wonderful bloggers and book clubs who have read and reviewed my books. Their passion for the written word is phenomenal.

To Maddy and the rest of the team at the Madeleine Milburn literary agency – it's a privilege to work with such dedicated people and I was thrilled to have *Truth and Lies*, the first in the Amy Winter series, optioned for TV recently. Thanks to Awesome Media for seeing the potential there. Amy has also been popular in the world of audiobooks, and I'd like to thank narrator Elizabeth Knowelden for helping Amy reach the *New York Times* bestseller list last year. Such milestones have meant the world to me.

Thank you to my publishers, Thomas & Mercer, for their unfailing enthusiasm for this series. To my amazing editors, Jack Butler and Jane Snelgrove, who have been firmly embedded in its creation, and to the team as a whole – I wish I had room to name you all individually, but you know who you are! Thank you for bringing my book to fruition. I could not have asked for more. To Tom Sanderson, thanks for creating another cracker of a cover.

A special mention to my author friends – Mel Sherratt and Angela Marsons in particular. Despite crime authors' devious minds and knowledge of how to hide a body and get away with it, they really are the nicest people you could meet. I'd urge all writers and readers to attend at least one crime writing festival a year. There is Capital Crime in London, along with Killer Women. In Harrogate there's the Theakston Old Peculier Crime Writing Festival, in Bristol there's CrimeFest, and in Stirling there's Bloody Scotland, to name a few. They're well worth visiting and I'm grateful to those who have invited me to attend.

To Billy Picton, who won the bid to have a character named after him as part of the CLIC Sargent fundraiser. Thankfully Billy is a good sport and was quite happy for me to portray the character as I saw fit. I take part in CLIC Sargent every year. It's a wonderful cause.

Last but not least, to the backbone of my world – my family. I've named you in every one of my books and it's getting to the point where you don't read the acknowledgments anymore, but I'm putting it in writing: you're the best and I couldn't do it without you!

ABOUT THE AUTHOR

 A former police detective, Caroline Mitchell now writes full-time.

She has worked in CID and specialised in roles dealing with vulnerable victims – high-risk victims of domestic abuse and serious sexual offences. The mental strength shown by the victims of these crimes is a constant source of inspiration to her, and Mitchell combines their tenacity with her knowledge of police procedure to create tense psychological thrillers.

Originally from Ireland, she now lives in a pretty village on the coast of Essex with her husband and three children.

You can find out more about her at www.caroline-writes.com, or follow her on Twitter (@caroline_writes) or Facebook (www.facebook.com/CMitchellAuthor). To download a free short story, please join her newsletter here: http://eepurl.com/IxsTj.